301

Praise for Cathy Kelly's irresistible storytelling:

'Honest, funny, clever, it sparkles with witty, wry observations on modern life. I loved it'
Marian Keyes

'Comforting and feel-good, the perfect treat read'
Good Housekeeping

'Th is book is full of joy – and I devoured every page of it gladly'
Milly Johnson

'A heartwarming story about family, love and love'
The Lady

'Packed with Cathy's magical warmth'
Sheila O'Flanagan

'Cathy Kelly shines an insightful light on female insecurity and the healing power of self-belief and family support'
Woman & Home

'Filled with nuggets of wisdom, compassion and humour, Cathy Kelly proves, yet again, that she knows everything there is to know about women'
Patricia Scanlan

'Love, laughter, tears and understanding are the perfect ingredients for a fabulous read'
The Sun

'An involving, heartwarming read about family, friends, love and disappointment'
Fanny Blake, *Sunday Express*

the wedding party

Cathy Kelly

ORION

First published in Great Britain in 2022 by Orion Fiction
an imprint of The Orion Publishing Group Ltd
Carmelite House, 50 Victoria Embankment
London EC4Y 0DZ

An Hachette UK Company

1 3 5 7 9 10 8 6 4 2

A CIP catalogue record for this book is
available from the British Library.

ISBN (Hardback) 978 1 4091 7930 6
ISBN (Trade Paperback) 978 1 4091 7931 3
ISBN (eBook) 978 1 4091 7933 7

Typeset by Input Data Services Ltd, Somerset

Printed and bound in Great Britain by Clays Ltd, Elcograf S.p.A.

MIX
Paper from
responsible sources
FSC® C104740

www.orionbooks.co.uk

For Angela Cowzer, beloved wife, mother,
grandmother, sister and friend.
And for Matt Murray, beloved brother,
uncle, godfather and friend.
You are both missed so much.

Prologue

The Invitation

The wedding invitation was a card fronted by that first photo of the Robicheaux girls, a picture as vibrant as it had ever been: four young women sitting on a back porch of the sprawling Sorrento Hotel, the girls lined up in age, smiling at the camera with the clear gazes of youth.

Even though it had been taken in black and white, colour seemed to leap from the photo, particularly from those young faces.

The twins were in the middle: just seventeen, lean and athletic, almost identical with what people knew was long strawberry-red hair, faintly curling around their faces. But they weren't identical, if you looked closely enough.

One had a dreamy gaze and fewer freckles, as if she stayed inside with her head in a book, lost in her imagination. She was twirling a strand of strawberry hair in one hand. Fey, you might say. Savannah.

Her name suited her, made her sound like a sweet-natured girl who'd lie on the grass with her friends and discuss what shapes the clouds made.

Her twin, Eden, looked altogether more knowing, as if books were the last thing on her mind. Eden Robicheaux was anything but fey. She wore very tight jeans and her shirt – the photographer had apparently insisted they all wore shirts and jeans – was opened just down to her breast bone from where perky, Wonderbra'd breasts pushed up.

Eden had nearly been expelled twice from the local school. She was on her last chance, by all accounts, but the arrogant look in her curious sea-green eyes made it obvious that she didn't give two hoots.

At the other ends, were the youngest and oldest of the girls.

The youngest was an altogether stockier girl of perhaps fifteen, who was staring at the camera with ill-disguised irritation: Aurora, who never answered to this fairy-tale name. She was Rory, she insisted.

You could easily imagine her snapping, 'Can you get a move on, Steve?'

She had a clear gaze, dark straight hair, wasn't yet as lovely as the others, if you wanted to be pedantic.

Steve Randall, the photographer, had taken a photo of the sisters every year since then: same positions, same simple outfits.

Steve had exhibited his photos – they were mildly famous in photographic circles, those Robicheaux girls, famous in a quiet sort of way for the twenty-something portraits of them as they grew up. Age, life, sisterhood in elegant black and white. The people who lived near the Sorrento Hotel who knew Stu and Meg, sometimes laughed that the Robicheaux clan were infamous.

At the time of the very first Four Sisters portrait, the photographer, Steve, was dating the eldest sister, the one on the far right: Lucinda or Indy Robicheaux, the one who looked like a model but wasn't one. Very tall, twenty-one, fair-haired, annoyingly exquisite in the eyes of any woman who wasn't born with limbs like a ballerina and the huge eyes of a startled deer in the forest. They were incredible eyes: a sea-green colour like her sisters' but with an explosion of amber around the pupils.

Kaleidoscope eyes, someone said. Or central heterochromia, as Wikipedia called it.

The photographer had married the stunning Indy.

Of course he had, the men thought. You'd marry that just to stamp your name on it: 'She's mine. Hands off.'

Now Indy was a midwife; she had two children, and yet she still looked as if she might slip onto a Milan catwalk at a moment's notice. No early-forties' weight gain there. Steve was a carpenter these days. The photography hadn't worked out but they seemed like a couple who'd found that elusive happiness in marriage, which annoyed everyone who hadn't found it.

One of the twins, Savannah, was married to somebody very rich, some clever advisor person – whatever that meant.

Money, the husbands said enviously. Money is what it meant. They lived in a big house with a guest bungalow and an indoor pool, and he drove a classic Jaguar. She had a business too – something to do with perfumes and candles, but he was obviously the real brains behind it all, people said knowingly.

Savannah was still fey and other-worldly – and thin, very thin. As if she might float away like dandelion fluff.

It was probably all the stuff for magazines – she was in papers and in articles a lot, so she'd have to be thin, wouldn't she?

The other twin, Eden, despite the up-for-anything look in her eyes in that first photo, had changed beyond all recognition in that she was now in local government, of all things, wore long, ladylike skirts and was to be seen on the television talking about green issues. She was a stalwart of kindly liberal politics, having married into a political family who owned half the pharmacies on the east coast. Her husband, who ran the pharmacies, was a hunky, smiling sort of guy, dependable and decent, not the wayward boy people imagined Eden would have hooked up with.

His father was the famous Diarmuid Tallisker, one of the elder statesmen of politics. She'd fallen on her feet marrying into that family, people said.

Luckily for Eden's political career, old boyfriends had never come out of the woodwork to talk about wild deeds, although there were certainly wild deeds in there somewhere, according to anyone who'd been to school with her. Mention her wild youth at your peril.

Eden Tallisker had never had her twin's dreamy eyes – she'd always looked like she had a taser on her person and knew how to use it.

As for the youngest one, still insisting on being called Rory, which was a boy's name, she worked in advertising but she said she was a writer first and foremost and that being a copywriter was just her day job.

What was the difference between the two types of writer, people wondered? Rory looked contrary, they decided. Her girlfriend, a petite girl who worked in a chichi boutique, was a sweetheart. Nobody could ever have called Rory a sweetheart. Plus, who wouldn't want to be called Aurora?

People who'd had unimaginative parents almost wept at the Robicheaux girls and their beautiful, memorable names.

The Marys and Janes felt stony-hearted. A smattering of Conceptas and Attractas were just enraged. The Sadhbhs were enchanted with their exotic Irish name but worried that if they had to go abroad, nobody would be able to *pronounce* it. Anyone could say Eden, Savannah, Rory or Indy.

But Sadhbh . . . it was tricky.

The Four Sisters' twenty-plus years of black-and-white pictures just added to their magic. The parents slipped in and out of the photos. For a few years, Stu and Meg together, holding hands, then, after the divorce, just Meg.

Surrounding the photo on the invitation was a hand-drawn golden line, unbroken writing endlessly repeating the words *Stu & Meg*. Getting married again after all these years.

Married at twenty-one, divorced at fifty.

And now, when other people were discussing having hips replaced, the Robicheaux parents were declaring their love again with a full court press. A wedding weekend in the place where so many weddings, so many parties, had taken place.

4

Having the first ever photo of their daughters on the invitation was pure genius: it was like saying: 'Yes, we know we split up for years, but look – look what we made. These beautiful women. Our remarriage is a testimony to them and to us as parents.'

Meg and Stu Robicheaux invite you to The Sorrento Hotel on Saturday, 29 of June at 3 p.m. to celebrate their marriage. Come as yourselves.

Everyone remembered that house – a big old Victorian pile close to the beach in Killiney. Killiney was a glorious slice of high-priced Dublin set on perilous roads that all led down to a panorama of rocky sea, expensive houses moulded into the cliffs so that the sheltered curve looked like a piece of the Amalfi coast, hence the Italian names running through the area. The family had run The Sorrento Hotel as a two-/three-star establishment for years, ignoring worn carpets because they were antique, damp on the wallpaper because it was *hand-painted Victorian*, for goodness' sake, and letting the army of delinquent peacocks grow more and more wild till they'd had to be cordoned off for fear of them mounting an attack on unwary guests or their pets. Legend had it that one small dog had had to be Xanaxed back to calm after the peacocks had cornered him. Who knew peacocks could get so inflamed? Or that dogs could take Xanax?

Life was curious.

Many weddings had been held there – Indy's, for a start – in the huge, mostly manicured gardens where there were Venus de Milos galore, a male nude with his willy long since knocked off, a pond with a giant leaping stone unicorn at its centre, and plenty of bowers in the flower meadow (easy to manage, no grass cutting, as Stu said every year when he threw another handful of seeds into it). There was a box-ball herb garden, also easy to manage as long as you went at it with the secateurs once a month.

The Robicheaux family had held many parties when the hotel was closed in the off season and everyone had at least one story of when the party went wild and when Stu – before he got sober – would get out his electric guitar, coax a song out of it and make everyone dance, even the kids, because what child could sleep with that noise going on?

The trees would be strewn with fairy lights, never taken down. It had all looked like an arty fashion magazine shoot but natural as opposed to contrived. The burned-down candles; throws flung half on, half off chairs; glasses of every stripe on tables along with the remains of the feast; bits of cheese and grape stems stripped of fruit; bowls of Mediterranean dips made by Meg and whatever jobbing chef they'd managed to hold on to at the time. It had been the stuff of magic.

People looked at their diaries when they got the wedding invitation. The 29th of June? They'd be there. *Come as yourselves?* That was so Meg and Stu. They used to be famous for the fancy-dress parties, Sixties nights, Charleston nights when Stu served all the drink from a bathtub. Were there fire eaters once . . .? The fire brigade, certainly.

The invited guests put their invitations where they'd be seen – on mantelpieces at the very front, on a large bare bit of fridge held up with the prettiest magnet – and began to think about what 'coming as yourself' meant? It was hard to know who you were, sometimes, wasn't it? The Robicheaux family had always known – that was what drew people to them.

'They'll think we're mad,' Stu had said the night he'd proposed – again – to Meg.

He'd gone the whole hog this time: a picnic on the beach in the evening, sparkling elderflower pressé, grapes, pears and cheese with real napkins. Rugs for them to lie on, a cushion for Meg's lower back which could be dodgy on hard surfaces.

And the ring . . .

The ring had caught Meg somewhere inside her heart,

holding it in a tender embrace. They hadn't managed the straightforward proposal route the first time. She'd been pregnant with Lucinda. The delicate rituals of courtship had been flattened by the pregnancy test with its two blue lines. The urgency and immediacy of it all.

'We'll get married,' Stu had said then, holding her close. 'We were always going to: it's just happening sooner, that's all.'

Stu, whom she'd never really stopped loving even if she hadn't always liked him, had known how she'd missed being wooed. She'd never told him. Never thrown it back in his face as they were divorcing.

In the last year, when they'd been spending time together, going on dates, letting people guess without actually saying anything, Meg had wondered what it would be like if they were together again properly. Man and wife. Thirteen years after the divorce.

Then he'd taken out the box with the ring in it: no perfect diamond in a loud princess cut announcing both a wedding and a surfeit of cash. This ring was a piece of the goldsmith's art, with a glittering green amethyst looped into whorls of curved gold, like a ring dug from an archaeological site in Brazil.

'Will you marry me, Meg?' he asked hoarsely.

Still, she stared at the ring.

'It's a rare stone, connects the heart chakras and is about love,' said Stu, holding it to her and Meg, who knew that Stu had never been in the slightest bit interested in crystals or stones or anything he couldn't pawn (his mother's pearls) for a bet, felt that this was indeed the man she wanted to spend the rest of her life with. He had changed after all.

'Yes,' she said, leaning forward and kissing him.

He slid the ring onto her finger, the one that had been bare for many years.

Then he kissed her fingers, one by one.

'Yes,' she said again.

PART ONE

I

Monday

Not many people can say they've been at their parents' second wed-ding – Eden Tallisker twirled her pen, stared out of the window and wondered if this sounded funny or sarcastic as the start to a speech. There was such a fine line between the two.

As a politician and the daughter most-likely-to-love-making-speeches, Eden had been picked as the Robicheaux daughter to speak at the wedding on Saturday.

'Please,' her mother had begged, holding on to Eden with her elegant, soft hands into which she'd obviously rubbed copious amounts of hand cream. Eden never had time for hand cream.

The *please* had two meanings – please speak at the wedding, darling, and please accept the notion of your father and I mar-rying again and at such speed. For Stu and Meg were only back together a year.

A year! Eden's father had proposed – was re-proposing a word? Eden wondered – in April and, suddenly, at the start of June, they'd set the date. For the end of June.

It was like a shotgun wedding without the weaponry.

'You want to get married in three weeks' time?' Eden had asked, aghast.

'Three weeks?' Indy had repeated.

Meg had brought her four daughters out for lunch to tell them. It was the first Saturday in June and the wedding would be on the last Saturday of the month.

Rory had been late.

Indy would have to leave early to take her daughters swim-ming.

Savannah said she wasn't hungry and Eden had a meeting at two-thirty.

'You're joking, right?' said Rory, the colour having leached from her face.

Meg had shaken her head mutely. It was as if she'd steeled herself to tell her daughters the news, that she was remarrying their father, whom they all loved but whose wildness had created chaos all their lives and ultimately had lost them their home.

'I know it seems sudden and it's hard for you all because of—' Meg paused; Stu's gambling and drinking had broken up their family many years ago – 'because of what Dad did but he's changed, he's different. He loves you all so much. And me, he loves me.' Her eyes were wet.

Indy noticed and felt a huge pull of love for her mother, who'd been so broken by their father's gambling and the loss of their home and yet had carried on taking care of them. Putting herself last.

Dad was great, Eden thought. They all loved him, for all his flaws. He adored his girls. But still – Dad and Mum remarrying . . .

Then she'd seen the tears brimming from their mother's eyes, the same sea-green as her own and the twins'. Meg never cried. She was a lioness, stoic and strong. Had taken care of them all when their home had gone, worked two jobs, been there for them emotionally and physically. Seeing her crying was like a blow to the solar plexus.

Indy stepped in. She'd risen and hugged their mother.

'We all want you and Dad to be happy,' she said, looking at her three sisters over their mother's silvery blond head. 'We hate thinking that you're lonely.' This, she said more sternly. None of them had the right to stop their mother finding love with their father again if it was what she wanted.

Indy was the peacemaker, gentle and fluid, Eden reflected. She was the voice of reason and expertly defused rows.

Rory caused rows. She was like their father: mercurial, although she'd be very annoyed if anyone said as much.

Savannah reached out to their mother.

'Happiness is everything, darling Mum,' she'd said hoarsely.

Savannah was so thin, Eden thought. Once, she and Savannah had looked the same, had the same body shape. They were very different in other ways but how they looked and how they laughed – a deep throaty laugh – were identical. Both had been ambitious, determined. When Savannah had been setting up her company, she'd been fierce in her way. Focussed. Still gentle with that belief that all people were good. But she'd been going places. Now Savannah had an air of transparency around her. Her drive, even her laugh, were muted. As if she had put up an invisible wall and was hiding behind it.

'Eden,' hissed Indy.

Eden stopped contemplating her twin. She worried about Savannah but then she always had. It was a mission for another time.

'Yeah, sorry, Ma. Course we want you guys to be happy. But three weeks . . . it's a bit sudden. You'll never get a venue,' she added, hopefully.

She had an election coming up in the autumn. And the letters. Oh hell, the anonymous letters. She thought of how the scandal could rip her career apart, so she needed to focus. Her parents' wedding would be distracting and it felt . . . she searched for what was niggling at her. For the correct word about the wedding. Nothing came. Nothing but a strange feeling in her gut that said her mother was rushing into this.

Now, the Robicheaux remarriage was only six days away.

Six days!

Eden had a speech to write, had endless work to do and still had to throw herself into the merry-go-round of a wedding week or else her mother would think she didn't approve of the wedding itself.

She would not be the daughter who was happily married and

begrudged her parents happiness. There was too much of that around. No, she would be smiling, waving and encouraging. A grown-up.

However, her schedule was manic. She also had to fit in a meeting with other councillors on the local drugs task force, visit a lady who'd just turned one hundred, and meet up with a local shop owner about dodgy street lighting outside her shop and how it was a security risk. That wasn't even taking into account her normal political surgery which she'd originally slotted in for Friday evening and which she'd had to cancel because of the rehearsal dinner.

No doubt about it: your parents remarrying was a pain but that wouldn't make a very good speech opening.

Unaccustomed as I am to public speaking, it's annoying to have to be here at the wedding of two people who are possibly better off not marrying each other again . . .

Er, nope. The tone was all off. Who was she to say they were wrong for each other? Pops – she was the only one who called him that and he loved it - did all that Gambling Anonymous stuff, didn't he? He even meditated.

Indy, Eden's eldest sister, was giving their mother away, seeing as there were no male relatives left to do this.

Indy was the beautiful and utterly perfect one of the Robicheaux sisters. Indy never put a foot wrong.

'That's not true,' Indy always said, showing a rare hint of irritation whenever this was said.

'It is,' said Eden, who prided herself on being the one who said it like it was. 'If you weren't my darling sis, I'd hate you,' she added.

Indy was genuinely beautiful: a tall, willowy blonde with a flawless face, a woman who could have been on the cover of any magazine if she'd wanted to and had chosen midwifery over a life of champagne, couture clothes and pots of money. She was happily married to Steve – also annoyingly perfect – with two exquisite little daughters, Minnie and Daisy, and a job where she brought actual human life into the world, coaxing tiny babies out of wombs, the ultimate in frontline nursing. She was like someone who'd get on the cover of *TIME* magazine – in an issue entitled 'Heroines of our decade' or something like that.

'Nobody's perfect, and you can't hate people for being nice,' their mother said, mildly shocked at the notion of one sister hating another.

Mum never got really shocked. It was being young in the seventies, she said, by way of explanation: nothing shocked you after seeing lots of people tripping on drugs and behaving with wild abandon. Aliens could land in Delgany, the village in Wicklow further down the east coast where her mother now lived in a pretty white bungalow, and Meg Robicheaux would wave them inside with a tanned, braceleted arm, gesturing to her all-white couches and asking which variety of green tea they wanted.

'You can hate people for being nice,' Eden sighed.

Actually, she hated loads of people – OK, not total hate, really, but certainly fierce annoyance, enough to make her grind her teeth.

It was a constantly evolving list: random people who rang her council office asking for ludicrous things, like permission to mimic Pamplona's bull run in a small village in a bid to up tourism; anyone who did their grocery shopping wearing full make-up; people who could eat what they wanted and not put on weight; journalists who asked her if marrying into a political dynasty gave her an unfair advantage in the upcoming election; people who automatically knew the right things to wear.

Savannah, her twin, might have fitted into the not-putting-on-weight category except for the fact that Savannah was thin because she didn't appear to eat, which was different.

And Savannah was always perfectly dressed too but that was for work and the fact that Calum, her husband and a man who

15

never let any part of their lives go to chance, had hired a stylist for her. Said stylist bought a whole wardrobe for Savannah every summer and winter.

Calum was spookily involved in Savannah's life, unlike most men, Eden thought.

'Wish I had a stylist,' Eden had moaned once to Ralphie, her husband.

'You don't need a stylist,' he'd said loyally. 'You look perfect the way you are.'

Ralphie wouldn't have noticed if she'd gone to work in her dressing gown but then that was because he utterly loved her. He didn't see clothes or hairstyles.

'You're a total pet,' said Eden, kissing him on his chin. She was tall but he was taller.

Calum might be good at hiring stylists but Calum was actually shorter than Ralphie and Eden had never seen him pull her sister into a bear hug, the way Ralphie routinely did with her.

'Ralphie, when you replace your glasses, don't get rid of the rose-coloured ones, will you?'

'Don't get rid of yours,' he'd replied.

Ralphie had insecurity issues as a result of having been brought up in a house that contained Diarmuid Tallisker. Diarmuid was the sort of competitive man who had to piss on every lamp post he ever saw. No young buck would ever take over his deer, so to speak.

Hence Ralphie never believed he was as wonderful as Eden knew him to be. She wondered how she'd got out of her family with her self-esteem intact: living with a sister as stunning as Indy would have flattened the self-esteem of most people but then Mum had been brilliant at making them all proud of their individuality.

Although – Eden grinned at the memory – Rory had hated it when their mother proudly championed Rory's lesbianism.

'Stop it!' Rory used to hiss when their mother sailed past wearing gay pride T-shirts and discussed, in all sincerity, getting one wall of the ballroom painted in the LGBTQ+ rainbow. 'I'm a person, not a bloody cause!'

Eden turned back to her speech.

'Nobody who was ever in the Sorrento Hotel forgot it—' she began and then stopped typing again because *that* was a total lie. A fair whack of the hotel's guests would have been in a stupor courtesy of her father's signature Martinis half an hour after they arrived. It would have taken a skilled hypnotherapist and photographic evidence to get them to remember anything.

The Sorrento had certainly enjoyed a ten-year-sojourn as the cool hotel for visiting movie stars and rock stars and such was the welcome they received from her parents that nobody ever remembered a thing about it.

Newspapers and magazines had lurked in the bushes trying to get photos of the great and the good, and, for a while, fashion shoots had been held there. Because Steve's photos of the four sisters had hit the papers with the first one, subsequent recreations of photos of the four sisters, wearing their individual necklaces, had been wildly famous in editorial shoots.

'You're famous,' one of the bullying girls at school had said to Eden once, unable to stop herself forgetting her role as bitch and currying favour. Eden had stared thoughtfully at the girl who picked on everyone, although never the Robicheaux girls or their allies. Nobody had ever had the temerity to bully Eden.

'Yeah, and when you're asking "fries with that?" when you leave school, loser, I'll still be famous,' Eden had replied sweetly.

In truth, she'd never felt famous, despite the papers publishing Steve's photos of her and her sisters for a few years running.

Savannah had been anxious about the anti-bullying exchange; Indy had been annoyed: 'there's no need to sink to their level', and Rory had been indifferent.

Even as a lowly first year, nobody had bullied Rory or her crew, which was all Rory's doing. The gang of just-coming-out kids, like fledglings all fluffed up and confused, leaving the hetero nest and finding their place in an LGBTQ+ world, they would easily have been picked on but Rory, lesbian and proud since she was eleven, when she'd cut her own hair short and thrown out all her girl's clothes, protected her people fiercely.

One bitchy comment involving the word 'so gay' and the commenter would find their head in one of the girls' toilets with the flush going. Male or female: Rory, physically strong and determined, took no prisoners.

Eden had never felt famous as a teenager chambermaiding for free. Plus, if she'd been a movie star, she'd have gone somewhere with more reliable heating. But then the Sorrento had easy access to nearby Dalkey's rock and movie stars, her father had been in charge of the drinks and he had a heavy hand with the vodka and tequila. Also, his pal, Redzer, who'd drive up in a pimped-up yellow Volkswagen beetle – wire tyres and zebra furry seats – brought drugs with him.

Eden wasn't sure how Mum tolerated it, but then she'd stopped tolerating it, hadn't she? When Dad's gambling and love of smoking joints and doling out ginormous drinks had got out of hand, Mum had pulled the plug. The hotel had been sold because the bank insisted, the family had broken up and . . .

Eden deleted all she'd written.

At thirty-seven, she didn't find her parents' break-up and divorce painful anymore but this remarrying – it was strange. It brought up the old feelings of fear of having to leave the hotel.

Yes, it was a nightmare looking after it, endlessly glueing down bits of wallpaper, scrubbing windows that really needed painting in order to hide the dark, creeping damp.

But it had been home,

Then the divorce – fierce, angry, horrible. Dad had been so desperate for it not to end but Mum had been angry. She'd loved the hotel, the security, and she could not forgive their father for losing it. It was the first time Eden had ever seen her mother really, really upset.

Eden knew that of the four siblings, she and Indy had clambered out of it best. Indy, because she'd had lovely, kind Steve with her. Steve was like a Dutch sea wall: he kept the ocean at bay and protected his beloved. Eden herself – well, she'd been made of tough stuff.

Also, anyone with a brain could have seen that Mum and Dad would implode at some time. But it had been hard. And they'd been so cripplingly poor afterwards.

Eden had been determined never to be poor again if she could help it.

Savannah and Rory, they'd definitely found the divorce very hard. And possibly the wedding too . . . Not my problem, Eden thought and felt a hint of guilt. But she wasn't responsible for her siblings, not anymore.

Eden thought of the wedding countdown. Today the four sisters were meeting Mum and Vonnie, her best friend, at The Beach Hut to iron out who was responsible for what.

As it was a wedding on a budget, they'd each agreed to take on a few jobs. Rory was in charge of getting the wine and Eden wasn't sure if this was wise: Rory with access to free wine was unpredictable. Though she was the youngest sister, Rory drank with the brio and hollow-legged ability of a much older person. Alarmingly like their father, in fact.

Savannah, Eden's twin, was involved in making the hotel beautiful as she had so much artistic talent. She and Indy were going to do the flowers on Friday because Eden had a meeting and couldn't get out of it. Eden was going to make sure the kitchens were clean and was going to, if necessary, organise dehumidifiers if the hotel was damp.

If the hotel was damp – Eden wanted to laugh. Of course it was damp. When was it ever not damp? Nobody had ever revamped it so dampness was a given.

Eden and Indy were also supposed to help with the silk

flowers Vonnie was making and which were to be draped everywhere in garlands.

As Eden hadn't been in the Sorrento for years, she wasn't sure what she was letting herself in for. First up, though, was her speech.

Unaccustomed as I am to public speaking, Eden thought and laughed out loud.

How many speeches had she given since being voted onto the local council five years ago? She couldn't count.

Her father-in-law, a politician who couldn't pass by a microphone or a camera, had told her that she needed to practise speaking at all times.

'Talk so that, eventually, your brain and your mouth get connected,' Diarmuid Tallisker had intoned, in that rich, grave voice of his that called to mind intense news reports on great matters. 'So many of our colleagues open their mouths, let hot air out and then spend the rest of their career being known for that one, car crash of a moment. Don't be that person, Eden, please.'

Eden looked down at her laptop and the embryonic speech for Saturday.

Diarmuid would probably delete what she'd written so far – then again, Diarmuid only liked speeches he gave himself.

She closed the file and looked at her watch. Half six. She'd been up with the lark, having showered quietly so as not to wake Ralph, dressed, eaten a small bowl of porridge, made a pot of coffee and gone into her small home office. She wanted to get a start on work before meeting her mother, sisters and Vonnie for the start of the wedding week.

Or, as Vonnie – her mother's oldest friend, a dizzy, skinny vision with white-blond hair – put it, 'The Wedding Party!'

Nine in The Beach Hut! Don't be late, Vonnie had texted them all on the group WhatsApp. Each of Vonnie's messages was surrounded by hearts, wedding flutes and emoji brides in vaguely Scandi headdresses.

Eden was not going to be late but she had much to do first. Nobody had any idea how many emails were involved in politics. Forty-seven new emails since nine the night before.

What she needed, Eden thought grimly, was a clone of herself to really manage all the admin, even though she had alleged help from her father-in-law's office. Diarmuid was always too busy feathering his own nest to let anyone help Eden.

He was like the iceberg that had broken the poor *Titanic*, she often thought: majestic but dangerous on the surface and bloody lethal on the seven-eighths hidden beneath it.

Diarmuid never had a moment for anyone in between all the dodgy property deals he was always doing, even though his public persona was that of much-beloved, white-bearded elder statesman.

If she'd known that politics was so dodgy, would she have got involved?

Yes, she thought with a smile. Politics was said to be showbiz for ugly people but you didn't have to be ugly, did you?

Eden's eye was drawn to the photo on her study wall – entirely beloved of the newspapers – of herself in the failed girl band, Allegra, back when she was twenty. She'd been the quiet, leggy one of the three.

'The quiet but hidden-depths one,' said Aidan, band manager, a chancer like her father-in-law, who'd failed to make Allegra famous but had managed with his next girl band.

Eden, with her wild red hair teased for the cameras, wearing jeans and tops that only hinted at serious boobage, was never to smile. Janie, who was just as wild but was allowed to be so, was the band's crazy chick.

'Why does she get to wear Lycra hotpants and I don't?' Eden had whined at the time.

'You're the quiet one,' Aidan had said again. 'Quiet one, sexy one, posh one.'

'Eden's posher than me!' said Gigi.

'You went to a private boarding school,' Aidan pointed out.

'Only for six months,' Gigi said, 'only cos Mum was house-keeping there.'

'It's the optics, innit?' said Aidan, who was from Cork but felt a London accent gave him an edge.

Optics worked just as well for politics, Eden thought, clicking into her emails, and, these days, she was glad she'd been the shy, quiet one which had never been her natural state. Out of the three of the Allegra girls, she'd been the wildest in reality but Aidan had had a plan and now, as a would-be national politician, Eden was glad of it.

Now she could play up the 'quiet and serious' version of herself.

She was running for a seat in parliament in September when Fergal Maguire (so rough he was nicknamed Feral) finally shuffled off into retirement. It was a safe seat for the party but still, it would require a lot of canvassing.

Creeping silently so as not to wake Ralphie, who was still asleep, she went into the kitchen to make more coffee.

Politics ran on caffeine. Local politics certainly did.

As she waited for the kettle to boil, next door's cat, a sleek Siamese with an Egyptian face and a howl that could wake the dead, appeared at the kitchen window.

Eden and Ralphie did not have children or pets. Eden didn't want kids and Ralphie, who adored her so much that he went along with everything she said, agreed that neither did he.

'I love children,' she'd told him. 'I just don't think I'm mother material. Is that OK? A deal breaker?'

Ralphie loved her honesty. 'You say it like it is,' he said. 'I've never thought about children.'

'If you do, later, then tell me.' Eden was adamant on this. 'If you want to go off and find a mother-earth person, give me a warning.'

'Deal,' he agreed.

Pets were out because they were messy and needed much taking care of.

'We're out all the time,' Eden had said.

But this cat, with her in-your-face screeching, had adopted them.

'I am not feeding you,' Eden said to it through the window.

The cat ignored her and kept up the waking-the-dead howl.

'Is this how you became revered in Egypt?' she asked it. 'For actually waking the dead?' For the sake of peace, she opened the window. 'I don't have anything for you,' she told the cat as it stepped elegantly in like a supermodel on a catwalk. It sprang onto the floor, then indolently rubbed herself along Eden's jeans. Next, it headed for the kitchen table, hopping up via a chair. It then positioned itself facing the larder cupboard and began grooming its back leg in a feat of hyper flexibility that made Eden stare.

'You don't listen to a word I say, do you?' she said to the cat, en route to the cupboard where she kept the cat treats she'd bought. Not that she'd told Ralphie this. 'This is a secret, cat,' she told the cat, who deigned to eat all the duck and raspberry treats, her raspy pink tongue licking them off the table. 'I suppose this is your natural, in-the-wild food? Duck and raspberry. Like duck à l'orange?'

The cat gazed inscrutably at her. She – it was a she: Eden had seen enough cats to know this – was very beautiful with that pale creamy fur and the dark Egyptian face, like a cat on an ancient tomb painting. 'I wonder what your name is? Raspberry?'

Nobody would call this cat Raspberry. She'd be named after a goddess.

But then Eden had always been quirky.

Raspberry began grooming herself again, then stopped and made a plaintive, one-note miaow.

'Raspberry,' agreed Eden, thinking that she wouldn't mention the cat to Ralphie just yet. His family home had contained a family dog and she wasn't sure if she was ready for the commitment of any pet.

Another secret. She thought of the letters in her desk.

I know your secret, Mrs Tallisker.

I know what you did.

There had been three letters so far, both dropped in her home letterbox, written on an actual typewriter. Eden had mentioned them to nobody.

Because she had a secret – didn't everyone? Except that secrets didn't go down too well for elected representatives. Secrets could ruin careers.

Of all the weeks for this to happen. She absently rubbed the cat's silky fur.

'What am I going to do, Raspberry?' she said.

2

Indy

Indy Ryan, née Lucinda Robicheaux, was dying for a pee. Dying. But she could no more leave the delivery room than she could fly to Mars. Peeing was for people in non-health care jobs where there was a very thin line between life and death and anything could happen while you were sighing with relief in the bathroom stall. People's lives hung in the balance when you were answering the call of nature or grabbing a quick latte. Being a midwife meant learning how to control your bladder for very long periods of time and Indy had worked many shifts where she'd gone from 8 p.m. to 4 a.m. without a sip of water, any food or a visit to the loo.

She was going to be late to the coffee-morning meeting in The Beach Hut with her mother and sisters. Very late, if she made it at all. She wasn't supposed to be working this week but someone was sick and the next midwife on the rota couldn't make it in till eleven because she was driving up from Kerry after a few days off.

'Of course I'll come in,' Indy had said at half five that morning when the call had come in.

Being a midwife meant mad hours. Indy's sleep had never really returned to normal once she'd had Minnie and Daisy, so she'd been awake at five, lying in bed beside Steve, thinking about the week ahead. Today, Monday, was the list day – according to Vonnie. Indy, as eldest daughter, could have felt put out that Vonnie had appointed herself organiser-in-chief but Indy had so much to do every week, that she'd delightedly handed it all over to Vonnie.

People always told Indy that she was well-balanced and she loved that: it had been handy in her home growing up when there had always been some drama or other, usually involving Dad or Rory.

Tomorrow was for the hotel, which they hadn't been able to get into up to now. In February, the last time they'd been into the Sorrento, when Mum and Dad said they were marrying again, Meg, Vonnie and Indy had trooped in to see the place.

'We'll sort out the damp,' said Frank, Dad's old friend, who'd bought the Sorrento with a view to turning it into an Airbnb. At the time, Indy had thought the Airbnb people would refuse to have it on their books as the previous owners – three since the Robicheaux family had moved out fifteen years before – had done nothing about the damp or the heating issues. Knocking it down was possibly the only way to sort out any of the issues but Frank, bless his innocence, thought he could do it. Tomorrow, the sisters were going home – Indy realised she still thought of it as home – to see how things looked.

'The ballroom won't be touched,' Frank had assured them, which was what Indy was scared of. The ballroom had been a beautiful room with hand-painted wallpaper, exquisite curtains that were falling apart with age and a walnut floor with a few bits missing.

If the builders had had a look at it and hadn't said it was a hazard, then there was some hope. Otherwise, the wedding was in trouble. Because all those years ago when they'd had to leave, it had been damp and in need of renovation and in February, nothing had changed.

In front of her now, in the stripped-down bed, lay a seventeen-year-old who'd been in the first stage of labour for nearly ten hours. Indy, a midwife with coming up to two decades of experience, had been with Tanya since eight that morning and said a silent prayer that her patient was leaving the first transition and coming to the delivery stage. But Tanya, who seemed like a child herself, was exhausted and Indy knew that it would be tough to get her through what might be another hour at least to deliver her baby. First births could take up to two hours at this point – second babies often slipped out like baby dolphins but first ones took a lot of coaxing.

'You're doing great, Tanya,' Indy said: calm, comforting, the voice of authority. Delivering a baby safely into the world meant reassuring the labouring woman, while inside her mind, the midwife's inner alarm system was running a constant check to make sure everything was going to plan medically.

Foetal heartbeat, presentation – at least Tanya's baby was presenting in the head-first position. She was slender and this was a big baby, so that rotating the baby for birth would have been tricky.

'You are doing amazingly well, Tanya, and you can stay strong,' Indy said, her midwife's reassuring voice speaking while her mind ran through what could go wrong.

There was far more back-up in hospital births than there was for the home births Indy specialised in but midwifery was about more than the mechanics of the process: it was about empathy, the ability to see what was holding a patient back, what was making them angry, afraid, who in the room was helping – who in the room was not.

Today, Tanya's birthing partner, her older sister, Mandy, was not helping. Her fear was enveloping the delivery room. Indy could understand it. Their mother couldn't come, Mandy explained, automatically closing her eyes at the sentence, when Indy had taken over at eight that morning.

Indy had worked as a midwife for far too long even to blink at this statement. Mandy's closed eyes had told her that Mama would not have been a help.

'We've got everything we need here,' Indy had said, smiling and shifting into the gear she used for young girls thrust into adulthood and parenthood too early. Mandy had a two-year-old, she'd said at one point. Mandy had had an emergency caesarean but was woolly on why.

This pinged an alarm bell for both Indy and Seema, a slight obstetrician with slender wrists and the uncanny ability to manoeuvre the most recalcitrant baby from its warm womb. Sisters often had similar issues birth-wise. The estimated foetal size meant that Tanya's baby was large for its age, and Tanya was a slender young woman.

She was getting anxious and so, according to the foetal heart monitor, was her baby.

Indy knew that an emergency caesarean was getting closer and it would not help Tanya, who would have to recover from major abdominal surgery as well as dealing with the emotional and hormonal flood of becoming a mother at the same time.

But the trick to being a good midwife was being able to project an aura of utter calm while, internally, shrieking: 'What is going on?'

Indy, a senior midwife for years, could put an amazing game face on, so none of this showed.

'Can you get Dr Patel,' she whispered to Clare, the junior midwife working with her.

Clare nodded, smiled and sailed serenely off.

She was only just out the door, when everything changed.

Indy examined Tanya's cervix again and found that, suddenly, she was fully dilated. The transition period was over. Indy felt herself breathe deeply again. With first babies, you never knew how long it was going to take but this baby had decided it was time to emerge into the world.

'You're ready to push,' she said. 'Let's meet your baby, Tanya, pet.'

'I'm going to call her Cecilia,' said Tanya forty minutes later, gazing at the tiny head with its tousled dark baby hair.

'How beautiful,' said Indy, settling the newly named Cecilia at her mother's breast. Breastfeeding helped deliver the placenta and that was the final step in the birthing process.

'I thought you were going to give her bottles?' Mandy demanded, phone out and taking photos of her sister from the waist up.

Indy kept her smile going. Breastfeeding was a hot-potato topic. She didn't ever like to pressure anyone, disapproved of women who looked down on those who didn't breastfeed. Motherhood was hard enough as it was.

'Even a few weeks of breastfeeding helps,' she said. 'But not everyone can do it or wants to, but if you can—'

'It's better for baby,' said Seema, coming into the room.

'You may not be able to, not everyone can. Or you may not want to,' Indy added.

'I'd like to,' said Tanya, still staring tearfully at her baby's little face with its perfect button nose, long dark lashes and rosebud mouth. She looked so blissfully happy.

Nobody went into midwifery for the money or the hours, Indy knew, but for this – this glory of delivering a new child into the world: that was the joyous pay-off. It was like hearing a foetal heartbeat for the first time and allowing the prospective parents to hear it too. No music was ever sweeter.

Indy never delivered a baby without thinking of her own two little darlings, Minnie and Daisy, and saying a prayer of gratitude for how lucky she and Steve were. Utterly blessed.

Savannah had one child, a superbright ten-year-old girl named Clary who stared at the world silently from behind thick glasses. She was like Savannah in looks, the long auburn hair, the same misty eyes, and yet Savannah had been such an eager child, eager to please. While Clary was silent and watchful.

Rory, the youngest of the sisters at thirty-five, had no maternal stirrings yet, although Indy could see it in Chantal, her sister's partner. Chantal got dreamy-eyed at family gatherings when Indy talked about work: Indy could spot baby hunger a mile away. She wondered if Chantal and Rory had talked about it. They must have, mustn't they?

Eden was open about not wanting a child. Not open with the electorate, of course.

Eden said that it was easier to keep some things to yourself when you were in politics. 'People judge,' she said simply. 'I say nothing about it. Let them speculate, if they want. I get asked, of course, but I look a bit wistful and say "not yet".'

Once, they'd have been confused by this but since Eden had been in politics for some years now, they understood. A person's whole life was on show and could rip into them like shards of glass.

'Sometimes I hate politics,' Eden said occasionally. 'Everyone thinks they have a right to know everything about you.'

'Tell them all to eff off,' was Rory's answer to this.

'You can't,' Eden would say, usually with a fierce blast of irritation.

Eden and Rory had been squabbling since they were small.

'Eff off is not a political answer.'

'It's what I'd say.' Rory was scathing.

'Yeah, and you're not a political representative,' Eden said.

'You're in local politics, Eden, not the UN,' Rory retorted.

'Are you slagging off the local council because we make the world move, you stupid cow!'

'Girls,' Indy would say at this juncture. 'Stop!'

Indy's own daughters did not squabble this way.

Indy had worked hard to make sure that in her home, open squabbling wasn't part of the way arguments were handled. Minnie and Daisy argued but lately, Indy felt they were old enough to be told that as they loved each other, they needed to sit down quietly and make friends again. So far, it was working. The rows were lessening.

Not like in the Sorrento.

But if it hadn't been for the rows in the hotel, then Indy might never have fallen in love with Steve. Her sisters were too young, Indy reckoned, to have known how bitter it got at the end. Once, she'd have spent time talking with Lori, the Cork nanny who'd lived in the Sorrento for years, helping out with the girls, doing shifts in the restaurant. Lori had always been a haven of peace in their lives and her attic room, with its cosy sitting room and old brass bed had been where all the sisters had gone for chats whenever Mum was out.

But Lori had left by then. So Indy had found another place where she didn't feel the tension between her parents. She'd spent hours with her friend, Carrie, in a house about an eighth the size of the Sorrento. In Carrie's house, peace reigned.

Carrie's mother, Anna, was a midwife and Indy had always found herself fascinated by stories of long shifts, of babies she'd helped into the world. Anna had been the reason behind Indy's career choice.

There was no wild glamour in Carrie and Anna's family life. No sense that a movie star would walk into Carrie's house and ask for a double-strength vodka Martini and a double room in that order. But the calm . . . nobody raised their voices. Nobody ever loudly proclaimed that they were sleeping in the spare room, nobody ever yelled that they'd only put money on two horses that day instead of the four they really wanted to bet on.

Then Steve, Carrie's brother, two years older than Carrie, came home from Germany where he'd been working with a master craftsman in handmade furniture and they'd fallen in love. He'd become her refuge, the love of her life. Steady, loving, emotionally intelligent.

'If the photography doesn't work out, will you still love me if I'm just a humble cabinet maker?'

'Yes,' Indy said. And she had.

A junior midwife popped her head round the door. 'Indy, if you could have a look-in next door, we've got—' her voice dropped – 'meconium-stained waters.'

'Tanya, I'll leave you with Clare and Fiona, who'll deliver the placenta.'

'Yuck,' said Mandy, moving right up to the head of the bed.
'Congratulations, Tanya, you were wonderful,' said Indy.
'I'll be back later to see how you're doing.' And she was off.
She'd organised a half-shift so she could be at the coffee meeting with Mum and her sisters, but that was ages away and she ordered her bladder to forget about peeing anytime soon.

3
Meg

Meg sat with her morning coffee on the sea-facing veranda of The Beach Hut, the ridiculously overpriced, boujis café on Hilton Road. The old Meg probably would have refused to enter into The Beach Hut on the grounds that it was selling coffee at inflated prices. The new Meg, the softer version, no longer sweated the small stuff.

That's what over six decades on the planet did for a person, she felt. Filtered out all unnecessary angst and left serenity in its place. She shifted in her seat to watch a swimmer bobbing out on an epic swim in the June sunlight.

Only six days to the wedding. The thought, unbidden, sprang into her mind again: was she mad? Marrying the same man for a second time seemed like an absolute triumph of hope over experience.

But in the past year, since she and Stu had begun seeing each other again – a ridiculous way of describing sleeping with a man she'd once been married to – she'd decided that they were destined to be together. Despite everything, their friendship had never wavered. Stu made her laugh like nobody else. Made love like nobody else. Held her at night like nobody else.

If she thought, in the dead of night, that she was marrying him because she didn't want to be alone anymore, she quenched that thought. She was perfectly able to be alone. Hadn't she proved that already?

When she'd married Stuart Robicheaux the first time round, she'd been four months pregnant with Lucinda, convinced that love could overcome any tribulations and her main worry had been that Stu's mother would explode with rage when she found out that after he married his pregnant, low-rent – his mother's words – fiancée, he was going to spend his uncle's precious inheritance on buying the run-down hotel close to the beach.

There was a far more beautiful and well-run hotel by the beach and theirs couldn't compete with that but they planned to run the house as a small, intimate place, a boutique hotel where nobody would expect silver service.

'Don't tell your mother about it today, darling,' Meg had wheedled as they drove a friend's off-white MG sports car – complete with the requisite *Just Married* written in shaving foam on the rear window – to the yacht club where Jacqueline Robicheaux would be holding court to two hundred of her dearest acquaintances.

'Why not?' said Stu, who liked winding up his mother.

'Because she already thinks I've trapped you by being pregnant,' Meg said. The widowed Mrs Robicheaux believed that Meg O'Reilly was nothing but a lower-class little tramp who'd sunk her predatory claws into innocent Stuart.

Meg's family lived just beyond the edge of posh Killiney, where the district became Ballybrack, not posh in the slightest. She'd been brought up in one of the old council estates with one sister, her mother and an often-absent dad. Now most of the homes were privately owned, like Ann O Reilly's, where she now lived alone, with handrails on the walls courtesy of the occupational therapist.

One could fit the O'Reillys' entire house into one wing of La Casa, the Robicheaux' Killiney home, with its rolling gardens, view of the sea and a summer house in front of which Jacqueline's Jaguar was parked.

Their wedding was only the second time Meg's family, the O'Reillys, and the Robicheaux clan had met. The first time had been pregnant with both silence and actual pregnancy.

Meg secretly wanted to screech to her new mother-in-law that she'd had plans before she'd got pregnant, that she had a degree in hotel management, that she wasn't after anyone else's money. But there would have been no point.

Jacqueline did not believe in social mobility and thought the have-nots infiltrated the haves by getting knocked up.

At least Mum had triumphed over Jacqueline in the style department at the wedding: Ann O'Reilly was a tall, lithe woman, like her daughter, and even if the dress she wore had come from a chain store Jacqueline wouldn't be seen dead in; it looked far superior on her than Jacqueline's eye-blindingly yellow Chanel-style dress-and-jacket-combo which served only to highlight her dowager's hump and the sparrow arms which rattled with expensive bracelets.

'They're not real diamonds, are they?' asked Vonnie, who had been Meg's best friend since she was four, staring in astonishment at the biggest bracelet on Jacqueline's crêpey arm. 'I mean, it's diamante, right?'

'Real diamonds,' confirmed Meg.

'Holy Mother of God,' said Vonnie.

St Gabriel's National School, where they'd met, had been heavily into religion. They could both still recite a litany of prayers in Irish as well as in English. 'You could buy a—' Vonnie scrambled mentally for a comparison – 'a car for that.'

'You could buy the whole garage of cars with what that woman has in jewellery,' Meg said.

Vonnie was silenced for a moment.

'No wonder she hates you,' she said, finally.

Jacqueline was now buried in the family plot, probably rotating at speed in it at the notion of the forthcoming nuptials, but at least she would not have to witness her son marrying Meg again, although the boot was somewhat on the other foot now. Meg's mother, less lithe these days, a formidable woman who'd just had her ninetieth birthday, had said: 'You sure, pet?

35

I love Stu like a son but he's not an easy man. Gave you the runaround a bit, did your Stu.'

'I'm sure, Mum,' Meg said. 'It's a bit different this time.'

'Make sure he stays on the porch, lovie, that's all I'll say.'

Ann O'Reilly had been as fond of Stuart as everyone else always had been, he was a charmer after all, but there was a bit of a naughty boy in there somewhere. Her Meggie had gone through quite a life with him, she told people. Time he settled down.

Meg's view of the sea was interrupted by a slim arm waving in front of her eyes.

'Can I sit or is this area reserved only for brides-to-be?' said a twinkly voice.

It was Vonnie, chief bridesmaid on Saturday, a notion which still made Meg wince a little. Did sixty-three-year-olds get to have bridesmaids? Was it tacky?

Vonnie had jumped up and said 'Bags be bridesmaid again!' when Meg had told her the news.

'Yes,' Meg had said automatically before she'd had time to think about it and say 'No! We want it to be classy and low-key this time. So no bridesmaids or matrons of honour, or anything . . .'

'It's going to be fantastic!' Vonnie had said that day, in utter delight. 'You and Stu – together again!'

Vonnie saw the world in complete black and white. Good and bad. Nothing in between. Stu and Meg had been good together once so they'd be good together again. And they'd all get to have a party.

'I'm thinking you in dramatic cream, very tanned – we'll have to have a pre-wedding weekend somewhere hot – and me in—' Vonnie had paused, considering.

Clothes were Vonnie's life. She'd worked as a seamstress since she was eighteen and still did. Gerry, her husband, was not one of life's great providers. It was his back – he couldn't get it off the bed, Stu joked.

'Sequins, spaghetti straps, a dress to the knee and my old jewelled sandals, the second-hand Jimmy Choos, although they're wrecked but I could add a few more glittery bits. The girls will be bridesmaids too, right?'

There was no going back about the bridesmaids, Meg reflected now, as Vonnie settled in opposite her in the café.

All four – Vonnie and three of Meg's daughters – were wearing bias-cut sheaths in colours that suited them. Savannah and Eden were in coral and Meg was anxious at the thought of how her beloved Savannah's thinness would be evident in anything strappy. Indy was going for turquoise and Vonnie had plumped for old gold. Rory had said she'd wear a dinner jacket like her father.

'Of course,' Meg had said. Meg had considered herself the champion of Rory's gayness since Rory was a little girl. Upsettingly, Rory did not want anyone to champion her.

'Muuuum,' she'd say. 'I want to be like everyone else! Leave me alone.'

Meg had sighed and cancelled plans to go to the Pride parade where she'd wear her own LGBTQ+ outfit with, well, pride.

Rory was a coolly androgynous person who owned nothing with rainbows on it.

'I couldn't sleep last night for excitement thinking about the whole week,' Vonnie was saying. 'A week of wedding!'

Vonnie had been one of the first people Meg had told about the remarriage on the grounds that it would ready her for the possibly tricky task of telling her four daughters. Vonnie was the test case. For a start, Vonnie had known her longer than her daughters and it would certainly be easier telling her because Vonnie was a) wildly, crazily romantic b) had always adored Stu and c) had never really understood what things had been like by the end.

The girls were another kettle of fish. They had gone through their father's gambling, drinking, the arguments, the stopping drinking, the starting drinking again, more gambling, the bailiffs, the promises – which never materialised – of rehab and, finally, Meg and her daughters moving without Stu into the old farmhouse they'd rented on the outskirts of Greystones where they knew nobody.

The farmhouse was 'charmingly distressed', which was clearly renting agent-speak for all the furniture flaking, for there being a wasps' nest in the tree just outside the back door and for hordes of mice to be convinced that it was their home too.

Nobody ever walked barefoot in the farmhouse or left a shoe or a slipper on the floor in case a mouse decided to set up home in it.

Vonnie had been a stoic presence in their lives then but she hadn't *lived* it. Being on the sidelines was not the same. Vonnie's husband, Gerry, bad back notwithstanding, had never gambled or drunk the family's home and livelihood away.

Telling Vonnie had been easier than telling Sandra, her older sister, who'd blurted out: 'Are you mad?' when she'd heard the news.

Meg, who rarely lost her temper, had hung up and hadn't talked to her sister until she'd apologised. Which she did – sort of.

'On your head be it,' Sandra had said. 'You never hang up on me. What's wrong with you?'

'I don't tell you how to live your life,' Meg had yelled down the phone.

'I wasn't telling you how to live yours,' Sandra said reasonably. 'It's just Stu and – ah, you know. The past. Marry who you like. I'll be there. But I won't wear heels. My bloody bunions are killing me.'

After that drama, telling Vonnie had been a balm.

'Do the girls know yet?' Vonnie had asked after a suitable period of squealing with excitement.

'No, I haven't told them,' said Meg.

'They'll be thrilled!'

Meg wasn't so sure. She'd endlessly gone over each daughter's prospective reaction in her head.

Her mental list started with Indy, who had serenity seeping out of every pore, saying: 'Whatever makes you happy, Mum.'

Indy was a midwife and reminded Meg so much of her own mother, a woman who faced calamity and happiness with the same clear-eyed gaze and determination to make the best of things. Indy was the family peacemaker.

Eden, who had always been a straight-talker, would stare at her and possibly blurt out: 'Seriously? You're remarrying Pops? Why?'

Eden did a lot less blurting out now that she was in local government and she was being groomed for national politics, was having media training, no less. It had been years since Eden had spoken first and thought afterwards. But still, Eden talked straight.

Savannah's reaction to her parents remarrying was the one Meg was most sure of – Savannah would immediately ask what she could do to help. That was Savannah's way: to do things for other people. Obsessively, almost.

Meg's youngest daughter, Rory, might easily shrug and say nothing – these days, Rory was a big fan of looking thoughtful so that nobody knew what she was really thinking. She'd been cagey when this was remarked upon.

'I'm observing stuff for my novel,' she said shortly. 'It won't be fresh if I tell you all about it before I write it.'

'Families share things, daughters share things,' Meg had said with a hint of irritability the last time Rory had grandly pronounced this. Rory had always been writing in note-books since she'd been a kid. Scribbled bits of poems, little stories. She could retreat to that dream world very easily and advertising had seemed the perfect job for her. But then she'd begun writing a book, which she'd been working on for years.

In truth, Meg was slightly anxious about the novel. What was it *about*? A memoir? Perish the thought. Yet Rory had wanted to see old family photos and had interviewed her grandmother at length. How was family history involved in a novel?

In the past year, Meg had barely seen Rory and Chantal apart from Ann O'Reilly's grand ninetieth birthday celebrations.

'They've got busy lives,' Stu said blithely, when she shared her sadness at not seeing her daughter. She'd kept her concern about what the so-called work of fiction was about to herself. 'They're young, Meg – having their lives. We're boring old farts to them now.'

And Meg, who remembered how she and Rory had been so close during the years when Rory had been coming out, had felt slighted. *She* had been her daughter's champion.

Now Rory insisted nobody should have to come out, that making an event of claiming one's sexuality was unnecessary. Which was true, Meg thought, except that it had been different when Rory was thirteen, and Meg, along with Rory's sisters, had been her strongest allies.

Meg had known she would physically murder anyone who hurt Rory or made homophobic remarks.

Stu had been the one who'd kept her calm, incredibly enough, despite the fact that he was merrily ruining the family's fortune at the time.

'Rory's a smart cookie, with brains to burn. She'll be fine,' he'd said confidently.

And she had.

Indy had hugged her and said: 'I'm so happy for you both.'

Eden's reaction had astonished Meg most of all.

'Married? To Pops?? I've got an election coming up, Mum.'

'The election's in the autumn. We'll be long married before that,' said Meg, hurt. What was wrong with the girls?

Eden was normally very empathic, but Meg wondered was the world of politics hardening her up? All that taking dogs' abuse from random members of the public and the nastiness of social media against female politicians – well, it had to hurt. But still. There was no need to take it out on her mother.

'You don't have to come if you object,' said Meg hotly.

Eden appeared to take control of her emotions. 'Don't be ridiculous. What would that look like? Of course I'll come. I just wish you'd consulted me is all.'

Savannah had embraced her silently, tightly, and Meg could have sworn she'd seen the glitter of tears in her daughter's eyes when the embrace ended.

Savannah had changed too. Children changed when they grew up. They had their own lives, which was why Meg had created her own life, but, still . . . It was a subtle pain mothers lived with.

Savannah's change was different somehow. She seemed fragile, almost bricked up in her own world, and Meg couldn't reach her anymore. But Savannah had always been an all or nothing person. She'd fallen so hard for Calum. He'd taken her over, almost. Now she had Clary and was running a hugely successful business. All of this would obviously take up so much of her time. But was the distance between them purely a matter of time?

'I get so emotional about weddings and imagine, you and Dad!' Savannah said as she wiped away the tears. 'What lovely news. We'll have to start planning! I love weddings and how many people get to say they've been to their parents' one?'

'Thank you, darling,' said Meg. 'You might have disapproved.'

'We all have our own lives to live,' Savannah said, which sounded like something she'd read on Pinterest.

Rory, of all people, had actually looked shocked when she heard.

'You and Dad are getting married again? Why? And why now? *Now?*'

'Why not now?' Meg had said, forgetting to be conciliatory.

'You all have your own lives. Your father and I are free agents.'

She felt guilty as soon as she'd said it. Rory was the youngest and, therefore, she'd been young when Stu's carousing had been at its worst. It wasn't like they'd been a dysfunctional family or anything like that. They'd all adored each other and love had been in abundance in their home. But, well, it had been tricky.

Stu was charming when sober and even more charming when he'd arrive home drunk, not that anyone but her ever knew he was: he had a startling capacity to hold his liquor and seem utterly sober. He'd arrive in, hug anyone who crossed his path, beguile the guests, and set the barman to wash up glasses while he, Stu, made elaborate cocktails on the house.

He had never seemed drunk, which was quite an achievement. Just more . . . more Stu. Like a larger-than-life version of himself. Hugging them all, telling them they were fabulous, the best family ever.

It had never been dysfunctional, Meg told herself. Stu had been a bit chaotic near the end, especially when he was gambling. Still loving but a loveable rogue.

The family had always survived financially but when he really got into gambling, Stu ran through money so quickly that they lost everything.

Rory, the youngest, had probably been most affected.

Meg had tried so hard to make their home a safe haven for her daughter and all her friends, but Rory had screamed that she wanted to be treated like everyone else. Not be the poster child for her mother's LGBTQ+ movement, as she'd once hissed.

Witnessing her father blazing an unhinged drink-and-gambling trail had made Rory furious with Meg.

'Why didn't you stop him?' she'd shrieked when the marriage was over and the five women were stuck in the Greystones farmhouse with the mice.

Meg had never known how to explain that one person couldn't stop another once they'd chosen a particular path.

The old arguments had restarted when Meg broke the news that she was marrying Stu. Again.

'Why get married – why now?' repeated Rory. 'My book—' She seemed on the verge of saying something and stopped herself.

Meg was briefly silent. Parental patience had always been her thing but it waned the older the kids got.

Plus, Rory had been writing the book for years. What had that got to do with anything?

Rory was thirty-five now, so if everything was to stop for said book to get written, they'd all have been frozen in time for quite a while. And what was this blasted book *about*? Why all the interest in old photos.

Still, she felt a tinge of guilt. Rory did look pale, as if she'd had a dreadful shock.

'It won't be a big wedding,' Meg soothed. 'Just something small.'

Rory, still somewhat ashen, had glared at her.

'You and Dad never do anything small, Mum. It all has to be an epic production where Dad's involved. He loves spectacle.'

This was true.

'Rory, you love your dad and you love me. We're adults, we have to do what's right for us,' Meg said mildly.

'Dad always does what's right for him,' Rory snapped. 'Other people have to cope with the fallout.'

In the end, Meg had been 50 per cent right about her daughters' reactions. Apart from Stu, Vonnie had definitely been the most thrilled of everyone with the news.

'I'm so happy for you both.' Vonnie's skinny arms had wrapped as far as they could round Meg's body, Meg being the archetypical volupté. Once, when she'd been working in an expensive clothes shop in the city, trying to make ends meet,

Meg had posed for swimsuit pics – her olive skin darkened in the sun till she looked Italian, her hair silvery white and long, sea-green eyes heavy-lidded in each sexy pose.

The pictures had taken flight virally and she'd been, briefly, the poster girl for the older, sexy woman.

'I wish they had a bar licence here,' said Vonnie now, adjusting herself in one of The Beach Hut's rattan chairs and organising cushions around herself.

The complete opposite physically to Meg, Vonnie was naturally a skin-and-bone person, was always cold and required cushions and blankets to warm her bony frame. 'I fancy Bucks Fizz. You're getting married in six days! We ought to be celebrating.'

Meg winced. She was understandably hyper-sensitive about alcohol.

'Bucks Fizz? It's only five to nine in the morning.'

Meg had already had a kale and cashew nut butter smoothie and had spent twenty minutes doing yoga. She worked hard at eating superfoods, keeping herself flexible and doing weight-bearing exercises. Her idea of a blow-out was nibbling some dark chocolate and having green tea too late at night. Green tea was a diuretic. At least life would be different to before when she and Stu lived together this time. No late-night drinks for a start. She liked the clean-living life she had.

Plus, the clothes shop she now worked in relied on her to look like a gorgeous Silver Surfer to sell their clothes. Meg herself was the best advertisement for the shop in Donnybrook, which sold expensive garments to wealthy older women, many of whom would donate an organ, any organ, to look like Meg Robicheaux.

'But it's your wedding week!' Vonnie complained.

'The downside of deciding to get married in three weeks is that we have to organise it all at warp speed. We have things to do today, to plan,' Meg reproached, knowing that if seven-stone Vonnie had a glass of champagne, even heavily diluted with orange juice, she'd be asleep in her cosy chair in half an hour.

Today was list making and then tomorrow, she, Vonnie, Eden and Savannah were going to the hotel, ostensibly to remind themselves of what needed to be done to the place before the wedding. Rory had said she had meetings and might not be able to get away, which sounded like an excuse. Indy was going to try to come if she could get cover at work.

The hotel had passed through many hands since they'd owned it and was now in the hands of one of Stu's old friends, Frank, who was threatening to turn it into apartments.

This could be the last time any big event was held in the old place, Meg thought fondly, remembering the family's life there. It had always been run on a wing and a prayer, once being saved from the bank because a Hollywood ghost story had been filmed there and the fee had got them out of the red.

'I have my list,' said Vonnie, reaching into the little pink basket she carried around with her in the summer.

'Monday – make list of all things to do, mainly phone people today. The flower people said to talk to them today about the peonies. If they can get them. Tuesday – hotel. Check for damp. Nothing's likely to be damp in June?' she asked.

Meg grimaced. Damp had been a constant issue during her time running the hotel. Old structures loved damp. Spiders loved old structures. Even bats loved old structures, she thought, remembering Stu making a makeshift plastic net and manoeuvring a baby bat off Indy's curtains and out into the garden one night, while the four girls had shrieked in the background.

Baby bats wrapped up in teeny blankets on social media: nice. Bats in real life: not so nice.

'The ballroom's tricky when it comes to damp,' she told Vonnie, putting bats out of her mind. 'There's one spot near the inner bar. But—' she closed her eyes and said a brief prayer

– 'it'll be fine. Eden's said there are a couple of dehumidifiers she can borrow if necessary.'

Vonnie went back to the list.

'Wednesday – the bridal shower! I can't wait. You're going to be so surprised. Although it would have been nicer if we'd managed a weekend away.'

Meg had nixed the idea of a weekend away with her daughters, Vonnie and her other old friends. Even when they were adults, daughters didn't like to be reminded that their parents had another life prior to their birth, which would have been impossible to avoid if in close contact with Meg's oldest pals, as rounded up by Vonnie.

No, far better to have one night out in the tapas restaurant on the seafront, where Gianni's stunning sloe-eyed nephew would smoulder at all the women and the food would be ambrosial. Sandra, Meg's sister, would have to be kept off the cocktails in case she started telling everyone what a mistake it was for Meg to be remarrying Stu.

Vonnie was still at her list.

'Wednesday morning – someone has to pick up Sonya from the airport. Should Stu do that?'

Meg paused. Sonya was Stu's older sister, who'd run away from the family home as soon as she possibly could, had worked as a nurse for the NHS for years and now only came back for weddings and funerals.

'He should but he's running a meditation session that morning.'

Meg noticed Vonnie smiling at the thought of Stu Robicheaux and meditation. Who'd have imagined it? The local wild man had grown up, finally, and it suited him. His tawny hair was still worn too long and he managed bad-boy stubble on his jaw most of the time, but he was a changed man. After all these years, he was tame. She'd managed it, finally.

For a brief moment, Meg too wished that The Beach Hut had a bar licence. She could hold a single glass of Buck's Fizz high and toast herself for managing to raise four beautiful daughters and for being able to keep her relationship with Stu so good that they were trying again. How many people got to do that?

4

Savannah

Savannah drove along the coast road listening to the mindfulness podcast as she zipped the car past houses with names that conjured up the Italian riviera.

'Breathe in and hold the sacred moment, that pause where one can let mindfulness in,' went the soft voice of the woman in the podcast.

Savannah was breathing the way she always did, which was shallowly and high in her chest. Actual deep breathing hurt and after that time last year when she'd done a yoga class and found out that she'd been shallow breathing her whole life, she'd tried to breathe properly.

But it felt wrong. The yoga teacher – who was young and sweet – had been lovely about it, said lots of people didn't breathe properly.

But Savannah had felt judged, she'd left early, had never gone back.

She was so useless, she couldn't even breathe properly.

So now she listened to mindfulness podcasts and breathing meditations, all the while trying to learn what she was doing wrong. Because Savannah was clearly doing everything wrong: it was the only conclusion she could come to.

The road curved. The white house with the overflow of jacaranda flowers was next and Savannah felt a hint of the tension leave her chest.

She'd walked along these roads to school, down to the shops with her sisters, along to the beach on summer days. It was home, familiar.

Eboli Road was set between Killiney and Dalkey, a winding road set into the cliff where some of the country's most expensive real estate lived. There were tiny cottages and giant mansions beside vast modern houses and bijou mews houses. The residents were people who'd lived there for decades and people who'd just arrived with a fleet of modern cars and moved into houses that were giant carcasses of Italian marble.

Savannah kept driving.

After the low stone wall where you could climb over it and down – perilously – to the rocks and the sea, was Savannah's and Eden's best friend, Rachel's old home: The Dolphin. A rackety old house that clung to the cliff and housed Rachel's granny on the top floor, The Dolphin was where they'd hidden out as kids.

Rachel had moved to Australia and was currently something big in TV in Sydney. Rachel was clever: she'd see what Savannah's life really was, wouldn't she? Savannah inhaled deeply. She had to stop thinking about random people coming into her world and seeing the truth. It was her deepest fantasy, the way she'd lived in a fantasy world as a child, a world she could disappear into when there were rowdy guests or arguments. In her fantasy world, a rescuer always plucked her from the scary bits of life.

As an adult, she saw that nobody could pluck you from your life; nobody rescued you. She had to stop hoping for someone to see what was happening.

Nobody would. There was no knight on a white horse: only her, battling away every day.

As she drove, she forgot about the mindfulness podcast and thought about the interview she'd just done for her business and about the wedding on Saturday.

Calum wanted her to wear the diamonds he'd given her for their tenth anniversary at her parents' wedding on Saturday.

'Non-conflict diamonds,' he told people proudly.

Calum was very keen on being seen to do the right thing

when it came to jewellery. When it came to everything, actually.

Savannah's engagement ring was a giant Ceylon sapphire sourced from an ethical mine and handcrafted by artisanal jewellers in Barcelona. It suited her long fingers and apart from her watch, the pale-blue stone was the only thing she wore every day.

Every time she did an interview about her business, Velvet Beauty, someone mentioned the ring.

'Oh, it's stunning! How many carats?' they asked.

Savannah always lied and said she didn't know, although she did. Knowing the carat size of the gem on her finger was not relatable.

When you ran a business, being relatable was very important.

Savannah, who'd been so truthful at school except when it came to talking about her home life – 'Oh, it's all fine,' she'd say to the guidance teacher who was head of the sixth-year class when the Sorrento was being mentioned in the gossip part of the newspapers in conjunction with 'things not going well' – had learned to lie marvellously.

She'd swiftly pass on the size and possible cost of the ring and breathlessly tell the interviewers that Calum chose it specially.

Actually, she made sure interviewers noticed it because it gave her something else to talk about.

Having a kitchen-table perfume business grow into the big company that candle-and-perfume business Velvet Beauty had become was not enough, it seemed, if you were a woman. You needed a 'back story'. Savannah didn't want ten-year-old Clary to be it. She refused point blank to put her daughter in lifestyle pics of the family, which annoyed magazine and newspaper people. They liked the whole family in their pictures.

But Savannah stood firm on not including Clary. It was just Calum and herself for publicity, therefore she needed other *hooks*. So she went with her ethical ring, the story of the Four Sisters photos which Steve had been taking since she and Eden were seventeen, and tales of how they all grew up in the beautiful Sorrento Hotel just off Killiney Beach. The Sorrento was famous because of all the parties rich and famous local people had there.

What she said was actually minuscule compared to what she didn't say. She never said to interviewers that she didn't know how to *be*. That other people, like her sisters, understood the world and that she didn't. She had a layer of skin missing or a flaw, *something* that meant she didn't know the rules, how to behave, anything: everything.

People, Savannah figured, didn't want to know that. They didn't want to know about her life, her constant anxiety, her *fear*.

Such utter truth made her sound a little unhinged or else totally self-involved and neither was right. The truth was far more complicated.

So she told the stories people wanted to hear: the Four Sisters photos always worked to pique interest. She also told people about her sisters, the women behind the photos.

'Rory's so creative, she works in advertising and she's writing a novel. Indy's the kindest woman on the planet – she's a midwife. Eden, my identical twin sister – no, we never had a shared language and I don't know what she thinks all the time! – she's our political star. Very passionate about climate change, a wonderful speaker. I want her to do a TED Talk.'

'I juggle,' Savannah would add, in the penultimate bit of her 'the real me' fantasy story. 'Like all working mothers. Defrosting dinner, school runs . . . the usual!'

She told them about the now-famous Italian singer who was a waiter in the hotel for one sultry summer.

Honestly, he never noticed her: he was totally into Indy, who was with Steve by then and she barely glanced at poor Maurizio.

Eden, who had two boys on the hook that summer, was enraged that she couldn't get Maurizio to so much as look at her.

Savannah didn't mention that, naturally. Her twin sister had been so much better with boys than she had. Eden could flirt with anyone and, sometimes, awareness of that made Calum freak out.

'But you're twins – you can do the same things,' he'd point out, biting his big bottom lip.

'I never flirt,' Savannah would say, which was utterly true. She never did. Ever. It wouldn't be worth it.

So, in case it set Calum off, she was always careful not to imply that she, personally, had ever fancied Maurizio, though she did, quietly. He was so handsome, utterly charming and kind.

There hadn't been a woman in a fifty-mile radius who didn't fancy Maurizio but Savannah was far too wise to say that. Instead, she stuck with praising his singing. 'Maurizio was always humming, always singing, such a beautiful voice,' she'd say to the reporters.

That was her other hook – being lovely. It was hard work, though. Because sometimes she wanted to scream.

Except she couldn't. Nobody would believe her if she told them the truth, would they? They'd look at her in disgust and wonder how could the woman who had everything want to sob or scream?

Eden arrived at The Beach Hut at exactly the same time as Savannah.

'Oh fabulous, you're here,' said Eden, getting out of her electric car and putting a beady eye on the mileage to see when she'd need to charge it next. She loved her car, but keeping it charged was a full-time job.

'I'm great. How are you?' said Savannah.

Eden looked carefully at her twin. On the surface Savannah did look marvellous, spectacularly slim in a way that looked good when she was dressed, but Eden reckoned she'd be far too thin with her clothes off. Eden was always drawn between wanting to be as thin as Savannah and knowing that somehow it wasn't a good thing. Because Eden was pretty sure that Savannah had an eating disorder. Not that anyone in the family ever discussed it anymore because Savannah blithely waved off 'you're a bit thin . . .' comments.

'You're a bit on the skinny side these days, you know,' Eden said, deciding that she'd say something again. She was wary of accusing her sister of anything in case Savannah fell apart.

'I just forget to eat,' replied Savannah.

And Eden, who was Savannah's identical twin, and had been close to her since they'd been in their mother's womb, although the gap had widened hugely in the past ten years, gave her a blank stare.

'You forget to eat?' she said. 'You're a stone lighter than me and we are the same height. Nobody just forgets to eat. I don't forget to eat.'

Savannah shrugged. 'I'm busy and I have lots of coffee. It's just the way I turned out. We're all different, you know. Just because we're identical on the outside doesn't mean we're the same on the inside. And I do have the running machine at home—'

As soon as Savannah began to bring up the 'just because we're identical, we're not the same' argument, Eden knew there was no point in continuing. Savannah's defences were up. Maybe she was just naturally thinner? Maybe she exercised herself to the bone – could that be it? What did you say or do when someone was thin in a world where thinness was such a distorted sign of success?

'Fine,' Eden said, backing down because she had no proof. Just a feeling. 'I worry about you, skinny malink. Plus,' she added, to calm her twin down, 'you're going to look totally amazing on Saturday and I'm going to look like I've eaten all the pies.'

'No, you're not.' Savannah giggled and Eden felt pleased. She'd defused things. One day she had to talk seriously to Savannah about her food/exercise issues but not today, not in this super-charged week where emotions were already heightened.

Eden marked it down in her mental diary: Talk to Savannah. A proper talk. She didn't know why everyone thought Indy kept the family running – she did, it was just that nobody noticed.

They hugged.

'What's the plan for this?' said Eden, dragging an enormous handbag out of the car.

'You're going to wreck your back with that rucksack thing,' said Savannah, whose own bag was a slim expensive-looking piece of high-quality vegan fabulousness.

'You're right,' said Eden as if she said this a lot and actually got bored with people commenting on her bag. 'I am going to wreck my back. But this has all sorts of work notes and notebooks and reports I have to read. Plus my make-up and a spare T-shirt in case I spill anything on myself. Loads of stuff. I've got one of those rollers for dog hairs because we've a cat that comes in now.'

'A cat, that's nice,' said Savannah. 'Is it your cat?'

'No, but I call her Raspberry.'

'Perfect cat name,' agreed Savannah and her twin grinned.

'I'd love a cat, or a dog. Do you remember Dexter in the hotel?'

'Yes,' said Eden fondly.

Dexter had been a young beagle abandoned outside the gates and instantly brought into the hotel by Stu, who could never resist anything sad and shivering by the side of the road. Including homeless people or drunks.

Meg had not been sure about the beagle. 'They're super clever,' she'd said, even as she wrapped the shivering dog in the blanket and snuggled it. 'They open cupboards and things, I've read about it. They can be destructive when they're alone.'

'I'm destructive when I'm alone,' Stu had joked. 'He'll be very good, won't you?' Stu had tickled the dog under the chin and then had gone off to do something else, leaving Meg, Eden, Savannah, Rory and Indy with the bedraggled, sad-eyed dog who had the unmistakable pong of roadkill on him.

'I suppose we should wash him,' sighed Meg. 'What will we call him?'

For some reason the name Dexter had been chosen. Dexter had been washed, and had not bitten anyone despite two soapings with an old bottle of baby shampoo that Indy had found. He was very gentle, they all agreed. He'd been fed with left-over cooked chicken and no bones, which he had adored. And had had a nest made for him in one of the halls of the kitchen. This had not suited Dexter, who had howled through the night as soon as he was left alone. Savannah had run downstairs, picked up the dog in his blanket and brought him up to her bed, which was where he had slept until he was very old and had gone off to live in doggie heaven.

'Why don't you get a dog?' said Eden now, thinking of how her sister had adored Dexter.

'I think Calum is allergic.'

'You either are or you aren't,' said Eden flatly.

Eden still wasn't sure if she actually liked Calum. There was just something not quite right about him. She couldn't help being her worst self when she was in his company. Which probably said a lot more about her than him. He was such an alpha male, so eager to leap into mansplaining, so full of himself. It brought out the worst in her.

'Dogs take up a lot of time,' said Savannah briskly.

'That is your "we are not talking about this anymore" voice,' said Eden.

Savannah shot her an irritated look. 'You know me too well,' she said as they walked into The Beach Hut.

Maybe not, thought Eden.

Indy was already there, looking exhausted after an early morning delivery.

'I did a split shift,' she said, 'so I could be here.'

She had a very strong coffee in front of her.

'Girls! You made it! Wonderful,' said their mother, rising like a silver-haired goddess from her seat and making everyone in the café look at her. Eden was used to her mother doing this: people looked at Meg the way they looked at Indy. They were both Valkyrie-style women. Tall, athletic, sensual. Meg was tanned with long white hair now and a body honed with yoga and clean living.

It had been hard growing up with a mother like that, Eden sometimes thought.

'Vonnie has lists of all the things we're going to do,' Meg said, after she'd hugged her twin daughters and sat down again.

'OK,' said Eden, 'hand them out.'

The lists were inevitably on pretty pink paper and Vonnie had stuck little paper flowers, angels and hearts onto each one. Her handwriting was the handwriting of a ten-year-old girl: all big loops and hearts over each 'i'. It was terribly sweet.

'You should come and be my executive assistant,' said Eden, looking at her list with pleasure.

'I'd love to be an executive assistant,' said Vonnie, pleased. 'What would I have to do?'

'Answer the phone, tell people I'm in a meeting when I'm actually having a sandwich. And what else? Oh yeah, never put anyone through to me if they call either you or me "pet" or "girl".'

'Why would anyone say those things?' said Vonnie in bewilderment.

'Because the Freedom Party is the most unwoke organisation in the history of the world,' said Eden, smiling. 'And I'm trying to change that.'

'Unwoke?' said Vonnie, confused. 'I don't understand—'

'Don't worry, Vonnie,' said Eden kindly. 'I can't afford an assistant, anyway. If anyone calls me "pet" or "girl" on the phone, I hang up instantly. Eventually, they get the message. If you explain it to them, they come up with all the reasons why I shouldn't get upset but when you hang up on them, it's like training a dog – the treat is to talk to me if they play the game!'

Everyone laughed.

Eden ordered coffee from a waiter who'd been hovering since Meg had risen, goddess-like from her seat. Savannah ordered tea.

'Anything else for you?' said the waiter, gazing at Meg.

Her mother looked luminous, Eden thought. No wonder the waiters were in love with her. She hoped she'd age like her mother and be full of vitality the way Meg was. But she also hoped that if Ralphie suddenly turned out to be a gambling man and ran through the family's money, that she wouldn't remarry him fifteen years down the road.

Now that was the very definition of insanity. Sure, Dad was all changed and did his meditation and stuff, but Eden was never sure if he'd have the stamina to keep it up.

Mum seemed so happy on her own, which was why the wedding was such a shock.

That's what seemed odd to her. She knew her parents loved each other. She loved them both but she could see their flaws. Her mother remarrying her father seemed to be a prime example of ignoring all the flaws. A true triumph of hope over experience.

Eden drank her coffee and remembered her maxim: *she could not fix them – she could not fix anyone.*

'What's first on the list?' she said.

Vonnie waggled a fluffy pen self-importantly. 'Today we're talking about the jobs we have to do. Tomorrow, we're going to the hotel to see how it looks and discuss the silk flowers I'm going to drape. Or some of you will drape,' she added. 'I don't know if I can get up on a ladder.'

'I can get up on a ladder,' said Eden, mentally running through the following day.

'Me too,' said Indy raising her head from her ultra-black coffee. 'Sorry, I'm a bit out of it here: after-shift exhaustion. I'll be fine once I have this pastry inside me.'

'I don't know if I can come tomorrow,' said Savannah, 'it's just a bit mental at work, but I'll do my best.'

'That's OK, darling,' said Meg. 'I totally understand.'

'Then, Wednesday, someone needs to pick up Sonya from the airport.'

'Why can't Dad do it? She's his sister,' said Eden.

'He has something on,' said their mother.

'Like what? Splitting the atom? Pops is retired.'

'It's his meditation class.'

'Really?' said Eden.

Indy's eyes met hers but Indy was smiling.

Eden held her hands up. 'Fine, it's his meditation. I can't do it. Even though it's summer, this is a busy a week for me.'

'No problem, I'll pick her up,' said Meg.

'Super duper,' said Vonnie, her pink pen with the fluffy thing on top bouncing as she ticked the task off her list. 'Now, Wednesday night, we have the hen party and that's all sorted out. But we do have to check with people about who's coming. I thought maybe you could do that, Savannah?'

'OK,' said Savannah, taking the list with the phone numbers of the people involved.

'Someone's going to have to keep an eye on Aunt Sandra to make sure she doesn't take to the floor and denounce Dad,' said Indy.

Meg looked gratefully at her eldest daughter.

'Oh, Sandra will be fine,' said Eden, 'absolutely fine. She's got over her strop. She loves Pops, really. Once she's made her point she moves on.'

'You think?' said her mother anxiously.

'I know,' said Eden. 'She'd a huge go at me when the party

voted in favour of putting that reservoir out near her home and there were compulsory purchase orders on several farms. But once she'd made her point and the council had passed the legislation, well, it was over. She doesn't hold grudges. She moves on. When are we going to hang all these flowery things?' she said to Vonnie, 'you know, the stuff for the hotel?'

'I was hoping for tomorrow, when we go to see the place,' said Vonnie. 'Or maybe later . . .'

'So you have all the stuff and you'll bring it in your car?'

'I've most of it. I mean, we may need more hanging equipment and possibly a ladder . . .'

'OK,' said Eden, taking out a normal pen and adding a few things to her list. She loved Vonnie but sensed that organisation was not her strong point.

'We'll sort it out. Just one thing—' she looked around – 'where's Rory?'

Rory

Rory had a hangover. She should be used to them, had had enough of them over the years and there was no doubt about it that since she'd hit her thirties, they'd got worse. But knowing you should be used to one never helped when one's insides felt like a boat on a roiling sea and one's head was pounding.

She'd woken at seven, Chantal was in the bathroom and Rory knew she'd have to drag herself out of bed to get water, paracetamol and coffee, in that order.

The night before, Chantal had watched her drinking with Louisa, Rory's recently acquired literary agent, and had pulled Rory aside anxiously. 'Rory, please. I know you hate me saying this but you're so like your father. You drink the way he clearly used to, wildly, crazily, I've seen it before. Darling, stop!'

Chantal was Irish with Vietnamese-French heritage: petite and beautiful with long dark hair that she coiled up in an elegant knot when they were going out. Rory was so in love with her, adored her.

Yet sometimes Chantal drove her mad – which was what couples did to each other, wasn't it? Saying Rory drank like her father. How insane was that? Rory knew she was nothing like her father.

This morning, though, in the cold light of both day and throbbing hangover, she admitted, with a flash of honesty, that Chantal was only worried because Rory did drink a lot. This thought drifted in and out of her mind like mist. Sometimes absent, sometimes not. It rippled in with guilt. Guilt over drinking, guilt over the one other thing she and Chantal disagreed about: children.

Chantal was the most maternal person on the planet. Rory wasn't ready for the responsibility. Wasn't sure she ever would be.

'You're going to be late for your mother and sisters.'

Chantal was wearing her scarlet and saffron vintage kimono and her dark hair was wet, pulled back from her face, making her look exotically beautiful.

'Sorry.' Rory crossed the room and held her girlfriend tightly. 'I'm a horrible old cow. You're right, I drink too much.'

Chantal leaned into the embrace. 'I only say it because of my worry about you.'

'I know.' Rory inhaled Chantal's own scent, a mix of the various potions Chantal applied each day and the scent of her lover's skin: something soft and flowery. How lucky was she to have found Chantal? She must never mess this up, never.

'Now, shower. I will bring you coffee. You have ten minutes to be gone. They'll all be waiting for you at the hotel.'

Despite the hangover, Rory was still on a high after the auction had concluded. She had told nobody in the family about it.

Telling them would be letting the cat out of the bag. They'd want to read it and she couldn't let that happen just yet. Not until she'd tweaked it.

It was fiction but like a lot of first fiction, there was plenty of fact in there too. Rory merely needed to remove any pesky little painful facts from the manuscript and then she could tell them. Now that the deal was done and the contract signed, things would move along speedily. And she could remove any particularly tricky bits, right?

Except for Chloe. It was going to be impossible to remove Chloe.

The other stuff could be fudged but the parts with Chloe in it, or the fictional version of Chloe, would be harder to tweak.

Rory felt the familiar ache in her belly.

Probably hangover, she told herself.

Before the drink had started flowing the night before, Louisa had explained that there'd be a lunch with the publishers and her new editor during the week, if possible.

'Of course,' Rory had said expansively, conveniently forgetting that her parents were getting married on Saturday and that she was involved because she was giving away the bride and had agreed to go to both the hen night and the rehearsal dinner.

If her parents were remarrying, she really wanted as little to do with it as possible apart from the actual ceremony but it was proving impossible to get out of it all. She was not, however, going to the 'let's pick up Ma's new wedding dress' morning out.

If her mother wanted to play dress-up, then Rory was not going along with it.

She peed, rinsed her mouth with mouthwash, managed not to look at herself in the bathroom mirror, then, pulling on her dressing gown, made it into the living room which smelled like a pub after a lock-in.

She and Louisa had got through so much drink last night, which was dreadful for a Sunday night. Louisa had flown back from London that afternoon after conducting the auction on Friday.

'We can discuss when to make it public,' Louisa had said as she'd arrived, with two bottles of champagne.

It transpired that Louisa knew how to party. When the champagne was gone, they had vodka-and-tonics with the delicately herbed omelettes Chantal had conjured up to line their stomachs, when it became obvious that neither of them was going to stop drinking until the auction was thoroughly toasted.

Then, they'd moved on to flavoured gin, which Rory didn't like on principle, but was perfectly capable of drinking when there was nothing else. Then that very weird brandy she and Chantal had brought back from Greece once, the sort of thing that tasted amazing when you were in Greece and suddenly not so amazing as soon as you got it home. She and Louisa had one glass but it tasted a bit off. Rory had then remembered a bottle of whiskey she'd been sent from a whiskey advertising campaign she'd worked on and even though she didn't like whiskey, needs must.

'Not bad,' she'd muttered as she sipped it first, knowing full well that mixing grape and grain was fatal the next day.

'Here's to Ireland's newest bestselling international novelist,' Louisa had said, triumphantly raising her whiskey glass.

She had triumphantly raised a lot of glasses, actually.

By the time she had finished with all the praise, Rory felt that a Pulitzer for her first novel was not out of the question. Which was amazing because in all the years she'd been writing or thinking about writing, Rory had been supercritical of her work. She'd write, stare at what she'd written and then delete it. Was this just her? Was she only pretending to be a writer?

And now this interest in her work, an actual contract: anxiety and joy mingled.

'Everyone will adore you,' Louisa said enthusiastically. Louisa was a portrait of enthusiasm.

She was the physical opposite to Rory: short to Rory's leggy tallness. Rory was five eight, although not as tall as her older

62

sisters. Rory had dark hair cut into a clever bob by a friend of Chantal's who made it look sleek and chic even when Rory ran her fingers through it and it became messy.

Louisa, on the other hand, looked like one of those girls Rory had seen coming out of the posh schools when she was a teenager.

Girls with long hair they flicked back, as well as rich parents and cars bought for them as soon as they hit seventeen and were able to drive. Rory's family had never been like that, for all that outsiders thought they were. Outsiders – neighbours, the press, everyone – bought the Robicheaux family story. They saw the glamour and assumed wealth went with it, when in fact, despite Stu Robicheaux having come from money, he had none.

But the hotel made people think they were rich – the Sorrento had been in the newspapers so many times because lots of glamorous people had parties there. When shabby-chic was fashionable, the quirky Sorrento with its genuine William Morris wallpaper, hand-painted silk Chinese hangings, and four-poster beds had an exotic and fabulous feel. Rory's parents had been so good as hotel hosts that nobody had ever guessed they were so absolutely appalling at handling money.

Mum would sail serenely through the hotel looking glamorous and elegant, kissing people on the cheek, making them feel as if she was inviting them into her home. Dad would be there mixing drinks, playing fantastic music in the background, giving people drinks on the house. It was where all the fabulous people wanted to come. And yet, they were always broke, despite always in the paper as the must-go-to destination.

It was partly the location. Set at an angle along the winding Eboli Road near Killiney Beach, close to the fabulous, successful and much better-run, Killiney Court Hotel.

Rory used to envy the girls from the private schools who came out flicking back their long hair, getting into their sweet cars bought by adoring parents and Louisa was typical of the breed, except that Louisa was unnervingly street sharp, a brilliant agent and had somehow, against all odds, managed an auction where she had sold Rory's first novel to British and American publishers. Not just her first novel, her second novel too. A novel which was largely unthought of because Rory had spent so long writing the first one.

'It's not really about all of you though, is it?' Louisa had said when they were well stuck into the champagne.

They'd had this discussion before, because Louisa, for all her long-haired, flicky-backy poshness, was at heart a ruthless business woman.

'No,' lied Rory, feeling her heartbeat race, 'it's just loosely based on a family running a hotel. I mean I wouldn't write it totally about us, but there are – shades of the family in there.'

She could hear Chantal in the kitchen getting cheese and crackers and some of those delicious little nutty biscuits they all loved. Chantal knew the truth; Chantal knew that the book was very largely based around the Robicheaux family and Rory's vision of it.

They talked about it endlessly. Fought about it.

'Writing about it is cathartic. People experience their childhoods differently,' Rory would say. 'I see my family one way and they see it another way. The book just vaguely sees a family in a hotel my way.'

'But Rory, it's a novel about a family in a hotel. It's your first novel. Everyone will think it's a thinly disguised memoir even though you say it's not. You must tell your family,' Chantal would say.

'I've been writing this book for years,' Rory had protested. 'They know I'm a writer at heart.'

'Perhaps,' Chantal had replied. 'Perhaps. But writing a book for years like a cathartic diary and releasing it as a novel are two very different things. If only you'd let me read all of it.'

'Nobody's read all of it,' said Rory, which was also a lie.

Because Louisa had read all of it, Louisa knew all the secrets. And the publishing company had read all of it and they adored it. Apparently, they loved all the thinly veiled references to the famous actors and bands who'd come to stay in the hotel and filmed their videos there.

Only the editor had asked her how much of it was autobiographical and would she be prepared to give in-depth interviews, and Rory, hyped up on the thrill of doing a huge deal, had said: 'Yes!'

She'd worked long enough in the advertising industry and knew enough about how the media worked to understand that the editor hoped this was the sort of novel that garnered vast features in newspapers about families and the experiences of them. And what it felt like to be a gay girl growing up in a dysfunctional household with such a macho father and beautiful mother amidst drinking and gambling which, ultimately, had cost them everything.

The heroine's story mirrored Rory's so well.

And it had a character like Chloe in it. A delicious twist.

Last night, before she'd gone off in a taxi, Louisa had grabbed Rory's hand and stared into her eyes.

'This book will make both our names, you know,' she'd said. 'It's so raw and truthful.'

Quite plastered at this point, Rory had let all her fears fade away and grinned. 'Fabulous,' she'd said.

But now, in the cold light of day, she felt a shiver of unease. The book was supposed to be fiction, yet it was so full of real life. She'd changed places, people, names and added in lots of stuff but still, if she was totally honest, the ring of truth was as clear as a bell in the novel to anyone who'd been there. To her family.

She'd have to make a lot of subtle changes before it was published, but that was fine, wasn't it?

*

Twenty-five minutes later, she arrived at the Sorrento with a Tupperware container of Chantal's date and cacao energy balls and her own third strong coffee in a keep cup.

She found everyone in the ballroom and conversation was going on about the curtains, wall washing and whether a lot of tealights strewn around the place would be a fire hazard or a very good plan indeed.

'From a fire safety point of view—' Eden was saying and Rory, despite hangover and unease, smothered a grin.

Eden noticed and grinned back.

They'd always understood each other, Rory thought, and then felt the pang of guilt. Eden would kill her when she found out: literally kill her. Eden had once gone out with a biker boy who'd had a swagger in his step and a deadly right punch. Eden always said he'd taught her how to street fight.

In hand-to-hand combat, Eden would undoubtedly win. For all that Rory liked androgynous clothes and her Zadig biker boots, Eden was waaay tougher.

Rory sighed.

What if she couldn't tweak the book to lessen the harder bits?

Eden would find out – they'd all find out and then what? The Chloe stuff? They'd kill her over that. To drop that into a novel and tell nobody about it first.

She hugged her mother and Vonnie.

'What have I missed?' she said. "I can do cleaning but don't ask me to do anything flowery. Chantal's much better at that.'

'Where is she?' said Vonnie.

'She's on the way to work,' Rory replied.

'I wish she was a bridesmaid,' Vonnie said wistfully.

'I asked,' said Meg, 'but she said no. Said she'd be better behind the scenes.'

Meg looked mildly upset now and Rory patted her down.

'Mum, Chantal would prefer to be behind the scenes. I

promise you. Now, I only have half an hour because I have a meeting—'

She didn't get to finish before Indy said: 'Rory! You're supposed to be helping.'

Rory held Indy's gaze for a moment.

Everyone thought Indy was wonderful but she knew what had happened and she'd kept it a secret. In a way, Rory reasoned, the revelations of her book were Indy's fault.

They'd been so close once because Indy had always mothered her. Being born each side of identical twin sisters, she and Indy had been special sisters. Youngest and oldest.

Until Indy had accused Rory of lying. It had been one of those defining moment of her childhood. A moment where the lovely world of childhood had been pierced by something sharp and painful.

'I am,' Rory said coolly to her sister. 'I wouldn't be leaving if it wasn't important. So, show me the list, Vonnie,' she added.

Chloe was waiting for her at the ice-cream shop on the seafront afterwards. They nearly always met there now because they both loved walking by the sea and there was a glorious little coffee shop that had all the weird milks just a few metres away from the rocky shore.

Chloe had two coffees waiting and an evil-looking almond croissant that would add five kilos from just looking at it, Rory thought.

'Hi, you,' Chloe said. 'Oat flat white with one sugar and a dash of hazelnut syrup.'

'Thank you,' said Rory with a sigh, kissing Chloe on the forehead and planting herself in the chair beside her.

When they'd first started meeting, they'd had to search to find a café that covered all Rory's bases: all the non-dairy milks so she could have oat, almond or coconut, depending on her mood. And an outside area for smoking that was screened so none of her mother's or her sisters' friends would see her and tell on her. Dad's friends were like Dad: they never noticed anything. Some sort of 'see no evil, hear no evil' thing operated with them all.

'How was it?' Chloe was casual but Rory wasn't fooled. Chloe was nineteen after all, despite her art-student chic and a studied air of 'I don't care what you think about me.' Rory did a good line in that herself and had used it to great effect as a teenager.

She lit a cigarette to give herself time to think, inhaled deeply then said, 'Oh fine. Squabbling. Mum wants Chantal to be a bridesmaid—' Too late, she realised that this might be the wrong thing to say, might highlight what had to be painful for Chloe. 'She doesn't want to be, obviously,' Rory raced on. 'So, tell me your news. The summer placement in the gallery. I want to hear all about it.'

Chloe, who didn't smoke, reached out for the pack of cigarettes and took one.

'Don't!' begged Rory.

Chloe glared at her with slitty blue eyes. 'I can if I want to,' she said.

Rory shrugged and took up her coffee. She could recognise a self-destructive instinct from fifty paces.

She smoked, drank too much and had written her family's deepest secrets in a book disguised as fiction. Who was she to tell anyone what to do?

'The gallery is just about making contacts. If I had the money, I'd go to Italy for the summer to one of the summer schools there. Tell me about the wedding planning?' said Chloe.

Rory breathed in and out and wished she was better at the whole deep-breathing thing. Mindfulness, yeah: that stuff de-stressed you. She needed a bit of de-stressing because she'd already said the wrong thing to Chloe.

'Ah, it's boring,' she began, hoping to ward Chloe off at the pass. 'You don't want to hear—'

'I do,' interrupted Chloe. 'Tell me everything. Everything.'

Rory gave up on the deep-breathing concept, took a slug of coffee and told her everything.

5

Tuesday

Eden

When interviewers asked Eden what it was like being a woman in politics, she always tried to gauge what sort of answer they were really after.

There were, in her opinion, three basic answers the press liked, depending on their readership.

The 'there aren't enough women in government or running companies' line.

The 'I try to juggle my family life with politics' line.

Or the one about the myriad nutters who were vicious to female politicians on social media and threatened them with every sort of abuse possible.

As a married woman without children, which, apparently, was a crime against humanity, according to some right-wing media, Eden never bothered with the whole 'juggling' schtick. But for the last six months, she could have written entire articles on the nutters. She'd dealt with social media insults before: randomers who said they wouldn't bother to rape her, which was a cunning ploy, apparently, because death or rape threats were actionable by the police and 'I wouldn't rape you' wasn't. And people wondered why there weren't more women in politics?

The nutter who had been sending personalised letters to her home since January was scaring her far more than any stranger on social media.

First, the letters were sent directly to her home – that was truly scary. Eden extracted the tell-tale yellow envelope from the normal post and wondered, as she always did, if it was worth handing over to the police.

I know your secret, Mrs Tallisker. Im going to tell.

Initially, she'd been shocked and then she'd decided that whoever had sent this to her home was clearly not the brightest bunny in the box because he or she didn't understand the use of apostrophes.

Then, she'd thought about what the letter said. That the writer knew her secret. And that thought really did scare her. If this was some person who was trying to push her out of politics through fear, that was one thing. But what if this was someone who actually knew the truth? That would destroy her.

'Is that the post, honey?' asked Ralph from upstairs.

'Yes,' she called back. 'Nothing important.'

A lie. The yellow envelope almost burned in her hand. 'I'm going to make coffee. Your father wants me to drop in on him this morning.'

'Why?'

Why indeed? Retiring from politics had not suited her father-in-law.

'You have your shower, honey,' suggested Ralph, 'and I'll make breakfast.'

Despite the letter she was holding gingerly in one hand. Eden smiled. Ralph was one of life's gentlemen, a darling of a husband and, luckily, nothing, absolutely nothing, like his father.

Former government minister and elder statesman of the Belfast Peace Process, Diarmuid Tallisker had once had two offices – his grand one in the Dáil, the Irish parliament, and the much less grand and much bigger premises in a townhouse in Wicklow town.

Now retired, he only had the Wicklow one. The ground

floor, suitably chic and with photos of the great man himself with the great and the good all over the walls, was simple and decorated in calming pale green because Agnes, his wife and the power behind the throne, said it was much used in counselling centres.

Initially, Eden thought Agnes was joking but after a few years working as a county councillor in local politics, she'd seen the point of it. Ninety-five per cent of people were perfectly polite when they approached their local representative but a good five per cent were grudges waiting for somewhere to settle and, if a bit of green on the walls calmed them down, Eden was all for it.

The man who'd kept her prisoner in her own office for fifteen minutes one day, having shoved her filing cabinet against the door before demanding she sort out his sheaf of parking fines and pointing out that, as he was the Messiah, he needed a pre-shrunk linen robe, thank you very much, had needed more than green paint.

After the first, hideous blast of fear and the terrifying thought of other brave politicians who'd been tragically killed on duty, Eden had realised the man was unwell, uncoordinated and not wielding a weapon. At that point, she'd tried talking him down and when this didn't work and he became agitated, she'd rather wished she'd had a stun gun. But, feeling calmer because four people were outside the door banging on it and telling her the police were coming, she'd hit the New Messiah on the side of the head with her *Irish Tatler* Rising Political Stars Award. The award didn't shatter – 'Amazing!' Eden had said in surprise, looking at it – but the New Messiah had groaned and fallen to the floor clutching his head and muttering, whereupon Eden had walked over his body, pulled the filing cabinet away from the door and said, in a shaky voice: 'We need an alarm button in here.'

'What were you thinking?' an anguished Ralphie had said. 'He could have hurt you.'

'I wasn't thinking,' she'd replied. 'I was scared – it felt very much him or me.'

Agnes had organised an alarm button for Diarmuid too but Eden felt he didn't need it. Diarmuid was never alone with any member of the public. His second in command, one-time political correspondent Rian O'Donoghue, was practically glued to him. Eden thought they probably went to the men's room together.

There was always a senator or two hanging around, looking for help/pearls of wisdom/a place in the photoshoot of the day. Then there were the big men of business who abandoned their Mercs, BMWs and Teslas outside the office and sat with Diarmuid on the top floor of the house, laughing, talking, doing deals on the backs of envelopes. Their eyes roved over Eden but it didn't bother her. Their eyes roved over anything female. It was pure instinct: she felt that many of them had lost the more thoughtful human qualities and were down to basic survival at this point. Business, she knew, could do that to a certain sort of man. Not all, but some of them. Rip off the tailoring and they were wolves, teeth bared, ready to fight for the deal or the sabre-toothed tiger.

Eden gave as good as she got. She eyeballed the wolves and generally made them lower their eyes first.

Diarmuid loved this. 'She's not lunch, boys,' he'd say. 'She's the next generation *me*.'

'She's a woman!' shouted one fella, who'd clearly missed the seminar on equality.

'Well spotted, Joe,' said Eden cheerily. 'Only the other day, someone was saying you were a muck savage straight out of the bog and only good for building houses but I said no, he's a champion of women's rights, dislikes all FWFs—'

'Obviously, I am—' began Joe, searching in the recesses of his brain for that speech on equality he'd learned the time he'd insulted the Lady Captain at the golf club. A senior counsel, no less. He still got the shakes thinking of it and what was an

FWF, anyway? He never admitted to not knowing things – it got you into trouble.

'She's only messing with you, Joe,' said Diarmuid, bored. 'Eden here will make mincemeat out of you all, so be nice to her. FWF means Fourth Wave Feminists, by the way.'

Today, Eden's father-in-law was not smiling at her when she entered the upper chamber with its smell of coffee, men and the illicit cigars that Diarmuid smoked in the back room with the door to the fire escape open.

His eyes alighted on Eden and narrowed.

'Gentlemen, I need the room,' he said.

The room emptied sharpish. They all knew that tone. Only Rian remained.

He was the exact opposite of his boss: Diarmuid was tall and stately. Rian was skinny, a bit haunted-looking, like a rat in human form.

Eden sat down warily. Rian leaned against the wall to one side of his boss. He was watching her.

'I had a phone call,' began Diarmuid, doing that steepling-his-fingers thing he did on important television programmes when he wanted to look statesman-like. Eden was having media training but she already knew all the moves. She was a quick study.

'Yes,' she replied, giving him her innocent faun look.

Diarmuid glared at her and dropped his steepled hands. 'Listen, you little madam, don't make the cow eyes at me. I got a phone call that the Indo have a juicy piece of gossip on you—'

Eden kept her face neutral but all twenty-two metres of her guts screamed with anxiety. The spasms rippled. How could he know about the scary notes? About what they referred to? Still, she stared neutrally back at him.

'About what?' she asked. Oscar-winning, definitely.

Diarmuid stared at her: grizzly grey eyebrows lowered, gauging her for lies.

'Someone told me that there's a freedom-of-information request on you.'

'Gosh,' said Eden.

She kept looking at him with what Diarmuid had already called her cow eyes.

'So do they have any idea what it's about?' she said, managing to look astonished.

'I know there was a lot in the papers about that water deal over in Baltinglass. But so much was written about that. There wasn't a thing wrong about it. It was just someone causing hassle.' She could sense Rian watching her now. She knew it would be dangerous to actually look at him.

Rian might look like a rat but he was a psychically enhanced rat, created in a laboratory to gaze at people with his predatory rat eyes and possibly had superhuman abilities to work out if people were lying based on what way their pupils flickered when asked a tricky question.

Instead, she looked at Diarmuid with as much innocence as she could possibly manage, desperate for him to believe her.

'I don't think it's about the water thing,' he said, a fleeting look of annoyance on his face.

And she realised he didn't know what the Freedom of Information request was about.

'What else can it be?' he said.

'I don't know. Could it be a scraping-the-barrel exercise just to cause trouble? Someone from the opposite side getting a tame journalist to investigate me? Everyone knows I'm going to be running for Fergal Maguire's seat when he retires in September. Is this how they normally do it?' she asked, going for the 'you are the senior politician and I know nothing' schtick. Diarmuid's ego was so big, it probably needed planning permission.

'I have nothing to hide, so are they trying to create something, make it sound as if I've something to hide?' Her guts clenched even more tightly. He couldn't know. But could whoever was searching for her know? While trying to look slightly confused, she racked her brains. There could be nothing official, nothing. The letters had been sent to her directly.

'Well, think; is there anything?' Diarmuid said.

'No,' said Eden, feeling on slightly firmer ground. He didn't know, he absolutely didn't know. She knew the party had investigated her before she joined. But even so political investigations into candidates were often desultory. Secrets came back and bit politicians in the bum all the time. Unbelievable secrets, things so huge it was astonishing that they'd never been revealed before.

Like the candidate who got elected and then it turned out he'd married bigamously and that his first wife was living happily in Thailand.

Or the fervently religious guy who'd been photographed buying hard-core bondage gear from a sex shop. On his own credit card.

If you had a secret, chances were, it would be found out unless you were careful.

Eden knew she'd been so careful. Plus, it was so long ago.

So while Diarmuid's people had examined her, they wouldn't have found this. Astonishingly, the examination she had had for the party was far more strenuous than any vague enquiries Diarmuid had made personally when he heard she was going to marry his son.

Personally, he didn't care what she was like, because she was good political material. Ralphie could figure it out on his own.

A sense of irritation hit Eden. She loved Ralph. And when she'd married him what had interested his father more – not his mother, but certainly his father – was whether or not she was as good for politics as she looked. Because by then, Eden had become interested in running for political life. Ralphie was a good man, she was a good person, this would not bring her down. Renewed, she stared at her father-in-law.

'Diarmuid, I don't know what they're looking for, but they're not going to find anything, are they?' She could see Rian, who had been leaning against the wall, straighten up and she repeated the sentence a little differently. 'They're not going to find anything.' God, that had been stupid, saying *are they*? But Diarmuid didn't appear to have heard it.

'No, no,' he said, 'they're not going to. And yes, if it's a tactic, you've got to know how to handle it.'

She was on firm ground again.

'Course I can handle it, Diarmuid,' she said. 'I've learned from the best, haven't I?'

She hated having to butter up his ego but it was the only way. Despite all their bluster about the Freedom Party being about uniting people, it was still run by grey men like Rian O'Donoghue with their freaky, emotionless eyes and by old school titans like Diarmuid, who could appreciate women but just didn't want to do political business with them. Women were part of the 'gender quota', unless they were his wife, Agnes, who was happy to remain in the background and work for the party.

The likes of Eden – still under forty, outspoken – scared them all.

The party, despite some efforts, was the least inclusive and all-gender-rights aware place she'd ever worked and that included a pub in the city once where the clientele were exclusively male and her signature move was flicking hands off her rear end as she passed by with a tray of beer.

Half of the party still went to church on Sundays, despite living life in a very non-church way for the rest of the week. Plus, they'd vote in Attila the Hun if he said he was pro-life because despite the Eighth Amendment making abortion legal, they were all terrified that the older populace was still wildly pro-life and saying anything about abortion at all would mess up their future election prospects. Which infuriated Eden beyond speech.

Women's bodies and their rights had taken possibly tenth place in the minds of the vast army of white, older male politicians for centuries, millennia.

Agnes had told her it would probably be a mistake to wear her 'Smash The Patriarchy' T-shirt to the last party conference but had added; 'your time will come, honey. I promise. You just have to wait for the right time.'

When was it going to be the bloody right time for her?

'Now is that it?' Eden said in her bored voice to her father-in-law. 'Because I've some personal time booked off – my parents' wedding . . .'

'Yes, yes, go,' said Diarmuid with a wave of his hand, an almost presidential wave. He'd love to be President, Eden knew, but there were definitely skeletons in his cupboard. Favours given to developers, donations from the same grateful developers.

Were his skeletons as big as her secret was? She didn't know. She didn't want to find out, either. This was a pivotal point in her career. With the next election in the autumn, she could be in national politics, finally. And could drag the Freedom Party out of the Middle Ages.

She could not, would not, allow some random blackmailer to ruin that.

Rory

The ring of the doorbell woke Rory.

She sat up in bed, realised she had the day off, then lay back down again.

Her boss at the ad agency hadn't been in the slightest bit pleased at her taking the week off but she didn't care. Rory allowed herself a small shudder that she wasn't sure was the remains of yesterday's hangover or a brief hint of anxiety. Not something she normally suffered from.

A memory from Sunday night hit her.

She'd been nursing her glass of whiskey, ruminating. Her childhood hadn't been perfect, she knew it hadn't been perfect. And everyone knew that, didn't they? But different children remembered childhoods differently. It was well known.

Eden seemed to think it had all been tickety boo. Indy behaved as though they'd been a happy family from TV sitcom-land. Savannah – who knew what *she* believed?

Rory had shuddered suddenly. Well, they'd know what she thought when the book came out. She could say that hints of the book had been inspired by her real life but that it was fictional. Saying that with a straight face would be tough, though.

And then – Rory cringed, as this went to the heart of the matter– Louisa had said: 'What do your family think about it?'

In a move she recognised as being exactly the same as her father's, Rory had downed her glass in one.

'Oh, they don't know that much about it,' she said quietly.

'Really!' said Louisa, suddenly sounding very sober. 'You do need to make them know what it's about,' she said. 'We don't want any tricky court cases, do we? Not when I just got you a six-figure deal.'

'No, it will be fine,' Rory had said far too quickly.

Why had she said that? When the book was part memoir, part cathartic novel, it had been lovely. The first piece of writing that had flowed out of her easily.

Therapy on paper: imagining the bits she'd have done differently, the bits her family might have done differently. But now – now it was very real.

Rory could still smell the cigarettes from Sunday night. They'd smoked so much even though she didn't smoke anymore except on rare social occasions. Yesterday's ones with Chloe were sheer nerves. But, of course, because they were drinking, she and Louisa had to smoke at the auction celebration. They were social smokers now which meant at least three packs during one drinking night, far more than an actual smoker would consume. The whole apartment still smelt like an ashtray instead of the bower of exquisite Diptyque candles Chantal liked to burn.

It was no good: she wasn't going to sleep now. She sat up in the bed as Chantal appeared with a huge bouquet of flowers.

'For me?' asked Rory.

'The publishers, perhaps?'

Chantal put the bouquet in its heavy glass vase on the floor and searched for the card, before handing it to Rory.

We are so thrilled to have won the auction!!! To The Eboli, *the novel of the year!!!*

Rory felt the shiver of nerves again.

'They're definitely calling the book *The Eboli*?' said Chantal, who was staring at the small card with something akin to horror.

Rory nodded.

It was hard to explain even to Chantal that after writing the book for so long, she'd become wildly wound up when Louisa had taken her on as a client.

The book had been going nowhere until she'd met Chloe and then, only then, had it come to life. Up till then, she'd been skirting around things. But Chloe's very existence had allowed Rory to mine her youth in great detail.

Then it had fallen into place.

Louisa had suggested calling the book *The Eboli*, which was the road on which the Sorrento Hotel sat. Another Italian place name in a place that seemed like a little piece of Italy.

Chantal had been horrified. 'It is as good as saying: this is the truth in fictional form. It will hurt everyone. Your parents, your sisters.'

This morning, she returned to her theme. 'You're going to have to tell them soon.'

Chantal dressed neatly in a navy dress and ballet flats, with her hair up and looking as beautiful as ever, spoke over her shoulder as she carried the flowers into the kitchen.

Rory got up and followed her partner.

'No, I'm not. They can read it like everyone else,' said Rory, sitting on one of the emerald-green bar stools. She still felt a bit ropey after Sunday's drink fest. Chantal always knew when to stop. Rory occasionally feared she didn't. But she wasn't going to think about it. She'd had enough pain. She deserved a drink when she was celebrating. Although now she was in her thirties, the hangovers seemed to last two days.

'It will be in the publishing magazines and then the newspapers will write about it. They'ill see it and everyone will be furious.'

Rory shifted and her dyed black hair, cut bluntly so that it accentuated her jawline, fell over one eye.

'They've no right to be furious,' she replied simply. 'It's all true. Mum and Dad might be living in cloud cuckoo land, where we're all one big happy family and 'oooh, let's get married again—' her voice had segued into the fake tone perfectly but now it clicked back into the sadness it always held when talking about her parents and the family breakup. She'd been the youngest, damnit. The most affected – 'but I know better. Now people can see my side of the story, even if I do tell people it's fiction and only partly based on my childhood. OK, so there's a gay character and it's set in a hotel, but that's it. I mean, all first novels are a bit about the writer, aren't they?' she added hopefully, not sure if this was always true.

In the IKEA subway-tiled white kitchen, Chantal paused at the sink. Rory was exquisitely gifted both in and out of bed. Superbly intelligent, analytical, thoughtful. But there was a self-destruct button in there somewhere and it made Chantal scared. The week-long wedding of her parents-in-law was always destined to be a wild affair but Chantal could not cope with it being angry. A little crazy, sure, she could do that – but anger, no. If Rory told them the truth, there would be much anger.

Rory could feel the vibes emanating from her darling. There was a sour, dangerous feeling in the air and Rory shivered.

Why was everything happening now? Why did bloody Mum and Dad want to get married now, for God's sake? she thought. It was ridiculous. Surely once had been enough?

Savannah

'Savannah, you're here, thank goodness: it's so exciting!'

Savannah had arrived early at the Velvet Beauty offices and Anthony, her second-in-command, was waiting for her.

'The new packaging has arrived and it's—' His voice faltered.

Savannah felt sheer terror.

It was wrong. She'd screwed up. Anthony was a very calming person to have around. But he looked quite wild eyed, his spiky hair standing up on his head because he'd been running his hands through it. And his tie was, for once, slightly askew, which was never the case. Anthony was the poster man for exquisite dressing. Even on his trip to the Burren, Savannah knew he'd have brought perfect merino sweaters to wear over his ironed chinos.

'What's wrong exactly?' said Savannah, evenly. She knew how to make herself sound calm.

'Nothing! It's fabulous!' Anthony hugged her and twirled.

Savannah allowed herself to be twirled, allowed herself to enjoy the glory of having made a clever decision.

The new boxes were a beautiful matte black and it had been a risk. She hadn't run it by Calum. He liked everything to be run by him even though it wasn't his company. He pushed his way into everything.

'The colour is glorious. This will take us to a whole new level. I can't begin to tell you how glorious it is.'

'Show me.'

Anthony was talking all the time as he led her through the

office, down to the marketing office where several boxes lay stacked against the wall.

'It was a genius decision,' said Siobhan, the marketing manager, who Calum hadn't wanted to hire because he said she'd go off on maternity leave soon as she was just married. It had been very stressful. Savannah had liked Siobhan from the first moment they'd met. It had involved a mild battle to hire her. Calum was still unsure: he was very tough on employees.

'Oh Savannah, you are a genius!'

On her desk lay the flat-pack boxes that would be made up for their products: their creams, their perfumes, their candles. The skin balm that one magazine had called 'nectar for the skin'.

In a move away from their clean, white packaging were these very elegant classy matte-black boxes with the rich cream writing.

'We can't wait to show everyone!'

'They'll be delirious,' agreed Anthony. 'I'm on my second expresso with excitement and I can't tell you what that's doing to my nerves. I think I'm going to go outside and have a cigarette to celebrate.'

'You can't,' wailed Siobhan. 'You haven't had a cigarette in months.'

'I need to celebrate!' emphasised Anthony.

'They're beautiful,' Savannah said.

Siobhan and Anthony had transferred many of the company's products into the new boxes and the effect was wonderful. She thought of the whole new campaign she had in her head to relaunch, to take Velvet Beauty to a whole new level.

Briefly, joy and pride surged through her and then it drained away.

There was one huge problem with this momentous business decision. What would Calum say when he saw this?

She hadn't mentioned the decision to change the packaging to him. She had gone ahead and made an executive decision.

Which was right, because it was her company and yet still nothing happened in Velvet Beauty that Calum did not oversee, did not OK. He had somehow infiltrated her baby and explained that his business expertise was what the company lacked.

He would be angry that Savannah had spent a vast quantity of the budget on something he knew nothing about.

That she'd made the right choice about the packaging was immaterial. If anything, it made things worse. Because Calum, who liked to think he knew everything, was King of the World, had been supplanted by her and he would hate that.

What had she been thinking?

The fear suddenly rose in her. It was impossible to explain the fear to people who didn't understand it. It was like being weakened by this creeping tingling that spread at speed over your body and into your chest. Every nerve cell pinged, sometimes she actually shook with nerves, a tiny vibration that people never saw.

Earlier in the year, for the first time ever, she'd thought she was having a heart attack and she'd gone to her doctor who'd said it was stress, contraction of the thoracic muscles.

Stress could mimic a heart attack but she was too young, her cholesterol was low, there were no other heart indicators on the expensive health checks she'd had in relation to her massive business loan. She was a healthy thirty-seven-year-old.

'OK,' Savannah said, feeling stupid and scared simultaneously. She tried to brighten the mood, which she was brilliant at. 'Gosh, must try and get less stressed.'

'Yes, that would be a good idea,' said the doctor, looking at her carefully.

'It's just work, you know work, oh, crazy,' said Savannah hopping off the doctor's couch. 'At least I know what it is now and I don't think I'm having a heart attack.'

'Stress affects your whole body and over long periods of time, it can seriously damage your health,' the doctor went on.

Savannah had given him her television smile. 'How awful,' she said. 'Better avoid that.' And she laughed, as if the very idea of her being stressed was ridiculous.

Now, she wished she'd been more honest with him because, at this precise moment, it did feel as if she was having a heart attack. There was a vice-like grip around her heart. Worse, it felt like there were hands around her neck and encircling her slim wrists, squeezing, angry, furious and she felt the intense fear of having done something wrong. Again.

'Anthony,' she said, still clinging to the notion that she needed to sound calm. 'I think I'll join you in a cigarette outside for a celebration.'

'You? Smoke?' He was stunned.

'Coffee and a cigarette to celebrate!'

She had to get out into the air and do something with her hands, take something, stop the fear. She hated smoking but it would make her feel ill and that would stop the fear . . .

'I'll make coffees,' said Siobhan, suddenly energised. 'I don't smoke but let's all sit outside!'

'Yes,' said Savannah as she pushed the door open. Outside. She'd breathe outside. She didn't want a blasted cigarette: Rory had been the smoker but she needed something to calm her and cigarettes did that, didn't they?

In the outside, the three of them sat with coffees on a little bench and smoked. The cigarette made Savannah feel sick. Why had she smoked?

She knew the answer to that: to take away the fear. She would have done anything to take away the fear.

Savannah had started Velvet Beauty before she met Calum. She often thought that if she had met him first, the business would never have happened, but then Calum probably wouldn't have been interested in her. He had been attracted to both her beauty and her success. Eden had once said this to her, a statement that had shocked her.

'You've got quite the package going there, sis,' Eden had said, idly and yet perhaps with a hint of envy. 'Me thinks the handsome Calum fancies you and your business. You'll be quite the power couple.'

It wasn't Eden's fault that she got envious, Savannah knew. She adored her twin sister. But they were so different for all that they looked exactly the same, the same hair that was dark strawberry with occasional blond hints, the same eyes, the same noses for goodness' sake, the same way their freckles came up when the sun shone.

Both of them slathered themselves in Factor 50 suncream, and it was really annoying that Indy and Rory took after Mum and Dad and were beautifully olive skinned.

'You must have adopted us,' Eden sometimes said when she was younger at the fabulous parties in the hotel when she'd sneak around taking little sips out of other people's glasses of wine.

'As if,' Mum always said, ruffling Eden's hair lovingly. 'Eighteen hours of labour; ask your sister what that must be like.'

But Eden had been born with that little hint of envy and Savannah understood that. Eden always wanted to be the best at everything.

She had been like that in school, even when she was going through her particularly wild phase. Savannah had wanted to blend in, which was why she knew it was odd that she had started up a business that seemed to require her to be front and foremost. It was just that the idea had come to her and being the front woman had come later, too late to back out.

'Fake it till you make it,' Eden had said before any presentations her twin had to make. 'The secret is to look confident and people think you are.'

Easy for Eden to say. She had confidence oozing out of every pore.

Savannah had had to force herself to be the public face of her company. But she loved what she did. It was her dream. She adored perfumes, creams and unguents. When she'd been young and Eden had been inexpertly layering their mother's black eyeliner on her lids, Savannah had been making creams with rose petals and lavender, although they generally separated into liquid and gunk in about two days. It had taken time before she learned how to make a proper emulsion the way the Nivea people had in the 1890s.

But she'd held on to that dream: the idea of starting a business using wonderful herbal recipes with the scents she loved as a child from walking around the old gardens in the hotel. That dream had kept her going through lots of difficult times.

She'd started the business with a loan from the credit union. Back then it really had been kitchen-table stuff.

She'd worked on it in the farmhouse in Greystones when she was studying chemistry in college, they were terribly broke and Mum was working all the hours. Savannah's first lab was out the back in one of the sheds, which had been a nightmare in every respect. And then, she'd got a proper business loan. Suddenly, Enterprise Ireland had taken an interest, she'd had a mentor. Everything had taken off. There had been terrible pain when her darling mentor Terry had left, had gone to New York to marry a wonderful man who worked for the UN. Savannah had felt so lost then.

And then Calum had come into her life and changed it. Utterly.

Twelve Years Previously

The Savannah Robicheaux of twelve years ago had a mane of long hair she sometimes plaited the night before so that it fell down her back in symmetrical ripples.

'The Beauty behind Velvet Beauty', one small magazine article had been headlined.

Raised in the glamorous Sorrento Hotel in Killiney, Savannah Robicheaux was chambermaiding from a young age: 'none of us are afraid of hard work,' says the young entrepreneur when we meet in her small offices in an industrial park outside Dublin.

It had been such a coup to get the article in the magazine. Eden had helped her with it.

Eden was a force of nature and could pick up the phone, ring absolutely anybody and ask them for anything.

'They can only say no,' Eden would say, shrugging as if this type of behaviour was entirely normal.

'How did we come out of the same womb at the same time?' Savannah said jokily.

Eden gave her a hard stare. 'You need to push your boundaries.'

Savannah shivered. 'No, I don't. You can do it for me.'

'Yeah, but I won't always be around to do it, sis. You need to be tougher, take no prisoners.'

Savannah hated the 'you need to be tougher' talks. Nobody ever said how to be tougher – did she need to wear chain mail, down two vodkas before she made tricky phone calls, what?

'I'm not like you.'

'S'pose.'

Eden had set up the interview and then another one, and suddenly, Savannah's company had momentum.

The beauty buyer in a glamorous store in Tokyo began stocking Velvet Beauty, which made it suddenly visible on the world stage. Then, an equally glamorous Irish store began stocking it.

'They only noticed you because the Japanese liked your stuff,' said Eden grimly. Eden had firm views about how fame in other territories made local stockists sit up and take notice.

'It doesn't matter.' Savannah was delighted. She didn't care what had come first: what mattered was the success.

'You don't get the nuance, it's insulting—' began her twin.

'I'm not insulted. I'm making money!' said Savannah happily.

She'd met Calum at a business dinner and he'd made a move on her right away.

She'd been wearing a dress Eden had made her buy: of heavy silk satin and the colour of moss on summer trees. It was high necked at the front with a cut-away back to reveal her elegant shoulder blades and the pale golden curve of her spine.

Calum Desmond, a dead ringer for a James Bond role in his dinner jacket, dark hair sleeked back, onyx studs in his fine Italian dress shirt, had walked up to her holding two glasses of champagne.

'I told myself that when I found you, I'd bring you champagne,' he said.

Charisma surged around him and Savannah, who rarely drank at work events in case she giggled at the wrong moment, found herself taking a glass from him.

'When you found who?' she asked daringly.

This handsome man, winged brows shadowing dark eyes, a hint of dangerous masculinity around him, seemed fascinated by her. Her! It was a dizzying feeling.

'You.'

He wasn't much taller than she was in her high silver sandals but his presence felt as if it filled the ante room beside the function room. He was quite dazzlingly handsome, was devilishly dark. All five o'clock stubble and hooded eyes.

'Me?'

This was flirting but she was really out of practice. She hadn't time for men as she tried to build the company. She sipped her champagne, licked her lips, then realised how clichéd this looked.

But the man didn't seem to think so. He was watching her

89

lips and she felt a surge of feminine power. He was watching her, entranced.

'You,' he replied simply.

'I know who you are,' she said.

He was often in the newspapers: an advisor to companies, on all sorts of Young Irish Entrepreneur power lists. He'd set up a protein shake company which was hugely successful, apparently. She was a bit muddy on what else he did exactly but he was somebody, of that there was no doubt.

'But I don't think you know my name . . .'

She risked a tiny smile at the game. She was winning it.

Eden had told her she looked amazing. She went jogging most mornings, sea swam at weekends. She hadn't had time for men. Not since that year dating Tom, who had turned out to be a bit of a control freak.

'He's a bit opinionated,' her mother had said when she met Tom and he'd launched into a 'my world vision' speech over dinner.

'Total gobshite,' Rory had said, more succinctly.

'And he kept holding onto you,' said Eden, 'as if you might fly away if he didn't keep a firm hold on your arm.'

They'd all been right, sadly.

Luckily, she and Tom hadn't gone so far as to move in together, which meant that it was easy to get out of it when he'd been transferred to the Limerick office. That was a year ago.

This new man, Calum, seemed a million miles away from Tom.

He was suave: he'd never deliver any speeches about his world view. He was possibly a year or so younger than her and his gaze was admiring. 'You're Savannah Robicheaux. Founder of Velvet Beauty. The photos don't do you justice. Any of them. You're more beautiful than your sisters. More slender.'

'Can I get you more champagne?'

He reached for her empty glass and their fingers met. The heat of his touch made her inhale suddenly.

So much of the night was engraved in Savannah's memory. She could replay it if she wanted to: how she'd thought he'd whisk her away, like a rescuing prince on a white charger. Instead, he'd brought her to her table and had taken her card.

'I'll be leaving early: I've an early flight,' he'd said. 'I'll phone you when I'm back. If you'd have lunch with me—?'

'Yes,' Savannah had replied, only just stopping herself from asking for his number. Men always said they'd phone and then they didn't and she wanted this man. The thought shook her. She really wanted him. He would whisk her away, take care of her, make sure life was safe . . .

'Good. Take care, Savannah,' he'd said, taking her wrist and kissing the inside of it.

Excitement trilled through her. This was like a fantasy scene in a film: a man kissing her wrist, this man.

She'd been on a high for days.

Every time her mobile phone rang, she'd grabbed it. Then he'd phoned.

'Did you think I wouldn't contact you?' was the first thing he asked, and she laughed because he'd got it exactly right.

'I did worry,' she began.

'Never worry. I am here to take all your worry away,' Calum had said.

It had been a fairy-tale courtship.

Calum had taken her out to expensive restaurants and for romantic weekends away. If there was a hotel with a four-poster bed in it – Savannah adored four-posters – then they went there. He paid for it all and Savannah, who had always worried about money since being a child in the fiscally-wobbly Sorrento, felt relief that this confident, generous man had come into her life. They graced every event in the city and posed for society photographers outside, with Calum standing proudly and protectively beside her, one arm clasped tightly around her waist.

'You make a lovely couple,' Eden remarked one evening when Savannah came over to her and Ralphie for dinner. 'When are we going to meet this paragon of romance, or are we only going to see him in the papers? You've been going out with him for ages now. I want to look him in the eye—'

'And scare him!' joked Ralphie.

'Yeah, if he needs it,' Eden agreed. 'Anyone going out with my sister needs the "if you ever hurt her, then watch your back for the rest of your life" warning.'

Ralphie laughed.

Eden didn't. 'You think I'm joking,' she said.

'You are,' Ralphie countered.

'I'm not,' said Eden, with a toss of her head.

'Calum's lovely,' Savannah insisted but, in truth, one of the only things about Calum that she couldn't get to grips with was his lack of interest in her family and lack of desire to meet them.

'Have you met his family?'

'I've met his mother,' said Savannah. Tonya Desmond was tiny, only five feet tall, with arthritic hands covered in jewels. They'd met at a dinner in town.

'Mama hates entertaining at home,' Calum said as if Savannah would expect a state dinner in her honour and his poor mother would not be up to such a thing.

'She could come to my place,' Savannah pointed out. She lived in the apartment she and Eden had shared for years before Eden had moved into a house with Ralphie: it was small and pretty, but big enough to squash all her family in to meet Calum and his mother if only he'd agree. The Robicheaux family were fine with pasta in bowls on their knees in front of the telly.

But Calum wasn't.

It had almost been a state dinner in the end: an ultra-posh restaurant with Tonya sending everything back because it was too hot/too cold/not what she'd expected. Calum danced attendance on her and appeared not to notice that his mother was rude to the waiters. He was rude to the waiters, too. However, he did notice that Savannah, embarrassed, was obsequious with all the staff to make up for the older woman's arrogance.

This had annoyed Calum, the first time she'd seen any irritation from him.

'It's their job to get things right,' he'd muttered angrily to Savannah.

And Savannah, who'd waited on tables in the Sorrento and knew exactly how hard it could be in a restaurant kitchen and how exhausting and rude people could be, had said nothing. His mother was difficult. He didn't want her upset. That was all.

Everyone had met Calum for the first time at Eden's and Ralphie's wedding.

He'd been the life and soul of the party, even sitting with her father and his pals, drinking soft drinks because the new, improved Stu didn't drink, singing along when Ferdie, her father's oldest pal, had taken out his acoustic guitar and a session had started up. Savannah felt Calum wasn't enjoying himself but he was doing a good impersonation of it and for that, she was grateful.

'Nice fella, that Calum,' her dad had said.

'Polite,' her mother had agreed.

'Very gentlemanly,' agreed Vonnie, 'and handsome. You wouldn't kick him out of bed for eating crisps.'

Eden had thought him charming enough but she'd said her own wedding was hardly the time to get to know him properly.

'Let's have him round when we get back from the honeymoon,' she'd said. 'I'll set Agnes on him: she'll unearth any dark secrets. Agnes is better than Diarmuid at that. She's like sniffer dog.'

'We don't need a sniffer dog,' Savannah laughed, a glass in her hand, as she watched her father's friends and Calum all chatting happily.

Rory was the only one not to be impressed.

'Bit of a showman and definitely a homophobe,' she said, her mouth narrowed.

'No, he's not.' Savannah instantly leapt to her boyfriend's defence. Then followed it up with: 'Why do you say that?'

'He shook my hand like I was radioactive. That enough of a hint for you?'

'He wouldn't—' began Savannah.

'He did,' said Rory bluntly.

Savannah said nothing. They just didn't understand Calum: not like she did. He made her feel safe. He was so interested in her business. In everything about her.

He loved it best when they were alone. That was love, true love.

6

Meg

The man on the radio said it was going to be the hottest week the country had seen in several years.

Too hot, he implied.

Stu had stayed over the night before and they'd both woken in the middle of the night, sweating in a tangle of sheets.

'I'll get us some ice water,' Stu had said, after he'd leaned over and kissed her very gently on one shoulder.

Meg had sighed voluptuously. The old Stu was always too hungover to do things like get ice water in the middle of the night. The new improved version was happy to prove how different he was.

At first, Meg had thought that people couldn't change but she knew better now. He really was a different man.

Stu came back with water and a small towel which he'd soaked in cool water.

'You are a genius,' Meg said, sitting up and mopping her face and décolletage with the towel.

'I wish,' he replied, getting back into bed and sipping his water. 'Is it worth installing air conditioning here?'

Meg's railway cottage on the hill in Killiney had the master bedroom in the converted attic and in summer it was unbearably hot. After the wedding and honeymoon, Stu was moving from his house into hers: their first time living together since they'd left the Sorrento.

'I couldn't afford air con,' Meg said, 'but when there are two of us, we might be able to.'

Inside, she'd felt a smile unfurl in her, like a flower in the sun. Together, again. Meg knew her daughters had misgivings about this wedding but she didn't. She wanted to be with Stu again, despite all that had gone before.

She'd known true loneliness. She knew she didn't want to live like that anymore.

Eleven-thirty was an OK time for everyone to meet at the hotel, Meg had decided, even Indy, who had another early morning shift but said she'd be off by eleven because she'd done a shift swap. She'd brought coffees and pastries for everyone as it was too late for breakfast but too early for lunch.

By the time she and Vonnie arrived at the hotel, Vonnie was already halfway through her pastry and was covered in croissant flakes.

Meg, who fought a hard battle to stay away from fatty things, felt hungry but flattened the feeling.

'Isn't this exciting,' Vonnie was saying, wildly excited with the day.

Savannah, eyes hidden behind sunglasses and clad in very dull taupe trousers and a white shirt buttoned up to the neck, took hers with pleasure.

'Thanks, Mum,' she said, a sweet smile on her small face.

Meg felt her motherly instincts prickle, as they often did around Savannah. Which was ridiculous, obviously.

Savannah was thirty-seven, a mother, a successful businesswoman. So why did Meg feel the urge to throw her arms around her daughter? She felt silly. It was the wedding, making her feel overly emotional.

'Where's Eden?'

Nobody knew.

'Saving the world, I suppose,' Savannah said brightly, still wearing her sunglasses, even though they were in the car park under the shade of the trees. 'I always forget how pretty it is here,' she added.

'I know.'

Meg squeezed her daughter's arm, and instinctively felt for extreme thinness.

Savannah didn't tense the way she used to – and her arm felt strong and muscled beneath her clothes. Letting go of a breath she had barely been aware she was holding, Meg smiled and looked around.

The hotel had always been pretty. Like a fading beautiful woman, it'd had good bones and was always able to put on a good show: Virginia creeper hiding bits of outer damage to the late Georgian structure; the stone wolfhounds looking suitably heroic in their pose by the door, the bay trees still elegantly standing sentinel at the steps up to the porch. If the Sorrento Hotel had been a lady, she'd have been one of those now stooping, yet still elegant, who wore Hermès scarves in their eighties, a real pearl necklace and nobody would notice bent, arthritic fingers or the fact that the cords in her neck were taut with age, while the skin around drooped and creped.

'Stand still!' commanded Vonnie, holding up her phone. 'I'm taking a photo. I'm the chief bridesmaid – this is my job.'

Obediently, Savannah and Meg held on to each other and smiled, then Savannah drifted off.

'Shall we wait for Eden, Rory and Indy?' Vonnie was walking towards them and checking the phone's pictures.

'No,' said Meg. 'Indy's on an emergency labour, Rory might not make it, she says and Eden . . .' She shrugged.

Politics was a crazy business: Eden was always saying it. She might have been on the phone frantically trying to find housing for someone or in a meeting about a bypass or discussing children's health services. Between running her weekly surgeries and her endless meetings, Eden never stopped. Ralph's mother had taught her well. Agnes Tallisker made Meg feel a bit of a time waster, which was something few other people could.

Agnes had raised four children, run a successful chain of pharmacies, and took care of the small stuff so her husband, Diarmuid, could be the great politician. Now Eden was doing it all, but Ralph – and Meg loved him but he was sweetly dizzy – would not be there sorting out the loose ends the way Agnes had done for Diarmuid.

At the edge of the circular lawn in front of the hotel, weeds were growing in the gravel. Meg bent out of habit to pull them up. She had lived here for twenty-five years, after all, and had never walked on the gravel without stooping to weed a bit. Saturday would quite possibly be her last visit, she thought, suddenly hit with sadness. She would not want to come back when her once-beloved home was turned into flats.

'Coming?'

Savannah was at the door.

Meg straightened up. No more reminiscing. This was not a time for sadness. It was a time for happiness. The Robicheaux family were becoming whole again in a wonderful, rich new way.

Eden found them in the ballroom where the smell of damp was faint but still there.

Vonnie was having a bit of a panic.

'I had no idea there could be this much damp. It never looked that way before, did it?' she was saying, pulling elderly brocade curtains away from the giant French windows that led into the gardens. The curtains were held together with thread and miracles while above, the curtain poles were draped in ancient spiderwebs. 'This fabric is ruined. We'll never get it ready for Saturday. Why did we say we'd have it here?'

'Because we're getting it for nothing, because it's a bit last minute and because it's romantic,' said Eden, kissing her mother on the cheek.

Meg perked up.

'No second thoughts,' Eden whispered.

'You've changed your tune,' Meg whispered back.

'I was a bit hormonal,' said Eden lightly.

Meg started and Eden quickly moved the conversation on.

'Plus, pulling this hotel back from the brink is what we Robicheaux women do, isn't that right, Ma?'

Eden was clenching her fists as she said this and spoke loudly, so that Vonnie could hear.

'Really?' Vonnie's eyes were as big as a nine-year-old's at Christmas.

Eden looked at Vonnie, who was like an aunt to her and yet was still adorably childlike, despite having two adult children of her own, three grandchildren, and a husband whose bad back had forced her into a life of bending over a sewing machine and occasionally cleaning other people's houses to make ends meet.

Vonnie had never done anything in her blameless life that would make her the target of blackmailing hate mail. Eden was sure of it.

Nobody would be sending her *I know what you did* letters. For a brief moment, she wished she was Vonnie, with a simple, blameless life.

But then she wouldn't be running to be chosen as a national candidate with a big political party, she wouldn't have a chance to make real change in the world and she wouldn't be married to darling Ralphie. His mother was great, too, she conceded, but she could do without his father right now.

'Yup, that's what we Robicheaux women do. We sort things out,' said Eden firmly. She looked around the room, pushing away all the memories the hotel evoked in her. This had been their home for so long and it was really quite strange being back. In fact, she wasn't sure why Mum and Pops had decided to get married again here, of all places. But – there was no point thinking about that now.

Keep moving forward.

'I'll just run out into the kitchen and see if there's a ladder lying around. There used to be a little step ladder hidden in one of the pantries.'

The kitchen was a warren of little rooms from back when

the hotel had been a grand private house. The plans to turn them all into cold rooms and clever storage places had never materialised.

Eden was gone before anyone could go with her.

Eden knew she was a doer. Other people talked about what they were going to do, but she did it, it had always been the same. That was why Ralph said proudly she was just a good politician, would make such a good person in government.

'You get stuff done, darling,' he said proudly.

'She does,' agreed his mother, just as proudly.

Eden adored her mother-in-law because Agnes saw a side of her that not many people did: that of a very straight arrow who wanted the best for other people, especially for women and children. Some thought that Eden had had a conversion when she'd found politics but, really, it had happened earlier than that. Eden knew how easy it was to have life hit you in the solar plexus.

With her own family, Eden felt as if her rather rackety youth was what they remembered. They looked at her and they didn't see the calm local politician. No, they saw the wild child and that rankled.

The kitchen smelled bizarrely of richly spiced Indian food. Eden tried to remember who had last had the hotel and could come up with nothing where Indian cuisine was the main dish and yet the scents were there: the mystical sweet scent of cardamom, layered with cumin, the hint of the smoky spice of the tandoor oven. But there was no tandoor oven. Everything was totally tidy but a film of dust lay all over the once-sparkling stainless-steel surfaces. Brushing away memories of how often she'd scrubbed the place down as a teenager, Eden shouldered into the door at the back hall, and after some searching, found herself in one of the old pantries where they used to keep tins and other non-perishables. There, as she remembered it, was a now slightly rusting small metal ladder. It would do perfectly, she thought.

Back in the ballroom, Vonnie was explaining her vision for the theme for the room. She had been, to all their great misery, on an Instagram account of a fancy wedding designer. Vonnie was a recent convert to Instagram but she loved what she saw and applied no internal filters to the unreachable, filtered photos of Malibu-tanned girl brides with flowers in their hair, dewy skin and vast budgets.

'When we talked about it ages ago, I was thinking swags of silk flowers,' Vonnie was saying, gesturing at the curtain poles in a fluid movement. 'I've been making them for other weddings over the years and once I heard about you and Stu, Meg, I started on your batch. But the ones I've seen . . . just lovely. Ombre is very in right now. You could buy them if you don't like mine or if I don't have enough. We should have started earlier . . .' she trailed off.

Meg was firm: 'We could never buy anything as beautiful as you make, Vonnie. What nonsense. Your flowers are exquisite.'

'But I hope I have enough. If only we had started earlier. I am fast, obviously, but it's all so rushed.'

Vonnie had hit the nail on the head, Eden thought, carefully putting down the ladder. Her parents had decided to get married, then did nothing for ages so that now, days before the event, they were staring at a once beloved but now shabby premises which would require fleets of people to make it decent. A Lottery win. Or both.

The most they could hope for was to hide the worst of the damp, light a million candles, set up fairy lights and pray the bougainvillaea and buddleia still threw off such strong scents from the garden that no hint of damp smell would linger.

Vonnie was back on Instagram. 'I mean I could have made silk-flower table settings too, I have so many off-cuts of material. Look at this – isn't it gorgeous?'

'We want it clean and fresh, that's all,' Meg said calmly. 'You are not to worry or overwork, Vonnie, darling. We are going to have flowers on the table and—'

'— and take down the curtains,' said Eden, deciding to put the ladder in front of the first set of French windows.

Worrying over the road not taken was Vonnie's speciality.

Eden had no time for it. Her life had always been lived going forwards, at full tilt. She adjusted the ladder and had climbed up before anyone could squawk about holding it steady. Eden had so much on today that there was no time for wasting. She had a meeting at two and it was already nearly twelve. She had an hour here, max, and she needed to get the plan made.

The heavy curtains unhooked and fell to the floor in massive piles, clouds of damp spores rising like puffs of smoke.

'We'll probably all get triple pneumonia,' she joked, staring down at the piles of fabric.

Savannah, who had been standing looking out at the French windows in a faintly vacant way, turned and smiled. An automatic smile, Eden thought. What was wrong with Savannah? It was like she'd checked out of her head, somehow.

Savannah caught her twin sister staring at her and pulled herself together.

'Yes,' she said, 'what should we do?'

'OK,' said Eden in the space where she knew she was best – in charge. 'I suggest we take down all the curtains, we get someone in to clean the walls, because it's a lot of work. Maybe get Dad and a couple of friends to clean.'

'Not the wallpaper,' said her mother, shuddering.

They all paused, thinking of the days when the old wallpaper was part of the Sorrento's charm.

'Shabby chic full of turn-of-the-last-century grandeur with painted walls and real William Morris panels scattered here and there,' someone had described it in a review.

'We need the walls cleaned with sugar soap or something,' Eden said.

'It's very old wallpaper,' Meg said.

Eden looked at her mother, feeling her patience ebb. Mum

was never like this – lost in the past. Mum was like her, moving forward. But then, Mum was remarrying Pops, which was the very epitome of being in the past.

'Mum, we've only a few days to get this ready, I don't know what Frank told you about how good it was, but nobody has looked after this place in years, possibly since we left it. You saw how shabby the hall is.'

'He said the people he rented it to ran, or were going to run, it as an Airbnb.'

'It must have been for people who had olfactory issues,' joked Eden. 'Or else he had the heating on full blast in the bedrooms.'

The bedrooms, eight of them in the hotel part of the house, had been beautiful, complete with four-posters, William Morris fabrics in some, heavy damasks in others. One half-tester entirely in pink watered silk, which was handy because, no matter how old it got, it still looked good as watered silk's very description implied someone had thrown a bucket of water over it.

'If we get all the curtains down, maybe get some bits of muslin and hang them over them, drape them with a couple of your silk flowers, Vonnie . . .' Eden said now, looking at Vonnie, who brightened up at this talk of her own involvement. 'We're hiring the tables, the tablecloths and the chairs, right?'

'Yes,' said Meg. Stu had organised that.

They'd been to a place which rented out fabulous party stuff – you could have entire tables ready decorated, with little gilt chairs, ribbons and napkins in every colour. Of course, they would then have to dress the tables and the chairs. They were saving money by doing the flowers themselves. Planned for Friday morning.

'That and the flowers will be perfect. Now catering.' Eden had a mental list.

'It's all organised,' said Meg. 'Lots of cold tapas and Gianni's doing us bruschetta. Ottolenghi salads, plenty of those roasted cauliflowers and two cold salmons, one plain, one honey and sesame seeds. And sourdough bread, obviously. Karen's going to make us lots of tiny cupcakes instead of a big cake. Much nicer.'

'Great, we do need to clean out the kitchen, though, because they won't want to come into it. It's clean but dusty. And if it's not up to scratch, they won't use it, you know that.'

In her work with the council, Eden had been involved in many cases where irate constituents had had premises closed because of health issues.

'Yes, I know,' her mother agreed.

Eden clambered down the ladder and moved it over to the next curtain. But before she climbed again, she went over to her mother and gave her a big hug.

'It's going to be fab, Mum, absolutely fab, just need to do a bit of work today. Vonnie, are you making a list of what you have to do?' Vonnie needed an actual list, Eden knew.

'Yes, yes,' said Vonnie, rifling through another mad sparkly handbag that looked like something a small child brought to parties.

Eden smiled at her. Every family needed a Vonnie to take people's mind off tricky issues.

'OK, will you write this down?' Eden went on. 'We need yards of muslin for the windows, we need your silk flowers and we need to get the walls washed down and cleaned. Dad can do that with his friends. It was his idea.'

'You know your dad has always been dreadful at cleaning,' Mum said, sounding anxious.

'I'll ring him,' said Eden, evenly.

What was wrong with everyone today? Savannah looked as if she wasn't up to organising a piss-up in a brewery, never mind running her own company. Mum was being all feeble, which wasn't like her at all. Rory hadn't turned up yet.

Only Vonnie, complete with sparkly small-child handbag

and now producing her pen with a purple fluffy top on it, was behaving as normal.

'Can you make two lists, actually?' said Eden to Vonnie. 'One for me, too.'

She scanned the room: dehumidifiers, definitely. They needed to draft in a few extra people on Friday to help set it all up. Otherwise, she and Indy would be doing it all on Saturday morning. Rory was being so useless she hadn't even shown up and Savannah – what was wrong with Savannah?

Indy was just getting out of her car at the Sorrento when Rory's car – very Rory, a sleek sporty thing in ice-blue – squealed to a halt beside her. Rory was talking loudly, clearly on the phone.

'I have to go, darling,' Indy said to Steve on the phone. She'd only phoned him when she'd parked: Indy didn't believe in using the mobile when driving. She'd seen too many phone-related accidents when she'd done her time nursing in A & E. Pity Rory had no experience of mangled bodies due to people taking their eyes off the road for a moment to look at texts.

'No, I'll organise dinner, honey,' she said. 'Love you too.'

She hung up and did her best not to bestow a disapproving glare upon her youngest sister. Apparently, she failed.

'It's hands free,' said Rory by way of greeting as she locked the car.

'Yes but—' began Indy.

'You're so holier than thou,' Rory interrupted.

Indy opened her mouth to speak and then shut it.

How was it that she dealt with all manner of stress in work where women laboured in intense pain to bring babies into the world, where funding and administration made life tricky, where she had to cope with difficult relatives and even more difficult births, and she could do it. But two minutes with her sister, and Indy felt like shouting.

'I don't mean to be,' Indy said, sucking in the irritation.

She wasn't sure when things had gone wrong between her and Rory but, lately, they couldn't be with each other alone without arguing. It had to stop and she, as the older sister, the peacemaker, dammit, had to stop it.

Rory glared at her and then seemed to subside.

'You been working?' she asked as they walked towards the hotel.

'Yes,' said Indy. 'We had a difficult breech presentation and—' She stopped.

Rory wouldn't want to know. Rory had no interest in babies. She was a fabulous aunt but said, loudly, 'Children only get interesting when they're about three.'

Chantal, on the other hand, loved hearing about Indy's work. Her beautifully expressive face lit up with any sort of baby talk.

'How's Chantal?' Indy asked.

Rory shot her a look that said she knew precisely how Indy's line of thought had gone: from baby to Chantal. 'Fine. Steve and the girls?'

'Fine. I hope there's not too much to do today,' Indy said.

Rory laughed. 'It's going to be Damp City in there. I don't know who's maddest – them for getting married or us for going along with it.'

They walked the rest of the way in silence.

Indy felt tired after her shift and relished the peace, even if Rory was stalking along beside her without speaking.

As for Rory, she was a mass of conflicting emotions.

Why did Indy always have to connect Chantal with having babies? Sure, Chantal wanted babies. But that was theirs to talk about, it was nobody else's business. And as for this wedding, it was insane. It always came back to the past. Not one person in the Robicheaux family wanted to look at the past except for Rory and they'd kill her if she talked about it.

Well, tough. Because she was going to. Writing her book had been so cathartic – it had helped her understand who she was and what had shaped her. They'd have to live with it, wouldn't they? Rory was going to own her truth.

Savannah

Timing was everything in Savannah's life. Everything had to run like clockwork and if it didn't, her whole day would fall apart. Sometimes, she felt like running away: leaving the car, running, barefoot, up to Clary's school and collecting her, and then they'd run together . . . silly, wasn't it?

Today, she'd gone to the Sorrento to see what needed to be done for Saturday's wedding and she'd felt almost spaced out there, as if all the excess emotion in her had flooded to the surface and she couldn't think straight.

She knew Eden had noticed but her twin had said nothing. Nobody ever did, Savannah thought miserably. She was locked in her own world, a world she'd willingly walked into and nobody was going to rescue her from it.

Rescue. The very words mocked her.

She'd loved films as a child where a hero rescued the heroine. Where love and valour made everything all right.

'You're my romantic girl,' her mother used to say fondly when she found Savannah curled up on a couch watching an old black and white movie, hugging a cushion and watching the heroine getting saved. In movies, eventually, someone would notice the person needing saving. Cinderella was her favourite fairystory and her favourite film plot.

In real life, though, the painful truth was that nobody rescued you.

You had to rescue yourself and first, you had to believe you needed rescuing and weren't just being overly emotional. Then, you had to actually change things.

Changing your life was like climbing the world's highest peaks: it took guts and strength.

There had once been a slender thread that linked Savannah to her reserves of strength and guts. That linked her to the woman she'd once been. But it was gone now. She was at the bottom of the mountain, unable to move. Trying to survive.

Arriving back in the office, two espressos banished Savannah's earlier spaced-out feeling.

She clothed herself in her office persona: smiling, warm, enthusiastic – and always with a list.

Her list was long: check the outgoing orders, make sure all the invoices were gone, say hello to the staff – fourteen of them – and admire the new boxes.

She felt a quiver run through her at her husband's reaction when he saw what she'd done. Calum was a brilliant businessman and he had the instincts for business, he always said.

He'd told her often enough that she was the arty head of things but that the business, that was all him. She recalled when things had changed. When his own business had gone bankrupt. He hadn't been broken – he'd been insane with rage.

That was when he'd gone from being her cheerleader to being the one in charge, the one who called the shots. His business and the kudos along with it was gone so now he grabbed onto hers.

Looking back, his control over everything seemed to have happened slowly, like the goldfish being boiled alive in water that kept getting gently warmer.

He got angry over the slightest things.

If she answered back, she got the silent treatment where he would simmer, raging silently, for weeks at a time. Not talking to her, making the atmosphere in their home toxic.

She learned to walk on eggshells, to do nothing to upset him.

But it was hard to know *what* upset him. Her laughing on the phone with her sisters – that could set him off.

Her taking so much as a glass of wine when they were out – another danger area.

'Your father's a lush,' he'd hiss. 'I don't want you to be one too.' And yet in public, he was polite to her father, charm itself.

The only utterly revealing part of this Jekyll and Hyde persona appeared with waiting staff, a person at a cash register: the people Calum didn't see as important.

She could only cringe when he spoke to them the way he spoke to her.

Calum now insisted on being consulted on all decisions. Savannah wasn't sure why she'd made *this* vital marketing decision without him but it had been last minute.

And – she admitted it to herself – when she'd delicately broached changing the packing, moving the brand in another direction, he'd told her she was stupid. That it was a ridiculous idea. Why replace what was not broken?

Savannah had known he was wrong.

She'd taken the risk. When he'd see it all, then he'd understand, surely? But she knew he wouldn't. He would be furious.

Except she needed her business to work, she needed that little bit of her to remain . . .

Savannah breathed deeply. In, out, hold in the middle. The sacred pause.

Calum would have to agree that the new marketing and packaging would move Velvet Beauty up another notch in the organic/pure perfume market. The old white and gold looked tired now. Savannah's instincts had told her that a matte black box with off-white lettering was the way to go.

And she'd been right. SO right. But at what cost? Why had she acted so impulsively?

Sometimes she did things like that – without thinking of the consequences and, then, the anxiety would cover her like a wave, stop her breath as fear inhabited her entire body.

'The chypre still smells a little synthetic in Capri Moment,' said Anthony, coming up behind her and making Savannah jump. 'I don't know why – it's the most expensive one we tried but I feel the base notes are corrupted by it. Capri is supposed to be so clear and pure.'

'Still synthetic?' asked Savannah, quieting the quiver of fear that had risen up in her when he'd startled her.

'You're so jumpy,' he'd once said in an unguarded moment and Savannah had laughed. 'Growing up in a hotel makes you jump when someone appears,' she'd said. 'We were all waiting staff, you know.'

Anthony had taken the comment entirely at face value. People did. People were remarkably trusting, actually. Nobody ever had any idea how much she lied. How she jumped if scared, how noises frightened her, how the fight or flight hormones flooded her body at all times. That was the secret to being thin, she knew: not diet or eating. Living in constant survival mode.

'I don't know if the chypre was good or not,' Anthony said. 'I didn't take it in myself. I was in the Burren.'

Anthony was a Nose – a trained one as opposed to Savannah's entirely untrained one and he liked trips away to refresh his senses. The Burren, with its moonscape beauty and hordes of plants found nowhere else on earth, was perfect for this. Also, it had some beautiful little hotels and Anthony was in love with a debonair older man who'd had far too few holidays in his youth and wanted to make up for it now. Savannah loved his stories of his and Phil's trips away.

Phil was always cooking exotic feasts for Anthony, who could barely heat up a can of beans.

'He cherishes me,' Anthony said, a phrase that made Savannah gulp every time she heard it.

Imagine being cherished? The thought crushed her romantic heart because she was not cherished. She'd married a man who told her she was wrong and useless every day in scores of different ways. Being cherished was a fantasy.

Examination of the lemon found nothing wrong with it,

which meant either some contamination on the lab floor in the early perfume-making process or, else, that the subtle building up of perfume involving base notes, and pinpricks of dazzling other scents had gone wrong.

They'd spent the afternoon discussing and smelling, until they were both miserable and incapable of smelling anything anymore.

'Time flies,' remarked Anthony, looking down at his phone. 'It's half five. Phil's making his pomegranate-and-blue cheese salad. Divine is not the word.'

'Shoot! Is that the time?' said Savannah, shocked. The afternoon had flown.

She was running late.

Late was never tolerated.

By the time Savannah got home, she was exhausted with the stress of being late – why did lateness make a person feel even more stressed?

Clary was sitting in the den with a book while Marie-Denise, the au pair, chattered on her phone in the kitchen. Savannah had been brilliant at French in school, the summer at Grasse had helped and, once, she'd have listened briefly in case there was a hint of 'the old bitch is home now . . .' But there never had been. Marie-Denise was as genuinely sweet as the meringues she made.

Eden never quite believed anyone could be that nice but then, Eden was a cynic. Savannah idolised Marie-Denise because she was so kind and seemed to understand the way Savannah's home worked without being told.

Make sure Calum is happy – that was the house motto. Unspoken but very present.

'Savannah's back,' Maire-Denise was saying now. 'I'll go and say hi. Talk in an hour?'

Never leave, thought Savannah, waving at Marie-Denise. She went into the den where she slipped off her high shoes and curled up on the maroon velvet couch with her daughter, who never took her eyes off her book but let her mother wrap both arms around her.

Savannah closed her eyes and let herself relax into her beloved daughter's little body.

'Hello, darling girl,' she murmured. 'I missed you. How was your day?'

'We had a test in sums. I think I got them all right but Ms McCormack only corrects the tests at night so I don't know. Daniel got the same answers as me. I have to draw a picture of an animal, a going-extinct one, and can you help me find one? Granny likes tigers, they're going extinct, aren't they? Granddad said men with motorbikes like him are going extinct and Granny said it was a Hardly Able To motorbike and it should go extinct, but motorbikes can't go extinct, can they?'

Clary put down her book and snuggled into her mother's thin frame, her little ten-year-old's body warm and scented with some of the rose perfume Savannah was working on. Savannah held her and thought that this was heaven, this moment when she was with Clary, holding her, when nothing could hurt her, when it was just them and Marie-Denise, who was such a sweet, benign presence.

Everyone thought Clary was a silent child but she wasn't – not with Savannah, with whom she chattered non-stop, or with Marie-Denise, or with Daniel, who was her best friend, a boy as clever as she who also wore glasses and read a lot.

'Granddad was just joking,' Savannah said, holding on to her daughter. 'He likes joking.'

'I know that,' said Clary but Savannah could hear the sliver of not-understanding in her daughter's voice. Clary did not understand light-hearted teasing, which broke Savannah's heart. Because she knew why.

She sat with Clary for a while and they talked, until Savannah looked at her watch and noticed the time for the second time in as many hours.

Half six. Calum was home by six forty-five most nights.

'Daddy will be home soon,' she said, getting up quickly. She planted a kiss on her daughter's forehead and ran into the kitchen.

Marie-Denise, tanned from sitting in the garden in her shorts and a bikini top, was defrosting an expensive ready-made goulash that Calum liked for dinner.

'You are an angel, Marie-Denise,' sighed Savannah when she saw the two tubs sitting on the counter. 'Shall we have wine?'

Marie-Denise, who came from Burgundy and had grown up in a family steeped in viniculture, beamed.

Savannah tried to limit wine nights to the weekend but this week felt so weirdly stressed, what with the time she'd have to spend on the wedding, and the thought of all the family dynamics at the actual event. And then the looming reveal of the packaging. She'd have to tell him soon . . . A glass of wine would relax her, relax Calum.

Quickly she decanted the goulash into one of her own oven-proof dishes, stuck it in the oven and rinsed out the tubs.

Calum liked it better when Savannah made dinner from scratch but she'd picked up this little purchasing ready-meals trick from Eden and it meant she had so much more time.

Her husband was ludicrously obsessed with home cooking for a man who could only make steak and chips, and even then the chips had to be oven ones.

Eden had laughed the first time Ralph realised she had never made Thai Green Curry and bought it.

Calum would not find it funny at all. He was simply a more traditional sort of man, Savannah told herself.

With the goulash heating up, the table laid with candles and napkins because Calum loved the formality of proper settings and abhorred the notion of eating off their laps in front of the TV, she just had time to race upstairs and shower.

Her heart was beating a little too fast, her watch informed

her as she sprinted up to the black granite-and-glass bathroom that Eden always told her looked like a hotel bathroom.

'I don't know why you picked this,' Eden had said in mild confusion when she'd seen the granite, the profusion of glass, the charcoal walls. 'You were such a fan of 1920s décor when we were young. You wanted a bathroom that would have fitted perfectly into *The Great Gatsby*, that's what you said. All white and gold, spindly chairs, plants and a pretty little bath with claw feet.'

'People change,' Calum had said equably, arms around Savannah, his chin resting on her shoulder. 'We love it, don't we, darling?'

'Love it,' Savannah agreed with a broad smile that didn't come close to reaching her eyes. Eden was opening cupboards and never noticed. Savannah didn't want anyone to notice. Nobody would understand. Calum was so brilliant at being charming in public. Everyone adored him. Who'd believe her?

The shower was set to stabbing needles, which was how Calum liked it and was far too spiky for Savannah but she didn't know how to change it and then change it back, so it was easier to leave it and get stabbed twice a day. Plus, it was fast.

Out, she dried herself, rewrapped her sore hand in its bandage, sprayed the perfume Calum liked – not one of hers – and put on the elegant skirt and blouse that Eden said made her look far too old. Lip balm, her hair up, her Apple watch off and her small Cartier one on, and she was nearly—

'Hello?'

Savannah's startled reflex did its reliable jerk and she was glad she wasn't wearing the Apple watch anymore. A new app she'd inadvertently downloaded meant it beeped when her heart beat became elevated. Which was useful for some people, she was sure, but not for her.

She hurried out of the bedroom onto the landing to greet her husband, who liked a proper welcome, all the while feeling her pulse increase. She could feel it in her neck: sometimes, she was aware of the blood pumping through her carotid and she wondered why nobody could see it? It felt as if it were leaping in her neck: *thump, thump, thump.*

'You look beautiful, darling,' said Calum, bending to kiss her.

Savannah smiled. 'Thank you.'

She allowed herself to relax a little. He was in a good mood. Thankfully. She allowed herself a moment of closing her eyes to say thanks to whoever was in charge. She had no idea where Calum's moods came from but the bad ones were always her fault and he was probably right when he said that.

She *was* oversensitive, anxious. That would annoy anyone, wouldn't it? She tried so hard not to annoy him but it was so terrifyingly easy to send him over from happiness to sheer rage. After rage, came the silent treatment which could last days and nearly broke her. Those times made her feel like a cowering animal, waiting for the rage to be over, waiting for even the faintest hint of peace in her life. Or what passed for peace.

But tonight, her husband was happy.

Savannah pasted on her magazine-cover smile and tried to quiet the ever-present feeling that something bad was round the corner.

'Where's my other girl?' yelled Calum, and Clary appeared at her bedroom door, her hair brushed and tied up with a velvet ribbon.

Calum pulled her into the embrace with Savannah.

'My girls,' he murmured. 'Don't know what I'd do without you both.'

Savannah held on to them both. She could feel the tension radiating up from her neck into the base of her skull. She always had a headache now: a tautness around her neck that made her feel as if she would shatter into a million pieces if she didn't control everything. Fierce control. Making sure everything in their lives was fine. Food in the fridge, the house perfect, Savannah smiling at her husband with her special smile, the one that said he was a giant among men.

Perhaps tonight would be a good night. A relaxing one.

PART TWO

7

People driving past the Sorrento Hotel that week could be forgiven for thinking it was open again.

Not like in the old days, obviously, because the stone wolfhounds were still a bit ivy-covered. Stu had always been marvellous at keeping the place going and perfectly maintained. The man had amazing energy, you had to hand it to him.

Meg joked that she never put a foot on the outside gravel without pulling up a weed, but old Stu had certainly done his bit. When word came out that he'd been a bit keen on tequila followed by the occasional snort of Columbia's finest, well, people understood where he got his energy from. The gardens, the box hedging, the parties. But he was hardly a serious sort of druggie. Nobody could run a hotel like the Sorrento and be sitting in a room getting stoned. No, he was a force of nature, that was for sure.

He and his old pal Ferdie were down in Dun Laoghaire a lot these days, people noticed, tanning their legs in their sailing shorts on friends' boats and pretending not to admire women speed walking on the piers.

More than one old neighbour had shared a coffee with them and a laugh at the old days.

'Fellows of our vintage are still allowed to look,' Stu liked to say, eyes following a blonde with lean legs and a pert rear end.

He was off the gargle he said, although some people knew this was not entirely true.

Lennie, husband of Lorelei Stanley, beautician and owner of La Maison Beauty Salon near the Sorrento, liked getting out of the house because the salon was very busy, what with all the pre-wedding customers, and when he was at home, Lorelei had a raft of jobs for him.

'I'm busy so can you go do the grocery shopping,' and the like.

Lennie hated grocery shopping.

He'd had a glass of wine with Ferdie and Stu, although Stu had stuck abstemiously to just one glass.

'Just one: I'm allowed,' he'd said gravely and Ferdie had nodded.

Weddings were tough.

They'd talked sailing and football, discussed why referees were all blind and why women went a bit mental after a certain age.

Ferdie felt they went mental at any age. He had two daughters and they let him away with nothing.

Stu said he was very lucky in that regard: his four were the best ever.

Lennie, who had one son, agreed.

Ferdie did not mention that his youngest daughter had told him he was not sleeping on the couch come September when the kids went back to school.

Stu did not mention that Meg would have his testicles in a mangle if she knew he still had the odd glass of wine. He'd promised her he was utterly clean and sober when they'd decided to try again last year.

Nor did he mention that he sometimes looked at Savannah and worried about her. She was so thin.

Stu's son-in-law, Steve, had done quite a few trips up to the hotel in his white van which had Ryan Carpenters written on it. Nobody, Steve felt, noticed white vans.

The wedding watchers didn't and neither did his father-in-law when Steve saw him during the week coming out of the pub with his mate, Ferdie.

The family, and certainly Indy, were of the opinion that Ferdie was a bit of a bad influence but Steve kept his options open. It could all have been innocent except for the fact that his father-in-law and Ferdie were staggering a little bit. Steve was a busy man. He'd been drafted into doing a bit of repair work up at the hotel and he was still doing his normal work.

Weddings were odd, he concluded. They made people act out of character, perhaps?

The wedding watchers who were going had already organised clothes and beauty treatments.

Lorelei herself said it was going to be the wedding of the season and that included some Hollywood young one who was marrying a rock star in one of the marble mansions overlooking the Killiney rocks. Bets were being taken in the local pubs on how long the Hollywood marriage would last.

Till his next tour, said one wag.

Till her next film with a studmuffin, said someone else.

What was a studmuffin, enquired one older lady who had long since stopped telling people her age but had embraced bright pink hair and no longer listened to any of that old clap-trap about taking off one piece of jewellery when she left the house. She was old enough to wear all her jewellery any day she felt like it and having a little Prosecco on the pub terrace with her Caprese salad was celebration enough.

Talk of studmuffins ceased.

The pink-haired-lady was going to the Robicheaux wedding and had her nails done in a lovely coral colour.

Lorelei in La Maison Beauty Salon was a big fan of coral.

Lorelei was out the door with clients.

The ones she liked, she told how she and Meg had been friends for decades and how she was delighted Meg and Stu were getting married again.

That would have been one in the eye for Stu's old bitch of a mother, although Meg had always been able for her.

The clients she didn't like, Lorelei told how she used to do all the beauty for the hotel when the rock stars and the movie stars stayed there and partied like there was no tomorrow. She could have told them of the time she'd been asked to do unusual waxing long before such a thing became the norm, but she didn't because, after all, discretion was important.

Everyone wanted to know about how Meg looked so beautiful.

At her age? The figure on her? Had she had any work done? This was always accompanied by a narrowing of the eyes.

Lorelei could tell who'd had work done from fifty paces and there were a few people she knew who were so addicted to filler that they permanently looked as if they were having an allergic reaction and needed emergency medication.

But she said none of this. Truthfully, she said, Meg had nothing done. She swam, did yoga, meditated and lived life to the full.

People sagged in their chairs at this.

Feck it: work was involved. How annoying. If only they could get the name of Meg's tribe of technicians, then they could look like her too.

Lorelei didn't say that Meg would have loved a bit of Botox, had confided as much, but hadn't the money for it. No need for this crowd to hear that sort of thing.

And the girls . . .?

Lorelei, who'd known the four since they were in their prams, said they were fabulous.

Indy was an angel; Eden was a force to be reckoned with in politics; Savannah had the most spectacular business – Lorelei didn't say that she thought Savannah's husband was a bit of an idiot and she wouldn't want anyone who belonged to her married to him.

And, of course, darling Rory had won loads of awards in advertising.

Lorelei loved the girls but secretly adored Rory most of all. When her Artie had been eleven, and the jocks at school had begun to make his life miserable because he was gay, Rory had been there like an avenging angel.

It had taken the school many years to understand homophobic bullying but Rory Robicheaux had got it straight off: she had her crew and she took care of them. Nobody ever said a word to Artie Stanley again. Not after the incident where two of the football team had limped out clutching their groins and their throats respectively, one side of their hair shaved off along with the opposite eyebrow.

The words written on their foreheads in indelible ink took some time to come off.

She'd taken photos with someone's Polaroid.

Yup, blackmail, she added cheerily, but she was laying down the rules now.

Next time, it would be worse. She would *always* be watching.

Rory made students in school understand that there was a battleground in existence.

They might not see it or be affected by it but it was there. People were bullied for their sexuality, gender, any basic choices in life. For not having money for nice clothes, for having acne, for anything that made them different.

Rory, who was superbright, tall, physically very strong and utterly fearless, said she would rule the battleground for kids who were different. The school wouldn't do it but she would.

She'd been terrifying, Artie had told his mother gleefully. She'd said she was getting a tattoo kit and was going to do rainbows on the hands of anyone who was homophobic.

Just let them try and prosecute me, she'd said.

Lorelei knew the world was a more accepting place now – or she hoped it was – but when her Artie was a young lad, Rory had saved him.

Artie now lived in London, was married to a fellow architect, and he said Rory was working on a book.

Lorelei didn't care what it was about, she'd buy it. Rory was an angel and the Robicheaux family were close to her heart.

She couldn't wait for Saturday.

8

The Second Photo

Rory could hear her mother calling her to come out in the garden for the picture.

'Rory, honey, come on, we're all waiting for you. Steve hasn't got all day, you know.'

There were so many things about this sentence that annoyed Rory that she couldn't begin to enumerate them. First of all, her mother calling her *honey*. She was sixteen, she made it perfectly plain that she was not anyone's honey.

No matter that her mother thought she'd invented gay pride all by herself, she still forgot herself and called Rory – Rory! – *honey*. Rory was the least 'honeyish' person she knew.

That wasn't who she was. Of course, her parents had been screwing up with names since they christened her Aurora. It was insulting to the person she was now.

What gay woman wanted to be called bloody Aurora, after a fairy-tale princess who was at the mercy of men. Huh! That was a laugh.

A new guy in school, who hadn't got the memo yet, had taunted, 'When did you first think you were queer, Aurora?'

'When did you know you were a moron?' she'd snapped back and she'd hit out like lightning.

Luckily, her instinctive blow to his throat hadn't crushed his larynx.

Rumour had it he still talked a bit hoarsely. Tough shit, Rory thought.

She should have said, 'When did you know you were straight?' but that was too subtle a question for some.

Indy was a bit freaked out when she'd heard. 'You'll get into trouble, Rory,' she'd said. 'You can't hit people!'

'I don't care,' Rory had replied mulishly. 'I won't hide who I am because other people's feeble brains can't grasp it. He won't go to the principal because then he'd have to admit that a girl beat him.'

'But violence—' Indy wailed. 'It's not the answer.'

'Gay kids get beaten up just for existing. It's not the answer then, either,' said Rory shortly.

She much preferred being called Rory to Aurora but certainly her sisters' names suited them.

Savannah was fey, ethereal. Even Eden suited her name – well, she certainly suited the Garden of Eden thing. Every boy within a fifty-mile radius wanted to go into the Garden of Eden with her and eat apples, Rory sniggered to herself. And Indy – Rory realised she was actually more cross with Indy than with anyone else, which was rare, because Indy never fought with anyone. But it turned out that Indy was well able to snap when the mood hit her. And the mood had certainly hit her on one occasion Rory couldn't forget. The snapping over hitting some moron's larynx was only half of it.

'Rory,' her mother's voice came clear and loud again.

Rory was in the back kitchen. She'd opened a bottle of wine. Nobody would notice, it was her father's wine and he went through it so quickly, how could anyone tell? She'd drunk two glasses and then she'd gargled a bit with some minty stuff she'd hidden for this purpose in one of the cupboards. Dad probably used it too to pretend he hadn't drunk as much as he had. Dad was why she and Indy had argued. It had been so innocent. Rory had gone to Indy with what she'd seen years ago. Rory had been little, eleven.

Now that she was totally sure about who she was, at least there were no arguments like some girls had about having to wear dresses on high days and holy days. Dad called her his little tomboy and she loved going off on adventures with him.

Indy was the oldest, six years older than Rory and she was like a second mommy. She knew stuff, she was wise and kind and gentle. Rory knew that Indy would explain what was happening.

'Indy, I saw something—'

'Yes, bubba,' said Indy, putting down her school book and hugging her little sister to her.

Rory had twisted the rope she'd been using to tie blankets to the rabbit cage so it wouldn't get cold. Mr Munch was not an outdoors rabbit. He should be in Rory's bed. She could clean up his poopies.

'It's about Dad,' Rory had begun and then she'd said it. Told the whole story.

As Rory spoke, a flush had risen up through Indy's neck and face.

'You did not see that,' she said, had hissed almost. She no longer sounded like Indy, kind and gentle. 'You're imagining it, you're creating trouble.'

'I'm not,' Rory said, upset. 'I wouldn't.'

'Yes, you would, I don't want to hear a word about this,' said Indy, 'certainly not to Mum.'

'I'm not going to say anything to anyone,' bleated Rory. 'But it's bad—'

'It's nothing,' interrupted Indy. 'Just stop trying to create trouble. There's enough trouble as it is, without you making up more.'

'I didn't make anything up,' hissed Rory fiercely now. Everyone said she had a worse temper than Eden and that was saying something. But today Indy matched her.

'I don't want to hear another word about this,' she'd said, her face frantic, angry, and she'd shoved Rory off her lap.

Rory had been shocked: Indy was never like this. Indy was kind, listened to her. Why was she being so mean?

'Hate you!' Rory had shrieked and then she'd clamped her hand over her mouth because Lori, lovely Lori, who minded them sometimes when she wasn't busy in the hotel and had long dark hair, shiny eyes and whispered quietly to them, said that every time someone said the word 'hate', a fairy died.

Rory cried then. A fairy had died and she couldn't even tell Lori about it. Indy had been horrid to her and Indy was never horrid.

Rory ran outside to Mr Munch's cage and wriggled him out, then hauled him upstairs to her bedroom where they both got into the bed and Mr Munch's dirty paws made the sheets dirty. Rory didn't care. Nobody loved her.

The roaring from outside was intensifying.

'Rory, the photo! We're all waiting for you.'

Rory narrowed her eyes. Do Indy good to have to wait, and Steve, who would be being all lovey-dovey with her eldest sister as he waited.

Everyone was outside. Everyone except Rory.

Rory could hear her mother instructing Eden to go and find her.

Hell, thought Rory, I might as well go out.

She hadn't dressed up for the picture, she hadn't the first time and she hadn't now. Eden always wore tight jeans and sexy tops so she was wearing that. Savannah wore her usual floaty things and Indy – well, it didn't matter what Indy wore because she looked stunning in everything.

She was one of those people who looked glorious no matter what, which made it harder to be annoyed with her but Rory still could. Rory had never forgotten that time when she was eleven and Indy hadn't believed her.

If she ever wrote a book – and she was writing poetry now, so there – *that* incident was going in the book. How Indy hadn't believed. How Indy had made it sound like she was making up tales. She'd held on to the secret for years, not trusting it to anyone because Indy had so successfully told her it was all make-believe. It hadn't been. She'd seen it with her own eyes and even if she hadn't understood what was happening at eleven, now, at sixteen, she sure did. Indy had lied to protect someone. She'd chosen protecting someone else over believing Rory. That had hurt and it still did.

'There you are. Are you hiding?' Eden said now.

Eden was brilliant at ferreting out secrets from people. She could look at you and know what you were thinking. It was like her superpower or something.

'No,' snapped Rory, 'I was having a drink.'

Eden was the only person she could possibly say that to.

'Oh,' said Eden. 'Having a drink *before* the photo. I was planning on having one afterwards to celebrate.'

'Don't see what there is to celebrate,' Rory rumbled. 'Just the four of us looking like idiots.'

'I think it's rather nice,' said Eden, fluffing up her hair. 'You know, for the future, something special.'

'What if I don't want to be special?' said Rory. 'What if I just want to be me and not part of some four-part Robicheaux daughter thing, just because Steve wants to make it as a photographer. And besides which, he's not a very good photographer.'

'The first photo was amazing,' said Eden, giving Rory an assessing gaze.

'That's what you think,' said Rory truculently.

But still she came out for the photo. They were all waiting for her.

'Where've you been?' Mum said, going over and rearranging her hair a bit. It fell just below her jaw bone. Made her look androgynous, which Rory liked.

Rory wanted it cut higher but she didn't think she had the bone structure for it. She still had a roundish face, what her mother lovingly called the curve of the teenager.

Rory wanted to be done with the whole teenager thing. Damn the curve of it. She wanted hollowed cheeks and an interesting face, plus short hair and a go-fuck-yourself expression, like Eden could manage.

Eden could look hard as nails despite the long-haired, pretty thing she had going on. Rory wished she knew how Eden did it. A certain narrowing of the eyes, a sense that Eden would strike when you weren't expecting it. Rory would never admit to anyone but she'd totally copied it in school for the protection of her crew. She had a reputation for being fearless. She wasn't fearless, precisely, but she couldn't bear injustice and bullying. Like the grief poor Artie used to get. That made anger bubble up inside her.

Lots of things did, actually.

She wondered what was wrong with her – thinking about stuff made her angry. She had entire conversations with herself where she told people exactly what she thought of them. Was that normal? Did anyone else's inner voice go off on flights of fantasy? Was that the writer in her? The conversations that started out one way and grew into stories of how she'd narrate what was going on around her.

'I do wish you'd let your hair grow a bit, darling,' her mother said. 'It looks beautiful just a little longer. Not because I want you to look more feminine, obviously, just because it would be beautiful. Beauty comes in all guises.'

'I know, Mum,' said Rory, leaning against her mother and feeling grateful for the love.

Mum was amazing and really did her best even if she was always putting her hetero foot in it. Mum was so behind Rory and everything gay that it was a miracle she hadn't had the whole hotel painted in the PRIDE rainbow.

Rory appreciated it but it was typical of her mother – over the top. Rory was a lesbian, not a cause that would involve the whole family, all of Eboli Road and the Sorrento Hotel.

Rory could imagine it now: 'The Sorrento Hotel – we've got free Wi-Fi, four-posters in some of the rooms, all mod cons, and we're one hundred per cent LGBTQ+-friendly.'

Cringe. She closed her eyes and wished there was no photograph. She wished she could sit with her mother and maybe Savannah and watch something on TV, something old fashioned like they used to watch and be happy. Or *Friends*. She loved *Friends*. It was calming, warm.

'Come on, everyone, I'm ready for you,' said Steve.

Rory turned and scowled at him. Normally, she liked Steve, he was sweet, but then, thinking about when she'd been eleven and how Indy had upset her made her cross with him and Indy. Emotions really didn't make any sense, did they?

'Have you got your necklaces on?' Steve said to everyone.

But he was really directing this at Rory, who was only into necklaces if they were leather thongs with shark teeth on them. The four gold necklaces, each with a different crystal or stone had been given to the girls when they were babies.

'Yes,' said Rory, reaching up to finger hers. It was a peridot, a dangerous green. She quite liked it. The others were all different, that was part of their charm. Indy's was a turquoise, which went perfectly with her hippie-girl look. The twins had different ones. Eden's was a citrine, while Savannah had an opal, which suited her: it was cloudy and hard to pin down what colour it really was, which suited Savannah to a tee. Savannah was a sensitive soul, easily swayed by other people, anxious.

'You have boundary issues,' Eden had told her once. 'And you don't,' she'd added to Rory, who was listening in.

'Thank you, Dr Robicheaux,' Rory had replied tartly. 'Are you handing out medication today?'

'No, I only psychoanalyse people,' Eden said. 'You have to deal with your own crazy.'

'OK, everyone, in place,' said Steve.

Rory went and joined her sisters. She was glad she was far away from Indy. Glad that Dad, who had been there last year for the photo, didn't appear to be around. Probably off with Ferdie, either in the pub or the bookies. Mum smiled at them all benignly.

'You look beautiful,' she said.

Poor Mum, thought Rory suddenly. Poor Mum, it wasn't fair, was it? Dad was off spending money or getting happily merry and Mum was here running the whole show, as usual. Rory wanted to tell her everything but how could she?

9

Wednesday

The Platts had a birth plan.

'There's music, candles, separate Swiss balls for both of them—' Andrea, Indy's partner in crime and the midwife who worked on the ante-natal care part of booking women in for either hospital or home births, had explained a few weeks before.

'Lovely,' said Indy, scanning the notes at the time.

'No bright lights,' added Andrea.

'What if it's night time? Are we delivering by candlelight?'

'Possibly,' Andrea deadpanned back.

They both had very mixed feelings about the lengthy birth plans that some mothers-to-be or couples arrived with.

These were often novella-length epistles on how the perfect birth was to be achieved, and involved a misty-eyed view of childbirth and how a seven-pound baby could emerge from what was essentially a very small part of a woman's body. There was always music, soft lighting, deep joy and no sense of the pain of getting a bowling-ball-sized object out of their vagina.

'First baby?' asked Indy.

'Yup. No complications, easy pregnancy so far and she's very fit. Which can be—'

'— good or bad,' agreed Indy.

Very fit people often thought that the painful bits of child-birth didn't happen if you could run a marathon and got quite a shock to realise that glutes of steel did not necessarily translate to an easy birth. The plus was that fit people were better able for the process.

At half five on Wednesday morning, Indy got the call from Flo, the junior midwife, who'd been with the Platts since half-twelve the night before.

'She's got to seven centimetres dilated,' said Flo, sounding a bit harassed.

'I'll be right there,' said Indy, swinging her legs out of the bed.

'You OK?' she added.

'Bit stressed,' whispered Flo. 'We're going a bomb on the incense and it's making me sick.'

'I'll be there in fifteen minutes,' said Indy. She was on emergency shift only today – she was sure there were more wedding things she'd be needed for.

Eden had said that hanging the silk flowers was going to take up a fair chunk of time and they still had to fit in going with their mother to pick up her wedding dress. Plus, tonight was the hen-night dinner. She'd have to slip in a nap at some point in the day or she'd be pooped before she even started this evening.

Indy was in and out of the shower and dressed in five. A slick of suncream, her hair tied back and a dab of lemon verbena on her elbows and collar bone, and she was done.

Steve, who could sleep through anything, moved in the bed.

'Delivery,' murmured Indy, leaning down to kiss him on the shoulder. She took his phone and set the alarm for six forty-five, fifteen minutes earlier than usual. When he was alone, getting the girls out of the house took longer. Minnie was seven, Daisy was six: they both had long blond hair they liked in plaits and Steve was not as quick as Indy at doing them. Almost, though.

Then, because it looked so inviting, she kissed his shoulder again. He made a soft growling noise. 'Temptress.'

'Beloved,' she replied, grinning.

She was in the car with an insulated cup of instant coffee and a protein bar in two more minutes, and onto the road towards the Platts' semi-D a moment later, having let Snickers and Twix out into the garden for their morning pee.

As she drove, she passed Savannah's house, which was a huge mock Georgian surrounded by a wall and security gates.

Indy was a big believer in living mindfully and not giving in to guilt, but she felt a hint of it now as Savannah's house appeared in her rear-view mirror. It had been ages since she'd seen Savannah properly. Indy and her mother met up every week, Eden too, and even Rory used to until she got into writing that damned book, which she was very cagey about. But Savannah rarely did.

Her business had become so successful and Indy could see how it would take up vast tracts of time, especially since she had Clary, and Calum was apparently very into his competitive cycling so Savannah had to do all the kid stuff but—

That ping was in her head again: the one that she heard when she thought about her sister. She couldn't put her finger on it but she kept thinking that something was wrong with Savannah. Calum was very charming when they all met up and he appeared to dote on her sister, never far from her side. It all looked great on paper but Indy worried that good on paper was not always good in reality. Ping, ping, ping.

All thoughts of her sister vanished when she reached her destination.

Chateau Platt smelt like a Moroccan souk after a wild weekend. When the front door was opened, Indy was assailed by what smelled like patchouli, oud, musk from several hundred oxen and what could easily have been marijuana. If there was a hint of marijuana at this home birth, she would go ballistic.

But despite the smell, Mike Platt looked entirely focused and not even vaguely relaxed, which at least ruled out drugs.

'You're here! That other girl is too young! Monica's in pain. It's not right!'

'Nice to see you, Mike,' said Indy calmly, following him up the stairs. The scent of dog was added to the mix. Two beautiful Afghan hounds lay on the floor outside the bedroom, their long silken doggy hair like something from a conditioner commercial.

Indy, who had been looking at dogs recently as she and Steve felt the girls were old enough to be good with pets other than hamsters, had a notion that Afghans were rare and cost a fortune. The dogs lifted elegant heads and gazed at her mournfully.

'She won't let the dogs in!'

'Dogs aren't that much help in labour,' Indy pointed out.

She stepped over the dogs, entered the room and took stock of the situation. The bedroom was clearly souk central, was lit entirely by candles and mingling with the smell of incense was the scent of sweat and stressed human.

Monica Platt was squatting over a Swiss ball and moaning, with Flo by her side.

Seeing Indy, Flo beamed a sigh of relief and Monica moaned more loudly. 'We're at eight.'

'Fantastic,' said Indy and relieved Flo. 'If you could open the window, Flo, and blow out the candles, please. And the incense. I think it might be better.'

'But the birth plan—' wailed Mark, holding up a document printed on pink paper.

'The baby hasn't read the birth plan and we need to see what we're doing,' Indy said, managing an even tone.

It was clear that Monica was exhausted after her night of labour.

'It hurts so much,' she wept, leaning against Indy's arm as she helped the labouring woman to the bed.

'You've been doing wonderfully and you're going to keep on doing wonderfully till this lovely baby is born,' said Indy. She looked around for water and a washcloth and saw an empty plastic beaker and no washcloth.

'Flo, I know you're shattered. You probably need a cup of tea,' Indy added, with a meaningful look at Mike, who stared at her blindly.

Another day in the front lines of being a midwife.

Sonya, Stu's sister, was on an early flight.

Meg knew that, actually, Stu wasn't doing any meditation, but she hadn't wanted to say that to their daughters.

'I'm out with Ferdie and Redzer,' he'd said on the phone, 'we're doing groom things.'

She'd laughed. 'Groom things, what does that mean?'

'You know, for the honeymoon and bridesmaids' trinkets, things like that.'

'Oh, darling,' Meg had said, 'I do love you.'

Stu had always been fabulous with presents. Not everyone was. Vonnie's husband Gerry was quite good with gifts. But Alicia, one of Meg's old friends from school, was married to a man who thought that a present only existed in the form of a gift voucher and not even a very big gift voucher. Roger truly believed that a twenty-euro voucher, or, when he was pushing the boat out, a twenty-five-euro gift voucher, would set any woman's heart fluttering. They were divorced now. And while there had been many problems, Meg always thought that the whole gift-voucher thing was part of it. She hated meanness and so did Stu. Ironically, Stu's hating meanness meant he'd gambled everything away. There was a sort of wild thing in Stu when it came to money.

Or there had been a wildness in him. It was gone now, she was sure. Thank goodness, she thought as she negotiated the roundabout at the airport. Thank goodness that wildness was gone. Those twelve-step programmes were completely amazing. She wished she could donate money to Gamblers Anonymous to say thank you.

When Sonya appeared at arrivals, she was pulling along two enormous suitcases. That was the first thing Meg noticed. Sonya did not normally travel this heavily. And Meg wondered for a fleeting moment if Sonya was coming back for good? She'd left Ireland years ago after fighting with her mother, which was very easy to do. Meg had rarely fought with her mother-in-law, but that was only because she tried to avoid her: it was the only way. But Sonya and her mother had fought constantly, although nobody ever commented upon this. It was just the way things were.

Sonya had eventually just given up and had left the country to work abroad. She'd been all over the place in her job as a nurse. Had worked in Saudi when it was the place to go to earn tax free money. And she'd finished up her nursing career in Northampton. She was older than Stu, sixty-six to his sixty-four. Sonya, Meg thought with a hint of pride, which she instantly identified as her vanity and felt guilty about, looked an awful lot older than Meg did. I'm a bad sister-in-law, thought Meg, as Sonya came towards her.

'Hello,' said Sonya brightly, hugging her.

She was a tall woman, well built with short grey hair cut in quite a mannish style and without a pick of make-up on her face. Not for Sonya the rounds of endless serums and creams. No.

She was a fan of the take-me-as-I-am approach to beauty.

'You're very good to pick me up,' said Sonya. 'What's that naughty brother of mine doing that he couldn't?'

'Bridegroomy things,' said Meg, taking both of the suitcases, 'I'll pull them both.'

'No, don't be silly.'

'You had the flight and everything, I'll do it.'

Sonya walked slowly to the car and Meg easily matched her speed pulling the suitcases.

'You seem a little stiff,' said Meg worriedly, after watching her sister-in-law's gait for a while.

Sonya had aged.

'It's just a lower-back thing. And my hip,' Sonya admitted with a grimace. 'I need a new one and I'm not looking forward to that. Nursed too many people with hips and knees and elbows and you name it. No fun. Mind you, hips are better than knees.'

'Are they?' said Meg. She'd never thought much about that sort of thing. She was flexible and she worked out, looked after herself. Then again, Sonya had had a lifetime of work as a nurse, so surely she must have worked every part of her body. But nursing was hard on the joints, on the back, or so Indy said.

'Was it work, do you think?' she asked now.

'Undoubtedly,' said Sonya. 'But it's fine, I don't mind really. Just makes me slow down a bit. I've joined a walking club and I can't walk anymore, not at the moment. I'll have to give in and have the hip done. But all medical people are bad patients and when I heard this was coming up, I said no way am I missing out on this wedding.'

Meg stopped pulling the cases to put her arm around her sister-in-law.

'Thank you,' she said, 'that means so much to me. I keep thinking that your mother would be going deranged with rage if she knew we were marrying again. If she'd been alive when we got divorced, she'd probably have thrown a party.'

'That she would,' agreed Sonya. 'But Mother was bitter and twisted at heart.'

'Sonya!' said Meg in surprise. Sonya might have moved to be away from her mother but she'd never voiced such a thing out loud. Therapy? Meg wondered.

'She was,' Sonya said firmly. 'I'm glad I'm able to say it out loud now. Nothing ever made her happy. Stu made her happy, actually, but one has to let go of one's children. Not that I know that from a practical sense, not having had any. But I can see it in other people. Mother wanted Stu for herself for always. The idea that you would come along, take him *and* be so glamorous and gorgeous – well, she couldn't bear it. She never supported you during the years Stu was going crazy.'

'She was very old then,' interrupted Meg, who had long since made peace in her own heart with her tricky mother-in-law. 'What could she have done?'

'She could have been on your side for once,' said Sonya.

The comment flew through Meg's aura of calm and, suddenly, she thought she might cry. She hadn't thought about the past for a long time. Yes, it flickered into her mind occasionally. But she had done her grieving for the marriage and the pain it had involved a long time ago. This was different, new. Stu was a different man. She was a different woman. They didn't have a hotel, their children were grown, Stu was sober, didn't gamble. He had made amends for all the things he had done and they had a chance of happiness. But Sonya had suddenly brought her right back. She shuddered.

'It was terrible,' she said, trying to breathe herself into calm again. 'But things are so different now. I'm different too.'

'I know,' said Sonya. 'I didn't mean to upset you. It's going to be wonderful and I can't wait to see the girls and the grandchildren.'

'Yes,' said Meg, 'they are fabulous, fabulous.'

Little Clary came into her head suddenly, little quiet Clary who was so different to her two cousins, Minnie and Daisy. They were like little dancing fairies full of light and energy. Clary was such a quiet, serious child, watchful. Watchful was never good in children. Sometimes people were born that way, she thought. That could be it. Clary could simply be that sort of child.

Rory and Savannah came into her head too. They'd been trickier children than Eden and Indy. But Eden, Rory and Indy coped with everything, whereas Savannah hadn't.

'You haven't seen them for ages, they are fabulous,' Meg said. 'They're happy.'

For a moment, she wasn't sure who she was trying to convince. Herself or Sonya. Her daughters were happy, weren't they?

10

Eden

Nobody, absolutely nobody, who didn't work in politics, had any idea of the endless emails, phone calls and meetings involved in it all. She'd thought local politics was bad but now, as she fought to get her name on the ticket for her constituency in national politics, she wondered how anyone without a wife ever managed political life.

A wife was what every politician needed. It had worked for Ralph's father. His mother was a saint, no question about it. Diarmuid Tallisker would not have reached the heights he had without Agnes keeping the home fires burning, doing the admin, soothing the ruffled feathers of constituents, raising the children, keeping the family's three pharmacies going and making sure her husband's shirts were ironed.

Diarmuid Tallisker was a famous name in politics. A man who'd been involved in the Peace Process, he was a statesman-like gentleman with a shock of white hair, a lugubrious expression and a reputation as a politician who could bring all sides together. But he'd have been nothing without Ralph's mother, Agnes, child of another politician and the one who'd held it all together.

Agnes Tallisker had run surgeries when Diarmuid was in Belfast or London: she'd got houses for people who'd needed them, sorted out tricky situations, organised for the local school to have emergency prefabs installed when the roof had leaked.

'My parents are going to love you,' had been one of the first things Ralph had said to Eden when they met in college and she was womanning the second-hand clothes stall for a home-less charity.

She was studying history and politics in the year behind him, although she was one of the older students in her year as she'd taken a couple of years out, 'because of the band,' she explained to people, because Eden liked being famous even if being in a failed girl band made her more infamous than famous.

As a girl who'd worked – unpaid – as a chambermaid in her parents' hotel, Eden viewed rich kids with something akin to loathing. Ralph Tallisker, with his famous friends of the family, his father's frequent trips to the White House and Number Ten, his skiing – imagine, skiing! – was all the things Eden thought she'd despised. She'd served the wealthy and privately educated in the hotel and she hated them on principle.

Yet she was astonished to find that she didn't mind any of this at all when it came in the lovely package of Ralph Tal-lisker. He was handsome yet didn't seem to know it, clever but not in the slightest bit elitist, friendly to all comers. If he had a euro in his pocket, he'd hand it to a homeless guy and sit down to talk to said homeless guy.

'Nobody talks to them – it's as if they're invisible,' Ralph said the first time she'd seen him doing it with a young man he'd clearly talked to before.

If Ralph had been born with a silver spoon in his mouth, it didn't show.

'Unlike all those other "my daddy's in the government" types, he's a total ride,' said her friend, Susie, who was studying arts.

Eden attempted to look shocked at these words, although she'd known Susie so long that it was hard to do so. She and Susie had been to too many parties together when they were at school. But Eden's reinvention for the failed girl band came in useful in college. She'd long since ditched the torn jeans and the tight tops. The new Eden worked hard in both the college library and the Bray garage where she did late-night shifts to pay her living expenses. Thanks to the band, she had a wardrobe of vintage long skirts that wouldn't have shocked a Victorian.

'He seems nice,' she said to Susie, secretly eyeing Ralph's sturdy rugby-playing frame, the face with the mobile mouth, the outrageously big eyes with long dark eyelashes like a girl.

'Nice?' said Susie. 'He's gorgeous. Look at that mouth too . . . Bet he's amazing in bed.'

'Not everything's about bed,' said Eden, in Victorian mode. Susie could be so crude.

Susie snorted. 'Yeah, right.'

Eden decided she ought to stop hanging around with old friends like Susie because if you were going to reinvent yourself, you needed to really cut the ties with the past.

Two weeks later, Ralph noticed her.

Eden, who'd never had to try to get a man to notice her in her life, found she'd been subconsciously looking out for Ralph between lectures. The old Eden would have been on his radar like a shot, but the old Eden wouldn't have scored a date with him. He'd have bought her a drink, maybe, and been warned off her by his friends. Scions of political families did not hang out with wild girls.

But long-skirted Ms Robicheaux, with her hair French plaited and books clutched to her bosom, was another thing entirely.

Another email pinged in.

Eden groaned until she realised it was spam. Still, most of the others weren't.

Politics took their toll on every part of her life, she thought, clicking into the first email which was a diatribe from a constituent on dog fouling.

She reached for her cup of tea and as she did so, her eye caught the drawer where she'd hidden the letters. Three now. Typed on what looked like an actual typewriter.

I know what you did, Mrs Tallisker.

Eden had found the third letter in her post at home.

I know what you've done.

One insane letter was normal. Two was worrying. Three was time to call the police – or her father-in-law. But she couldn't. Because it would end her career in an instant. There were different rules for women politicians. Like in everything.

The Platts had had a little boy.

'Mark Junior!' said Mark proudly, holding up the baby in a way reminiscent of the birth scene in *The Lion King*.

He'd only just been stopped from letting the Afghan hounds in to smell the baby. Indy loved dogs, and these were beautiful ones, but felt they were better outside the field of birth.

Once everything was finished and their notes were written up, Indy and Flo left.

'I could kill for a cuppa,' said Flo, finally allowing herself to relax out of her smiling 'it's all fine!' midwife mode, 'but I had to get out of there.'

Indy grinned. 'Dog scent and a lot of incense is not a good combo. I can't join you for tea – I'm racing off to the hotel where my parents are getting married. Myself and my sisters are helping get it ready.'

'The Sorrento,' said Flo fondly. 'My mum remembers it. Lucky you growing up there.'

'It was magical,' agreed Indy.

She thought all about her childhood home as she drove there. Mum and Dad had bought it with some money Dad had inherited, which had driven Granny insane. Her parents tried their best never to discuss family bitterness but Indy had heard enough. Granny Robicheaux and her family had made money out of a series of launderettes but apparently had sold out when the going was good and Granny's subsequent occupation was looking down her nose at the rest of the world.

Either way, Mum and Dad bought the Sorrento, which was painted a rich honey colour and sometimes, when the light shone a certain way, hints of a previous rosy wall colour could be seen. The big old house was a little bit Georgian, with a hint of Edwardian on one wing. A dining room and a veranda that were very California 1960s round the back – complete with several egg-shaped hanging chairs – completed the structure. Dad had had great plans to turn the old barn into apartments but the hotel took up so much time and money, that he never had.

Indy had loved the Sorrento the way it was: as a child, she'd sit in the garden under the oak tree, half hidden from the house by the white tangle of the rose bushes and play fairies with the doll's house Dad had made her out of a tea chest. The fairies were her small collection of dolls and their clothes were sometimes rain-soaked petals, sometimes oddments of fabrics from the attics where previous owners had left old suitcases stuffed with elderly garments.

When she was older, Indy played fairies with Savannah, who mixed the flower petals in the curved hollow of a cut-down beech, and sniffed the mixtures delightedly.

Eden was never one for playing in the grounds. She had a vast network of friends and was keen to go to other people's houses so she wouldn't have to wipe tables or polish sideboards.

And Rory . . . Indy had been that much older than Rory, so it was like their childhoods hadn't overlapped. When Rory was twelve, Indy had been eighteen, heading for nursing college, feeling grown up.

Rory, Indy thought guiltily, hadn't had as much of the idyll in the Sorrento as she had. If her youth had been during the halcyon years, when Mum and Dad were happy and nothing could spoil it, Rory had grown up in an altogether trickier era. Phone calls from the bank, arguments about money, arguments about drinking, white-faced rows over gambling debts. Families could have totally different experiences of childhood depending on where they sat on the family tree.

Indy

It was an hour after the allotted time when Indy finally parked in front of the hotel and allowed all the feelings to flow through her. She'd grown up here. It had been home, an eccentric home, for sure. Most girls she knew hadn't gone home from school and then had had to race to clean bedrooms because money was tight and there weren't enough chambermaids.

'You live in a hotel! It's cool!' her friends at school had said, much the way Flo had.

It was cool – sort of. Except when it wasn't, when Mum and Dad were working every weekend, Dad charming the guests and Mum doing her swan impersonation: all fluid elegance on the surface and frantic moving parts underneath. Mum could simultaneously cook for twenty, help Eden and Savannah with their homework at the kitchen table, and dry the current au pair's tears because Rory had just thrown a bowl of baby slop at her.

Indy knew she was like her mother because she had the same caring nature, the same calm-in-the-storm thing going on.

'You never lose it,' Steve had murmured to her in admiration.

'Losing it doesn't help,' Indy said.

She'd just reached the front door when it opened and out came her mother, twin sisters and Vonnie.

'Late as usual,' she said apologetically. 'Babies are notoriously bad with timing.'

They swarmed close to hug her.

'What did I miss?'

'Muslin and silk flowers, all draped. It's going to be beautiful,' said Vonnie breathlessly.

Indy realised that Vonnie was holding a notebook and pen, which had a purple feather at the tip. Dear Vonnie.

Eden was holding on to her phone and texting, but stopped long enough to wave at her sister. She was holding a piece of ripped-off notepaper covered with Vonnie's distinctive purple writing.

'It will be beautiful,' agreed Meg.

Indy and Eden smiled at her as one.

'Of course it will,' said Indy.

Rory

Rory was lost in thinking about the book.

One single photograph from years ago, one of those background shots where nobody was really in focus, had changed everything. She'd been thinking about her beloved book when she'd asked Mum for some of the old Sorrento photographs. Mum had lots of boxes in the attic and Rory had braved the spiders' webs to find them.

'I just felt like doing some family-tree stuff,' she'd said to her mother which had been a complete lie.

Rory had felt a smidgen of guilt because she wanted to look at the photos to remind herself of what it had all been like. Had she really had a corduroy coat in bright pink? Was there evidence of that time Eden had pushed her into the pond?

Wading through them all, there were plenty of photos of all four sisters as children, no giant gaps where a person could say 'why were there no photos of me when I was four or six?' Rory had been photographed just as much as three-year-old Indy had been. She had begun to feel guilty over the feeling that her childhood had been different to theirs.

'People see things differently,' Chantal had said wisely as she'd looked over her partner's shoulder at the mass of photos on the table top

And then, Rory had spotted her.

Lori. Their one-time nanny, beloved friend with the attic rooms where the four girls used to hang out.

The scene was a random party and there were many people

in the shot: it was a slightly blurred one, with somebody toasting something in the middle and a birthday cake. It was hard to date the photo but there was no mistaking Lori, standing in the distance with one single hand cradled around her belly. Rory, who had never been pregnant but who recognised that classic stance, had known. She'd remembered the long-ago conversation with Indy when she'd seen Dad kissing Lori.

Rory, with her head in a notebook, saw everything – it was like her inbuilt radar was tuned to a higher frequency than other people. She saw her father that day. With Lori. And she'd raced to Indy to tell her.

'Indy, I saw Daddy kissing Lori! Why was he kissing her? Why?'

Instead of hugging her close, Indy – her surrogate mother-figure - had been furious. 'You don't know what you're talking about. You're a silly little girl. Dad was just – hugging Lori, because she was sad and don't tell lies about it—'

'No, I didn't lie,' cried Rory, stung.

'You did and you're not to go around repeating it or you'll get into trouble with me and Dad and Lori. Lies are bad,' said Indy.

But surely Dad kissing Lori was worse?

The incident had created a slight fracture in her relationship with Indy. Rory hadn't had the words to explain how she felt.

On the surface, she'd calmly ignored her eldest sister the same way she ignored the jocks in school who were beginning to realise she was different from the other girls, the ones they teased and half-fancied. Inside, she'd ached.

Even then, Rory had known how to hide hurt with an angry face.

She'd put it in the back of her mind, the way childhood things receded into distant memory, until now.

Looking at the photograph of Lori, a woman in her late

twenties, then, in the pose of the newly pregnant. Rory suddenly gauged it had been taken some years after she'd seen her father kissing Lori.

Was that when it had all really fallen apart? When another Robicheaux sister had come into the world?

Rory didn't allow herself to process any of this – she simply wanted proof. If she had another sister, she was going to find her and to hell with the consequences.

It was easy enough to turn private detective. In the days of the Internet with Facebook, Instagram and LinkedIn, it was no trouble at all to find people by finding other people who might know them. It was a circuitous, snaking route but that's how Rory had found Chloe.

'I'm trying to contact a Lori Riordain, who worked for a family in Killiney,' Rory had written in an Instagram message and, to her astonishment, Chloe had accepted the message request and responded..

'Maybe we should meet up. I know who you're talking about,' said Chloe, not giving anything away.

Intrigued and against Chantal's advice because who knew who this Chloe girl was, Rory had driven to the city centre flat where Chloe lived.

Young, vibrant, quirky, when she opened the door, Rory had inhaled quickly: Chloe looked exactly like Savannah and Eden, if only they had jet-black hair, the same shade as Lori's had been.

'Hello,' she'd said, standing at the street door of her flat with a cup in her hand, dark hair tied up, wearing a paint-splattered apron over jeans. And a necklace, the same necklace Rory and her sisters wore, each with a different semi-precious stone.

Chloe's was the blue of lapis lazuli.

'You're my sister,' said Rory, staring at this girl. Chloe. Her sister, well – half-sister. But that didn't matter. This girl had been kept from them all. She started to cry and she never cried. Chloe patted her on the back in a friendly manner.

'Come on in. It'll be fine,' which was exactly what Lori used to say to them during their teenage disasters.

'I wondered if any of you would ever come looking for me,' said Chloe, moving aside to let Rory into the house. 'I'm on the top floor. No lifts in these old houses.'

She was nineteen, she said. An art student from Cork and currently paid the rent on her small flat by selling seascapes with mystical sea creatures in them.

As she led the way up the stairs, she said, 'I wasn't going to come to see any of you. I have a life and if none of you ever contacted me, then that was the way it was meant to be. I believe that destiny lets people drift in and out of our lives in a very random way. What happens is the universe letting people in and out.'

'But the necklace—' said Rory. 'Did our father come?'

'No,' said Chloe. 'He gave this to my mother when I was born. She didn't want to see him. Didn't want any of the running around and hiding anymore. They were having a thing forever. Sorry - hard to hear but that's the truth. She always said she was sorry for doing it because she loved your mum but she was happy because she got me out of it. I've never met your father. He's tried loads of times, but I didn't want to.'

'And Lori? We all loved her. Now I understand why she went. I'd love to see her—' Rory, normally so self-assured, felt wrong-footed in this situation.

'Mum died,' said Chloe softly, leading the way into a one-roomed flat where a scrawny black cat stood on the kitchen counter and stared in an accusing way at Rory.

It felt like a blow to hear that Lori was dead. Rory reached out for the only comfort and picked up the cat. It nestled into her, wound its way around her neck, then leapt onto the floor in a neat move.

'I'm so sorry. I loved her.'

Chloe's face was not good at hiding things. It softened and she reached out and hugged her sister, making Rory feel like the younger instead of the older. 'She loved all of you. Told me about you. Said she'd learned how to be a mother by taking care of you when she was in the hotel. My mother was an amazing woman,' Chloe went on while Rory sobbed.

'She married an incredible man, Harrison, my father, and he raised me as his own. I have two younger brothers who live with Dad. Do you want to come and meet them? They live in Cobh.'

'Yes!' said Rory joyfully, then: 'Will you come and meet your family too?'

'Do they want me?' asked Chloe with a hint of hauteur that reminded Rory utterly of Eden.

'I have twin sisters and you are SO like one of them, Eden. She's feisty.'

'The politician?' Chloe grinned with pleasure. 'I'm very like my mother and apparently quite like my birth father too.'

'You don't drink or gamble, do you?' asked Rory warily. 'Genetics and all that.'

'Guinness with blackcurrant on high days and holidays and, occasionally, the lottery. My addiction is painting supplies! I plan on graduating top of my class in art college!'

'My family are going to love you, ' Rory promised. 'But they don't know anything about you. We're going to change that,' Rory added.

Chloe shrugged. 'Artists need complicated lives,' she said.

Rory laughed. 'We can give you complicated,' she said. 'We specialise in it.'

Savannah

It was the postman's fault.

Savannah always chatted to him if he had a package. Today, he had books for Clary and Savannah was downstairs putting on lipstick at the hall mirror when he arrived. Crucially, Calum hadn't left for the office. Since his protein business had failed, he'd started an investment firm with some old school friends. It meant travel, lots of dinners and many meetings. Savannah never asked how it was going or how the finances were: she wouldn't dare.

Calum wanted to run her finances but his were off-limits.

Most days, he was gone by half seven, which meant Savannah and Clary could have a leisurely breakfast together and chat. Savannah had known Calum was running late. He hated lateness.

He'd made coffee and toast with a certain coiled anger about him and Savannah felt it swirling like dragon's breath on the kitchen floor.

Once he'd left the room, she could feel herself breathe again and tune back in to what Clary was talking about.

This morning, it had been the 'could we get a dog?' conversation.

'Just a teeny one and it could sleep with me.'

Clary looked just like her aunt Indy had at the same age: those stunning eyes with the amber centres, the full mouth, the long hair with hints of blond and a bit of strawberry in there too. But while Indy had been a free spirit, Clary was a quiet little figure who watched adults carefully.

'Let's talk about the dog later, darling,' Savannah had said quietly to her daughter, and winced as Clary's little face fell. There was no way Calum would allow them to get a dog, simply no way.

'Dogs smell,' he'd said flatly. He hadn't grown up with a dog, didn't understand the comfort animals brought.

Savannah felt it was time she confronted him about this even though she quaked at the thought. But she had to do it, for Clary.

Their daughter was an only child, she needed another presence in the house, a little creature she could love, be a big sister to.

After breakfast, Clary ran upstairs to get into her uniform and Savannah checked her big bag for notebooks and tablet, and fixed her lipstick in the mirror.

The gate bell rang.

It was Kev, the postman and Savannah greeted him cheerfully.

'How's the baby? Is he sleeping yet?'

Kev, young and a new dad, leaned against the wall and settled in for a chat on how his four-month-old still wasn't sleeping more than two hours at a time.

Clary came down, said a shy hello to Kev and then Savannah looked at her watch.

'Shoot! Look at the time!' she said.

'Yes,' said Calum's voice from behind her. 'The time. We're all running very late indeed.'

'Morning, Mr Desmond,' said Kev.

'Morning,' Calum replied.

Savannah's gut clenched. She felt the familiar spasms. The different tones of her husband's voice were connected to her body. She was a blank canvas on which he could paint any colour, trigger any emotion. To an outsider, he sounded friendly. She knew differently.

Her body knew differently. It could hear his displeasure.

Kev was waving and hopping into his van, Clary was telling her mother about something she'd forgotten: a charity thing where they had to bring two euros into school '— and we'll get a muffin. Please, Mum?'

And Calum's hand was on Savannah's left arm, sliding down its slender length until it reached her left hand.

He was very strong and when he touched her little finger and pulled, she had to muffle the gasp of shock. Pure pain arced up her hand as he hyper-extended the finger, pulled and twisted sharply. She felt something crack, a tiny bone shriek.

'He's over familiar, that post guy,' Calum murmured. 'But you like him, don't you?'

Savannah couldn't speak for pain. Her eyes closed.

Don't frighten Clary. Keep her from seeing this.

'He likes to talk about the baby. I'm sorry,' Savannah said. 'Sorry. I won't talk to him anymore. It's just the baby thing—' She was babbling now. Pain mingled with anxiety that Clary would see what was happening at the door.

It was what drove her daily: keeping Clary safe, unaware.

'Good. He's over familiar. I don't like it. But you know I don't like it.'

Calum was brusque now as he walked her back in, shut the door. Nobody listening to him or looking at them – the family tableau of three of them in the hall, waiting to leave the house for work and school – would think there was anything amiss.

They wouldn't see the undercurrents. Nobody ever saw. The years of put-downs, insults, so-called jokes at her expense. Nobody saw any of it. He was like a magician with how he fooled people into thinking him charming.

'See you later,' Calum called to his wife, then to Clary: 'Have you a kiss for your dad?'

Savannah heard Clary mutter, 'Love you, Daddy.'

Did Clary love him? Savannah felt the wave of pain from her hand overwhelm her but she kept it inside, even though she was now shaking with pain and anxiety.

Leaning against a wall in the hall, she decided that was both strong and weak at the same time. How could a person be both?

'Nearly ready, honey,' she called to her daughter and she ran upstairs. In a box labelled 'tampons' where she kept painkillers, she found paracetamol. She had much stronger painkillers from that time in the bathroom when she'd banged against the bath.

Her ribs had been fractured and the A & E doctor had taken her word for it that she'd slipped getting out of the shower. He'd given her ten opioid painkillers and she'd used most of them. They made her sleepy, though. She couldn't be sleepy today. Plain paracetamol would do. Or maybe the one with the codeine in it that made her feel sick. She'd take nausea over pain right now. Her finger was swelling and she thought that perhaps the best thing was to neighbour strap it to the next one, yet it was too painful to do that right now. It was bent at a funny angle. She clumsily wrapped a bandage around it and stuck medical tape on top. She might say she'd shut the car door on it? People did that all the time.

The front door slammed.

He was gone.

Savannah let herself sag against the bathroom sink and threw the codeine and paracetamol combination tablets into a glass, added tap water. A shot of caffeine would help too. And some sugar, just a hint. She and Clary could be a bit late today, couldn't they?

As she drank down the medication, she caught sight of herself: her face a little clammy from the pain but, otherwise, she looked like she always did. Her hair perfect, the elegantly androgynous grey linen shift dress hanging perfectly from her shoulders. Calum's big engagement ring glinted in the morning light.

Another beautiful day shone in through the windows. Savannah closed her eyes for one blessed moment and tried to breathe. As always, her breath stayed in her chest, high up. She found it impossible anymore to breathe the way she used to in yoga, deeply into her belly. It was as if her very breath was just about reaching into her body, keeping her alive, but always alert. Alert for danger.

Honeymoons were supposed to be wonderful. And this one was.

'It's bliss, isn't it?' she'd asked Calum when it was just the two of them alone in the beautiful villa with its view of the beach in Thailand and its own tiny infinity pool just outside.

Savannah unpacked her suitcase which had been beautifully packed by Indy, the family's best packer. Indy used tissue paper.

Imagine: tissue paper, thought Savannah happily.

The tissue-paper-wrapped garments were themselves enclosed in little suitcase bags in pale purple, special cubes to keep things separate. It was part of Indy's gift to her.

Each was zipped up with different types of garment inside: a zippy cube full of her bikinis; one with light T-shirts neatly folded; another with a couple of pretty camisoles to be worn with long flowy silk skirts in the evening, not a crease in sight. A cube filled with her lingerie.

Nobody could pack like Indy.

Calum had gone into the bathroom and while he was in there, Savannah had walked over to the double doors and opened them out, so that all she needed to do was step out onto the decking and walk into the pool. She thought, with a grin, perhaps they could skinny dip. Calum was tired, he hadn't slept on the flight. Thailand was such a long way away, which was partly why she hadn't wanted to go in the first place, because even though she was dying to see Thailand, it was such an enormously long trip for eight days. They were both so busy, both businesses manically busy. But Calum had insisted.

He had a friend, a wealthy friend, who'd gone there for his honeymoon.

'It sounded completely amazing, you'd want to have seen the pictures,' Calum said. 'No, it's got to be Thailand, I won't hear of anything else.' And she laughed.

'You old romantic,' she said, 'wanting to go to the best honeymoon place ever.'

Eden had disagreed.

'You don't want a long flight, Savannah.' She looked disapproving. 'Why are you going so far if you're this busy, if you're going to come back absolutely shattered. And eight days is not enough to go that far.'

Eden didn't get it, Savannah thought. They'd manage the jet lag. Together, they could manage anything.

She walked back in and called her husband. *Husband*, even the word excited her. How absolutely fabulous. He must be in the bathroom, she realised, and went back to her suitcase, looking around for the best bikinis. Here was a wonderful one, sort of a tie-dye thing that Indy had found for her. Trust Indy to find something so utterly wild and delicious. But the idea of skinny dipping thrilled her.

The villa was so hidden and secluded that nobody would see. So she stripped off her travelling clothes and stood naked at the double doors facing the beach

'Savannah.' It didn't sound like him, his voice was guttural, low, angry. And then the flat of his hand slapped her across the face. 'What the fuck are you doing stripping off in front of an open door? Anyone could see you.'

The floor came up to meet her. Savannah found herself sitting painfully on her hip and her hand went wonderingly to her face. Calum had hit her. It was like having a beloved friend turn around and scream at you, then turn into a face from a horror movie. And she was naked on the wooden floor of her honeymoon villa, with the painful imprint of her new husband's hand on her cheek. None of it made sense. Her mind could not compute. How had this happened? Had she said something strange? Done something? Was it against the law to take off your clothes if all the doors weren't locked in Thailand? Was that it, was he saving her? And then he was on the floor beside her.

He was stern: 'Anyone could see in.'

She let him put his arms around her, but she was suddenly very aware of her nakedness and her vulnerability. She pulled herself into a ball but Calum wouldn't allow this and was dragging her to her feet. The towel he'd had draped over one shoulder was wrapped around her. As if she was a creature to be covered up.

'Go into the bathroom, sort yourself out.' He was brisk, no nonsense. Not a word of apology. No 'Oh gosh, what did I do? Are you hurt?'

'You'll be fine, ' Calum went on in the same brisk voice. 'Perhaps we'll eat in our room tonight.'

Her hand hovered around her face. He hadn't said sorry that he'd hit her.

Or had he hit her? Was she imagining it?

No, she thought: she wasn't. Calum's hand had rapped against her face, palm first.

But he loved her, didn't he . . .? You didn't hit people you loved.

In the bathroom, she shut the door. She considered locking it but then thought that might make him angry because he'd hear the click of the lock. She didn't want to do that. No, no it would be better not to make him angry. Better just to pretend that this hadn't happened because he wasn't saying sorry. It was a mistake, obviously it was a mistake, because he loved her.

She looked at her face in the mirror, fingers tenderly feeling around the livid red mark on her cheek. It ached. Her whole head ached, actually.

Calum was strong.

Would she have a bruise? The fingers touching her face began to shake.

A bruise.

'You all right in there?'

'Yes,' she replied and she didn't sound like herself.

She wet a corner of the hand towel and held it to her face to cool the skin.

Concealer would tone the red mark down a bit. They could eat in their room for a few nights, that would be lovely. People expected honeymoon couples to eat in their room. Yes, that was it. Nobody would know, it was just one of those things, wasn't it?

She wouldn't say anything to anyone. It had been an accident. A one-off.

Savannah smiled at herself tremulously in the mirror of the beautiful villa, the best place ever for a honeymoon. It would all be fine.

II

Wednesday Evening

Eden and Savannah walked into the restaurant together. Eden looked preoccupied and was withdrawn, Savannah thought, which was odd, because nobody did public performances like her sister. She stopped herself; that sounded cruel and bitchy and she hated being like that. But they used to be so much closer and . . .

Savannah bit her lip. Her fault. She knew exactly why they weren't close anymore. Nobody could be close to her. She pushed people away, subtly. It was easier that way, easier to stop people seeing. Tonight was going to be different. Tonight Clary was at home with Marie-Denise and Calum was out at a work event. So it was like a free night. Nobody minded that she was out. Nobody would be timing her evening out, waiting with annoyance for her to be home. Her sore finger still throbbed but she barely noticed it now. Calum rarely hurt her, after all. He said things, yes, but he didn't hurt her physically. So it was OK.

The unexpected thrill of free time out made her giddy and she reached over and grabbed her sister's arm, so that they were linked going through the restaurant.

'Will we sit together, and we'll be safe among all Mum's crazy friends?'

Eden grinned and held on to Savannah.

'Sounds like a good plan, actually. I'm terrified Vonnie's going to start some longwinded story about what they were like when they were younger. Vonnie is,' she paused, 'deliciously eccentric and getting more so as she gets older.' The sisters giggled. They both loved Vonnie, an ersatz aunt. But she lived on her own adorable planet, a place full of unicorns, sparkly pens and little handbags that girls might bring to their First Holy Communions.

'I'd love to be like Vonnie sometimes,' said Eden wistfully. Savannah looked at her in surprise.

'Really?'

'Just sometimes,' said Eden. 'You know it must be so relaxing in there, in Happy Fairyland with no worries.'

'She has got worries,' said Savannah, thinking of Gerry of the bad back.

'I know, but nothing major. Everything is simple in their world.'

Savannah couldn't help but shiver.

'You don't know what's going on in other people's lives,' she said dully.

Chantal probably should have gone to the hen night, Rory thought as she got out of the taxi outside the restaurant. Mum and her sisters would have loved Chantal to come. They probably got on better with Chantal than they did with her, Rory thought irritably. But that wasn't the reason she hadn't brought her partner. No, Chantal was still hassling her to discuss the book with the family and Rory felt unaccountably anxious. She wasn't used to this: anxiety wasn't one of her primary emotions, not like Savannah, who was always quivering. Rory felt an unaccustomed pang of guilt at thinking of her sister in that way. Savannah was as much a survivor of the Sorrento as she was.

Eden and Indy seemed untouched by it all, delighted, happy to be the children of Meg and Stu Robicheaux. And it wasn't that Rory was unhappy with her parents, per se, it was just that it had been chaotic and chaos was no fun. She'd wanted stability – not her mother wanting to paint one wall of the ballroom in a rainbow-pride mural.

Her mother had never understood that Rory wanted to discover her own path in life without Meg in front of her, strewing rainbow symbols all over the place, being Mama Lesbian while Rory was still trying to live a quiet life with her friends. And yet, her mother *had* been Rory's safe place. All the love her family and Mum had given her had made her strong enough to fight the bullies.

They had made her who she was: unafraid.

No matter what she did – forcibly tattooed some homophobe with a rainbow, perhaps – they'd have stood up for her. Their strength had been her strength.

There needed to be another chapter in the book. About how fabulous her family was. The family of the fictional Rory character.

She paid the cab driver and marched into the restaurant. She could hear the squeals and the laughter even before she got down to the back.

'Rory,' squawked a delighted Vonnie, who threw herself around Rory and clung on as if she was a limpet holding on to a stone. 'It's so lovely to see you, I've missed you at all our little meetings. Are you very busy?'

Rory hugged her back. Vonnie was sweet, harmless. She'd always been there in Rory's childhood.

'I am busy,' she said. 'I'm involved in—' she was about to say 'a book project,' but quickly amended, 'lots of work. It's very busy.'

Hell, she was going to have to tell people soon, she couldn't keep lying and it was going to be in the papers and the unaccustomed anxiety shimmered within her again. She had to contact Louisa and tell her huge changes needed to be made.

'Hey, sis,' said Eden, appearing beside her.

Eden put an arm around Rory's waist and squeezed. She knew Rory wasn't into girly kissing. Eden understood her, Rory always thought. She loved her sister at that moment.

Eden was the best. Tough as old boots and straight as a die.

How was it that four sisters – actually five – could be so different?

'You do know you're organising the wine for the wedding, don't you?' Eden said cheerily.

Rory shot a glance at her.

'Yeah, the wine, sure.'

'Have you done it?'

'Er – I—'

'Thought so,' said Eden. 'Do you want me to do it?'

'No,' said Rory, outraged. 'I said I was going to do it and I'm going to do it.'

'You need to have it organised pronto, Rory. We've already agreed the corkage for the catering company. We need to get a time from the vintners to say when they're delivering it.'

'OK, I'll get onto it,' said Rory. She caught sight of her mother looking beautiful as always, surrounded by old friends. And there was Savannah sitting talking to some of Dad's old sailing buddies, or rather, their wives.

'Just going over to say hello to Mum,' she said and escaped Eden.

Despite her plan, Savannah ended up sitting as far apart from Eden as it was possible to be. The table was long and the assembled hen party was noisy. She hated loud noises. Every clanging glass, every dropped knife made her jump. The more the evening wore on, the more it seemed to intensify.

Vonnie had a plan for people to move around after the main course and sit with someone else for dessert. Since she was several glasses of wine in when she announced this idea, it was amazing she was able to manage it. Clad in what looked like something an off-duty tooth fairy might wear – an outfit made up of pale-green gauze decorated with fake white marabou – Vonnie stood up and tried ineffectually to get people to move, her skinny little brown arms waving.

'No, you sit over there, that's right, because you haven't talked to Meg yet. Sonya, why not sit here!'

Savannah found herself sitting beside Miranda, one of Mum's old friends from the many years when her father had dallied with sailing. It had always been a limited dalliance. Because sailing cost money and the Robicheaux clan had never had much of that. Dad had crewed a lot and he loved it but had never managed to own his own boat, to his eternal misery.

Miranda, a woman who could sail through any gale, had stuck with the Robicheaux family through thick and thin.

'Oh, Savannah, look at you. I have to say, I'm loving your new range. What's it called? Safari Pleasures, I love it. The candles are divine. It's got oud in it – is it oud?' Miranda had a carrying voice and Savannah thought that possibly the people at the next table could hear her, or possibly even the people two tables away.

'Yes,' said Savannah, 'there is some oud in there.' Not much because oud was one of the most expensive perfume ingredients in the world. But just a little hint of it was wonderful in the candles and room diffusers.

'We're working on it for a perfume range,' she added. Perfume was still just an embryonic part of the business, with two scents for sale so far because getting into perfume was expensive. And Savannah knew it could be make or break time for many businesses. She and Anthony had discussed it many times.

A perfume launch was a huge thing and they were a small company. Only the huge cosmetic giants could really afford to launch perfume. But Calum was against it.

'Oh no, I love it. I'd buy it in perfume form,' Miranda was saying, her eyes glazed happily with the look of someone who had had a fabulous meal and probably too much red wine.

Gianni was doing the rounds, checking who wanted after-dinner cocktails or liqueurs. He was an excellent restaurateur, Savannah thought absently, watching him walk around, polite, kind. She felt herself ludicrously drawn to him. Kindness was just an underrated quality. Look at the way he was putting Vonnie's wrap back on her chair, gently, not remonstrating with her for letting it drop in the first place. But maybe he wasn't like that at home, maybe Mrs Gianni got shouted at when she dropped things.

He was at Miranda's and Savannah's end of the table now.

'I could kill for a Grand Marnier, Gianni, sweetie,' said Miranda, who was obviously a regular. 'That would be fabulous.'

'How is Robbie?' said Gianni, referring to Miranda's husband.

'Oh, Robbie's great,' said Miranda. 'You know him – as long as he's sailing, he's happy.'

Gianni beamed at her. 'Yes, he's a happy man, your husband. Even if he is not sailing, I think he is happy.'

'Yes, he is,' said Miranda mistily.

Gianni hit a button on his iPad. 'And you?' Gianni turned his attention to Savannah and she felt his warmth encompass her. Ludicrously, she felt herself tear up. She was so receptive to any sort of kindness. A cashier in the supermarket talking to her. Another driver letting her go on the road and waving at her. All these things made her want to cry. It was ridiculous.

Gianni was waiting patiently for her order.

She began to panic. Calum hated it when she dithered over menus. 'I don't know—'

She hadn't had much to drink. Drinking was always a mistake. She felt so sad when she drank and then she cried—

'An amaretti, perhaps?' said Gianni.

She looked at him gratefully. 'Yes, yes, an amaretti, I'd love that.' She loved almonds. How clever of him to know.

'And how is your dear husband?' said Miranda, when Gianni had moved on.

Savannah looked at her.

'He's such a charmer. Robbie and I met him recently at a fundraiser. Such a darling. He's doing incredible things with the business, I believe. You are so lucky to have him at the helm. Handsome man too. You lucky thing.'

Miranda patted Savannah's knee and Savannah swallowed down any number of thoughts and emotions. Calum was not at the helm but he controlled so much. And lucky? If she was so lucky, why did she feel so scared all the time?

'Yes,' she said automatically, 'he's a lovely man.'

Her eyes glazed over and her finger began to hurt. She simply wanted an evening out and here she was, having to talk about Calum again. Nobody could see who he really was. But then, there was nothing to see, was there?

It was all her fault. She was imagining it.

That's what he'd told her anytime she'd tentatively said that perhaps they might try marriage counselling. It had been years since she'd tried that.

'You're over-emotional, Savannah. Everything has to be a drama with you. You can't complete the simplest tasks, either. I have to do everything,' he liked to say.

Now, that was untrue: she knew it for a fact. He did nothing round the house. Never bought groceries. But was she so bad at everything? Was she hopeless as a mother the way he said she was?

Two years ago, she'd begun to search on the Internet to see if anyone else lived the way she did. She searched on her private tablet which she hid, even from Clary. Especially from Clary. Her daughter already seemed older than her years and Savannah didn't want to make it worse. When she was very stressed, she'd sit in the car outside the office, hotspot her iPad off the phone and look at the sites again, the ones she came back to again and again.

These sites seemed to be speaking directly to her: 'Are you walking on eggshells? Do you spend your life in a state of tension trying not to upset somebody? Are you scared, frightened in your own home? Are you financially controlled by your partner?'

Sometimes, Savannah read the various articles so quickly that she scanned them in moments. They all said the same thing. They all talked about her life, about her.

Women who lived in fear. Men who told them they were crazy.

Emotional abuse, they called it.

And yet was it her? Was it her fault?

And if it wasn't her fault, was her life so bad?

She didn't know anymore. Maybe having your husband get angry with you and not talk to you for a week – maybe that was normal?

Perhaps Ralphie did that with Eden and Eden just never said it. Had it been like that with Dad and Mum? She tried to remember. She didn't think it had been like that when she was growing up. No, nobody ever gave anyone the silent treatment. Although, Rory could be very grizzly and sometimes would sulk in her bedroom, but normally it was for no more than an hour.

Then she'd come downstairs, stomp around a bit and everyone would make up.

Dad never got angry with anyone. He did sometimes shout at the TV during horse races.

No, it hadn't been like that at home. Yet, marriages were different, weren't they? Nobody knew what went on when the doors shut.

Savannah thought of what it would be like to ask Eden. How would she phrase it? What words could she use? *Eden, does Ralphie ever make you feel very, very scared? Do you worry about upsetting him? Do you dance around him in case he screams that you're a stupid bitch and everything's your fault? That you're over emotional/stupid/annoying? Do you read his every mood hoping to cheer him up?* And then: *Has he ever hurt you?*

Her finger throbbed. He'd only physically hurt her three

times. That first time was the honeymoon. It had been an accident; she was sure of it.

She had trained herself to think that way because to imagine anything else was staring into utter horror.

He did sometimes shove her out of the way in the kitchen or open drawers on her hips. He liked doing that. But it was never obvious, never an action anyone would see and think was anything other than clumsiness.

He'd once shoved her in the bathroom against the sink during sex; had been so rough. He knew he was hurting her, knew her head was banging against the wall: she'd had a lump on the back of her head and her ribs had hurt. That had been the time they'd gone to A&E.

She'd lied that she'd fallen because how could she tell anyone what had happened?

This week with the postman – that had been no accident, Calum had meant to hurt her. He was jealous. The thought overwhelmed her.

She had been talking to the postman about his new baby and Calum was instantly jealous, some men were, weren't they? And that was his way of proving it. He hadn't said sorry. He hadn't asked her how her hand was. It was all forgotten, unmentioned, like it had slipped under the floorboards, a dirty secret that everyone would walk over.

Eden had been collared by a woman who was having trouble with planning permission. She was not part of the hen party but had followed Eden into the loo and was now haranguing her about why politics was such a crooked business, why the planning people were all corrupt and that all she'd wanted was a conservatory.

Eden washed her hands, gazed at herself in the darkened mirror in Gianni's small ladies' room and wished that the woman was drunk. Drunken constituents were far easier to handle: a smile here, a mention that she and the constituent should talk urgently on the phone and then a quick getaway with the person happily forgetting all about it because they were in a haze of wine.

This woman – a harridan wearing a diamond cross necklace that would probably buy her another house with an already-installed conservatory – sadly was not drunk.

Eden decided there was only one way out: she grabbed her phone and looked at it intently, as if she'd just had a text come in.

'Gosh, so lovely to meet you. Do phone me at the office, but I have to go.'

And she slipped out of the loo, belted off to their table and hid herself in a corner.

Wine, she decided, was the answer.

In another corner, she could see Rory holding a vast brandy balloon filled with what had to be a double.

No, Eden reflected. Alcohol was not the answer.

The problem with the book, Rory decided, as she looked around for a waiter to get her more brandy, was that nobody would ever believe that she hadn't meant to hurt them all from the very beginning. Rory knew the story would shatter the family. Except that she hadn't planned it that way. Sure, she'd been writing the book – a book – for years. But then she wrote for a living. That's what working in advertising as a copywriter meant. You wrote adverts. And lots of advertising copywriters went on to write novels, so it was nothing very new or unusual for her to fiddle around on her laptop. Chantal had been so encouraging.

'You express yourself so beautifully,' Chantal had said. 'This is a very good thing for you to do, to get rid of some of the sadness.'

'I'm not sad,' Rory had said, which was a lie, because sometimes she was sad. She was a human being: humans were complex and had so many different emotions. The book had been this blissful cathartic way of writing about a character quite like her, who'd grown up in a chaotic and loving family, and who'd then discovered a secret which had shocked her.

So the book had been her therapy. It was fiction, yet the fictional family lived in a big old house that they sometimes used as a B & B. One wouldn't need to look very far to see the similarities between the Belloc family in the book and the Robicheaux family. It had been marvellous therapy at first, writing down how she'd felt as a young lesbian. What life had been like, how she'd found herself with her group of friends, all a little different, all the little edges of the school groups. And then she began to do research into the family, just for the sake of it.

Which was how she'd found the photo of Lori, which led her to Chloe. Dear Chloe who was pretending to be cool but who really wanted to be accepted by this other family. If that wasn't proof that things had been mixed up, then Rory didn't know what was.

Lori had worked in the Sorrento for seven years when Rory had been little. From Cork, Lori had been a strong, tall woman with rippling long dark hair, amazing cheekbones, finely crafted eyebrows and a strong nose. She had been fiery and fun, stern when she needed to be. Had taken care of the four sisters, driven them places, served at table, in the restaurant dealt with tricky guests. She'd been like a fabulous big sister. And Mum loved her, loved her like a little sister probably. And then Lori had gone, left. It had been so sudden, one minute she was there, the next, vanished. As the youngest, Rory had felt it the most.

It seemed to Rory that Lori's departure had marked the beginning of the end for the family. It was when her father's gambling had become worse. When his drinking escalated, when their mother stopped tolerating his behaviour. When Lori left, everything had fallen apart. And now, Rory knew why. She had written about it. She had written about it in the book that Louisa had just sold for hundreds of thousands and her family were going to read it and find out. She could hear Chantal's voice in her ear: 'You have to tell them.'

These past six months, Rory hadn't been able to think of anything else. It was why she had been so angry when her parents said they were getting married. Now, at this moment with everything that was happening with the book, it was making a mockery of everything she had written. It was ignoring the truth, the facts. And she paused at the most horrible thought of all: if the book came out – *when* the book came out, she corrected herself – everyone would know, they'd be distraught, humiliated, and it would be all her fault.

But they had helped her be who she was. Her family had helped make her this strong woman. How could she hurt them?

Savannah

It was one in the morning when the taxi dropped Savannah home. There was no sign of Calum's Lexus. Just her Golf sitting outside the house. She couldn't help it, she felt herself breathe a sigh of relief. Wonderful, she could be in bed asleep – even pretending to be asleep – when he came in. She paid the driver, raced out of the car, was in the door, and then a familiar voice stilled her.

'You're home late.'

Oh no. He'd left the car because he'd obviously been drinking. Not that Calum ever drank very much. But even a glass of wine magnified everything when he was annoyed. He was standing in the doorway of the study, his study, not her study. She didn't have a study in the house. She didn't need one, he insisted. What did she need one for? So she did her work at the kitchen table.

'Looks good,' he always said when he saw photo shoots

where she was sitting at the kitchen table. 'Really good, you working there.'

Sometimes there were pictures of him in his study in the articles and he loved this: his two computers on the desk, looking like a business magnate.

Now his tie was off and he had a couple of shirt buttons undone, his suit jacket gone. He wasn't tall, her husband. Not tall like Steve or Ralphie. But he carried himself well and he looked after himself. He leaned against the door jamb, lithe, in his grey suit trousers and pristine white shirt. He was a study in darkness: he needed to shave again and his skin, always tanned, was brown.

He held a tumbler of amber liquid. Scotch, she figured. His little finger was tapping on the glass. Other people wouldn't notice those details. They wouldn't notice the glitter in his dark eyes.

'Were you drinking?' he said.

'A couple of glasses of wine, a glass of amaretti,' she said. Her heart was racing.

'You shouldn't drink, it makes you emotional.'

'I'm – I'm not emotional,' she said, trying to sound cheerful. 'It was a lovely evening, Mum's hen night. You'd have loved it. Oh, a lady called Miranda, Robbie's wife, was asking after you, said you were handsome.'

'Really.'

It was hard to describe how cold a person could sound.

'Is she the blousy one with the bad skin?'

She shivered internally. He could be so hateful about other people.

'No, the one with the big boat, you went out on it with them once.'

Calum hadn't been good at sailing, he had been seasick. She shouldn't have mentioned Miranda.

'Oh yes, I remember. The husband had a big job.' He was talking about Miranda's husband. Calum liked people with big jobs as if some of their lustre would rub off on him. 'He's retired now.' He took a sip of his drink. 'I suppose everyone was flirting with the waiters, everyone does in Gianni's. Were you?'

'No, no, I don't flirt with people,' she said, desperation creeping in.

'Oh for God's sake,' he said. 'Don't get your knickers in a twist.'

She grasped about for something else to talk about.

'How was your event?'

'Fine.'

He walked towards the kitchen and she knew she was supposed to follow him. He sat down at the kitchen table, sprawled in one of the chairs, making himself bigger. It was something he did. He made himself bigger and she, Savannah thought, made herself smaller.

'I dropped into the office earlier and guess what I found.'

Savannah felt her stomach disappear, as if it had been vacuumed out.

Calum held up one of the new packages: the elegant black that she'd ordered, the packaging she'd been hiding from him.

'You've managed to keep this a secret from me. How do you think this makes me look, Savannah? I'm your husband and I didn't know about this. How fucking dare you go behind my back?'

She was frozen for a moment and then she began to stammer: 'It was just an idea I had.' She wouldn't throw Anthony under the bus. 'We can junk it, but—'

'But everyone think's it's amazing. I saw them all there and they are so proud of you. Our Savannah has done it again.'

She began to cry now. The rage in his voice did something to her.

'Don't give me the tears,' he hissed, contempt in every word. 'Jesus, you definitely shouldn't drink. And I don't know what you're getting so over emotional about. There's always some big whiney drama with you, isn't there? You just listen to me: I'm explaining the facts to you. I make the decisions. You know fucking nothing. You think you'd have got where you are now without me?'

Savannah looked down, his eyes were glittering dangerously now.

The terror was upon her.

The fear.

She felt trapped. As if every word was a step in a field of land mines.

'You're just useless, you can't do anything.'

He leaned over her, trying to dwarf her, coldness emanating from every part of him. 'You are nothing without me. *Nothing*,' he hissed. 'You just spend money and ruin our kid, because she is ruined. Why the fuck is that? Because you're making her into a little fairy princess and you're too fucking stupid to see how that's a mistake. I didn't get where I am today by being mollycoddled. I got there by hard graft. You understand? Hard graft.'

There were beads of sweat on his forehead now.

His eyes looked crazed. He was like a rat, she thought: a rat that had turned on her, had grown in size and was going to kill her one way or the other.

'How do you think it makes me feel when my wife goes behind my back?'

'I didn't,' she whimpered.

'I'll show you how it makes me feel,' he said. 'I'm going to bed, coming?'

Sex, he wanted sex. Rough sex. It was the ultimate weapon. His ultimate weapon.

Savannah's brain processed it rapidly. Sex might make everything better.

'Of course, darling,' she said, ignoring the fact that she was shaking with fear.

She had the barriers totally up now. She was insulated – the real Savannah hidden inside the shell of the physical person.

The act of insulation was like bringing down shutters and when she did it, she was safe because she blanked out the real Savannah, put on the mask. The masked, shuttered Savannah could smile and get through this, so she did.

Insulated Savannah pulled back those unshed tears, her face almost frozen, palely expressionless.

She followed her husband upstairs to bed but took a detour to stick her head in the door to see how Clary was. Her daughter was curled up in a little ball. She always slept curled towards the corner of her bed, like a shell around the comforting mound of her teddy bears. Calum said she was too old for teddy bears, but then he would. Savannah never let him win when it came to this. There were a couple of things she would fight over.

'No. She's a little girl; little girls need teddy bears and stuff like that.'

Fighting for what Clary needed were the only times she disobeyed him. It was so much easier to go with Calum, agree with everything he said, because life was easier. But for Clary, she had to be strong and sometimes disagree with him.

She planted a gentle kiss on her daughter's forehead knowing that Clary wouldn't wake. Then she went into the grand master suite, an area Calum had decorated to his own taste. It wasn't the pretty bower that Savannah would have liked. It was very much a man's room, all dark wooden wardrobes, dark wooden floor, grey walls, charcoal bed covers.

He was at the dressing table taking off his cufflinks. She went into the bathroom hoping she might remove her make-up, but steeling herself because this was an endurance test, had been for a very long time. She put a soaked cotton pad on one eye and had removed the mascara and make-up from it and was just about to start on the second one, when he appeared behind her.

'Stop that,' he said, 'come to bed.'

It was his different voice, his sex voice.

She knew better than even to attempt to take the mascara

off the other eyelashes. She dropped the cotton wool pad where it lay and let him take her hand and lead her back into the bedroom. He stripped her clothes off, kissing her shoulders, neck and her mouth. She put her arms around him and did her best to make it seem as if she was joining in. Because this was the way to make things better. He wanted sex. She would give him sex or passion or whatever it was he desired; he could have anything. Anything but her soul, her heart. She'd locked off those parts of herself long ago.

'You're so beautiful,' he said, 'so beautiful.'

Suddenly she was lying on the bed and he was on top of her. And she felt so dry inside because how could she feel anything else? Arousal was a thing of love and desire, not of fear.

He pushed inside her, pumping away, ripping into her arid body, Savannah holding on to his back and quivering with fear and pain. Her eyes were wide open, staring up at the ceiling but not even seeing it because soon this would be over and he'd sleep. He'd be happy.

For Calum, sex was winning.

Forcing her to have sex was a control mechanism and it excited him beyond belief.

'Don't go behind my back again,' he grunted.

'No.' Her voice was automatic. No. Yes. Anything.

'Tell me you want me.'

'I want you Calum,' she said mechanically.

As he moaned and moved over her body, grinding himself into her, she wondered if he could hear how like an automaton she sounded. She wondered if he could feel that her body was a vibrating carcass that had nothing to do with sensuality.

She was nothing but a vessel to be used.

He thrust into her, again and again, getting more aroused.

Savannah kept staring at the ceiling. This was paying a price, nothing more. Anything to keep him happy.

When he was finished, he rolled off her.

'I love you, you know that,' he murmured, and she replied, 'Yes, love you too.'

Her reply was as mechanical as the whole act because she was acting the way he wanted her to act.

He wanted the obedient wife who took his angry words, his commands, his insults, his cruel silences. Fear made her that woman.

Her sisters wouldn't do it, she thought, a flare of wet in each eye.

Eden would have screamed back at him in the kitchen. Rory might have hit him. Would have hit him. With the copper saucepan, perhaps. On the side of the head.

Indy – Indy would never have married him because she'd loved wonderful Steve for so long. But Savannah couldn't. So she paid with her body. Anything to keep the peace. To keep the fear at a minimum. To keep her and Clary safe.

'Wonderful, I'm going to go to sleep, OK?' he said and planted a kiss on her cheek, as if none of the scene in the kitchen had happened.

She lay there a minute more and got up, went silently into the bathroom to take the make-up off the other eye. She could hear his snores. He fell asleep instantly after sex, always had. So she took off her make-up slowly, creamed her face and her neck and the tears dripped down into the sink. But she didn't wipe them away. All that mattered was that it was going to be OK in the morning. Things would be better; she'd seen to it.

12

The Third Photo

Eden stood in her bedroom and looked at herself in the mirror. Her outfit was totally different to the one she'd worn for last year's photo. In fact, she was so totally different from the person she'd been last year. So different, it was hard to imagine that the girl from then and the girl from now inhabited the same body. She'd been eighteen then, whereas now she felt about a hundred. She felt changed by life and knowledge. Changed by the secrecy. She wished she'd been able to tell people, but, how could she? There were some secrets people didn't want to know. Secrets that therefore made shame bloom around them. When, in reality, Eden thought sadly, there shouldn't be shame, there should be understanding and kindness. But secrecy flattened all that. It was like damp mould creeping through life the way it crept along her now blackened windowsill. Damp was clambering over the Sorrento again. Old homes were the worst, her mother said.

She tied her hair back and looked in the mirror again. Gone were the cute breast-enhancing shirts she used to wear. She didn't want to be associated with that Eden. She wanted to start again, be the person she had been years ago, before excitement and craziness had been a part of her life. The manufactured girlband, which she'd joined after reading about it on a college noticeboard, had given her elegant, sedate clothes because that's who she was in their vision. And now she wore those clothes in normal life too. It was like trying them on for size: high-neck blouses, long skirts. She felt like a suffragette from the turn of the last century, ready to fight for her cause.

Where she'd fought for her cause, but she had had to fight it alone, because Jimmy was no use.

She'd known he wouldn't be. As soon as the words were out of her mouth, she could see it on his face: shock and a desire to be as far away from her as was humanly possible was what she'd seen.

She adjusted her hair a little now and found her necklace. She liked the citrine. It was an unusual stone, could stand in for a yellow diamond. But then she wasn't really into diamonds. No diamonds for Eden, she thought grimly. She'd have to buy them herself. She went downstairs out the back into the late summer sun.

The sun was shining through the trees, casting beautiful golden light on the back of the little barn where they took the pictures. When they'd started this years ago, the barn had been prettied up covered in twinkly lights and more of a cabana where Pops could serve drinks to people having parties outside. Now it looked faintly decaying like everything else about the Sorrento.

She took her place beside her sisters. Savannah was beaming into the camera. Eden loved seeing her twin happy. College had been the making of Savannah. She was blossoming under the business course, coming home at night to share new things with them. And talking about this idea that she had for a natural beauty company.

'You'd need a lot of money for that,' said Steve thoughtfully.

'It's all a load of rubbish, making women think they're ugly and have to buy things to make them look better,' Rory had said.

Rory, on the other hand, was going through a difficult time, Eden reflected. It was her place in the family; she didn't know where she fitted in. It was, Eden kept telling their mother, absolutely nothing to do with her sexuality.

'Rory's perfectly happy being gay, Mum,' Eden had said. 'It's us who are the problem. She's suffering from being the last born. Indy's the lovely one and I'm the minxy one.' Eden had winced slightly as she said this. 'Savannah is the dreamy but clever one. And where does Rory fit in? So far, the only role seems to be the irritable one. And she's not irritable – well, she is a lot of the time, but she'll get over that, it's just being a teenager.'

'I know,' Mum had said. 'But I worry, darling, I worry so much. I don't want life to be hard on her and—'

'Mum, stop. Life is hard on all of us.'

Eden thought of the secret she now carried. She should have told Mum from the beginning, but she didn't because she felt so stupid and Mum would have done anything to support her, she thought, and yet she'd kept it to herself. Because she felt ashamed of being so stupid; such a cliché.

Eden hated being a cliché above all things. No, it was better the way she'd done it, easier. Easier not to upset Mum and Pops. He'd have gone out and drunk himself insensible with shock and misery. No point in telling Pops.

Eden had thought of telling Indy, but no. Indy would have been far too upset given her work; it was easier the way she'd done it.

Savannah? She and Savannah had once been so incredibly close, but even identical twins weren't conjoined. Eden didn't want to add to Savannah's burdens. She was so happy now, seemed to have got over all the anxieties and self-doubt. How her sister had such low self-esteem, Eden didn't know, but Savannah was a mass of insecurities.

Eden took her place in the line-up.

'Your hair is nice,' she said to Rory, who looked at her in surprise.

'I don't know,' said Rory, 'it's just tricky getting it to sit properly.'

Eden reached out a gentle hand that flattened the tendrils gently.

'You are so good-looking you could model, you know.'

'No,' said Rory as if such an idea was crazy.

'Course you could – you're tall and slim, you'd be fabulous. And you're skinny. Look at the legs on you.'

Rory was wearing her normal uniform of ultra-black jeans, flat boots and a woolly black jumper, even though it was late summer.

'I couldn't model,' said Rory mulishly.

'You can do anything you want to, you big moron,' said Eden fondly. 'Just need to believe in yourself a bit more.'

'I do believe in myself,' said Rory as if this were a competition.

Eden smiled inside. Once this was the sort of thing she'd have said. Trying to look tough. She knew that, inside, Rory was an old marshmallow putting on a stern exterior to help her cope with life.

'Just saying you could,' she said.

'Are you all ready?' said Steve.

Indy, who'd been looking at the first quick shots on Steve's laptop, hopped back into place.

'Ready,' she said.

13

Thursday

Meg arrived at the coastal walk before Stu. She parked in the little car park and looked out towards the sea, thinking of the days when this was the view she saw every day. But the past was the past, she told herself firmly. If there was one thing she had learned over the past few years, it was that life kept changing and you have to change with it. Meg felt she was spectacular at changing. And now this huge change, remarrying Stu. Today she was picking up the dress and the girls were coming with her. She wanted a morning with just her girls, even though Vonnie had looked like a slightly sad puppy when Meg had said this.

'I just want it to be me and the girls, Vonnie,' Meg had said. 'You do understand?'

'Course I do,' said Vonnie, ever amiable, 'course I do. You know me: I'm just a big child. I love being in the centre of everything, but this is for you and the girls. You should have a nice breakfast first and then go in and try on the dress and bring it home. Oh, it will be wonderful.'

'We can't have breakfast,' Meg had explained, 'because Savannah has to go into the office, and Eden has a few appointments.'

'They're so busy all the time,' said Vonnie wistfully. 'Big jobs.'

'I know,' said Meg, 'but we can be proud of them, can't we?' She gently included Vonnie in the sentence. Vonnie didn't have daughters and instead had two sons. One of whom was an incredibly hard-working physiotherapist and the other was often prone to the same bad back as his father. He lived with his girlfriend just down the road and she was expecting their first baby.

'Yes,' said Vonnie, 'we can; our girls.'

Vonnie would have loved a girl, Meg knew this. Dressing a little girl would have fulfilled all Vonnie's own missed childhood fantasies. Meg wondered if adults always tried to recreate their own missed past with their children. Perhaps they did.

Her mother had been strong and powerful, but a little straight-laced. So, she'd been different with her girls, more relaxed. You couldn't have got more relaxed than raising them in the Sorrento Hotel. Her daughters had blossomed there, grown from toddlers to skinny girls, to pouting adolescents, into young women. Having the run of the place, helping out, cleaning, cooking. It had been a very different sort of childhood to her own. But it had turned out well. They were beautiful women and she adored them.

'Thinking of me?' said a voice.

She turned around to see Stu peering in the open window at her. He was wearing his old straw sun hat, one he'd worn for walks on the beach since time immemorial.

He was dressed in a white linen shirt over beige shorts. He was tanned and looked happy.

Meg unwound herself from the car and could feel Stu's eyes on her which was pleasing, nice that she could still make him watch her, she thought. She wouldn't have married him otherwise, not if he was indifferent to her. She knew too many people whose marriages had moved long ago from intimacy into some sort of mutual sticking together for the sake of it. Meg, had never wanted that. She was marrying Stu because she loved him, cared for him, desired him. And she knew he felt the same.

'You look beautiful, darling,' he said, his lips briefly meeting hers.

'Oh this old thing,' teased Meg. She was wearing a dress

he probably hadn't seen before, a sleeveless one that showed off her tanned shoulders. It was a turquoise colour that made her eyes stand out and made her beautiful long silvery plait look even more exotic. Round her neck she had wound some turquoise beads and on her feet she wore sensible runners for the walk.

'I can't believe it,' said Stu as they strolled down the beach holding hands. 'To think we're doing it again.'

'You're not having second thoughts, are you?' she asked. 'I have to know.'

'No, don't be ridiculous.' Stu let go of her hand and put his arm around her shoulders. 'I'm crazy about you, crazy. Are they going to do that bit, if anyone here has any reason why these people can't marry?'

'I don't think so; that's more of a church ceremony thing,' said Meg, laughing. 'We're not getting that experience with the civil ceremony but we can ask for that, if you want, in case you're hoping that some of my old lovers will appear.'

Stu grinned. 'Are there any lamp posts I need to piss on,' he said, 'just to show that you're mine?'

'No, darling,' said Meg, 'no lamp posts; you're mine and I'm yours. Besides, I'm the one who should be looking for lamp posts, you old charmer.'

'Ha!' His arm moved from her shoulder and slid round her waist this time. 'You're the only woman for me – always were, Meg, even if I was a bit wild on occasion.' He turned her around and they were facing each other.

Meg could hear the lapping noise of the water against the beach as Stu kissed her. There was something about being with a man who could kiss. Stu had always been the most amazing kisser. His mouth made every part of her body sing and she arched towards him. Her eyes opened; he was watching her almost lazily.

'I know we're supposed to be doing a walk,' he said, 'but do you fancy . . .?'

Meg grinned. 'I fancy,' she said, 'I do fancy.' She slipped a hand inside his shirt, caressed his chest, reaching over to touch his nipple.

He jerked and laughed.

'Still sensitive there?' she said.

'As if you didn't know.'

'I think it's been two weeks since we've been to bed together,' said Meg.

'You've been busy and I've been busy. It's not that we planned it,' said Stu, sounding slightly affronted.

'No,' said Meg, 'let's go there now.'

She knew what she wanted, always: it was lovely to have reached this stage in her life when she knew what she would and would not accept, what she needed and how to ask for it, simply. More people should try it. Expecting your significant other to be a mind-reader was always a mistake.

Savannah was determinedly keeping her mind off the night before.

The wedding dress: they were picking it up later today. Her mother had gone for something almost Grecian, which would suit her body, with a fall of soft pleats and a knotted snake belt in gold leather around her waist.

Savannah thought that the wedding dress was one of the most important parts of a wedding. Irony of ironies, she could remember her own so well and her joy at wearing it: an Art Deco piece of beauty, a bias-cut silk that shimmered around her hips, falling beautifully to the ground. She wore long pearls, and, of course, the necklace. Hers was a beautiful opal set in gold, worn high on the neck, a delicate little droplet that emphasised her slenderness. She'd worn her hair up.

'Twirl it like this,' Eden had instructed the hairdresser on the morning of the wedding. And Savannah had laughed.

'Eden, you can't tell her how to do my hair, we've gone through this.'

'Yes,' said the hairdresser glaring at Eden.

Savannah had smiled. Eden really could drive people nuts because she had to be in control of everything. Savannah and the hairdresser had practised this hairstyle.

'It really suits you,' Fiona had said, 'and it's in keeping.'

Savannah had gone for pretty jewelled combs in her hair and had worn an old, cloudy veil, that sat at the back of her hair, like a proper 1920s bride. The church had been amazing. She'd felt so lucky to be marrying Calum. Mum and Dad had sat together, not fighting, which was amazing because at that time they did fight a lot, were separated, barely speaking to each other, everyone still stinging over the sale of the hotel. Things like that lasted a long time, Savannah knew. Indy had been wonderful that day. Making everything flow smoothly, because that was the way she was. Even Aunt Sonya had come over from Pembrokeshire, which was a great honour. She hadn't come over for Eden's wedding because she had been ill. And Eden felt a needle of disappointment, Savannah could tell. She knew her twin's face like nobody else did, because they were identical after all. Apart from Eden's freckles and entirely different way of dressing, they could have got away with swapping out for each other. Not anymore, Savannah thought now as she drove to the shop where they were all meeting to pick up the wedding dress. Now, she was very thin.

Being thin was, at its easiest, something she and only she was in charge of, because there was absolutely nothing else in her life that she felt any control over.

She had long since stopped thinking of her disordered eating as any type of control, it was just the way it was. She rarely ate. She ate to survive and barely.

The thinness had bad points, obviously.

As she drove, she considered her life the way she often did, as if from afar, as if she was telling an audience of people what her life was like. *He doesn't touch me, he just shouts at me, belittles*

me, tells me I'm useless and frightens me. Oh, the fear. I fear dis-
pleasing him.

I feel his anger and his rage and it comes so quickly now. And I
do everything I can to spot it, but it just comes and I can't stop it, no
matter what I do, no matter how I behave. I'm powerless over that.
But I have to keep trying because I can't lose him and he's there, he's
there for me and Clary. Isn't he?

But last night . . . Last night she'd locked herself into the safe
place in her head while he'd frightened her, while he pounded
into her. It took a while to come out of that place. Like being
an animal creeping out of a burrow when the danger was gone.

Her body kept her in a type of fear-ridden stasis and even
though she could smile at Clary and talk normally to Marie-
Denise, she was acting. With Calum, it was different. She
never knew which way it would go, how he'd react after a
rage-attack.

He never said sorry. Hell, no. He'd said sorry to her twice in
their whole marriage, both times when he was with old school
friends and was drunk. He'd had to be out of his head to apologise for what he put her through.

'Sorry – I can be hard on you,' he'd said. Or something.
She'd been so stunned, she'd almost misheard. Had thought
she'd imagined it.

So there would be no apology, no 'actually, the packaging is
good'. Instead, he would punish her for days with his silence.
The withdrawal of speech, the silent treatment like a minus-
forty wind from across the Arctic.

As she drove to the office after dropping Clary at school,
she thought of telling her sisters all this. What would they
do? Would they rescue her? Would they tell her she was being
stupid the way Calum did? Possibly.

Because, people couldn't see.

That was the hardest thing, nobody could see into her life.
All they saw was her smiling face, Velvet Beauty doing so well
and the lovely house. They saw that she wore nice clothes, that

Clary went to school and Calum was handsome and smiled at people; he could be charming. That's all people saw. The dark, scary underbelly, the walking on eggshells: they never saw that.

Eden had a list as long as her arm for the morning. She had a meeting with Diarmuid and the hated Rian. There was a drugs task-force meeting, which she wasn't looking forward to. Because three young people had recently died from drugs on just one housing estate and Eden had been to visit all their mothers. None of Diarmuid's preparing her for politics all those years ago had prepared her for that. Agnes, on the other hand, had been the one who'd told her how to handle it.

'There's nothing you can say that will take away the pain,' Agnes had said. 'They've lost their child to drugs or drink or whatever it is. You are there to go and pay your respects. They might hug you, they might tell you their life story, they might shout at you. But you have to go.'

'OK,' said Eden.

God she'd been innocent back in the day, the days when she'd thought that politics was about giving interviews to newspapers and pontificating about all the wonderful things she was going to do. She had been so innocent. Now she knew that much of local politics was made up of planning permission and trying to get a homeless person off the streets, organising carers for an elderly lady. Trying to push some sort of legislation through that might get a couple of hundred grand for a special school that was falling apart. That had damp in all the corners. A school where children who had terminal diseases went every day to be looked after. None of it was what she'd expected. This morning there were no devastatingly sad visits to families who'd lost a young son or daughter. There was a visit to a marvellous woman who had just celebrated her one hundredth birthday. The leader of the local Cumann was coming with her to that and they were bringing a cake. Eden was dying to know how anyone lived to be a hundred. The first time she'd had to do a visit like that, she'd expected some delicate little flower of a lady telling her that she'd never drunk, never smoked and had never got married. Instead, she met a very vibrant woman with a shock of silvery white hair with a purple streak in the front, who'd told her that lots of sex was the answer. Everyone had laughed and Eden had laughed loudest.

'You're not what I expected at all,' she'd said.

'Isn't that the way,' the woman had said. 'Keep them guessing.'

Since today's hundred-year-old lady was a nun, Eden expected there to be less of the purple streaks and lots of sex. But you never knew.

As she got dressed, she thought about what sort of outfit would look right for this. Sometimes she laid her clothes out the night before and it was easier. But this had been such a mental week, what with the hen night and all the wedding palaver. She also had to drop into the women's shelter because there were, as usual, fundraising issues. It wasn't scheduled but she'd have to make time. It was important.

'You're not up already, are you, love?' said Ralphie.

One of the great things about their house was that they had been able to transform the upstairs anyway they wanted. There were no rooms for kids: there was his office, there was Eden's office, and there was the lovely dressing room they both shared, but that, realistically speaking, was mainly Eden's.

'I'm sorry, did I wake you, honey?' she said. 'I'm trying to figure out what to wear that will do a meeting on drugs and one with your father and Rian. And seeing a hundred-year-old nun and telling her she's amazing.'

'Ah, go with the stripper costume,' Ralphie joked from the bed.

'Oh yeah, that would go down very well.'

'Well, it probably would with Rian,' said Ralphie.

Eden grimaced.

'You've put me off my breakfast and I haven't even had it yet.

Rian does not think about sex. Rian just thinks about politics and power. Sex doesn't even come into it. I don't know what he'd do with a woman if he ever saw one.'

'He is married you, know.'

Ralphie had been brought up in the world of politics and knew everything.

'I always find that so hard to believe,' said Eden, holding two tops up against her. One a bright fuchsia that clashed with her hair, and yet somehow worked. And the other a dark green that might be more sedate for meeting an elderly nun. And then she could put on her grey jacket over it for the meeting on drugs.

'Everyone knows you're married to me,' said Ralphie playfully.

'Yes, love, they do,' said Eden. 'Ya big ride, ya.'

'Councillor, I am shocked at your language,' said Ralphie from the bed.

'I am a disgrace to the council,' she said idly, deciding that the green was the best thing. 'Are you making the coffee or what?'

'You're a slave driver, you do know that?'

'Yeah,' said Eden, 'and you love it.'

'Love you,' said Ralphie.

'What's your day like today?' she called after him.

'Ah just the usual,' said Ralphie, making it down the stairs.

'No, seriously.' She began to tie the bow on the green blouse and followed him downstairs.

'I don't want to be one of those women who tells her husband exactly what she's doing in minute detail and then doesn't ask him what he's doing.'

'Your life is more exciting than mine,' Ralphie said. 'Today I'm talking to the accountant. And I thought I might bring my mother out for a spot of lunch.'

'Can we swap?' said Eden, 'I'd much prefer lunch with your mother than your father.'

'He's not a bad old stick,' said Ralphie.

Eden said nothing. Diarmuid had never quite forgiven his eldest child for not wanting to be involved in politics. Ralphie had two younger sisters, one of whom was a dog groomer. The other a physiotherapist. Neither of them wanted anything to do with any of the family businesses, pharmacy or politics.

'What time do we have to be at Fergal Maguire's retirement dinner tonight?' said Ralphie.

Eden clapped her hand over her forehead. 'I had totally forgotten it was tonight,' she said. 'Oh shit. I'm supposed to be at the motorway meeting—'

'You're not, I cancelled it.'

'You cancelled what?'

'You're supposed to be at the motorway planning meeting and I cancelled on your behalf – or rather, to be precise, my mum cancelled on your behalf. Because I knew you'd forget.'

Eden went over and hugged him.

'Thank you, and send on the hug to your mother. Do you think she'd come and work for me?'

That was one of the reasons why Eden really wanted to get into politics on a national level, because then you'd have people to help you. So far, she was doing so much of it on her own.

'I'll ask,' said Ralphie. 'That green suits you, you look very much the colleen at the crossroads of the 1937 Constitution fame.'

'Do you think?' said Eden, laughing. The colleen, an Anglicised version of the Irish word for girl, was an imaginary dancing girl in a green dress dancing at a rural crossroads, seen as the epitome of happy, traditional Irishness by Church and State of the time. She wasn't mentioned in the Constitution but her innocent obedience to all rules, especially the moral ones, made the colleen the perfect ideal of the genuflecting politics of the day.

'Yes, beautiful, you'll knock them dead.'

She grinned. 'As long as your father's henchman, Rian, dies, I don't care how it happens,' she said.

Green turned out to be exactly the right colour for the centenarian. She herself wore a long black nun's habit with silky pearly white hair creeping in little curls from under her headdress. She did not mention a lifetime spent drinking whiskey, smoking and running after strange men. Although she said she'd heard how that had helped other people.

Prayer, she told Eden. Prayer works – and honey, always have honey. It cured everything. Walking and gardening helped too.

Sister Agatha had a list of things that had helped keep her going for a hundred years. Humour was certainly on the list – she had the most glorious sense of humour and was delighted to see Eden with her shoulder-length red hair in the green silky blouse with the pussy-bow neck.

'I had a thing just like that,' she said, 'before I was professed. It was my sister's but I used to borrow it.'

'Really,' said Eden, sitting down and taking a sip of her tea.

'Oh yes, my sister had all the best clothes,' said Sister Agatha. 'All the best clothes. They thought she was going to marry a local farmer and the money went on her.'

It was funny, Eden thought to herself, that even eighty-five years down the line, Sister Agatha could still sound like an aggrieved younger sister, irritated with the older one for getting the better outfits.

'Yes, but I borrowed that one from her once, the green one like the one you've on there. She went pure mad, pure mad is all I can say. I did plenty of penance for it, but I had my offers when the local fellows saw me in it.'

'Did you now,' said Eden, grinning. She loved this woman.

There was a photographer from the local paper there, but the reporter was late. A few nuns bustled around, all small and elderly like Sister Agatha herself.

'She'd still steal any outfit you had if you didn't keep an eye on it,' said another nun, a Sister Rita, whose hair was a quite improbable shade of red under her headdress.

Eden giggled.

'Don't mind her,' said Sister Agatha, beaming. 'What do we have to steal?'

'I have that Aran cardigan and you've taken it plenty of times,' Sister Rita said.

'If it was mine, I'd lend it to you whenever you wanted it,' said Sister Agatha. 'I only took it that one time, a year ago when I was ninety-nine.'

'And you didn't feel the need of it today?' said Eden, the corners of her mouth twitching up.

'No,' said Sister Agatha, rolling her eyes. 'She gave out yards to me for it the last time. I said, "Rita, when you get to be my age, you have to borrow the odd thing, you know, because you're not going to be around long enough to go through the effort of knitting another cardigan. Or indeed buying a cardigan." Anyway, look at these hands.'

She held up frail but arthritic fingers. 'I couldn't knit another cardigan, not like that one.'

'My niece gave it to me,' said Rita with a martyred look. 'It was a Christmas present.'

'I can't knit anything. I can sew, though,' said Eden. 'My parents ran a hotel and things were always getting ripped. I was very good with a needle.'

'There you are,' said Agatha. 'You need a bit of a skill when you are in here, praying.'

The reporter arrived and both nuns adopted vaguely pious, stern expressions.

'What happened?' said Eden, startled. 'You've both stopped smiling.'

Sister Agatha talked out of the corner of her mouth: 'We don't want them thinking we were joking all the time or they'd only make fun of us. It's either that or let them think we're dry auld sticks in here. And that's sort of easier, to be honest with you.'

'No one is going to think you lot are dry auld sticks,' said Eden. 'Sure, haven't you taught all over the world? You've seen everything.'

'Everything,' agreed Sister Rita. 'There's not a thing we haven't seen between the lot of us. Burying small children from preventable diseases in missions in Africa, all for the want of a few pounds. But people like their religious folk to be more otherworldly, you know.'

'That's true,' said Sister Agatha.

'I've seen some things too,' said Eden, surprising herself. 'I've got to go to a local meeting on drugs later, I'm not looking forward to it. Too many people lost to them. And I'm nipping into the women's shelter.'

'God bless you for the things you do,' said Sister Agatha, and put one papery soft hand over Eden's. 'Come in on your way back and we'll have a little pray with you. And if you're not into that sort of thing, we'll just hold your hand and pray for you.'

'Well, I can't tonight or tomorrow,' said Eden, definitely torn. 'Because tonight I've got a retirement dinner and my parents are getting married again and they're having a rehearsal wedding dinner tomorrow night.'

'That sounds very exciting,' said Sister Rita.

'Were you going to have a rehearsal dinner?' said Sister Agatha naughtily.

Eden looked around in surprise.

'She was stepping out with a young fellow before she entered the convent,' said Sister Agatha.

'She never lets me forget it. You'd swear that we had been running around like mad things. This was a long time ago. If you held a man's hand it was the height of excitement. There was none of that rehearsal-dinner carry on. You were lucky if you got an engagement ring. If the fella's mother was dead, you might get hers, but not every woman liked that. A wedding ring was good enough to show people you were wed.'

'They were different times for sure,' said Sister Agatha. 'That's exciting, your parents getting married again, isn't it?'

'Well,' Eden could see the reporter making her way over towards the two elderly nuns. 'It is and it isn't,' she said. 'Part of me thinks it's a great idea and part of me thinks they're completely mad, because they did fight a lot back in the day. And my father lost every ha'penny on gambling and beer.'

'That happens with men,' said Sister Rita knowingly. 'But you have to give people another chance.'

'Do you?' said Eden.

'Your mother is giving him another chance, and isn't that lovely for all of you. Are there many of you in the family?'

'Four sisters,' said Eden.

'And grandchildren?'

'My older sister has two little girls and my twin sister—'

'Oh, you're a twin,' said Sister Rita delightedly. 'I always wanted to be a twin, an identical twin, so we'd be able to play games.'

'Actually, I am an identical twin,' said Eden. 'But I haven't played any games for a long time.'

'That's just a waste,' said Rita, shaking her head. 'Think of the fun you could have.'

'Well, Savannah has a little girl, but I don't have any children, I don't want any children.' She waited for a moment. She rarely said it out loud, because saying out loud that you didn't want any children was a bit like saying you tortured small animals. No matter how many strides feminism had made, women were careful about saying they didn't want children. People looked at you with shock and horror.

But neither nun looked shocked.

They were, after all, Eden considered, women who had chosen a vocation where not having children was a prime requisite.

'I liked teaching children,' said Sister Agatha thoughtfully. 'Getting that lovely little mind and helping shape it. There was sheer joy in that. But as to actually having a child myself, no. My sister, the one who had all the better clothes, she had ten. Ten children are too much for any woman, is all I can say. She was always pregnant. I think I did better out of the whole bargain.'

'Ten children!'

'And none of them twins,' said Agatha meaningfully. 'I told her that she should lop it off in the middle of the night, so he'd keep away from her.'

Eden burst out laughing.

'The reporter is coming over,' said Sister Rita out of the side of her mouth.

'Right, OK, grand.'

'Well, we're here every evening,' said Sister Agatha, 'if you need a bit of a pray and a bit of peace, we're here. We've seen it all too and we understand how it can weigh a person down.'

'I came here to wish you a happy birthday. I didn't know whether to bring a cake or maybe a bottle of wine, so I brought a cake.'

Sister Agatha looked at her. 'I don't have a sweet tooth anymore but a bottle of whiskey would be nice,' she said. 'We're allowed to have a little tot occasionally and it helps me sleep. When you get to my age, sleep evades you.'

'Bottle of whiskey coming up,' whispered Eden and she hugged both nuns before they all posed quickly for the photographer.

Savannah sat outside the office in the back and let the cigarette smoke slip deep into her lungs. Ever since the time before when she'd had the cigarette with Anthony, she had had three more, which was ridiculous. She didn't smoke. But there was something about the self-destructiveness of this, something that Calum would hate, that made it terribly attractive. She tried to blow a smoke ring and failed. She'd never smoked. Eden had dabbled with it, could blow smoke rings. Eden was the perfect bad girl archetype. Not me, thought Savannah. She'd been good, sensible, the twin that everyone asked for when they needed something done. No need to get Eden, you'll do, people would say. It had been lovely being the sensible one, because it meant you were never in trouble and it was calming. Calming in a chaotic world, when Dad had been wild and Mum had been acting like a swan, serene on the surface and paddling madly underneath. Being sensible felt like the right choice. It meant being in control, but now, as she tried to blow another smoke ring, now she wasn't being sensible. Her being sensible had got her nowhere.

She felt so fragile and shaken. Unhinged almost. She held up the hand with the cigarette and it shook. The veins were blue.

'Savannah,' came a voice.

She looked up to see Leonora, the receptionist, waving a mobile phone at her.

'You left your phone and it's been going bonkers. I was on a call and I couldn't answer it.'

'Oh my God,' said Savannah, leaping to her feet. She never left her phone out of her hands. She grabbed it: the school had rung twice and Calum once. What had happened? Something had happened with Clary. She rang the school and got through immediately.

'Mrs Desmond, yes, we tried to get you, but we got your husband after all.'

'Well, I'm here now, what's happened?'

'Just an incident with your daughter, it's fine, it's sorted.'

'No, I'm coming over. What happened? Did someone hurt her?'

'No, it's more that she got upset for no reason really. And we thought maybe you should take her home.'

'I'm on my way.'

'Your husband said he'd do it.'

Savannah felt her insides freeze.

'I'll be there too,' she said, and hung up.

She grabbed her things and was in the car in less than sixty seconds. She tried to think of what Calum was doing today, where he'd be, how long it would take him to get to the school. Because she needed to be there first. If Clary was upset, she wouldn't want him. She'd want Savannah hugging her and holding her.

Parked right outside the school, in a place where only the principal parked, was Calum's car. Savannah, who'd parked in a normal parking space, ran past the car and into the building. She raced all the way down to the principal's office and saw Clary sitting there, outside the door, which was half open. Calum and the headmistress, Ms Turner, were talking.

'Yes, oh you're wonderful, wonderful, I wish all the fathers were like you,' Ms Turner was saying to Calum.

Savannah mouthed. 'I'm so sorry I'm late,' she said, 'I had my phone somewhere else, I was having a meeting.'

Calum's eyes met hers and they were cold, like the tundra, and flat like – no, not like a tundra, like a shark's eyes, she decided. She knelt beside her daughter and hugged her.

'Are you all right? What happened?'

'I'll tell you at home,' said Calum in measured tones. In a way that said, we will not have this conversation here now.

'But I need to know.'

'No, we'll talk about it at home,' he said. 'I know everything, Ms Turner told it all to me. We'll sort it out there.'

Clary had put her arms around her mother, clutched a little tighter.

'Of course,' she said.

Clary wanted to go with her mother, but Calum insisted she went with him. And somehow Savannah found her voice.

'No,' she said, smiling, aware that she was safe, that teachers were all around.

'I need to know what happened, darling,' she said. She pecked him on the cheek. 'You are so good for coming so quickly, I'll bring her home.'

'I'm coming home too,' he said.

'Great, well, you know what's happened, I'll find out now and then we can all have a lovely cup of tea at home.'

She put Clary into the car, did up her seatbelt like she was a child again. And they headed off.

'Tell me what happened, darling,' she said.

'I got upset and I think I screamed. I don't know. The girls were playing that chasing game, you know, the new one? And it was loud and I was tired; I just sat down and I didn't mean to scream, just somebody ran up behind me and tapped me. And then my teacher came out and she got Ms Turner and then the nurse.'

'Did you scream for long?'

'No, no, I didn't. And someone said I did, but I didn't, I didn't do anything wrong.'

'Of course you didn't do anything wrong,' said Savannah. 'Don't be silly. Now, we'll go home and we'll have – let's see – hot chocolate?'

'Yes, Mum, but Dad—'

'Oh, Dad might have some hot chocolate too,' said Savannah.

'He'll be cross.'

'No, he won't,' lied Savannah. Cross? He was going to be incandescent. The dirty laundry of their family had been washed in public and Calum would not be able to bear that. Because what he hated above all other things was people seeing anything wrong with them. Calum liked it best when nobody saw any side of him that he didn't personally choose.

Savannah turned on the radio to her daughter's favourite channel and turned it up a little bit.

'We don't have to talk about today,' she said, 'but we can, if we want.'

'It's that,' began Clary and then she stopped.

Savannah waited.

'It's that there was shouting and it was scary.'

Savannah understood. Fighting, shouting, they would evoke a response in Clary, a sensitive child who'd grown up listening to shouting. Knew that shouting meant something bad. Who knew she was unsafe on some subliminal level when it started.

'That must have been frightening,' Savannah said. 'Where was Daniel?'

'Daniel wasn't in,' said Clary. 'He's got a cold. Martina told me I was a cry baby because I was scared. She laughed and kept laughing.'

'She did? OK, I'll tell the teacher. You didn't do anything wrong, honey,' said Savannah.

Clary had behaved precisely as a scared child would.

Calum's car was, of course, there when they drove in.

Savannah got out of the car, stealing herself. She would not let him bully Clary. She would not. Could not let that happen.

Calum didn't start immediately. He let Savannah come in and chatter to Clary as she made her some hot chocolate.

'Now, let's make you nice and cosy in front of the telly,' Savannah said to her daughter, filling the air with talk so Calum wouldn't have a moment to break in.

Clary said nothing. Just sat mutely, while her mother arranged her all squashed up on the couch, blankets around her, even though it was warm, and put the TV on quite loudly in case there was shouting. Up till that point, Calum had almost smiled.

He was waiting for her in the kitchen. Smiling time over.

'What the fuck was that about?' he hissed. 'Did you find out?'

'I don't know. There was a lot of shouting and she got upset.'

'Was she involved? Who did it? Did someone hurt her?'

'No, she wasn't involved, she just heard it and it upset her.'

'Ah, for fuck's sake. It's all your fault, you know.'

Savannah could have written the script and yet even though she knew what was coming next, every part of her, every muscle, every cell in her body, tensed in expectation of the onslaught.

'She's totally spoiled. She won't hang around with the kids in school except with the little fucker Daniel, and his family are so low rent.'

In his rage, he wrenched open the fridge, started pulling things out, throwing them on the counter. 'Look at this, shop-bought ready meals.' He started throwing them on the floor.

'I suppose that's what Daniel's family are into – ready-meals. How is she going to grow up into a woman to take her place in society, to go out like a person with a bit of class. Ballet, that's what she should be doing: not playing with bloody Daniel. She's too introverted, has her head stuck in a book too much.'

'Books are good,' said Savannah. She was trying to fight back.

'She's hanging around with the wrong kids because she has a stupid mother like you. You're useless. My mother said you ruined Clary. She needs a decent girls' school, not one with boys where she learns to be a hoyden.'

His face was contorted now, full of rage and contempt. And one part of Savannah knew this was unacceptable, one tiny part of her and yet all the other parts of her quailed at his anger and his fury, all this rage directed at her.

'You've got to do something about her.'

'I will,' she said and instantly felt shame flood her. She was letting Clary down.

'I expect something new in this house this summer. Ballet camp or something, where she can mix with the right sort of girls. You need to sort that out.'

'I will, I will.'

'You always say you will,' he said. His voice dripping with contempt, she could feel it sliding off each word like acid burning into the ground. 'But you never do anything. How often have we had these conversations?'

Conversations, she thought. These weren't conversations, these were diatribes.

'How many times have we had this talk about her making new friends and you do nothing? Nothing.'

And the absolute fear swept over her. Of course, he was right. She was stupid; it was all her fault, she was failing Clary, failing him, and she had to do better, had to do the right thing. And her eyes flooded and the tears began to drip down her face, like the monsoon.

'Oh, spare me the tears,' he said, 'just do something. Do something. Really, you make me sick. I'm going back to work. I'll be late.' He swept out of the room and Savannah leaned against the wall and slid down it until she was crouched down, like a child, her face buried in her dress. She felt like nothing. She was failing, failing Clary, failing Calum. Just a failure. But she had to do something. For Clary. She had to.

Rory was suffering from hen-night hangover. She'd lain in bed till late thanking all the goddesses in the world and in the heavens that she'd taken the week off. There was no way she could have got up for work.

'Goodbye, *chérie*,' Chantal had said this morning, kissing Rory on the cheek as she left. 'I won't leave you a cup of coffee, not yet, go back to sleep.'

'Love you,' Rory had muttered and had sunk back into a deep sleep full of crazy dreams involving the hen-night guests and then her father, herself and Eden shouting at each other. She woke up at half eleven, hot, sticky, thirsty. Why did she never remember to bring water to bed when she'd been drinking?

Half eleven, she realised with a shock. Today she was having lunch with the publishers. The triumphant, isn't-it-wonderful lunch. In a fancy restaurant, the sort of place that clients got brought to in advertising agencies. Not somewhere the lowly copywriters went to.

She dragged herself out of bed, went into the kitchen to drink about two glasses of water straight down. Then she went into the bathroom and stood under the shower for a climate-change battering ten minutes. When she got out, she felt more human. The long hot shower, cold at the end, had done the trick.

Something human faced her in the mirror. Normally Chantal was brilliant at telling her what to wear at these events. But, she was on her own today, she thought, as she rubbed a bit of wax into her hair, making it stand up because she didn't have time to dry it, and rubbed moisturiser on her face. Chantal wore the make-up; Rory didn't bother. Although, she did have her eyebrows shaped. They were great, her eyebrows: strong, like her face. She liked her strong jawline and so did Chantal. She loved running her fingers along the edge of it up to Rory's full bottom lip and sliding her finger inside. She was lucky, Rory thought, lucky to find someone as beautiful, wonderful, giving as Chantal. In the bedroom she realised that Chantal had thought of an outfit for her. It was her tux-approximation suit, a dinner-style jacket and similar trousers. Because it was warm, she wore a sleeveless white shirt that showed off her shoulders and her arms. She had great muscle tone, she was lean, fit. A splash of cologne and she was ready.

They were all there at the restaurant when she arrived.

'Sorry I'm late,' said Rory, uncharacteristically for her. She was a big fan of the never-explain, never apologise school of thought. But for this, eating with publishers who were going to pay her a lot of money, she thought she might just modify her behaviour. 'Got caught up doing something,' she said. There was no point explaining too much, didn't want to confuse people. Nobody seemed to mind.

'We ordered champagne,' said Emily, the editor.

'Oh good,' said Rory approvingly. This was her kind of party.

She sat down, allowed her glass to be filled and they all toasted her.

'To the wonderful Rory Robicheaux. The newest superstar writer. This time next year, everyone will be reading your wonderful book, *The Eboli*,' said Emily.

Everyone raised their glasses again. And Rory felt the faintest hint of a shiver. Everyone reading her book, yes, that's what happened. People wrote books and people read them and they made judgements. She thought of the story. Judgements on her and her family. It seemed so long ago that she'd had a thought about writing about her life and how she'd come through everything, and how that had morphed into something else, something that would now hurt the people she loved.

Immediately, the grand publisher, a stately lady with a slight purple tinge to her hair, who was definitely wearing Moscow Red MAC lipstick, was talking about something and Rory got caught up in the conversation.

They were onto pudding, cheese for Rory, who rarely had anything sweet except when it came from alcohol, when Emily finally turned to Rory and hit her with the big question.

'I know it's tricky, but how much do you think you'll want to get into about the autobiographical parts of the story?' she said.

Rory felt her face freeze. 'Em—' She was never at a loss for words, never. But here, now, she felt tongue-tied. 'Em—'

'Because people will want to know, they're going to ask you that.'

'But it's not autobiographical,' Rory said, the words tumbling out of her mouth. She could see Louisa looking at her with mild concern.

'But it's quite a lot about you and your family, isn't it?' said Emily.

'Hints of it, but, you know, one takes the real world and . . .' Rory cast around desperately for some explanation and then realised she was with people who worked with writers all the time, and there was absolutely no way she'd get away with fudging this here. 'And one puts them into the story, but you know nothing in fiction is taken from the real world. I mean, it couldn't be.'

She could see the grand-dame publishing lady looking at her, eyes hooded.

'Yes,' Emily said, 'I understand that, absolutely.'

And suddenly Rory felt seen and not in a good way. She felt as if she was found out. People were going to be reading this book and it hit her even more forcefully that what had been a way of working out her thoughts as well as combining her love of writing, and of finding out her family's truths, was not a triumph of literature. But something akin to the worst betrayal of all time.

Just beyond the restaurant was a stone wall and beyond the stone wall was the most beautiful view of Dublin Bay, the sea glistening like the Mediterranean. Lots of little yachts were out in the Bay, sails bobbing. There must be some sort of regatta going on, Meg thought fondly. The restaurant had put them outside and they sat on the veranda with an umbrella shading them from the sun and a glorious breeze taking away the heat of the June day.

'I love this country when the sun shines,' said Sonya, stretching luxuriously.

'So that's why you left it,' said her brother.

Meg glared at Stu. 'Stu,' she hissed, 'what is wrong with you?'

'Oh, it's just a bit of sibling teasing,' he said.

But Meg was not convinced.

He sounded irritable and she didn't know why. Sonya, however, didn't appear in the slightest bit put out. All those years nursing, Meg thought. First Sonya and then Indy had shocked her with stories of patients who had screamed and yelled at the nurses caring for them, demanding to see doctors, their superiors, the boss of the hospital so they could complain in their attempts to go outside for a fag/have a nicer dinner/get more painkillers than was recommended for a human being in a single day.

Meg never knew if Sonya and Indy were so calm as a result of their years nursing or if they were, or had been in Sonya's case, such good nurses because they were calm. Either way, Sonya bore an air of such serenity that Meg always felt her sister-in-law wouldn't be upset at anything. Now she peered at her brother over the top of her water glass and smiled.

'Stu, I got out of this country because I wanted to work abroad and because I didn't want to spend the rest of my life in jail for murder. And if I had spent any more time with Mama, I would have been in jail. And, at that point, we were running out of money for really good lawyers.'

Stu gave in and laughed gracefully.

'Sorry, Sonya,' he said, 'I didn't mean it. Just woke up on the wrong side of the bed this morning.'

'Oh, we all do that sometimes, brother dear,' said Sonya. 'Anyway, it's lovely to be here, to help celebrate this day.'

Meg looked at her suspiciously. 'Celebrate this day?' she said, eyes narrowed as she looked at her sister-in-law.

But Sonya stared back guilelessly.

'Yes,' she said, 'I want to celebrate your marriage. I think it's marvellous that you've come back together again, because I always felt that you were made for each other. Not really like me and James.' Sonya had been married for twenty years and was now divorced. There was never any mention of subsequent boyfriends, lovers or partners. And Meg had always got the feeling that Sonya liked her life on her own. She was free to travel, spend time with her girlfriends, do whatever she wanted to.

'The girls seem very happy about you getting married again.'

'Why wouldn't they?' said Stu, faintly belligerent again.

'God, you're like a bear with a sore head,' said Sonya crossly. 'You put the family through quite a lot, Stuart. So, I think it's reasonable to discuss how marvellous it is that your children don't appear to be too upset by you remarrying. They could hate you, Stu. You bankrupted them, broke up the family.'

Meg felt her mouth fall open. None of these things were things she hadn't personally said to her ex-husband. But she hadn't said them for a long time and she'd never put it quite so severely – or had she? she wondered, thinking back. Certainly, she'd never let Stu off without telling him exactly what he had done to the family. But it had been done in a constructive way because he'd done his best for her and the girls when he'd stopped drinking and stopped gambling. He really had.

'Look, Sonya, I don't want to be lectured to by you,' said Stu.

'I'm not lecturing you, I'm just saying it's amazing your daughters are still pleased with this.'

'Well, why wouldn't they be pleased?' Stu grumbled.

A waiter materialised and Sonya seamlessly moved from staring coolly at her brother to ordering.

'I'll have some elderflower cordial in sparking water,' she said.

She wasn't much of a drinker and she never drank around Stu, Meg noticed. Meg had never put herself through such torment. She'd drunk glasses of wine in front of Stu. It wasn't up to her to stop drinking, it was up to him, in the same way that it wasn't up to her to stop gambling, either. Occasionally she did the lottery, not that she'd expected to win, but it was sort of fun thinking about what she'd do with the money if she won. Rory had once told her that there was more chance of the entire planet moving to Mars in ten years' time than there was of her winning the lottery, but that didn't put her off it. Instead, she'd laughed at Rory and said she was an old spoil sport.

'A glass of Sauvignon Blanc,' Meg said once she'd finished ordering a salad.

'And you, sir?' said the waiter.

Meg looked at him and realised he was staring fixedly at the drinks part of the menu. Oh gosh, she shouldn't have ordered wine. It was too much. Everyone knew that people who didn't drink could fall off the wagon in times of stress and there she was, ordering wine, taunting him.

'Non-alcoholic beer,' said Stu, 'and a steak, rare.'

Meg let out a breath.

Vonnie had organised champagne to be ready for them at the shop. And Meg, who had developed a slight headache on the way in, which she felt was due both to Stu's very enthusiastic lovemaking early that morning, when she'd twinged her neck a little bit, and the glass of wine in the heat at lunch, felt there was nothing she would like less than champagne. What she really wanted was a cup of tea.

'Anyone for champagne?' Meg asked, holding the bottle with a sigh.

Indy and her mother's eyes met. Indy looked tired. And something else.

Meg tried to translate the look on her daughter's face but couldn't. That was the thing about children, she thought. For a long time, you could read them, read every emotion across their face, and then, suddenly, it changed and you couldn't. You had literally no idea what was going on. She'd been able to read Indy for years and then that had stopped. Rory, last of all, had gone slightly blank from when she was fourteen. Those were the 'Don't call me Aurora, call me Rory' years.

'You just don't understand me,' Rory had said many times.

Which made Meg so sad as she'd done everything she could to be there for Rory. Chantal made her so happy now, though: that was a blessing. Chantal should have been here this afternoon, Meg thought.

'Why didn't we ask Chantal?' she said to Indy, who looked at her blankly.

'She probably has to work.'

'I know, but she should be here.'

'Rory should be here,' Indy said.

The shop's second-in-command was desperately trying to get someone else to drink some of the champagne because there was an entire bottle. Meg had a vision of herself being forced into transporting a nearly full bottle of champagne home in the car and spilling it all over the precious wedding dress.

Crystal, who ran the shop, appeared full of the joys of spring and smelling faintly of cigarettes. She had recently doused herself in some sort of grapefruit perfume to hide it, but the scent was definitely there.

'Now, are we ready to try it on for the last time before the special day?' said Crystal.

Meg's headache increased. 'Yes,' she said, 'just hold on a minute. Indy,' she turned to her eldest daughter, 'do you have any paracetamol?'

As a nurse, Indy always had something. But, as a nurse, she was very keen on leaving drugs to the very last minute.

'I have a murderous headache. My neck, you know the way it goes sometimes,' Meg said. The lie came remarkably easily. Lies did when you were a parent, she thought. There was no way she was going to say, 'I had sex with your father this morning, so my neck hurts'.

Indy produced some paracetamol and an energy bar and prevailed upon Crystal to get some water.

'You need to eat when you're taking tablets,' Indy said in her nurse's voice.

At that precise moment Savannah and Eden arrived in. They hadn't come together.

'Sorry I'm late,' said Savannah.

Her eyes were red and there was no other word for it, she looked dreadful.

'Are you all right, sweetheart?' said Meg.

'Fine,' said Savannah. 'Just didn't sleep well, absolutely exhausted. And I had to pick Clary up from school.'

'Is she sick?'

'No, no, it's a long story.'

'Well, where is she?'

'At home with Marie-Denise.'

'What happened?'

'Oh, I'll tell you another time,' said Savannah.

She felt so fragile, as if a blast of wind would push her over. As if harsh words would make her fall to the floor and cower. Harsh words did make her fall to the floor and cower metaphorically. Since this morning, Calum wasn't talking to her. It was a very bad week for this to happen because, normally, when he gave her the silent treatment – and she now knew what it was from looking at the websites, she knew that men like Calum withheld affection, withheld conversation, withheld everything as a control – it lasted weeks.

A week of this was enough to turn her to an absolute quivering mess of anxiety. Because the power he wielded over her was such that she could barely function. She managed well enough for Clary and Marie-Denise's sake, for them she could be strong and pretend everything was OK.

She smiled and talked and behaved as if everything was normal, when in fact Calum was speaking in a perfectly normal voice to Clary and a perfectly normal one to Marie-Denise. But he was blasting the coldest, iciest breath upon Savannah. It was like winter. Winter blowing in from the Steppes. It froze her, unhinged her.

The event with Clary had started it and then, just as he was getting into his stride, her father had phoned him. Calum had always been so odd about her father, because Savannah loved Dad so much.

In the early days, when she was telling Calum how the family used to be, how they had run the Sorrento, how it had been fun and how Dad had lost everything, he'd stared at her. His father had died when he was young, he'd only had his mother. He didn't seem to understand that you could love a parent and still see their flaws. If only she had that time back again and she hadn't told him that stuff.

Because she knew what it was now. She'd told him how amazing Dad was despite everything and how they'd all loved him. And how, despite everything, everyone probably thought it was a reasonable idea that he and Mum were getting back together, because they did belong together. Not that Savannah would say that now, no, she never talked about her family now, not to Calum.

But Eden had told her that Dad was ringing the sons-in-law to arrange some sort of a stag night. Calum wouldn't like that. Calum would want something special. An elegant dinner in the most expensive restaurant in town where he'd pay with the company money, with Velvet Beauty money, and write it down for tax. Something that Savannah hated because it made her nervous, because it was wrong, because it wouldn't have been a tax thing, it was a wedding thing. But Calum always got angry when she said stuff like that.

'Don't tell me how to run the company. I understand this stuff; you don't.'

And she'd meekly say, 'Yes, of course, darling,' even though it wasn't his company. Even though she had been running it before he came along. Because she didn't know any of that stuff, he'd insist. She was stupid. But now, to add insult to injury, Dad was trying to organise a party. Steve would think it was a great idea and Ralphie would go along with anything. But Calum wouldn't like it. There were loads of things Calum wouldn't like and Savannah was very careful to avoid them all.

He couldn't continue the normal week of silent treatment with the rehearsal dinner on Friday night and the wedding on Saturday, could he? But then he could, she realised. Her husband could do anything he wanted to because who was going to stop him? Not her. She was too terrified, too cowed. She was failing her daughter and she hated herself for it.

*

212

Eden knew where the women's shelter was because she'd helped them fund raise and she had done a lot of work packing Christmas hampers for them. The exact location of the shelter had to be kept secret, or else the women and children who sheltered there were at risk from furious partners and husbands turning up, screaming, shouting, doing anything to get their person back. Or to scream rage and say they were going to break them. There were two women who ran the centre and Eden was in awe of both of them. Her mother-in-law had put her in touch with them. Agnes had been on the board of the shelter for years. And now, Eden wanted to come in and help in a more formal way. There were always times when she walked in, and she felt both the joy and happiness of the place – and yet an undercurrent of fear in some of the women. So many of them kept their eyes down.

'They're the newer people,' Barbara told her. Barbara ran the centre.

'When women and children come in here, they're traumatised. It's like being in a war zone for them. They've endured years of fear. Because, for a woman to leave her home, it takes enormous courage and yet once they've managed to escape, there's not this big gasp of joy and freedom: there's more terror. Because they have done the very thing their partner told them he'd punish them for.'

This was a place where Eden listened rather than spoke. She knew the difference.

'What about the funding?' said Eden, that was one of the reasons she was there. She needed to make sure there was more funding for the shelter, despite the increasing rise in the number of women who were seeking emergency accommodation because of domestic abuse. Government and council funding was not always forthcoming.

Violence against women was increasing and yet nobody was making it a priority. Every world news bulletin had more and more women being hurt, violated, killed – and what was being done? Talking – that was what was being done.

'Funding is always going to be a problem,' Barbara told her simply. 'The problem is that when other people don't understand what's happening, they can't imagine it and they can't put their hand in their pocket for it. I've heard people ask why the women who get beaten haven't the backbone to leave. As if it's that simple.

'As if torture – and that's what it is – leaves a person with the ability to up and walk away. They think someone can walk away when they've been beaten up so badly, that they can't walk. That they can up and leave when they're terrified, cowed, living in absolute fear. Ordinary people can't imagine life like that. So they imagine it happens to only a very few people, only a very few poor, sad people. But this,' she gestured around her office, 'this knows no bounds. No bounds of society or people. The nice man you might see in church one day, he could have his wife locked up at home, go home after church and beat her or scream at her for hours, because he feels like it.'

Barbara sat down behind her desk with its overflowing loads of paper.

'I'm simplifying it, but that's at the bottom of this: power, control, rage and the ability to hide it all. Plus, we're seeing an increase in the number of emotional abuse cases, because people are finally coming forward with that. And coercive control – financial coercive control, that's a big area.'

'OK,' said Eden.

She sat down in front of Barbara's desk. There was a manila folder on top of one of the piles and Barbara hesitated for a moment before opening it and showing some pictures to Eden. First up was a picture of a pretty-looking woman with blond hair, although her roots were dark. Her prettiness, however, was marred by the absolute defeated look in her eyes.

'She came in two nights ago with her little girl. The little girl is a baby and since she had the little girl, the husband gets irritated because he's not the centre of attention. He's treating her like she's a piece of dirt. He wasn't actually physically hurting her until about six months ago and then it started with Chinese burns, pinches. Then it moved on to a few slaps, just a few slaps,' said Barbara. 'It's amazing how often I've heard that in court: 'It was just a few slaps, Your Honour'.

She showed some pictures of the woman's body to Eden.

'It goes against all the regulations but I'm showing you this so you understand what we're up against.'

One side of the woman's rib cage was a murky bruised green-and-yellow mass. It was hard to imagine the pain of it and how difficult it would be to get up off the floor after a beating like that. To pick up her baby, to keep her safe in the midst of such anger and violence.

'She didn't go to hospital for that and she didn't ring us when he started picking on her, when he started belittling her. She didn't phone us when he began to control the money, when he told her that she was stupid, that she was imagining things, that she was always whining, that she was too sensitive, that she wasn't to go out without his permission. She thought it would get better and then, if she tried harder, it would be OK. She rang one day because she was worried he'd start on her daughter when she was older. This woman couldn't protect herself but she did the thing she feared most for her child. So that's what we're up against. But this is what we deal with every day.'

'There are just no words to say the right thing here,' said Eden. 'Except that I want to help.'

'Your mother-in-law, Agnes, has been amazing to us. Not Diarmuid,' said Barbara, with a wry smile. 'I don't think Diarmuid is aware of what domestic abuse, emotional abuse, is. Agnes has been our saviour. But the Freedom Party never really did anything but pay lip service to our work.'

'That's changing,' said Eden. 'There are so many changes to be made. Women need to be at the forefront of this party.'

For a moment her head flickered back to the blackmail letters. Damn whoever had sent them. She was not going to let that stop her, she wouldn't. These women needed help and she was going to give it to them.

14

Friday

Clary's nightmare woke Savannah. She slept lightly; anything could wake her up. But the sound of Clary in distress seemed to have a special frequency in her head and she sat bolt upright in the bed. Calum was sprawled beside her, taking up a lot of the bed. Savannah generally slept on the edge, close to her phone, her reading glasses and anything she needed. She slipped quickly out of bed and pulled a fleece top on over her silky dressing gown. She ran barefoot into Clary's room. The little night light plugged into the wall shaped like a ladybird was glowing beautifully. In the bed, Clary lay turning, twisting, muttering something. Her skin gleamed with sweat. Savannah raced to the bed, touched her daughter's forehead and felt the heat.

'Mum, Mum, I can't stop it, I can't stop it.'

It was a night terror, not just simple waking up and making noise, but one of the terrible night terrors. Savannah knew exactly what to do.

'It's all right, darling,' she said. It made no difference when she tried to hug Clary when she was like this. Only one thing worked. Savannah ran into the bathroom, grabbed a face flannel, ran it under the cool tap and came back in with it. Somehow, gently waking Clary into a slightly less frantic sleep took her out of this pain. It was the only answer.

'Now, Clary love, you're OK.'

Savannah was in crisis mode. She was the best person ever in a crisis and she knew it. Her life was one big crisis, after all. She kept rubbing the face flannel over Clary's face and arms and the back of her neck and her legs. She could feel it getting warmer and warmer. But did she need to wet it again? Sometimes it took two or three rushes to the bathroom to get cool water into the cloth before Clary came out of the darkness. It must be dark in there, Savannah thought.

'Mum?' Clary was back, no longer locked in the horrible terror of a dream.

'It's all right, love, you just had a bit of a nightmare.'

Savannah knew her daughter wouldn't remember any of this in the morning.

She reached into a drawer and pulled out a fresh nightie, ripped off the old damp one and pulled on a clean, fresh-smelling one over her daughter's head.

'Now, sweetheart,' she said.

Clary always just wanted to sleep after the night terrors. She was never really awake after them. Savannah settled her and then curled up in the bed beside her. It was a single bed, but not the narrowest, even though Clary's teddies took up a fair percentage of the space. She'd sleep now. But Savannah didn't want to leave her: she wanted to be there holding her for Savannah's sake. For her own sake.

She lay there in the dark listening to her daughter's deep, contented breath as Clary slipped back into beautiful dreams.

It was getting worse; the night terrors were increasing. Savannah knew what they meant, knew absolutely what they meant. She lay in the bed, the comfort of her daughter's body close to hers. And she thought of the puppy, the puppy that Clary wanted, something really small. Calum didn't like dogs, he said he was allergic, although Savannah didn't really believe that.

Savannah allowed herself to imagine a world when she was in a tiny little apartment, not this massive, beautiful show house, just her and Clary with a puppy. And it would sleep on her bed. Her and Clary's bed. Of course, that was ridiculous – because Clary couldn't sleep with her. But she wanted her to, because she wanted to hold her tight and keep her safe forever.

Savannah wondered if she'd go back to sleep. This evening was the rehearsal dinner and right now, she could think of nothing worse. She'd organised it with Marie-Denise to have a special evening in with Clary. They were going to watch some sweet kids' film and have popcorn. But Savannah felt the bone-deep tiredness of having to stay awake for the rehearsal. Of smiling and being lovely. She leaned her face close to her daughter's, inhaled the beautiful scent of Clary's hair and thought, even if she couldn't sleep, she could rest close to her beautiful daughter. That was enough, wasn't it?

'Did we have a wedding rehearsal dinner?' said Steve, turning over in the bed and readjusting his arm, so that he was holding Indy even closer to him. She loved lying like this just after they'd made love, when their bodies were warm and there was a faint flush of sweat on them. She was proud of that, proud that they still wanted each other. Proud that she felt her heart leap every time she saw Steve and she knew his heart leapt when he saw her. So many people in work moaned and bitched about their partners and she never did. Didn't need to.

'No,' she said, 'we didn't. We were going to, but it was expensive and I was training.'

'I wasn't sure,' said Steve. 'I just couldn't remember it.'

Indy looked at him fondly. Steve was in great shape, she thought. It was the carpentry work. You didn't see many overweight carpenters, Steve liked to say. Occasionally, Indy wondered if you saw many overweight photographers. Because she knew that's what he'd love to have done with his life. But it hadn't worked out that way. Life took its own path. Steve's father had been ill, Steve had taken over the family carpentry business and suddenly being a photographer was relegated to a hobby, something he did at weekends. Photography had brought them together. But would they have stayed together if she'd ended up as a model and he'd been the man taking the pictures? No, she didn't think so. Besides, she'd never wanted to be a model.

She'd been fascinated by women's bodies, fascinated by nursing. And it hadn't taken her long when she was in college to realise that midwifery was where her future lay, like it had for Steve's mother. No, who knows what directions they'd have gone in, if they'd stayed stuck in those strange roles in the beginning.

It was dawn on the Friday morning of the rehearsal dinner. And one of the girls had woken up in her sleep, which, of course, meant that both her parents were now awake.

You never sleep properly once you have kids, do you? Steve always said.

Not all men agreed with him. Through her work Indy knew plenty of men who did not wake in the middle of the night when their small children woke up. She saw this on second and third deliveries.

Many labouring mothers reached the point of no return and screeched at their husbands and partners. *I don't know why you want this baby so much when you never got up for the last one.* It was incredible what people said in the pain of labour.

Steve had never been the sort of person who'd abandon the hard part of baby rearing to her. Indy could remember exactly the first time she had fallen in love with him, when she'd known he was different. When she'd asked him what his favourite colour was and then, instead of saying blue or red like a Ferrari, he'd looked at her thoughtfully. 'I love that faded red of old second-hand books – you know, the ones that are covered with fabric and sea-glass, the blue of sea-glass. I love that. And green leaves, when you can't work out if they're lime or an acid-green.'

That was the moment. Indy was glad she had been able to pinpoint it. Steve was a thoughtful man and that translated through to the love he felt for her and their daughters.

'We're very lucky,' she said, letting one long, naked leg wrap itself around his legs.

'I know,' said Steve.

Indy thought that perhaps they might sneak another hour of sleep before the girls woke up. Just one hour would be perfect, because they were going to be late tonight. The rehearsal dinner. It did make her laugh. Her parents really pushed the boat out whenever they did anything. It had been the same when they'd been running the hotel: everything was an enormous spectacle—

Steve interrupted her thoughts. 'There's something I've been meaning to tell you. I mean, it might be nothing.'

'What?' she said, suddenly quite abruptly awake.

'It's about your dad.'

Indy's awakening sensors which had been at about 75 per cent, were suddenly at 100 per cent. She untangled her legs from her husband's and sat upright in the bed.

'What about him?'

'It might be nothing.'

'Steve, just tell me.'

'I saw him coming out of the pub the other day with Ferdie.'

'Which pub, was it Mickey Macs? I mean, you know, they're friends, always have been. He goes in there sometimes – just for a coffee, though.'

'It wasn't Mickey Macs,' said Steve. 'It was one of the ones behind the old housing estate – you know, where we've been doing that kitchen. The sort of place you wouldn't think you'd see him. Sort of place you'd only go into if you wanted a drink.'

Indy slumped back against the pillows. Steve wrapped himself around her.

'Honey, it might be nothing,' he said. 'He might have been meeting some of his old friends, that's all.'

'Or he might have been drinking,' she said. 'You know Dad – in times of stress, he goes straight to the old problems.'

'He's not gambling anymore, though,' Steve said hopefully.

'We don't know that,' she said, sighing. 'It's all connected, Steve, the whole thing. The gambling, the drinking. Mum would not marry him if she thought he was drinking again, because that will lead to the gambling and they've already lost everything. They can't afford to do it again.'

'We don't know for definite.'

'True,' said Indy.

But she did know for definite. If Stu Robicheaux had been seen coming out of a less-than-savoury pub just days before his wedding, it was unlikely to be a social call. Far more likely to be a few swift scopes with some old mates in a place where he didn't think he'd be seen.

'Was it just the two of them?'

'Him and Ferdie,' replied her husband.

'That bloody Ferdie,' said Indy.

'It's not Ferdie's fault,' said Steve.

'I know, I know. You don't need to sound judgemental.'

'I'm not being judgemental,' he said, holding up his hands. 'You know how fond I am of your father. But I saw what all this did before. I had a front-row seat, Indy. He doesn't need help – he can drive himself to drink quite happily with no help from anyone.'

'I know,' she said quietly, 'I know. Sorry for biting your head off. Should I tell her?'

There was a pause. 'Maybe talk to your dad first, check it out before we say anything.'

'Perhaps,' said Indy. 'But he'd lie. Why did he have to go and do it now?'

'He's getting married,' said Steve. 'Marriage is stressful for some people.'

'Why did he ask my mum again, then?'

Steve shrugged. 'People are mysterious, darling.'

'True.'

They lay there pondering the mystery of people until they finally gave up all thoughts of going back to sleep. Steve got up to make green tea for Indy and coffee for himself. Indy lay in bed. Over in one corner hanging on the wardrobe door, wrapped carefully with tissue paper because the girls kept going over and petting it, was her bridesmaid's dress. She really wanted to wear it. But not, not if wearing it meant she was participating in some big fake plot against her mother. Not then. Her mother had been through enough.

Eden drove up the winding drive to the Sorrento Hotel. It looked magnificent in the early morning sunshine when, with a slightly cool eye, all the flaws were hidden. Sunshine hid an awful lot of stuff like the falling-off plaster and the fact that the beautiful Georgian windows had missing bits of wood on the sashes. Beside her sat Indy, leaning back with her eyes closed. Today was one of Indy's days off. But because poor Vonnie had actually hurt her back making endless cream flowers for the wedding, Indy and Eden had been pressed into service to bring them up to the hotel and finish the decorating. Then, they were racing off to look at the flowers.

'We're probably the two worst people to be doing this,' Eden remarked as she pulled to a halt and reached blindly with her left hand for the flat white she'd insisted on getting.

'Are we?' said Indy.

'Yep,' said Eden.

She clicked her sister's seatbelt open, grabbed one of Indy's hands and put it around her coffee.

'Get this into you, you'll feel better.'

'I'm just so tired,' said Indy but her face was clouded over.

Eden wondered what Indy was hiding but decided not to investigate. She was tired too and not up to family drama.

'Of course you're tired; you've a job that gets you up at all hours. I'd be tired.'

'I know, but I love my job,' said Indy, holding on to her coffee, still with her eyes closed.

'You can love something and it can be tiring,' Eden said equably.

It was what Agnes, her mother-in-law, always said to her: 'Politics is wonderful, but tiring, just remember that.'

Agnes had said a lot of other things, including the fact that the tiredness that came with having children didn't kill you and the like. There was no doubt Agnes was very keen for Ralph and Eden to start a family. She would, Eden thought with a sigh, be waiting.

'Come on, take a few big gulps of that, it's got two shots,' she said to Indy.

Indy didn't move.

'Lucinda.' Eden could do a very creditable impersonation of their mother in full commander mode.

Her sister's eyes shot open. 'You're scary.'

'I know,' said Eden, smiling. 'That's why I'm in politics and you're a midwife. Somebody told me midwives are pit bulls with lipstick.'

'That was rude,' said Indy, outraged.

'Aunt Sonya.'

'Ha!' Indy laughed, offence gone. Sonya was a nurse, so she could say what she wanted.

'You do have to tell people what to do,' said Eden. 'It's very important knowing when to say, no, this is how we're going to do it. I think it must be like being a surgeon; you're God or Goddess at that exact moment. What you say goes. Like not letting dogs into the delivery room,' she added.

Indy laughed again.

'I shouldn't have told you that, you do not know these people. That was just a random bit of a story, I'm not supposed to tell you things.'

'What, like, midwives anonymous?'

'Yeah, exactly,' said Indy.

They leaned against the car and looked at the hotel.

'It's so pretty in this light, isn't it,' said Indy dreamily. 'Do you remember everything?'

'Oh, I remember so much,' said Eden, taking a deep gulp of coffee. 'It was wonderful and different, made us resilient.'

'That's for sure.'

'Having to clean bedrooms. We broke the child labour laws, I'm pretty sure about that,' said Eden.

'Nothing wrong with a little bit of child labour of that sort,' said Indy. 'It was nothing very much, a bit of scurrying in and out of the dining room carrying toast and extra butter to people. You know we weren't down mines or anything.'

'Excuse me, I was scrubbing bathrooms when I was eleven.'

'I'm sure that was a punishment and Mum was with you. It's not as if you were left on your own at the mercy of pervy guests.'

'True, Mum was good that way.'

'And Lori.'

'Oh Lori, she was brilliant.'

Lori had lived in for seven or eight years and had practically taken over when their mother had broken her arm. She'd been cook, cleaner, general factotum, and had looked after the girls too.

'Lori never wanted bleach or anything like that in the hotel. It was all natural stuff,' Eden remembered.

'Yeah, said Indy, 'she was a bit of a hippy, ahead of her time in terms of climate and everything.'

'And she fancied Dad.' Eden laughed at the thought.

'No, she didn't,' said Indy, too quickly. She remembered Lori and her father laughing. Lori's slender arm lying upon her father's. Lori always had brightly painted nails, impossible colours, sky-blues when nobody wore blue nail polish. And her hair, jet-black and glossy, rippling down her back.

'She was very young, wasn't she?' Eden was saying. 'Probably only in her late twenties.'

Indy didn't want to talk about Lori.

Eden was continuing with her trip down memory lane. 'And she left the summer after you met Steve? Or was it the year after?'

'We weren't friends at first, you know.'

'What you mean is you weren't his friend, but he seriously wanted to be your friend,' teased Eden.

The two of them had always got on brilliantly teasing, joking, like delicate fencing, never hurting, just fun.

'Lori, she was very beautiful, wasn't she?' Indy felt herself tear up. Lori, dear gorgeous Lori.

'Yeah, I suppose,' said Eden.

Indy finished her coffee, put it back in the car and opened the boot.

'I suppose we'd better get these boxes inside,' she said.

The boot contained the remainder of the boxes of hand-sewn flowers all looped together with ribbons to form great garlands. It must have been back-breaking work to do more. No wonder poor Vonnie's back was gone.

But Indy wasn't thinking about Vonnie's back now: she was thinking about Lori, how she'd been young and beautiful and definitely in love with their father. Indy didn't want to think about it. It was a long time ago when she'd imagined love at every corner. She hadn't been in love with Steve when Lori was first on the scene but she had seen him, noticed him, wanted him to like her. It was like she wanted him on a string in the distance so that if she pulled, he would come. She'd forgotten that: it had got lost the way the truth sometimes did get lost. The truth got lost in the stories people told themselves, she realised. In the story of her and Steve, they'd fallen in love at first sight, but it hadn't been like that. And there'd been so much going on that summer. She didn't want to look too deeply into those years.

*

Indy and Eden walked up to the shop where Chantal worked.

'You'd know it was run by French people, even if it didn't have the sign,' said Eden, looking up at the sign now: *La Mode*.

'Yeah,' said Indy, looking at the window which was so beautifully understated that only the very discerning customer would enter into the shop.

Indy had had some experience of clothes shopping in France when she'd gone on holidays with Steve pre-children. Everyone had been terribly nice to her because she had been beautiful and had clearly looked like a model. But she'd seen other people being given the Parisian shop-assistant treatment. Whereby it seemed as if said assistant did not want to sell anything, purely because the customer didn't look like they deserved it. Steve had thought this was hilariously funny. Eden would kill them, he'd said at the time and Indy had agreed. Luckily, they were now in a shop where their sister-in-law was running things. Chantal had both exquisite taste and the absolute charm that meant she was very keen to make a sale. She hugged both women when they came in.

'I have put some stuff aside in the large changing room,' she said.

'You mean beautiful, gorgeous, elegant stuff that will make me look fabulous and ten pounds thinner,' said Eden.

Chantal laughed. 'You don't need to be ten pounds thinner,' she said. 'You are beautiful.'

'Oh, I love the way you say that,' sighed Eden, and she went over to a rail where sparkly things dangled.

'No, no, that is not for you,' said Chantal sternly. 'They are for the *jeune filles*, not for a grown-up. The young girls who come in here, they can wear that sort of thing, but we must go with elegance and gravitas.'

'Enough of the we,' said Indy indignantly. 'You're ten years younger than me. If you can go with dignity and gravitas, I need to go in long trailing dresses like an elderly lady.'

'Don't listen to a word of it. That one can wear anything,' Eden said in mock despair.

'True,' said Chantal, 'but so can you.'

'You're definitely my favourite sister-in-law,' said Eden, giving her a hug.

In the dressing room there were lots of beautifully cut exquisite clothes hanging up and Indy and Eden had a glorious half-hour examining things and going, 'Oh, I'd never have picked that up.'

Chantal stood outside and said, 'No, I know you wouldn't have, but trust me, this is what I do, this is what I see.'

Which is how Indy came out wearing a very elegant dress with a scalloped, deep neck which went into a boned bodice and out to a flowing skirt. It was an elegant sky blue colour and she twirled around admiring herself.

'I'd never wear something like this,' she said, 'never.'

'I know,' said Chantal. 'You wear jeans, flat shoes and Steve's sweatshirts.' She shuddered.

'And your uniform,' interrupted Eden.

'But it's handy, it's handy to put on Steve's sweatshirts,' said Indy looking at herself from behind. 'I look—'

'— wonderful.'

Then it was Eden's turn. The trousers were so beautifully cut that they made her look the ten pounds lighter that she'd hoped to be. And the tiny jacket made of silk and cashmere clung to her like a little cardigan and yet with the shape of a jacket. The entire ensemble was a dusty-pink colour, like peony petals about to turn, a colour she'd never have worn, never have picked.

'I'm amazed,' she said, 'literally amazed.'

'This is my job,' said Chantal.

'Truly my favourite sister-in-law,' Indy said again, and Chantal laughed.

'Now we're paying full whack for this, no discounts,' Eden went on.

'Excuse me,' Chantal could be stern when she wanted to be, 'let this be my gift to you; a discount. It is my discount from the shop.'

Once everything was parcelled up and both Indy and Eden had looked with relief at the discount because the shop Chantal worked in was not cheap, the three of them went off for coffee.

'I only have twenty minutes,' Chantal said.

'I've got to pick up the girls,' said Indy.

'I've got a meeting,' said Eden, 'I wish I could wear this. That's the thing about new clothes, I always want to wear them now.'

'What are the girls wearing at the special dinner, the rehearsal dinner?' Chantal asked Indy.

And for a moment Eden could see the longing in Chantal's eyes, the longing of a woman who adores children and can say nothing.

Before she even thought about it, she said, 'You love children, don't you?' And Chantal's face suddenly closed up. 'It's OK, we love you, you can say it to us.'

'I've always wondered,' Indy said, 'why you and Rory don't have any.'

The closing up of her face, which had been so efficient a minute earlier, changed and Chantal's big eyes filled with tears.

'It's private, I can't talk about it,' she said as the tears began to roll down her face.

'But you want children. It's something I see a lot in my work,' said Indy carefully. 'Generally, I see people when they are giving birth or about to give birth. But, quite often early on in the process there are couples where one person wants a baby and the other one doesn't, but that's normal, it happens. And yet by the time the baby is being born, they're both eager.'

'You mean I should somehow con your sister?' Chantal said laughing, half laughing and wiping away the tears. 'That

229

might work in straight relationships, but not when there are two women involved.'

'No, that's not what I meant at all,' said Indy. 'But Rory's tricky.'

'Rory's difficult,' interrupted Eden, 'always has been. She gets fixed ideas in her head and I know now she's so into this book that she won't think about anything else. But time is not always on your side.'

'Exactly,' said Indy. 'Women's fertility does decline and if you want children and,' she paused, 'it kills me to say this because I love you, but if you want children and Rory doesn't, that's a serious problem; you will regret it.'

Chantal looked quickly at Eden.

'I don't want children,' said Eden, holding her hands out. 'Never have. I just don't think I'd be a very good mum and Ralphie's ambivalent either way. It's a choice. We've talked about it, but with you and Rory . . . I get the feeling Rory doesn't talk about it. She always clams up if anyone mentions it to her.'

'That's exactly what happens,' said Chantal sadly, 'she clams up, she doesn't want to talk about it. But I do want children.'

Indy reached forward and placed both hands around one of Chantal's.

'We will support you all the way. If you need help in talking to Rory, we'll be there with you. We love you, Chantal, we love having you as a sister-in-law. But, you have to do what's right for you and it's not fair of Rory to make you be childless just because she hasn't reached that point yet.'

'Thank you,' said Chantal, 'thank you.'

The questions were terrifying. Rory stared at the email with horror.

'Do you think you could have complex post-traumatic disorder after your upbringing? Because that's the sense I get in the book.'

Rory was sitting at her desk in the apartment. She'd carved out a little space for herself and Chantal kept it perfectly nice. A cabinet that opened where Rory could put her laptop, where her pens and paper already waited. Where a lovely IKEA lamp beamed warm light down and she could work at night. Now she sat at the desk and felt an absolute fear the likes of which she'd never felt in her life. The question hadn't come from some random person: this was a respected interviewer from a publishing magazine who wanted to ask her these questions and, because they were so sensitive, had actually sent them over in an advance.

Rory thought fear would kill her.

A cigarette. And a drink. That's what she needed.

Who cared that it was just after twelve and most normal people never touched alcohol at that hour of the day. Totally immaterial. She went to her and Chantal's pretty little drinks trolley. She grabbed a bottle of the blue gin and a little tin of tonic, then sat out on the small terrace which Chantal had made beautiful with little baskets decorated with willow and greenery spinning out of them. She sat at the small metal table where there was an ashtray that wasn't supposed to be used much. Chantal hated smoking.

'I only smoke occasionally,' Rory had said in the early days. Which was true. Then. This week, she'd been smoking all the time.

Now Rory threw a fast glug of the blue gin into her glass and added only half the tiny tonic tin. She had no time for the niceties of the lemon and ice now. She lit a cigarette, sucked it into her lungs. The gin barely touched the sides. She drank deeply, as if it was water and she had been crawling through the Sahara for two days. What was she going to do? How could people ask her questions like that? It was ludicrous. The book was fiction. A little bit of it was about her family, sure, but people made stuff up.

It sounded like an excuse, even to herself. Rory sat on the

terrace thinking of the chapters in her book. Chapters about arguments at home, chapters about how it had been so difficult to be a young gay woman in a sometimes-homophobic world when her family were in turmoil because her loveable rogue of a father was addicted to gambling. When her mother was pretending to ignore it all but clearly exhausted from carrying all the weight on her shoulders. That part wasn't in the book. Rory could remember her mother's tears and Savannah and Indy comforting her.

Rory poured another gin. She didn't have time to worry about her mother. Mum always bounced back. Look at her now, getting married to him *again*. She must have been absolutely mad. Dad would never change. Rory didn't believe his *I'm not drinking* crap at all. He liked his drink. Gambling was his real problem. Gambling was what had lost them all their money, lost them the hotel. Lost Rory her safe place, so that she'd been searching for it forever, and she'd found it with Chantal. And now, because of the book, that safe place felt as if it was under siege. Here in her lovely home, beautifully decorated by her darling Chantal, sat an email full of questions she couldn't answer.

'Do you still speak to your father? Is the book an indictment of what gambling and alcoholism can do to a family today?'

None of this was what Rory had expected when she was writing. None of this. How dare they ask her this stuff? Yes, how dare they? They'd go on that radio show and she'd tell them that, of course, she didn't have post-traumatic anything. What a stupid question. Families were complex, this wasn't all about her real life.

She poured herself another enormous gin, adding only a little bit of the tonic now. Who needed tonic? And she lit another cigarette. She looked at the pack between narrow eyes. They were mild ones. She'd buy a pack of stronger ones later; she was going to need it. After all, there was the wedding, there was the book. She needed her cigarettes. She threw back the gin. Nobody was going to ask her horrific questions about her family; it was none of their bloody business. She had written a book, it was fiction. OK, some of it had been taken from her life, but how dare they imply that the whole thing was true, was her, because it wasn't. Or was it? said a tiny voice in her mind. A tiny voice that Rory chose to ignore.

Claudia brought Indy, Meg, Eden and Sonya into the cold room in the florist's.

'Oh, it's freezing in here,' said Vonnie, shivering dramatically.

Eden put her arm around Vonnie.

'I'll keep you warm, Aunt Vonnie,' she said.

Behind her she could hear Sonya snort.

'More clothes is what you need, Vonnie,' she said loudly and Vonnie and Eden giggled.

'More clothes aren't the point, Sonya,' said Eden, still holding on to Vonnie's skinny shoulders.

'Exactly,' agreed Vonnie, 'I don't do lots of clothes, I do fashion,' and she waved her arms around dramatically with a clinking and tinkling of bracelets on her spray-tanned arm.

'Oh wow,' said Indy, looking around. One entire part of the cold room was full of peonies, beautiful, just-about-to-blossom, blossoming full-bodied, and exploding into blossom of the palest pink imaginable.

'These are amazing,' said Meg. 'Claudia, thank you, how can we ever thank you enough.'

'You've always been there for me, Meg,' said Claudia.

'Now we need to get these out of here and you can go off and organise them. I've got blocks of oases soaking, I've got twenty-five square vases, I've got some bamboo leaves to wrap around the oases on the insides of the glass, and Bob's your uncle. Plus, I'll have your bouquet for you tomorrow morning and the bouquets for the girls. And we're doing very pale pink roses for the men's boutonnieres? Yes,' said Claudia, 'it's all under control.'

'Wonderful, wonderful,' said Meg, looking at the flowers. She hadn't had peonies on her first wedding to Stu. It had been so different. They'd been broke and Jacqueline, Stu's mother, had hated her and she'd been pregnant. She felt herself tear up; this was going to be so lovely.

Indy put an arm around her mother. 'Why don't you go out and organise some boujis coffees for us all and the rest of us will get these into the cars.'

'OK,' said Meg.

An hour later they were up at the hotel, Eden sighing at her second visit of the day to it.

'It's a pity we don't have Savannah with us this morning.'

'She is coming,' said Eden. 'I texted her and she said she is.'

'Great.'

They set themselves up at one big table. Everything looked so much better now that the place had been cleaned. Whoever Stu had got in to do it, had done a marvellous job. The silk flowers that draped all over the place and the lovely muslin curtains that floated off the windows looked spectacular. All they needed to organise were the flowers on top of the table-cloths, which Indy was racing around putting on. And then the caterers would dress the tables. The flowers would be glorious in the middle with mirrors that Vonnie had sourced on each table and little delicate tea lights in little old glass containers, shining beautiful lights.

'Here she is now.'

'Sorry I'm late,' said Savannah, 'work.'

She walked stiffly Eden thought, as if she were in pain or something.

'Hiya, honey,' she said, 'you've missed the coffee and the scones.'

'Oh no problem, I had an espresso at work,' said Savannah.

'Sorry I'm late, it was just terribly busy.'

'Can you help me put the things on the chairs?' said Indy.

'No, she's much better at doing flowers,' said Eden, deciding that her sister looked exhausted and that rushing around wrestling with chairs and trying to wriggle them into creamy skirts would be exhausting.

Savannah was wonderful with flowers.

'I'll put on some music,' said Vonnie suddenly. 'Wouldn't that be lovely. Disco music, Meg?'

'Yes,' said Meg, 'gorgeous.'

Eden's phone pinged.

'Rory's coming with the wine,' she said.

'Fabulous, I thought she was getting it delivered?'

'Well, maybe she's coming along with the delivery people, I don't know,' said Eden. 'Either way, as long as there's wine, we're doing fine.'

When Rory arrived twenty minutes later, she found them all busy. Already some of the tables were dressed with mirrors, delicate candles, delicate tea lights and beautiful square vases of exquisite peonies and foliage on each table.

'It looks wonderful,' she said in surprise, 'really wonderful.' She looked around. 'I didn't know the place could look so good.'

'Well, if you'd been here during the proceedings before,' said Eden acidly, 'you'd know that.'

'Don't be such a bitch, Eden,' said Rory. 'I've been doing things—' She stopped herself abruptly.

'Yeah, what've you been doing? You could have helped, you know, we're all busy, not just you.'

'Yeah, of course, sorry,' said Rory.

And Indy, Savannah and Eden looked at her in surprise, Rory did not do apologising normally. Sonya, Vonnie and Mum did not appear to have noticed.

Two young guys appeared behind Rory carrying crates.

'Wine.'

'Ah fabulous,' said Eden. 'OK, I've got a locked room for you.'

'You have?'

'I have been up here,' said Eden, 'and I've got a locked room sorted out because when there's loads of booze involved, you need to be able to keep it under lock and key, OK?'

'I have all the bottles counted,' Rory explained. 'I know you've sorted out the corkage with the caterers, so we're good to go.'

'Respect,' said Eden.

Rory shot her a grin. 'Thank you.'

Sonya sat down on the veranda at the back of the hotel. A wind chime made up of seashells hung and moved faintly in the breeze. It was still so pretty, the dusty white-painted wood, and a couple of old storm lanterns grouped around the pot plants that Meg had once lovingly tended.

'There you are,' said Meg, coming out to her.

'I've been sitting remembering what it used to be like and how much I love Ireland. Is it a cliché to come home?'

'Moving back,' said Meg astonished.

'Yes. Now that I've stopped working, I have been thinking about it. And I thought I'd like to change my life, come home, live by the sea again. I can just see me alone in a beautiful little cottage like yours, get some cats.'

'Ah, you need the crazy cat lady starter kit,' said Meg and she reached for her phone to pull up the picture of ten cats in a box that Vonnie had sent her one day.

Sonya laughed at it. 'Yes, that would be me, I'd be very happy, maybe not ten, possibly too much effort house training them all. But a couple of lovely little moggies that would sit beside me on winter nights. I just want peace and—' she looked at Meg – 'I think that's what I don't understand, darling,' she said quietly so the others wouldn't hear. 'I don't understand why you're giving up your peace, your life on your own, to marry Stu again.'

Meg was astonished. 'You can't mean that,' she said, 'I love him, he's your brother. What a crazy thing to say.'

'I love him and he's my brother, absolutely true,' said Sonya evenly, 'and I love you. I just don't know if Stu is ever going to settle down. He might always lead you a crazy dance.'

'Ah,' said Meg, 'I understand,' and she did.

She had realised that that was what was frightening her daughters. That was what was frightening Indy and Eden anyway. With Rory and Savannah, it was harder to tell. They both had something going on in their lives that was making them distant. When the wedding brouhaha was over, she'd talk properly to them but this week was proving to be crazy.

All her daughters were probably scared that Stu would go wild and lose all her money. He wouldn't be able to get it – she was financially independent now and would remain so. She had learned many lessons.

'This will be different, Sonya,' she said. 'Stu knows that. He comes into my house with his own money and it is my house. He has no claim to it, and if he screws up, he will have to leave it. *But*—' and she emphasised the 'but' – 'I've been on my own long enough to know what it's like to be lonely and I don't want to be lonely anymore. I love Stu, and I think I've always loved him. Even when he lost everything for us, even when I was angry, even—' she broke off for a moment, as if she was going to say something else, but didn't – 'I still loved him. There's not an ounce of malice in your brother. He's a free spirit who needs reining in sometimes. I know how to do that. But he's coming into this marriage in a very different way.'

'Are you sure?' said Sonya.

'I'm as sure as I can be,' said Meg. 'But he knows that if he goes crazy again, it'll be over and I'll join you in the crazy cat lady starter kit. If we get the whole box between us, we can have five each.'

Sonya put back her head and started to laugh.

'I think five is too many for me.'

'OK, maybe three each and a puppy.'

'Three kittens and a puppy,' said Sonya thoughtfully. 'You do like a challenge, don't you?'

Meg grinned. 'Yes,' she said, 'I love a challenge.'

*

On Friday afternoon, after an hour at the hotel, Savannah found that she couldn't face going back to work. The stress of the last few days was swirling around inside in her head, gripping her temples in a vice-like grip. Her hands were shaking: they shook a lot. It still astonished her when she held them out to see the minuscule vibrations. Her stomach ached. Not the howling ache of hunger, because she'd conquered that one long ago. But the ache, the clawing ache, of naked fear. She couldn't face the office. She couldn't face smiling at everyone, being the cheerful boss, the person with a kind word for everyone. She felt completely depleted. Clary was in school, safe and loved.

Savannah had coaxed her in that morning and, once there, with the teacher sitting beside her and her best friend Daniel in class, Clary finally relaxed.

Calum had meetings all day – she knew because she'd asked.

No matter where he was, she was always conscious that he would want to know where she was, what she was doing. Otherwise, she rushed so much, because if he was at home, she had to be at home too. If she was late, he wanted to know why. At the weekend, if she needed to leave the house, he looked at her, querying it.

'Why?'

'I just need to go to the supermarket.'

'What do we need?'

She'd list the things they needed. And he'd tell her that they didn't need them.

'OK, isn't that great,' she'd say. 'You're so clever.'

The thought of how she pandered to him made her slightly

sick. But that kept everything even and happy. She knew that they didn't need groceries, she just needed to get out of the house briefly. Those times when Clary was on play dates or had a sporty thing on, on a Saturday, Savannah loved that. It meant she and Clary could get out together, could escape. For all that he liked to tell Savannah how to raise their daughter, Calum wasn't very interested in watching his daughter do anything. He was currently in a competitive cycling phase and went out every weekend clad in head-to-toe in lycra on a wildly expensive racing bike.

In Clary's school, they played camogie, but she wasn't an amazing player. Savannah loved the sports-morning days. They'd be up early, down to whatever place the team were playing. Savannah sometimes helped with the teas and coffees along with the other mums, and she smiled and laughed and waved like the other mums. There were dads there too, some of them definitely playing vicariously. 'Get on the pitch, come on,' they'd shriek at their daughters. It made Savannah jump and she didn't understand their point of view. Winning was not the only thing. She just wanted Clary to be happy. Her being the best player on the pitch didn't matter.

She was glad, though, that Calum so rarely came, because he'd have been angry if he had seen that Clary was not a particularly gifted camogie player. This didn't worry Savannah in the slightest. Happiness was all she wanted for her daughter. But Calum liked his daughter to win.

'Is Calum not with you?' the other mums would sometimes say. Because quite often both parents of a child would be there, often with another child, younger, with them. Or sometimes there would be parental tag teaming between a couple on different pitches: the little boys playing hurling and the girls playing camogie.

'No, he's busy,' Savannah would say. 'Running your own business is a full-time job.'

Her face ached as she said things like that.

Actually, if Calum wasn't cycling, he was probably reading the financial papers. He would then mansplain something. His absolute favourite thing when reading was to name some person in the paper and say, *Do you know who that is?*

She never did. And he'd want to know, *How could you not know who that is? I mean really, how?*

He'd look at her with bemusement and contempt. It was the contempt that was like a knife under the ribs. There were loads of people she knew of that he didn't know anything about. People who worked in the beauty and perfume industries. And Calum, who thought he knew so much about the business, hadn't a clue. He wouldn't have known who they were.

Or artists, for that matter. He knew nothing about art and, consequently, refused ever to discuss it because Calum only liked talking on subjects about which he knew lots.

She pulled up outside the shopping centre. It was small but it had two expensive boutiques, one for shoes, one for clothes. She knew she shouldn't go in. But the gaping wound inside her said, go and buy something, fill the wound. She could feel her heart racing. She paid for the parking with money. She was never quite sure if Calum could track where she was by her parking. She knew he'd been able to track her on her old phone on the *find my phone* part of it. But when she'd got this new one – which had driven him insane with rage because he hadn't chosen it and she'd gone out and bought it – she set it up herself. And disabled the find my phone bit. It had been worth the raging that she must have done it wrong and that she was stupid.

'You've no idea how to do things like that. I'm sure it's all wrong. Have you backed everything up to the cloud? I'm sure you haven't. So don't come running to me when it all falls apart. You know you're useless at that sort of thing, impulsive, you're totally impulsive, there was no need to spend that money. There's nothing wrong with your other phone.'

All delivered with anger. He had just bought a new phone. He never denied himself anything. And it wasn't that Savannah couldn't afford a new phone, the old one was four years old. It was that he hadn't bought it, he hadn't set it up, he hadn't been in control. With this new one, the *find my phone* option was not connected to anyone else. So she knew that Calum did not know where she was. He might ring the office, though, he sometimes did that. She'd go in and the girls would say, 'Oh your husband was on.'

He was always so nice to the people on reception, except when he wasn't, of course.

At the clothes shop, she walked in and ran her hands over the sweaters folded beautifully on a table: cashmere. She loved cashmere, but it was so expensive, she felt terribly guilty buying it. She was careful with money; her childhood had taught her that. Mum was brilliant at bargains and putting outfits together on a shoestring.

'You don't need money to look good,' her mother always said. 'See this T-shirt? I dyed it and this navy really suits me, doesn't it? Of course, the stitching wasn't right, but I went over it with my navy fabric pen.'

Nobody who'd ever looked at the glamorous Meg Robicheaux would ever think that her wardrobe was full of things she had dyed herself or bought in charity shops or, latterly, in TK Maxx, the discount store. Mum never lied about her clothes, but when they had the hotel, she never precisely told the truth either. She had managed to make it look as if she had a beautiful wardrobe with glamorous, expensive things, even if, in reality, the family were always broke. Mum had managed to keep it all a secret, Savannah reflected as she held up a pale-pink cashmere polo-neck, soft as angel wings. But then, Savannah thought to herself, she was pretty good at keeping things to herself. The difference was that they'd all known: Indy, Eden, even Rory, they'd known that Mum was fabulous at putting together a dress she'd got in the Vincent de Paul shop and a pair of shoes she had from aeons back that were actually designer.

But in Savannah's life nobody knew, nobody saw. Her secret was perfectly hidden. She herself kept it that way.

'Are you happy to browse or do you want some help?' said the woman in the shop. A woman who reminded Savannah a little bit of her mother, except this woman's silvery hair was cut much shorter. She wore the classic sales lady outfit of an elegant black dress and low pumps. She wore one fat Perspex bangle on her arm. The bangle was an unexpected bright turquoise colour. It was her only jewellery and looked both stark and fabulous at the same time.

'I love your bracelet,' said Savannah, 'it's wonderful.'

'We stock them. I got them in because I liked them so much myself, see.'

She showed Savannah a display of rings, necklaces and bracelets all in the same Perspex in a variety of colours. Acid-green, lime-yellow, bubble-gum pink, pillar-box red.

'They're fabulous,' breathed Savannah, running her fingers over them.

'Now this one,' said the woman, picking up one of the acid-green rings and holding it towards Savannah, 'would look wonderful on you with your hair, your colouring.'

Savannah generally wore only her engagement and wedding rings and the little delicate gold watch Calum had bought for her. He liked delicate, elegant jewellery. In the same way, he liked feminine clothes, which was why Savannah wore flowing things that twirled and swung around her ankles. Flowing clothes also hid how thin she was. She slid the ring onto her ring finger on her left hand, but it was far too big.

'You're quite slim, aren't you,' said the woman assessingly. Her voice was very kind.

'Yes,' said Savannah, who'd heard this before. People often

wanted to comment on how thin she was and she laughed it off saying that it was exercise and running around and being a busy mum and entrepreneur.

Nobody really wanted to know about her disordered eating. Or how sometimes she stared into the fridge and thought she might get sick if she had to eat anything. When the last bit of control in her life was about drinking coffee and never touching a biscuit.

The sales lady got a smaller ring.

'Try this one.'

It fitted perfectly. Savannah held her hand out and admired it, admired this new version of herself. But then the dress she was wearing, a floaty floral thing, looked so wrong with a modern piece of jewellery. To wear this ring, to be this woman, she needed different clothes.

'That dress you're wearing,' she said, 'I love that. I'm sorry, that sounds a bit insane, I love your bracelet, I love your dress, I want to take over your body.'

The woman laughed. 'No, this would suit you. And, besides, it's my job to show off the wares of the shop so that you'd go, oh I'd like that.'

'I used to come here all the time,' Savannah said, 'but somebody different worked here.'

'Yes, I bought it recently. Eleana.' The woman held out her hand.

'Savannah,' said Savannah, shaking Eleana's outstretched hand.

'Do you want to change your look, perhaps, try something different? Because the clothes here used to be more your style. But I prefer a leaner, more sculptured, tailored silhouette.'

'No, I love this,' said Savannah, surprising herself, and she did. Apart from the cashmere sweaters and some very comfortable-looking velvet track pants, everything on the mannequins and on the rails seemed sculpturally shaped. There were no florals here, no leopard print, either. Eden always said leopard print was a neutral. Savannah used to agree with her, but Calum hated leopard print.

It's tarty, he said.

Savannah had let it go.

Eden wore leopard print and it looked fabulous on her. She had a leopard-print dress that clung to her curves and she wore it with purple shoes. Calum was good at both implied and straightforward insults. To imply that her sister wore tarty clothes was very him.

'I would like something different,' said Savannah.

Ten minutes later she was ensconced in a large changing room with hangers of clothes. There were dark greens and navies and some rich creams, tailored trousers, shaped jackets, tanks that didn't cling to the body, but had a firm business-like look to them.

Everything looked amazing. She wanted it all. But when she'd added up the total, it was too much. Maybe a few pieces, Savannah thought. She was dressed in her own clothes, had pulled back the dressing-room curtain and was working out what she would like to buy, when Eleana appeared.

'There is no pressure,' she said. 'There's nothing worse than shop owners who refuse to let you leave the premises without offloading everything in the shop onto you.'

'Thank you,' said Savannah, gratefully.

The kindness was there. Instinctively, she knew Eleana meant it. If she walked out without anything, it was fine, and Savannah rarely felt as if she could do that. So often she had bought things in shops because someone had hovered over her and made her feel she had to purchase, because she might get into trouble with somebody if she didn't.

'Forgive me for saying this,' said Eleana slowly, 'I sometimes see things about people.'

Savannah looked up rapidly. 'What?'

'I see things and I see the pain in every part of you. I see the way you stand, as if you're afraid. The way you move. The way you jumped when the bin lorry was outside the shop and clanged. You're scared and I hate to see that. I'd just like to give you my number, if you ever want to talk.'

She reached out with a small card, with both the shop name and her phone number on it. 'Now you can go, you don't have to buy anything, there is no pressure. And I'm sorry if I upset you by saying that, I just felt I needed to say it to you.'

Eleana's eyes, which were a lovely warm brown, the deep mellow of chestnuts, were on Savannah's face gentle, assessing.

Savannah took a deep breath and said, 'No, no, I'm fine, I'm fine.'

'You're not fine,' said Eleana kindly. 'But we can do the "I'm fine" thing if you want to.'

'No, really, I am. I think I'll take the trousers, the skirt, these two tops and the jacket,' Savannah said.

Nothing was as expensive as she'd thought. The shop was cheaper than its predecessor with the floaty dresses that did not make a woman look business-like. Something which annoyed Savannah, who'd like to look business-like. Susy, the stylist Calum employed for her, went into frenzies of delight at all the flowing garments. Susy herself was very feminine – that was probably why Calum had picked her. She dressed the wife of a friend of his and he'd seen Susy's look and decided that was what he wanted for Savannah.

'Thank you,' Savannah said to Eleana, hoping to shut down the conversation.

'No problem,' said Eleana. 'I'll pack these up, then.'

'Will I put the stuff back?' said Savannah, looking around the dressing room, which appeared to have everything in the shop hanging in it.

'No, that's fine, I'll do that; I'm sure you have somewhere you need to be.'

'I do,' said Savannah out loud. She looked at her watch anxiously; she'd been enjoying herself and she needed to get home and get dinner ready.

Eleana put one hand on Savannah's arm.

'Whoever he is, he's not worth this,' she said. 'I don't know exactly what you're going through but nobody should make you feel this way.'

'I don't feel any way,' said Savannah. And then she thought of all the times she wanted somebody to see and now somebody had seen and she was lying, backing away frantically.

'You're right,' she said, suddenly, surprising herself with the blast of honesty. 'I just don't know how to escape and I'm terrified all the time.'

'Please ring me,' said Eleana. 'I can help you. You're so thin, your eyes are haunted. Does nobody else see this?'

Savannah could feel her eyes brimming over with tears. But she put on her public smile.

'I'm fine,' she said. A tear fell on one side of her face. 'That's what people see,' she said, 'me smiling, and they see him being charming and lovely.'

'Charming and lovely in public and not at home?' said Eleana.

'How did you know?'

'I recognised the signs,' Eleana said. 'I've been through it myself. I think that's how I recognised it in you. I've seen you in magazines.'

'Oh God.' Savannah took a step backwards. 'Please, please don't tell anyone.' She thought of it getting out, that she'd spoken about Calum like this, and he would kill her, he would kill her.

'I'm not going to tell anyone or do anything,' Eleana said gently. 'Only you can get away from it, but if you need help, please talk to me.'

Savannah sat on the stool in the dressing room. She felt winded.

'I'll add everything up,' said Eleana. 'Would you like to come back another day and decide if you'd like to buy these things or not? You're emotional and I'll not take advantage of you.'

'No, I want them, they make me feel strong,' said Savannah.

'Clothes can do that. Clothes, make-up, they're our armour,' said Eleana.

'Armour,' said Savannah, 'wow, imagine what I could do if I had armour.'

*

The call for the TV show came on Friday just as they were heading off for the rehearsal dinner. Chantal answered Rory's phone.

'Louise,' she said, 'so nice to hear from you.' Chantal didn't feel it was that nice to hear from Louise, because she was a little tired of picking up the pieces in connection with Rory's book, and Louise seemed to be a part of that. Yet it would mean money and money would mean a settled life, would mean them being able to buy a house and – Chantal let out a breath – have a child.

But first, Rory needed to face up to her past and to let it go, to make peace with her family over this book, to stop drinking so much. So much needed to change.

'Yes, of course I'll get her for you. It's the rehearsal tonight for the big wedding.'

'Gosh, yes,' said Louise on the phone. 'Terribly exciting. Take lots of pictures. Put them up on social media. You know we talked about that. Rory's really got to get it together, it matters a lot in this business.'

'Yes,' said Chantal, already feeling like the dismissed spouse.

Rory put down the phone from Louise ten minutes later, her eyes wide.

'I'm going on a TV show on Friday night, next Friday night,' she said.

'Oh lord,' said Chantal.

'Yes,' said Rory, half smiling, half grimacing. 'To talk about the book, to discuss the deal and what it feels like and how marvellous it is and how there's interest from Netflix.'

'Wow,' said Chantal. 'This is huge.'

'Yes,' said Rory. And then she sank onto their emerald-green couch and suddenly seemed much smaller. 'Oh, Chantal, what am I going to do? I'm going to have to tell the family.'

'You are,' said Chantal. 'You are going to have to tell the family and you're going to have to decide in your interviews whether you say this is fact or fiction or a mixture of both, because they're all in it. They all deserve to read it. I want to read it.'

'You're not in it,' said Rory. 'It's not about now, it's about then.'

'Everyone remembers their childhood differently,' said Chantal. 'I know I do. My brother has one vision, I have another. It's the way it is. You must make this right before the book gets out there or you will lose them all, Rory, the way you are losing me . . .'

'What do you mean, the way I'm losing you?' said Rory.

Everything stilled in her brain. All thoughts about the book floated away. None of that mattered. What mattered was what Chantal had just said.

'I love you,' said Chantal, 'but I don't know if we have a future.'

Rory was rarely lost for words, words were her tools, her weapons. The things she used every day and she felt as if she had no words for this conversation.

'We want different things,' said Chantal. 'I want to be with you, to marry you, to have children, a happy home, and that is not going to happen because none of this is on your list. You are content to continue on the way we are. You want the fame and fortune of your book and no children. We are too different. I didn't realise it for a long time but I do now.'

'What do you mean I want fame and fortune? I don't want

that.' Rory tried to work out how to say it. 'I want to talk about how it was—'

Chantal cut her off: 'Talking about how it was is one thing, but you have become obsessed. Your life, your childhood, the big secret of Chloe and what that means. You think no other family has secrets. All families have them.'

'But—'

'No buts,' interrupted Chantal. 'What happened happened to Lori, to your parents, to Chloe. She is happy and she would like to meet everyone. Your father has tried to meet her, he will not be so shocked, and your mother—' Chantal shrugged. 'Your mother must know. She is the wisest woman. She must have known that your father was out at night. It is not your trauma, Rory. You are holding the secret, that is all.'

'But what's any of this got to do with you leaving me? I love you,' said Rory.

'Do you love me enough to have children with me?'

'Of course,' said Rory and Chantal stared at her.

'You're just saying that to get what you want.'

'No. No,' Rory repeated. She thought about how to phrase it. 'I think that Eden not having children always made me feel that perhaps some of us weren't good at it, but I'd like to have children with you.'

'Huh. You always say little ones are not interesting until they are three,' snapped back Chantal.

'Oh, that's just rubbish. You don't want to listen to half the things I say. I do it for effect. I'd love our babies, but I think you'd be better carrying them.'

A big smile split Chantal's beautiful face in two.

'I think I would too. I am not holding you to ransom here, then? If so, I will walk away now rather than let you throw this back in my face. And the drinking.'

She eyeballed Rory. 'You drink too much. I can't live the life your mother lived.'

Rory reached out and pulled the only woman she'd ever

loved into her arms. 'I love you, Chantal,' she said. 'I want us to have babies. I will get up in the night, I will change nappies, I'll do feeds ... I'm sorry. I've been so selfish. About this, about the book, about the drinking, about everything . . .'

Chantal's smile turned into tears and hiccups as she began to cry and laugh at the same time.

'I am so happy,' she said, 'so much happiness. There are two things, though. The book—'

'I know. And Chloe. Later. For now, let's just sit and hug.'

An hour later, Rory got up, leaving Chantal lying in bed, smiling sleepily at her.

'Definitely needs to be your biological child,' said Rory, looking lovingly at Chantal. 'You are too beautiful for words.'

'You want me to have the stretch marks?' Chantal said.

Rory laughed. 'Of course. I'm going to phone Chloe,' she added, 'and to introduce them all. No time like the present.'

'You want to invite them all over here?'

'The sisters,' said Rory. 'And not here. Everyone's getting ready for the dinner. Nick's is beside the Fisherman's Shack. I'll get a table from him outside and we can all sneak out.'

'But your parents—'

'I'm still figuring that bit out,' said Rory.

Steve zipped up Indy's dress.

'What should we do?' she said. 'Should we tell Mum?'

'No, I don't think so.'

'But she can't go marrying him, and if he's still drinking, if he's gambling, it would be crazy; that's what broke them up in the first place.'

'It's not the only thing that broke them up, though, is it?' said Steve.

Indy turned to face the mirror. She was wearing a silky dress in a floral pattern. Her work clothes were so plain coloured – blue scrubs – that she quite liked wearing colourful things when she wasn't working.

'No, it wasn't the only thing, but it was the big thing. I just don't know what to do.'

'We've no proof, though,' said Steve, 'no proof of what he was doing.'

'No,' said Indy. 'No proof at all. But can we let Mum go into that, can we let Mum marry him tomorrow not knowing?'

Steve stood behind her, wrapped his arms around her waist, leant his chin on her shoulder.

'I don't know, darling, it's up to you, she's your mum, he's your dad.'

'You're lucky your parents are so normal,' she said.

Steve laughed. 'Nobody thinks their parents are normal,' he said.

'Do you think Minnie and Daisy will be talking about us like this in thirty or forty years' time?' she said.

'Oh totally,' said Steve, 'totally.'

And they both laughed at the very idea.

A text pinged in on Indy's phone.

It was from Rory.

'She wants to meet me and the girls outside the restaurant,' she said, and shrugged. 'Who knows what this is about.'

Eden was driving.

'Darling, we'll get a taxi or I'll drive,' said Ralphie as they left the house and got into the car.

'No,' said Eden, 'it's absolutely fine; I really don't want to have a drink tonight, darling. I'd far too many glasses of wine at the hen night on Wednesday. And I couldn't cope with to-morrow if I had a headache. A bit of sparkling water will be fine for me tonight,' and she smiled at him.

'Well, if you insist,' he said, 'I quite fancy a pint.'

Eden started up the car and they drove. She thought of

the fourth letter that she'd found stuffed in the letter box this evening. *I know what you did, Mrs Tallisker.* She was absolutely fed up with it. Fed up and annoyed. No longer scared. No, she'd reached a point where the anger was growing. She'd spent weeks being terrified of this anonymous individual, who'd taken over her life, taunting her with her secret. And she had had enough. That's why she wasn't drinking tonight; she was afraid that if she had a couple of glasses of wine, the rage might encompass her and she might scream it out at the whole table. Which was not what she wanted to do. Tonight was a special night, a family night. They were all going to be there, even Rory, who'd been so notoriously absent from so many of the wedding events, apart from the hen night, of course. Eden felt quite annoyed with Rory. She wished she knew what was going on with her. When she'd rung the other day, Chantal had made some off-hand comment about Rory's agent. And Eden had been utterly astonished. She hadn't said agent, what agent, but she wanted to. Because it was clear that Chantal assumed she knew. So something was going on and Chantal assumed the whole family knew about it and Rory hadn't told anyone. Typical Rory. Yes, thought Eden. It was just as well she wasn't drinking tonight, because she would be a danger to everyone if she was.

Her phone pinged with a text: Rory.

She certainly wanted to talk to Rory, all right.

Meg looked around her family sitting at the huge table in the Fisherman's Shack. Anything less like a shack, you'd be hard pushed to find. The Shack was a chichi restaurant on the outskirts of Dalkey, set on a bit of cliff where some marvellous cantilevering meant that a tiny part of the restaurant actually sat over the rocks, and there was a glass floor where you could see the surf dashing against them. Meg always found that quite scary. It was like the Grand Canyon: you didn't want to get too close to the edge. Now, she believed, the Canyon had a glass platform where you could walk out and stare down. It hadn't been like that years ago when she and Stu and the girls had done a three-week American road trip. She smiled; everyone said she was crazy, including her sister Sandra, for bringing four small children around America at Easter.

'They're little, they'll never get a chance like this again,' Meg had said. 'Indy's going into senior school in September and once she's in the senior cycle you can't take them out of school on holidays. But now, this is the perfect time and we can do all the things we've always wanted to do.'

'Yes, but Rory's only two; you're going to schlep around America in a big car with four children and the littlest one is two, and you think that's a holiday?'

'It will be a holiday,' said Meg.

She and her sister were very different. Sandra took offence easily. Although, Eden was right: Sandra did get over things quickly. But boy, when she got angry, she got very angry.

Sandra was there tonight and Meg was thrilled. Ann O'Reilly, their mother, was there too. Still strong and tall, despite being ninety. Sandra, Eden and Ann were sitting together chattering. Ralphie was beside Eden, one big hand on her shoulder as he leaned in listening, smiling. He was a gorgeous man, thought Meg fondly. Her daughter had chosen well. Calum and Savannah weren't there yet. Indy and Steve were, both turned and talking to their neighbours, having highly animated conversations. Steve had been part of the Robicheaux family for so long – since the photos. That, Meg thought, cemented his being part of the family in her mind. Because before that, he'd been Indy's first serious boyfriend and Meg had been a little unsure of the whole concept. Because Indy used to say, 'I want to be with him for the rest of my life, Mum.' And Meg would wince. Girls of Indy's age shouldn't settle for their first boyfriend. And yet – it had all worked out in the end. They were so happily married and Minnie and Daisy were the most adorable little girls.

Steve had coped with his dreams of being a photographer not being realised. And even though he still took pictures at the weekends and had taken the family photo up until last year – this year's one was imminent – he didn't appear to mind. He liked being a carpenter, he said, doing things with his hands. Indy and Steve had the most beautiful inlaid coffee table that Steve had made in his work room. It was a piece of complete beauty.

'You are an artist,' Meg had said when she'd seen it.

'Wish I could do things like that, son,' Stu had said. 'It's amazing.'

Down at the other end of the table was Stu. He looked wonderful, Meg thought. He was tanned and his hair was brushed back from his face. He had a strong face with strong planes, high cheekbones, a long nose and that mobile mouth. In his day he'd given all the rock and movie stars a run for their money. Which was probably why they liked coming to the Sorrento. Glamorous people liked to be around other glamorous people. Of course, she'd had a huge part to play in it, she knew. She'd made it beautiful. Having that beauty taken away had been definitely part of what had made her so angry with Stu all those years ago. But she was over it now.

Nick, who owned the Fisherman's Shack, sidled up beside her.

'I said it to Stu already, should we start taking the orders?'

Meg looked around. Still no sign of Savannah and Calum. Who knew what was delaying them?

'Yes,' she said, 'let's start.'

Marie-Denise had been anxious as Savannah and Calum were leaving.

'Clary won't settle,' she whispered quietly to Savannah. 'The thing that happened in school is still on her mind and she's anxious. Anxious she's in trouble.'

Savannah felt the familiar tightening in her chest, her

254

breathing shallow. Where was the precious breathing pause now?

'It's time to go,' said Calum, looking at his watch. He'd dressed up especially in his version of smart-casual and he was wearing his shoes with the slight lifts on the heels. He wore his trousers low, so he thought nobody could see the shoes. For his sake, Savannah wished he was taller because then he'd be happy. Maybe that was it, maybe that was the problem.

'Just running upstairs to er—' she hastily cast around for a lie that would satisfy him – 'get my bracelet, the one you really like.' And she ran up the stairs.

He liked her to wear jewellery. Jewellery showed people how much money they had. And he liked that. Sometimes she felt ridiculous when she went out, with her diamond-drop necklace, the big Ceylon sapphire, her gold watch. Not that Calum bought her the jewellery. He'd bought the Ceylon sapphire but she'd bought the rest.

They'd be away and he'd spot something that he thought was appropriate and she'd snap down her credit card.

She ran into Clary's bedroom. Her daughter was sitting on the bed, still dressed, her feet curled up around her, teddies near her.

'Mum, don't go out tonight, please.'

'I have to, sweetheart,' said Savannah, sitting down on the bed. 'It's Granny's and Granddad's special dinner and it's for grown-ups only, darling, or I'd bring you, but it's going to be fine. We won't be late, I promise.'

'I know,' said Clary.

And Savannah could see the stoicism come into her little face. It was the stoicism of a child who knew that her needs did not come first. And that wasn't about tonight's dinner, it went much deeper than that. It was because Calum's needs always came first, what he wanted, what would make him happy. They were the rules by which they lived their life. He ran their lives and they danced on eggshells around him.

Savannah had been trying for so long to make it all work and, still, she couldn't.

She curled up on the bed beside her daughter, not caring that her flowing floral frock would get creased.

'I promise I won't be long,' she said, 'I'll tell Granny you're not feeling well and I'll get away early.'

'But Daddy will be sad,' said Clary, with unerring accuracy.

'No, he won't,' lied Savannah. 'Don't be silly, he won't. Now, you go downstairs and sit with Marie-Denise, and I'll text you every half-hour to make sure you're OK and you can message me back on Marie-Denise's phone and tell me how you're doing. And at the first hint of you not feeling well or feeling sad and lonely, I'll come home.'

'OK.'

Savannah ran down the stairs and it was only when she got to the bottom that she realised that she hadn't retrieved the extra bracelet that she was supposed to have been looking for. Calum looked at her wrist.

'Where is it?' he said.

He was like a sniffer dog sometimes, she thought wearily, noticing everything.

'I couldn't see it,' she said. 'It's very odd. I must tidy out my jewellery box.' She put a hand on his arm. 'You're so generous to me, darling. I've so many things I can't find them all.'

'Mm,' he muttered. 'Come on, let's go.'

They were taking his car but it was an unwritten rule that Savannah would drive back afterwards so that he could have a couple of glasses of wine. It was like a rule of life: the man had a drink and the woman drove home and the man criticised how the woman drove. They were the rules. Savannah thought he'd be irritated if she left early to go home to Clary. What would he do then? He might have to accept a lift from somebody else or get a taxi. He hated taxis. But then he'd got one the other night, hadn't he? She'd say something like, 'that company you used the other night'. But then that might bring up the other night and he'd be annoyed. She got into the car, put on her seatbelt and made herself as small as possible. It didn't make any difference, generally, but it helped, it helped her.

She didn't notice the text at first and when she did, she didn't read it. She'd see Rory at the restaurant.

The Shack was buzzing when Chantal and Rory arrived.

'I will get Savannah,' said Chantal, 'if you can get Eden and Indy.'

'Deal.'

Chloe was going to wait outside.

'Do you think this is the right time to do this?' Chloe said, anxiously.

Rory was astonished. In the time since she'd known her, Chloe never looked anxious. She was so self-contained, happy within herself.

'Yes, it's the right time. You need to know your sisters and your dad and it would be lovely for you to be at the wedding.'

'I do want to go to the wedding,' Chloe said, 'but your mother—'

'Mum will not mind.'

'I agree,' Chantal echoed. 'I will tell you one thing about Meg – as soon as she knows of your existence, you will be part of this family already.'

A big fat tear dropped down Chloe's young face.

'Stay here and don't run away,' Rory ordered.

Chantal crept quietly up to where Savannah was sitting, staring off into the middle distance. She looked so sad, Chantal thought, although it was no wonder, being married to that odious man.

Chantal made it a point never to discuss Calum with Rory but she always felt there was something wrong with him, something cold, assessing.

Savannah was so thin, so edgy. Carefully, so as not to startle her, Chantal laid a delicate hand on Savannah's wrist—

'Oh, you frightened me,' gasped Savannah, jerking away.

'I am sorry. Can you come outside?' she whispered.

Savannah looked around. Calum was talking to someone on his other side, ignoring his wife completely, which was rude and unnecessary.

'It will only take a moment.'

'I'm just going outside, darling,' Savannah said brightly to her husband, as if asking permission like a child. Chantal winced. There was nothing normal there.

Outside, Eden and Indy had joined Rory.

'What is it?' said Eden.

Rory looked around.

To one side of the Shack, there were tables used during the day when the sun shone on the front of the restaurant. At night, people liked to sit at the back and stare at the view over the sea, watch the sunset. But now, only a couple of people sat at one of the nearby tables, sharing a glass of wine, talking quietly among themselves. At the furthest away table, under some sparkling fairy lights, sat Chloe.

'There's someone you need to meet,' said Rory.

Eden realised it first.

'You're Lori's daughter, aren't you? Lori and – Pops,' she said. She could recognise that shape anywhere because it was like looking into a mirror at herself: the same height, the same legs stretched out in jeans, even the same sort of trainers that Eden herself liked to wear. Only the girl's hair was different. Long, dark, glossy under the lights. Lori's daughter. Their half-sister. She knew it.

She had begun to run before anyone else had moved.

'I knew it!' Eden said, grabbing the girl's hand. 'I knew for years. When Lori left, I just knew because—' She broke off and realised that she was gabbling and she held out her other hand and the girl took it.

'I'm Chloe.'

'Oh, my sweet Lord,' said Indy, putting a hand to her mouth.

'It's true. It was always true,' she said, looking at Rory.

'I did tell you,' Rory said, 'but you are now forgiven.'

Indy hurried over to Chloe. 'Hello!' She leaned in to enfold the younger woman in an embrace. 'I'm Indy. It's so lovely to meet you. How is Lori? Is she here?'

'She died a few years ago. Cancer,' said Chloe.

There was silence and Chantal crossed herself.

'I am so sorry she never brought you to see us,' said Indy, overcome with emotion. 'We loved her, and if Dad stopped her coming here—'

'Your father tried to visit but Mum didn't want that. She wanted a new life. She knew he adored your mother and she needed to get away. He did his best.'

She held up the lapis necklace. 'He sent this.'

Savannah sat down on the seat opposite and put a shy hand in Chloe's.

'Welcome, sister,' she said gently. 'I'm a little tired. My daughter is sick, so I'm not effusive, but it is so lovely to welcome you.'

'Clary's not well?' said Indy.

'A little off,' Savannah said. 'I'd like to go home early to her. She'll love you,' she said to Chloe. 'You look like me and Eden, only with hair like hers.'

'My mother would have loved to have met your children. She loved you all, talked about you, but she got sick when I was twelve and she was ill on and off for a long time before she died. It wasn't possible then. I'm sorry. Indy, she told me you were elegant and beautiful and kind. "A born midwife", she said when she heard you had qualified.'

Indy glowed at the compliment.

'The twins, so different, so brilliant.'

'Hardly,' said Savannah softly.

Eden patted her twin's hand. 'Stop that,' she said, sounding gruff when she really felt like crying. Why was Savannah like this? Her beautiful twin reduced to this pale, sad woman.

'And Rory, who found me.'

'Rory found you?'

'When I was writing the book. I was looking through old photographs and there was one of Lori and I was sure she was pregnant.' She stared at Indy. 'I knew there was something going on, Indy.'

Her sister ruefully rubbed her forehead. 'I knew it too but you were so little. I had to say there was nothing, that you were imagining it. You were a kid, Rory, and so was I, really. What teenager wants to think her father is having an affair?'

'The book?' said Eden.

'The book she's been writing,' said Chantal. 'She's sold it and it's about—'

Rory shot her a look but Chantal was determined. 'If secrets are coming out, they need to come out properly. It's about a woman coming to terms with being gay, a woman who grew up in a hotel who has an unknown sister.'

Everyone turned to look at Rory.

'What?' said Indy.

'Any more secrets in it?' asked Eden sharply.

Savannah started to laugh slightly manically. 'Does it have everything in it? All the secrets?'

'It's fiction,' insisted Rory.

'Faction,' said Indy crossly.

'I'll let you read it and you can decide,' said Rory suddenly. 'I'll give them the money back, if you hate it.'

'There's money in this book?' Eden looked pleased.

'It doesn't matter if there's money in it – it's all family secrets,' said Indy.

Savannah spoke in a voice that was less dreamy than before.

'Nobody ever knows what your true life is,' she said. 'People wrote about the Sorrento as if they knew and they didn't. They made stuff up. I live a life where I pretend things to sell my business. Only we know the truth and if you say you made it up, then you made it up.'

They all stared at Savannah. 'You control the narrative. People can do that, you know: say one thing when the reality is different. You can say you hung your story around the bones of our life but that it's so different.'

'What she says,' agreed Rory.

'Totally a fair point,' said Eden. 'I'll have to write a book someday. Politicians do. And they'll want to know about me. I'll give them the truth of who I am.' She paused. The truth – she had to do that. Tell the truth and not let some anonymous letter writer wield a sword over her head.

Her past would not ruin her political career. The world was a changed place and women like her were changing it. 'As long as I come out of this book looking lovely,' she added, giving a big fake grin to Rory, 'then *no problemo!*'

'I wondered where you all were,' said a voice.

Everyone swivelled.

There, her silvery hair lit from the fairy lights, stood their mother.

Chantal smiled first because she, as the outsider, could see most easily what the others could not.

That the existence of Chloe was not a surprise to Meg and that she was relieved to see her here.

For a moment, Meg stared at Chloe, tears in her eyes. 'I so wish Lori had come to me and told me. I understood why she didn't. She didn't want me hurt but your father had hurt me so much and I could have helped Lori. You look so like her – and like Eden and Savannah.'

The sisters parted and Meg stooped to kiss Chloe, who started to sob and threw her arms around her.

'My mother loved you and she was so sorry—'

'That's in the past,' murmured Meg, stroking Chloe's hair. 'Now, lovie, it's going to be fine. Your mother wrote to me near the end and she told me that, one day, you'd want to come and I said I'd welcome you with open arms. I know you have a real father but you have a birth one here who'd love to see you.'

'You knew and Dad knew you knew?' said Rory finally.

'Told you,' said Chantal with a hint of smugness.

'Nothing gets past me,' said Meg.

Savannah smiled to herself, a sad smile, and thought that some things did.

Her eyes rested on Eden who had precisely the same smile on her face.

'Come in,' Meg went on, her arm around Chloe. 'We're having a party and you need to be there.'

Meg brought Chloe back in with her and sat her down in her own place, then got a waiter to bring another chair. Stu had been deep in conversation with Vonnie and he turned round and went pale under his tan at the sight of Chloe.

'Now, darling,' Meg said quietly. 'This is Chloe and I know you've been wanting to meet her for a long time. We're not going to make a big deal out of this now, but here she is, your beautiful daughter.'

'Oh my God,' said Stu, 'Can I—?' He stopped and threw his arms around Chloe.

'He's a bit of a hugger,' said Meg, extracting her newly acquired soon-to-be stepdaughter from her ex-husband, soon-to-be-new-husband's embrace.

'Now, Stu, hold it together. You're having a sedate family dinner.' Meg looked around the table. Everyone seemed to be enjoying themselves, except Savannah, who'd just sat down and was smiling over at them in a wistful, lonely way. Beside her sat Calum. He was now tapping his fingers on the table, irritated, waiting for something.

'I know this isn't the time, now that you're here, Chloe,' Meg said quietly, 'but, Stu, there's just something about that man that worries me.' Meg looked across at Calum.

'Er, Calum?' said Stu. 'Yeah, he's a bit of a cold fish, all right. I mean, I tried to get him to come to my stag night but he said he had some big business dinner on. One of those restaurants in town where it's all meat and costs a fortune for a lump of beef the size of a small car. I dunno, bit of a show-off, I think, but, you know, Savannah seems to love him.'

Chloe and Meg stared across at Savannah and Calum.

'Does she?' asked Chloe. 'She looks scared, actually. Like a wisp of a person who wants to float away. She seems different from the way Mum described her to me.'

'I can tell you're an artist,' said Meg, squeezing Chloe's hand, 'and yes, she does look scared, doesn't she?' she added grimly.

Savannah insisted on leaving early and drove home. There was no way Calum was going to get a taxi. No, he wanted to arrive and leave in his Lexus, and, of course, he would want a drink at the rehearsal dinner, so under no circumstances could Savannah drink. She'd barely been able to eat anyway. She'd kept looking over at beautiful Chloe, fascinated to see her own features but with a different skin tone and that rippling, long dark hair. Mum had kept Chloe between her and Dad for ages and then Eden had rescued her and taken her away and then Indie had wanted a go, then Rory and Chantal insisted that they talk to her but Savannah hadn't, not because she didn't want her beautiful half-sister with her but because she felt as if there was nothing left of her even to move a finger towards Chloe. She felt as if her heart was bashed in, as if her ribs were crushed and there was nothing to her. She didn't know how she was going to get through tomorrow smiling at everyone, trying to be normal when inside she felt lonely, broken, crushed, almost dead, but she had to keep going. She was going to keep going for Clary, but it was so difficult. Once they were in the car Calum stopped talking to her. He'd spoken a few words to her at the dinner, loudly, so other people could hear. Once, when he'd seen her staring off into the distance, he'd painfully squeezed her knee under the table. 'Smile,' he'd hissed. 'You look like you're going to the scaffold.'

'Sorry,' she'd said, and she'd tried to be merry but it was so impossible.

'Turn your full lights on, this is a back road,' he commanded, so she did and then she didn't turn them down quickly enough when another car approached. 'For God's sake, that's stupid, you're a bloody useless driver,' he'd snarled. Somehow, her hands shaking, they'd made it home. They got in the front door and she could feel herself quake. He might want sex. She couldn't bear it. She couldn't bear the thought of him touching her. But he stomped upstairs without saying a word to her. She ran up a minute later and went into Clary's room. Her daughter was asleep, all curled up with her teddies. And Savannah, unable to help herself, stripped off the beautiful clothes she'd bought, down to her under things, and curled up in bed beside her daughter. Here she could keep her safe. Here she might sleep.

Eden and Ralphie drove Chloe back to her B & B.

'You can stay with us tonight,' said Eden.

'No,' said Chloe, 'it would be crazy, I've paid for the place.'

'Well, how about you stay with us tomorrow night?'

'Why are you welcoming me into your home?' said Chloe. 'I came and I disrupted everything.'

Eden and Ralphie laughed uproariously. Eden was stone-cold sober because she hadn't been drinking. She needed a clear head, she'd told Chloe. But Ralphie had had several pints of beer and a whiskey with Steve.

'That's so funny,' he said. 'Disrupting things. You don't know what you're getting yourself into. This family is mad.'

'Ha, mad,' retorted Eden. 'Who's got the mad family? Do you know, Chloe,' she said, 'his father is a very famous politician and—'

'Oh I know,' said Chloe, 'I've looked you all up.'

'Really? What do we sound like? It's very interesting to know what you sound like from someone who's looking you up with a real interest. I thought you were studying art not history?'

'Yes,' said Chloe. 'Actually, I studied your father-in-law in history in school.'

'You'll have to meet Diarmuid, he's going to love you. I studied history in college, that's how I got into politics. Because I met darling Ralphie and he introduced me to his family.'

'And they fell in love with her,' said Ralphie. 'Like I'm so in love with her,' and he leaned his large frame over to put his head on Eden's shoulder as she drove.

'No, sweetie, you don't want me to crash, go back on your own side.'

Chloe grinned. They were terribly sweet together. Nothing she'd expected at all. Eden was sharp and clever but warm, funny.

'You didn't look surprised when you saw me.'

'No,' said Eden. 'Because Rory told me something years ago. She'd seen Dad kissing Lori. And I believed her. She told Indy as well and Indy didn't believe her, because Indy doesn't like things that aren't lovely. Well, she didn't then. She's more real world now.'

'She's very beautiful,' said Chloe, 'so gorgeous and nice.'

'We call her the perfect sister.'

Chloe giggled.

'I'm the imperfect sister. Rory is the deeply tricky sister.'

And Savannah, Savannah was the troubled sister, she thought to herself but didn't say it out loud. 'And Savannah is the business-lady sister. So what are you going to be? You can be the wildly famous artist sister.'

'I can be a sister?' said Chloe, who'd had none. 'I've never had a sister before, or even four. I have two brothers.'

'Do you want to ring them, text them? You could ring them from the car so they know you're safe, so they know you're with us.'

Chloe burst into tears. 'You're being so lovely,' she said.

'You're my sister,' said Eden in a matter-of-fact voice, 'what else would I be? Families are weird these days, just telling you. And the one you've got yourself involved in, we're weirder than most.'

'Yeah,' said Ralphie.

'Ralphie Tallisker,' said Eden, sounding tough, but there was a lot of humour in her voice. 'Stop saying we're weird; your family are really weird, your father is nuts.'

'I know, but who's going to tell him that?' said Ralphie. 'Really.'

'I might,' said Eden, starkly. 'One day I might tell him.'

Ralphie giggled. 'As long as I can be there when you do it, honey.'

15
Saturday

Eden was half asleep in the morning light, in the lovely zone between dreaming and waking. It was an important day, she knew, and her mind searched for the reason. Then it hit her. The wedding. Today Mum and Pops were getting married again. And, she sat up in bed, smiling, she had a new sister, a half-sister. How absolutely amazing.

Chloe was gorgeous. Mum knew about it, astonishingly, and everything was going to be OK. Except the thought of her own secret clunked inside her.

I know what you did, Mrs Tallisker.

But her secret seemed transformed, somehow. Last night had done that.

She thought back to Lori, dear, lovely Lori, who'd been part-chambermaid, part-nanny, part-family. She'd been in the bosom of the Robicheaux family for perhaps seven years, always smiling, dark-haired and dark-eyed.

Then Eden thought of Lori getting pregnant. The moral majority had still been standing on the high ground, belittling women who were pregnant and single. Being a single mother was never an easy option and Lori had been in her twenties.

Women were always having to go through hard stuff and having to hide it, because it didn't suit the patriarchy, Eden reflected grimly. She picked up her phone from where it was charging on the bedside table and looked at it. It was only half seven, probably too early to wake her new sister.

Ralphie was asleep beside her. He slept well. Since the arrival of the anonymous letters, she hadn't slept well, at all.

Slivers of anger rose in her. She was fed up with the letters, fed up with hiding. Why should she hide the truth?

Her phone rang and she knew the number because the phone flashed it: Rian O'Donoghue, Diarmuid's henchman.

Oh heck, she thought, her finger hovering over the button. The phone was on silent and it was sheer fluke that she'd seen the number come up. She slipped out of bed, answered the phone and said: 'Yes,' quietly, hurrying out of the room so as not to wake Ralphie.

If this was the moment when Rian told her he knew her secret and she was out of the party, well, she'd tell him exactly what he could do with himself. She was pretty sure it was anatomically impossible, unless he was triple jointed, but that was his problem.

'Eden, it's Rian,' he said somewhat unnecessarily.

'Good morning, Rian. It's a little early at the weekend for social calls.' Eden did her best to sound professional.

'Not a social call,' said Rian.

He really needed to work on his people skills, Eden thought, but said nothing.

'I know this is not really in my brief, but I know your parents are getting married today.'

Eden stared at the phone. 'Yes,' she said cautiously. 'What's that got to do with anything?'

'One of my, er—' Rian hesitated over the words. 'A friend of mine met your father late last night and he was a bit over refreshed, shall we say. I know he doesn't drink anymore and—'

Eden realised that Rian, hard man, second-in-command to her father-in-law, was embarrassed, which was almost sweet. He was trying to be helpful.

'So he was on the piss last night after the rehearsal dinner?' she said.

'Yeah, I knew you'd want to know. I'm sorry, I'm really sorry, it's not fun having that in your family,' said Rian.

And again Eden stared at the phone. She wanted to say *who*

is this Rian and what have you done with the old one? But she
didn't.

'Thank you,' she said, sighing. 'That's helpful to know. I'd
better get over there and sober him up. He's supposed to be
marrying my mother in a few hours, if she wants to marry
him.'

'I'll tell you from experience,' said Rian grimly. 'If they don't
want to stop, you can't make them. Good luck.'

And he hung up. There was the turn-up for the books,
thought Eden. Rian was an actual person after all and not a
robot. But that was immaterial right now, because apparently
her father had gone out and got completely trolleyed after the
revelation that he had a fifth daughter emerged.

'Why did you do it, Dad? You complete moron,' she said.
'Mum said she knew, we were all OK with it; why would you
go and get drunk because of it? Especially when you've been off
the drink for so many years, why?'

She needed Ralphie. She went back into the room.

'Honey,' she said, shaking his shoulder.

'Errgh,' he said sleepily.

'You've got to get up. Dad went on the piss last night and,
we need to find him, if we can, sober him up and—' she
stopped for a minute – 'and I don't know if my mother will
want to marry him. But at least if she sees him she can make
the decision.'

'OK,' said Ralphie, sitting up, trying to focus. 'OK, I'm with
you. Do we have time for coffee?'

'Hell, yes,' said Eden, 'I think we're going to need it.'

Ralphie was parking the car in his normal neat fashion. Eden
had already undone her seatbelt and was attempting to get out
before he'd stopped.

'Stop,' shrieked Ralphie, 'you're going to get killed.'

'I'll be fine,' she said.

He'd braked as soon as she'd opened the door.

'Maniac,' he said.

'You're a good driver: you won't squash me.' She leaned over and gave him a long, lingering kiss on the lips. 'Thank you.'

'I haven't done anything yet,' said Ralphie.

'Yes, you have, and there's more to come,' said Eden with a grimace.

All she had was her phone on a hastily constructed phone-holder around her neck and the little useless bridesmaid's bag that Vonnie had insisted on purchasing for all of them. There was no room in any of these fairy bags for something as prosaic as a mobile phone, which was why Eden's now dangled on an old long-forgotten ribbon and container yoke around her neck.

Her father's flat was not somewhere she'd ever spent a lot of time. She and her father walked together, that was their thing. They walked along the seafront, up Killiney Hill and then they'd get a coffee or have something to eat. Walking, that was it. Now, as Eden fumbled in the useless little hand-bag for her father's spare apartment keys, she wondered was it because she didn't like where he lived? It was an odd, perilous building set up in a cliff, but ancient, looking as if it might all crumble into the sea because climbing plants had practically occluded all brickwork at the front. It took her a minute to figure out which was the front-door key. And she shoved her way in, leaving it on the latch for Ralphie. Then she bounded up the stairs. Her father's apartment was on the third floor, the top. And, needless to say, the crumbling old wreck that was Liffey Heights did not have a lift. There was a smell of cat pee and dust and food stuck to microwaves. There were two doors on Pop's floor and she paused to catch her breath outside his. It was painted the same dull matte cream as the rest of the woodwork in the place. She knew her father had a cleaning lady who came in occasionally. It didn't look as if the cleaning lady had ever applied herself to the front door. Eden knocked.

'Pops, are you in there? It's me, Eden.'

It was eight o'clock in the morning and she knew there was

an old fellow who lived in the apartment opposite, who might or might not yet be up. Might think eight on a Saturday was practically dawn. But she didn't care if he was up or not. She began shouting louder.

'Pops, it's me, Eden, let me in.'

There wasn't a sound.

'Feck.'

She grabbed the keys that she'd dumped back into the useless little handbag. Found the actual front-door key and let herself in. Not for her father any of the folderols like security chains. No, Stu Robicheaux had always been convinced that he could take on any burglar, which was why they had no burglar alarm in the Sorrento Hotel. There was nothing to steal, her mother used to say. It didn't look or smell like there was anything to steal here either, was Eden's first thought as she went through the door. The smell was of eau de brewery.

Oh, Pops, thought Eden, what have you done, you bloody moron. The place was different from the last few times she'd been there. Obviously, her mother had stayed over and her father had been making more of an effort. Or else her mother had actually cleaned the place up and put flowers on the table. Eden was quite sure she could remember a bowl of roses on the table. Now there were cereal bowls. The family jug – a milk carton – sat there along with plates, bits of toast stuck to them, flies buzzing happily around. Maybe Pops was dead on the bed, she thought. Jesus, where was Ralphie? She moved back to the door and she could hear him coming, bouncing up the stairs. She'd wait for him, because, if something had happened to her father, she wasn't sure if she was able for it.

'Eden,' croaked a voice.

The bedroom door had cracked open. And there, in pyjama bottoms, a very wrecked old Rolling Stones T-shirt and beard stubble, stood her father, leaning against the door jamb. The door jamb seemed to be supporting him, because it looked like he mightn't be able to stand up on his own.

Behind her, Ralphie's hands slid around her waist.

'You all right, love?' he said.

'Yes,' said Eden, looking at the wreck that was her parent. From across the room, she could smell the bang of alcohol. It was like walking into a wine tasting and having someone throw the slops of the previous week's wine tasting all over you. Not just wine, possibly whiskey and beer too.

'Oh man, Stu, what have you been doing?' said Ralphie.

'What do you think he's been doing?' said Eden, marching in properly. She was glad she was here; she was always the sister who could handle difficult situations.

'You do know you're supposed to be getting married in five hours, don't you?'

'What time is it?' said her father. His eyes resembled two tiny currants in some unproven dough. His nose was red. His cheeks were red. The rest of him, though, was a deathly white colour, even despite the legendary Stu tan.

'Why did you have to go on the piss again now, Dad?' said Eden, aware that she was wailing.

'I didn't, I didn't. I – I mean – I didn't—'

'Stu, man,' said Ralphie, 'there's absolutely no point lying at this stage, none whatsoever.'

Ralphie went to make the strong coffee Eden had said they needed for her father, and she sat him down at the table for a serious talk.

'Spill,' she said fiercely.

Stu looked blearily down at the table.

'I just felt so bad for everything I'd done to your mother and all of you. And Chloe. That was all my fault. It all came back to me. And I just – it just meant that I thought I'd need a drink.'

'Yes, but a drink was going to make it worse,' emphasised Eden, 'not better.'

'I know,' said her father, putting his head on the table, putting his arms around his head. 'I just felt so bad, about Savannah and that asshole, and Chloe and your mother and we can't tell her this happened or she won't marry me . . .'

'Dad,' Eden said, so he'd know she meant business. She, alone, always called him Pops. 'Mum knows everything, which is great, because if she didn't, none of us would stand by and let her remarry you. So, she knows about Chloe, and she has the biggest heart in the world, so that's good. The fact that she is willing to marry you amazes me no end, but she is, and I love you. I say that with love. But she's willing to marry you. So why the hell you went out and got trolleyed is beyond me—' Eden stopped.

What had her father said? Something about Savannah . . .

She thought of her twin the night before and when she'd left because she was worried about Clary. Calum hadn't been pleased.

And Eden had thought for a moment that his fingers were digging into Savannah's slender arm. She was sure she'd been imagining it. But now, the more she thought about it, the more she thought she hadn't been imagining it.

'You didn't gamble, did you?'

'No, no.'

'I don't know if you can gamble late at night,' said Ralphie innocently from the kitchen.

'You can gamble at any time,' Eden said. 'You must know; we're always trying to get anti-gambling legislation in. Did you lose any money?'

'I didn't gamble.'

'OK, so it was just drink, a lot of drink.'

'But I haven't been drinking, you know, before now; I've been really good.'

Eden looked at him and suddenly she thought he wasn't telling the truth.

'That's a lie,' she said and he had the grace to look down.

'It's up to Mum now,' Eden said.

Eden would get Pops delivered to the Sorrento and her

mother could take over. But she needed to sort out Savannah too. Her father talking about how he'd taken Savannah's arm roughly had suddenly clicked everything into place in her brain: Calum was an abuser. It was as clear as daylight. Eden was going to kill him.

Indy answered the phone on the first ring.

'Hello, Eden, is everything OK?'

'No,' said Eden. 'Ralphie and I are at Pop's and he's hungover, still drunk.'

'Ah,' said Indy slowly. 'I don't think it's the first time he's done it this week.'

'You knew?' said Eden in an accusing voice.

'I didn't know for sure, Eden, but Steve saw him coming out of a pub during the week. One of the pubs in Ballybrack, somewhere he thought we wouldn't see him.'

'Why didn't you tell me?'

'There was nothing to tell; Steve was driving past and saw Dad coming out, that was all. I mean, he could have been fine, he could have been meeting someone for a coffee.'

'Very likely,' said Eden sarcastically. 'I mean, so likely that a raging alcoholic with a gambling addiction was in a pub just to have a coffee. I'm sorry, he's pretty hungover and I've to get to the hotel and make sure everything's OK. So do you. I was hoping that maybe Steve could come over and help Ralphie sober him up, babysit him until the wedding so he doesn't go on another bender, and then get him into his suit.'

'Good idea,' said Indy. 'The girls and I are ready. And Steve just has to throw himself into something respectable.'

Eden could hear Steve in the background, laughing.

'What's this about me throwing myself into something respectable? That sounds like a very X-rated conversation altogether.'

'It's Dad,' Eden heard her sister say. 'He got drunk last night. Eden's hoping you're going to go over and help Ralphie sober

274

him up, while myself, Eden and the girls go to the Sorrento and smile and make sure the place is ready.'

'But your mother will have to know,' said Steve.

In unison, Eden and Indy said: 'She'll smell it off him.' They laughed.

'He does smell a bit like a brewery,' said Eden. 'Not a chichi craft one: one of the giant ones with vast tanks of beer.'

'Figures,' said Indy.

'It's up to Mum now; she's got to make the call.'

'Yep,' said Indy.

'I did tell her she was nuts to even consider remarrying him. I don't think he'll ever change.'

'You don't know,' said Indy, 'people do.'

'Whatever. The thing is – there's something else. It's Calum. He's an abuser. He's emotionally abusing Savannah. I don't know how I haven't seen it. Jesus, I've been working with a women's shelter, for God's sake, and I didn't see it. We need to get her away from him.'

Eden heard her sister's sharp intake of breath.

'I'll meet you there. Will you phone Rory?'

'Yes.'

Meg

Meg moved quietly through the hotel. She was getting married in a few hours. Her hair had been curled and rippled down her back in glossy curls. Her make-up made her beautiful sea-green eyes look bigger and the make-up artist had been amazing at using products that gently disguised the inevitable creeping of skin around the eyelids. She had a bit of a tan so she'd rubbed something glowing into her skin. Once she'd got the wedding dress on, she knew she'd look as good as she could. Which was all she wanted to be – as good as she could be in everything, especially today on her wedding day with all her family there, her beautiful girls, Stu, her sister and her mum. Ann O'Reilly was a bit fragile and Meg worried about her. But today was going to be special, her three little granddaughters, Minnie, Daisy and Clary, were going to be bridesmaids.

There was even Chloe, Stu's daughter.

Meg had always known about it, about him and Lori.

Lori had been beautiful and young. Lori had always hero worshipped Stu. But nothing had ever happened until the last few months of Lori's time at the hotel and it had been the final nail in the coffin of their marriage for Meg.

That her husband had gone off with a younger woman. But the very fact that he'd gone off at all . . . she could never forgive that.

She'd always known that Lori had ended up pregnant but Meg had not been able to be her best self about it at the time. She had not been able to put her own pain aside and think about Lori and the innocent baby. Not then, anyway. She'd been grappling with keeping her daughters safe and their financial heads above water. Later, she'd been able to move on and talk to Stu about it, help him understand that when Chloe wanted to come to him, she would.

He'd begged forgiveness then but it had taken years before she'd been able to let it go.

Seeing Chloe last night, Meg had known instantly who she was. Chloe was so like Lori and Meg's twin daughters. In the flesh, Chloe had been a young, innocent girl who needed love and support from her other family. She was young, scared, keen to meet her family, and Meg, the Meg who had lived many lives and understood that life was complex and always drawn in shades of grey, had willingly held out her arms. Chloe was part of the Robicheaux family: it was that simple.

Stu's mother, Jacqueline, would have hated it all, Meg thought with a grin.

Now, before the absolute madness started, Meg wanted a wander around the hotel, to breathe in the atmosphere of this special day and say goodbye to the Sorrento. Soon it would be turned into apartments. Their friend Frank was having trouble getting money from the bank, but he would eventually, he insisted. And this little slice of heaven where she and Stu had raised the girls would become a different slice of heaven for more families. People who could look out onto the beauty of the water, smell the sea, feel the rain lashing against the windows and the rocks on windy nights. It was a magical place.

The kitchen was beginning to get busy. But Meg was used to walking through kitchens. She didn't feel uncomfortable in them. At the height of its fame and business, the Sorrento had had plenty of staff in the kitchens. And although the chef of the day was always in charge, Meg was adept at travelling through, making a suggestion here, a comment there, soothing frazzled nerves because kitchens could be very frazzled.

This lot didn't look as if they were frazzled – yet. There were cold canapés and precooked hot food for those who'd want it. And she knew that a refrigerated truck with the salmons and the cold meats was coming soon. Because the fridges in the Sorrento were long past their sell-by date. No amount of bleaching would bring them back up to proper culinary standards.

'Everything going all right?' she asked a girl hauling in a big pile of lettuces.

'Yes, great,' said the girl. 'Oh, you're Mrs Robicheaux?'

'Yes,' said Meg, 'well, the ex, and soon to be the current.'

The girl laughed nervously. She looked about twenty-five and probably thought there was something absolutely insane about people in their sixties remarrying or getting married at all. Meg wondered if younger people assumed that sex stopped once you hit thirty or forty. They probably assumed they'd stopped it ten years ahead of their own age, a bit like middle age. Middle age was always defined as being ten years older than yourself.

Meg vaguely remembered that when she and Stu were young and wildly in love and lust, they'd felt sorry for old people.

People like they were now. They'd blithely assumed that their lives were over, because how could they possibly have a sex life or romance or anything to say to each other?

Yet Meg had so much to say to Stu; she loved his company, his charm, his wit, his cleverness, his kindness and his love-making – that was a part of it. The years they'd been apart had been unusual in that she'd always had a longing to be back with him. Had always known that he was the one. But his behaviour had taken him off the list.

And now, now he was back on the list, now he was on top of the list. And yet . . .

She left the kitchen behind and walked quietly into the ballroom where all the work she, Indy, Eden, Savannah and Vonnie had done was obvious in every inch of its beautiful, silk-bedecked beauty. The hired linens and tables and chairs with their pretty covers and peony-pink silk bows on the back looked beautiful. Savannah, who'd always had a marvellous eye, had decorated the tables with tea lights and mirrors and tiny little vases with clustered rosebuds. It was all completely gorgeous and nobody would guess it was done on a shoestring. Meg still had the beautiful old silver from the hotel and the marvellous linen napkins with an elegant cursive embroidered in teal in one corner.

There was nobody in the room and Meg stepped out into the garden breathing in the scent of a summer morning. Three hours, it was ten now and the ceremony was to take place at one. The girls were expected soon. But, for now, it was just her and the caterers. She walked around the garden feeling the sun dusting her skin. She could see the place where the girls had had their photos taken. It had been against a little barn-like structure, one that had been hung with fairy lights and decorated with trailing wreaths, depending on the season. Storm lanterns dotted the steps. How many pictures had they taken there? Fifteen? Twenty? Meg could remember them all.

Could remember the fights and arguments. Could remember the mood from different photos.

The ones where everyone was in marvellous form: the ones where there was tension, like after Savannah's and Eden's weddings. When Eden glowed with an inner beauty and Savannah, who Meg had expected to blossom, had looked as if frost had crept up on her in the night and frozen her face into a mask, not of fear, but of tension: that was it, tension. Indy might have been the out-and-out beauty of the family, the one who looked like she could be on the cover of *Vogue*. But all her daughters were beautiful, Meg thought. Savannah and Eden identical in so many ways visually but so different inside, had very different sorts of beauty. Eden's was a rich, confident, sensual beauty, an awareness of who she was and what she wanted. And Savannah's beauty had always been that of a mythical creature with her long rippling hair and her far-away gaze, and that was all gone now. She was dressed in floaty clothes but the far-away gaze was now the gaze of someone who had shut down. Meg paused, Savannah was shutdown, that was it, and she, Meg, had done nothing about it.

Then her mind roved to Stu: there was something not quite right with Stu, she knew it. It wasn't to do with Chloe. He wasn't himself. Or he was – he was behaving like the old him. Meg didn't want Sonya to be right. She just wanted everything to be lovely again, just wanted a simple life with Stu, and why couldn't she have that, why did everything have to be so difficult?

Indy, Eden, Minnie and Daisy arrived at the hotel at exactly the same time. Rory and Chantal had just turned up and so had Chloe in a taxi.

'No Savannah?'

'She texted to say she's running a bit late,' said Indy.

'OK,' said Eden, eyes narrowed. 'Thought she was going to get her make-up done here with us?'

'Well, maybe not.'

'OK.'

'Do you think it's all right me being here, now?' said Chloe.

'Don't be ridiculous,' said Eden, putting her arm through Chloe's. 'Come on, you've got to meet your nieces. Daisy and Minnie, this is your Aunt Chloe. In fact, Aunt Chloe is going to play with you this afternoon.'

'She's not being a babysitter,' said Indy firmly. 'She's a sister—'

'I don't mind,' said Chloe. The girls looked up at her and smiled. 'I'd like it.'

'Well, we might have a lot of people for you to baby-sit,' said Eden, 'including your dad.'

'Why?' said Chloe

'Don't worry, we'll tell you later.'

Eden

Eden kept trying to tell her mother.

'Mum, I've got to talk to you for a minute.'

'Not just yet, darling, it's a bit busy. Can we leave it till later?'

'OK,' said Eden, 'but you need to know, I do need to talk to you.'

She tried several times and each time Meg slipped out of the way.

'Just need to go down and check with the caterers. Go and see if your Aunt Sonya's all right.'

'Mum, all I need is five minutes,' said Eden.

Her mother turned and looked at her.

'Are you coming to tell me that your father got very drunk last night?'

Eden wasn't often lost for words, but she was now.

'Yeah,' she said.

'I thought as much,' said Meg. 'I tried to ring him this

morning and his phone was off. His phone is never off, except when he's AWOL.'

'Oh Mum, I'd have once said you'd be crazy to go through with this but nowadays, I judge less.'

Meg looked at her in delight.

'Good girl!' she said. 'It comes to us all. Once you stop judging people, life is easier. We all have our paths. You can't understand me marrying your father again but I have my reasons. Besides, I'll decide when I see him, when I talk to him. He's going to be here at one o'clock.'

'I hope so. Ralphie and Steve are trying to sober him up.'

'Your father was always pretty good at sobering up,' Meg said calmly as if she were talking about something very simple.

'I'm not sure I understand you, Mum,' said Eden.

'It would be very dull if you did, darling,' replied her mother.

'I love you,' Eden said, 'but you're quite nuts, you know that?'

Eden thought about Savannah. She couldn't tell her mother now. Not before the wedding. That would be cruel.

Eden wandered through the hotel, thinking. The family was awash with secrets.

She thought of her own and how she'd been so afraid it would derail her career. But would it? Women in politics had a lot to contend with. The Great Enraged who hit social media with viciousness every time a woman said something they disagreed with. Mention women's fear of walking alone at your peril. Mention the MeToo movement and someone would shut you down. Her secret was all about the intricacies of being a woman and how women had to carry the can.

In her rambling walk, she found herself in the old library. It was only a bit of a library now. The books were mainly long gone. Her parents had kept lots of fabulous books in here, books they'd found in old bookshops and second-hand shops and charity shops. With some bought by the yard, the way decorators did. Gibbon's *Decline and Fall*, bits of sets. Some

Dickens, a few *Reader's Digest*, with their abridged versions of novels. The old cabinets were incredibly dusty.

There was one very elderly moth-eaten couch that nobody had taken. And some stools and an armchair that possibly housed mice now. It was still a beautiful room. The rich, dark green walls, the long sash windows, the view out to sea. Sometimes, when there weren't guests like at Christmas, the family would come in here and play games. All sorts of games, Monopoly, Mine a Million, which had been Pop's favourite game and some sort of casino thing he had, which had a genuine roulette table. He loved that.

She found out she was pregnant at Christmas. She'd been scared, the way only a seventeen-year-old could be scared, she thought. She'd sat in her and Savannah's room, quaking, feeling utter fear. What if she was pregnant?

Stress could make periods late, she knew that. And Jimmy had pulled out. It couldn't have happened. He hadn't had condoms, they hadn't planned it. It was stupid, she'd meant to go on the pill. But that meant going into town to a clinic because she couldn't go and see old Dr Timmy, who was the doctor they'd all gone to see as children.

Indy, who was studying nursing, had said she'd bring Savannah and Eden to a clinic to get them fitted out with the pill. Then Mum had suddenly decided that she would.

'You're my daughters, it should be me,' she'd said. 'If you're going to be sexually active, I think we need to take proper precautions.'

Eden had found her mother's involvement in the whole thing slightly freaky. There was so much shouting at home now. Mum was stressed. Dad was a nightmare. Every night was a drinking night. And there were rows, such rows. Getting out of the house with Jimmy, climbing on the back of the motorbike, pulling on her helmet and roaring down the roads had been such an escape. Jimmy's parents were never home.

They worked very hard and now that Jimmy was nineteen, they expected him to get on with things. He was in college, first year, doing business. Eden was doing her final year in school. So far, they'd had sex, but Jimmy had used condoms.

That night, Jimmy had none. She hadn't been to the clinic to get the pill. She just wanted to get away from home, to be held, to be in someone's arms and feel safe. Jimmy had lit the fire in his parents' house in the basement and they'd sat looking at the TV, trying to figure out what stuff they'd watch.

'Got this DVD,' Jimmy said and found *9½ Weeks*. 'Mum and Dad had it upstairs. It's ancient, sort of dirty, but not too dirty.'

'I don't want to see anything dirty,' Eden had said irritably. 'I want nice.'

'Fine,' he said, 'you pick. I'll get the wine and the glasses.'

Jimmy would be driving her home. He regularly drank and drove the motorbike, something Eden knew was wrong, even though she told her parents that he would never do such a thing.

'He's really safe,' she'd say.

He'd only have a couple of glasses of wine and maybe a beer. But Eden knew it was risky. Still, risky was good, risky would show them; what if she did have some horrible accident and was lying in hospital? Maybe then they'd think about her, maybe then her parents would stop fighting with each other. Maybe then it wouldn't be the *Meg and Stu Show*. Maybe then they'd have time for their kids.

She and Jimmy had lain down on the couch and drunk and talked and eventually they'd forgotten about the film. It was *The Bodyguard* with Whitney Houston, another of his parents' films because *9½ Weeks* had gone missing. The Bodyguard was lovely and sad. It made Eden cry even before the end, because her emotions were so up and down. But that night they hadn't got as far as the end.

They'd made love and, due to the lack of a condom, Jimmy had pulled out. But still Eden felt pinpricks of anxiety afterwards. They lay there naked, wrapped around each other, films of sweat over their bodies. And she was trying to think how beautiful this was and at the same time she was thinking, *Shit, shit! That pulling-out thing doesn't work, we should have used a condom. Oh shit, shit, we should have waited, why didn't we wait?*

Two days before Christmas, Eden had gone into the city and bought a pregnancy testing kit.

Why are these so expensive? she remembered thinking. She'd got one with two tests, and she couldn't wait until she got home to try the first one. She'd gone into a department store with toilets and peed on the little stick there, waiting for three minutes.

It didn't take three minutes; she could see the second blue line creeping up slowly. It had to be a mistake, it had to be a mistake. She came out of the cubicle, reeling.

Somehow, she'd got home.

The second test was waiting, screeching in her handbag to be used. The first one, proof of what she didn't want to know, was also in her handbag. On the train home she kept looking at it in the depths of her handbag so that nobody else could see. It must have been wrong, there were bound to be false positives, she thought, trying to think herself out of it.

There'd been a friend of hers who'd got in the train at Sandy-cove. Jill, she sat beside Eden and chatted away. They were in the same class at school, Jill was doing chemistry.

'I don't know how I'm going to do this, it's very difficult, the higher level. But I love to do science.'

Jill wittered on and on about exams and college points and Eden couldn't have cared less. She listened with about a quarter of her brain and made the right noises but all the time she was thinking, *What do I do if the second test says the same thing?* Because in her heart of hearts she knew it would. She was pregnant. And for a pregnant seventeen-year-old, there was only one option. The boat to England for an abortion. Single women with babies did not have the best time in Ireland. Illegitimacy was still on the statute books.

Eden could not bring a child into the world now. She was a teenager. How could she be a mother? She still needed her own mother. No, she thought, she couldn't, there was no way. She could not have a baby, not now. She didn't know if she wanted kids anyway, full stop.

Which made it stupider to have sex without a condom, without the pill, without *two* condoms. She was never having sex again and she could not have a baby. She looked out the window and listened to Jill discussing whether Hamlet was a hero or an anti-hero.

'Don't you think that's an interesting way of looking at things?' said Jill. 'I mean, he's paralysed by his indecision. Is it an oedipal thing with his mother? I don't know, I've been doing research. I know they only want you to answer the way they want you to answer. But still, there must be extra points for thinking outside the box.'

Eden dragged her gaze away from the window.

'There are no points for thinking outside the box in exams,' she said, 'not in your Leaving Cert. Get real, Jill. Tell them what they want to know.'

Jill startled. 'You're very grumpy,' she said.

Eden laughed, she would love to have said, 'I've got my period, so I'm hormonal.' But she hadn't. She was hormonal all right, but nothing to do with her period.

The question was: how would she get the money to go to London for an abortion? Because that was the only sensible option now.

Savannah

Savannah's bridesmaid's dress was a pale-pink sheath which showed off the faint dusting of sun on her shoulders and probably, she thought, showed up the boniness of her chest too much. She wished she'd brought a shawl to put over herself. She knew that, beside her sisters, she'd look very thin. But it was going to be fine, it was going to be a lovely day. She thought if she said it enough to herself, she would convince herself and she had to smile. Because Clary was there, dressed in her pretty princess flower-girl outfit, looking adorable beside Minnie and Daisy, her cousins. Because she was older than them, Indy had put Clary in charge of the two smaller girls.

'Now you're the grown-up cousin,' she'd said.

And Savannah had wanted to hug Indy at that moment for being so kind. Savannah couldn't stop thinking about what had happened at school during the week. She knew, intellectually, that whenever Calum got very angry about something, it took her a few days to get over it.

After perhaps a week, things would somehow have slipped back into normality. Their normality. He would be fine and calm and she would finally begin to unclench her body and let some of the stress out. But that week was always hell, and now they were right in the middle of it.

She'd gone earlier to the hotel with Clary and it had been lovely because they'd played music along the way and sung. But now she could see Calum had just arrived and he was walking in with Anthony and Philip, of all people. Anthony and Philip were beautifully dressed. Anthony had the most exquisite taste. And today he was wearing a lilac shirt that showed off his Mediterranean dark, good looks.

'Must have been the window cleaner, darling,' he'd often said laughingly to Savannah. 'My dad's a redhead,' and they'd both giggled.

She thought that Anthony quite liked Calum, which was both good and bad and the three of them seemed to be joking and laughing as they walked in. And then she could see it, that infinitesimal change in her husband's face as he heard something he didn't like. It was so subtle but she recognised it: his expression would change, just a tiny fraction. Only she and probably Clary would be able to recognise it. To everyone else he'd still be the smiling, charming Calum. But she knew better. What had Anthony said to him? Against her better judgement she rushed over to find out, because it was better to know now and then maybe she could try to fix it. If she fixed it, it would be OK and then he wouldn't be angry with her. Because she couldn't cope with his anger on this important day. She could feel her heart racing. She knew that thoughts were spiralling around her head at speed.

She raced up to Anthony, Philip and Calum, said, 'Hello, hello, Anthony, Philip, you look wonderful. Darling.' She laid a hand on Calum's arm and he jerked his arm away.

Nobody else would have seen it, but she felt it and she knew what it meant. He was angry, ragingly angry. He shot her a look, rich in fury, and she quailed, felt herself move backwards until she was banging into the wall.

'Oh, sorry, sorry.'

She moved again and nearly toppled over some flowers, ones she had put there herself only yesterday.

'We were just talking about the new packaging,' Anthony said. 'It's stunning. Savannah is a genius, isn't she?'

'Of course,' agreed Philip, smiling down at his partner. Philip was very tall, something Anthony loved.

Normally, Calum did not like to stand near tall men, but he had no option at this exact moment. He'd move away soon, naturally.

Savannah knew Calum hated being five foot eight, which is why she didn't wear heels anymore.

'This place is absolutely beautiful,' said Philip, looking around, 'I've always wanted to see inside it.'

'It's a bit run down now, though,' Savannah said sadly, looking around. She almost wasn't sure what she was saying, she was rattling the words out.

'Yes, you'd need millions to make this liveable,' commented

Calum, looking around with contempt in his eyes and in his voice. 'Savannah, a word.'

She thought she was going to pass out.

Sometimes, when he was angry, he waited until they were at home before he said anything. But today, clearly, he was going to say it here and she didn't know how she was going to cope.

'This way,' she said. 'Everything is all right, isn't it, darling? I mean, the old place looks lovely.' She was overtalking, she knew: compensating. Trying to make him forget.

He walked along behind her.

'The bloody packaging, they're all *still* talking about it.' His voice was menacing and low. 'Nothing about what I do. No, it's all "Isn't Savannah brilliant"—'

Savannah led him into a small hall off the breakfast room. It was a little room where she and her sisters, as waitresses, used to keep cutlery and fresh glasses when they were helping out in the hotel. It was a little hidey-hole where nobody could see you, but you had to keep your voice down. Savannah didn't know why she'd led him in there. It wasn't the most private place, they wouldn't be seen but they might be heard.

'Anthony was telling me how they all think you're a creative genius. That humiliates me,' hissed Calum.

He couldn't bear people to think that she had talent – it had to be all him, the focus must remain on him. 'You've made me look stupid, you bitch.'

Eden came out of the library, the decision made. She would not keep this secret anymore. She felt freer for having made the decision.

Idly, she wondered if they'd done the right thing in delivering her father to the wedding. Had it been a massive mistake? But her mother seemed happy enough with it as a concept. The way she'd put her arms around Pops had made something in Eden sigh with happiness. They loved each other and her mother was prepared to marry her father in spite of everything.

Eden could not argue with her, not now, not today when her mother was determined. Weddings brought out heightened emotions in everyone, and even though Indy, Steve, Ralphie and herself had calmly pointed out that there was a certain risk involved, Mum wanted to go ahead.

Who was Eden to stop her?

She arrived in the ballroom, which was steps off the breakfast room, and looked around. It was nearly time for the wedding to begin and where was everyone? The guests weren't all here, which was typical for people going to the Sorrento. Everything started late – they probably thought the wedding would be Robicheaux-style late too.

The musicians were playing, there were drinks being circulated, fabulous smells were emerging from the kitchen and the old place looked pretty amazing, she had to admit it. All the flower arranging yesterday and the hanging of bits of muslin and Vonnie's lovely silk flowers, and even those bonkers fake feathers that Vonnie had come up with – it all looked fabulous. There were probably enough tea lights spread around the place to constitute a fire hazard, but whatever. And then she saw Savannah with Calum in the small hall. He looked furious, his face a mask of rage.

Indy and Rory were beside her in an instant, with Chantal bringing up the rear.

The four of them looked over at where Savannah was standing with her husband.

'He is not a nice man,' said Chantal. 'Cold. I think he hurts Savannah.' There, she'd said it.

'He couldn't,' began Indy. 'She'd tell us, surely?'

Eden looked at her. 'No, she wouldn't. People don't. That's the whole point, people don't. He might be beating her or he might not. There are lots of different forms of abuse. But look at her. She's like skin and bone, she's frail, she could float away. And she's scared. I've been trying to figure out what it was all week, and now I know.'

They all kept watching.

'She's scared all the time. Did you see Clary today? She's the same. They're like two beautiful little scared creatures wandering through the world, waiting for someone to save them. And I never noticed.'

'I'll fucking kill him,' said Rory.

'No, that's not the way we're going to do it,' said Eden, icily cold. Everything was coalescing in her brain. There were so many things she had to sort out. The abortion, her political career, moving forward, abuse against women. Making sure that that bastard got what he deserved.

How had she missed it? Her own sister. Her twin. But then again, as the woman in the shelter had explained to her, this always hid in plain sight. Street angel/house devil.

Not anymore.

Eden was still trying to figure out exactly how to prod Calum when she saw it happening in front of her eyes.

Quickly and quietly she made her way over to the little hall. It was open from both sides, an open doorway into the hall towards the ballroom and kitchen or into the breakfast room itself.

'You stupid fucking bitch. How dare you make me look stupid.'

For a second, Eden just listened in absolute astonishment. And then the part of her that functioned at a high political level clicked in. She reached for her mobile phone, which she'd hung around her neck because of the tiny little bridesmaid's bag, and clicked on the record button. Indy and Rory came quietly up behind her.

Calum was ranting.

'First, you make the decision without asking me and then you take all the credit, making me look foolish. How dare you, how dare you treat me like this. You'd be nothing without me, you bitch, nothing!'

'It was just an idea,' Savannah stammered, 'and I can say it was your idea.'

'No! They all know you came up with it, you vicious bitch.'

'I'm sorry,' Savannah was saying, crying with apology.

Eden felt her heart ache at her sister's distress.

'You know fuck all, Savannah. You play with scents with Anthony but that's just messing around. I understand business, not you.'

Eden listened coldly. Savannah had set up that business long before she'd met Calum, it wasn't his idea. Stupid prick. He'd been hanging onto Savannah's coattails, pretending he was the big business man while he frightened her to death.

'Don't think you can hide things from me ever again, you know I'm in charge of the finances. You know I'm the one who takes control; me, not you.'

'I know, I know, it was just an idea. We can change it if you like—'

'No, you won't, I'll take over, you're not fit to run something like that. Just the way you're not fit to bring up our daughter. Like what happened this week when she freaked out in school, that's all your fault. It's all your fault.'

His voice was so full of rage: it was breathtaking. Eden knew of nobody on the planet whom she would speak to in that way and yet here Calum was, speaking to his wife, darling Savannah, like she was dirt on his shoe.

'I don't know why you can't get anything right, you're such a useless bitch.'

'I know, I know, I'll do better,' Savannah said, craven, crying. 'You know Clary's doing really well now and we're going to do the ballet camp this summer and—'

Eden thought she might go in and stab her brother-in-law, but she waited. She had the steel in her soul now. A cold steel. Waiting was a good political tactic. She would give Calum enough rope to hang himself in every court in the land.

'I don't want this ever to happen again. We need rules,' he was saying, hissing. 'Rules that you do not break. So, in future, you do not spend money in the company without my say so. In fact, I need to be at all the meetings in future.'

'Of course,' said Savannah.

'Nothing happens that doesn't go through me. Have you any idea how I felt when that little moron Anthony was telling me about how the packaging was your little secret, do you know what that was like?'

'No,' said Savannah.

Eden really wanted to kill him. She could hear the abject fear in her sister's voice. She understood everything now. She understood that Calum was a bully and was emotionally abusing her sister, coercively controlling her. Imagining that he was in charge of her business, a business that she'd set up. And he was putting boundaries around that. What had happened with Clary earlier in the week, why hadn't Savannah said anything to her? But then Eden knew. Women who were abused didn't talk about it. They thought it was all their own fault, they kept the silence, because the abuser had convinced them that they were useless.

It was a clever, complex piece of manipulation: another type of domestic abuse where the abused thought they were in the wrong.

'I'll tell you something, you stupid little bitch,' Calum was saying, 'it's going to be all changed now.'

'Of course, of course,' said Savannah.

'I'm in charge. If you so much as make a decision to order printer ink without my say so, I'll rip your fucking head off.'

'Will you?' said Eden, standing at the door jamb, ice in her voice. 'That's a very interesting statement, Calum. Very threatening, actually, I have to say. I'm really astonished you speak this way, because I've never heard you talk like this before. But I get a feeling—' she looked at his blazingly angry face and then at Savannah's terrified one – 'I've a feeling that this isn't the first time you've spoken like this to my sister.'

'It's none of your business,' he said.

'Oh, I see the mask takes a minute to go back on,' said Eden, cheerfully. 'That's interesting to know. Because clearly this sort of thing happens all the time and you're all sweetness and light afterwards to the rest of us and poor Savannah is in bits.'

Savannah was shaking, Eden could see it. She reached over and held her sister's arm.

'It's OK, Savannah,' she said, 'this won't happen again.'

'No, it's fine, she doesn't mean it,' said Savannah in desperation to her husband. 'Everything's OK, really, everything's OK.'

'Oh, everything *is* OK,' said Eden, and she held up her phone. 'Everything is OK because I've been taping you, Calum, and it's a very interesting tape. Before you try and grab my phone, I've already emailed the tape to a friend of mine in the police. So, it's sorted. Do you want to go now? Or will you wait until the police get here?'

'What do you mean, the police?' he said arrogantly. He didn't look in the slightest bit upset.

'There's legislation,' said Eden softly. 'Legislation against coercive control. It's a criminal offence now and you are clearly inflicting abuse upon my sister. Abuse does not have to mean physical attack. It can mean an emotional attack, controlling, abusing, screaming at, that's all abuse. And you're doing it to Clary, too. People are going to be really interested to read about the court case about how you abuse your wife and ten-year-old daughter too. Locking up isn't good enough for people like you—'

He was backing away now.

'You're a fake, Calum: a big fake. Full of pretentions, delusions of grandeur and entitlement. You want to be someone and if you can't, you want to destroy the woman who loves you.

'You hate anyone knowing the truth. That's the thing, Savannah,' she said, looking at her sister, who was now struck dumb with fear. 'He's a bully, at its most simple. I can guarantee that Calum will go now and he won't be back, because,' Eden waggled her phone towards him, 'he's on tape threatening you. He's on tape threatening you in a coercively controlling manner and it's obvious he's doing the same to your daughter. They are criminal acts,' she repeated, 'criminal. Do you understand that, dickhead? So why don't you leave, go home, get your things, and don't think about wrecking the house or destroying everything that belongs to Savannah,' Eden said. 'Because I'm going to ring my friend in the police now and get them over to the house. You should go quickly in case they're there to arrest you. Diarmuid will phone them too. Get your stuff, just your stuff, and leave. Leave your keys too, because you won't be going back. I'll throw everything else out on the road later when the bin truck's due so they can drive over it, OK?'

'You can't.'

'Oh, I can,' hissed Eden. She looked at Calum and her eyes were full of rage and hate. She saw that he was afraid. 'Look at him,' she said, 'look at him, Savannah, he's scared.'

'I'm not fucking scar—'

'Shut up, you dickhead. You've only got one more thing to say,' said Eden, 'and that is that you're sorry.'

'I won't say it.'

Eden stepped forward. She was taller than Calum because she was wearing high heels. She stared down at him. 'Say you're sorry to my sister,' she hissed. Without him knowing, she clicked the button on her phone again, the button to record; it was handy being so adept.

'You're a coward,' said Rory unable to stop herself.

'Oh yeah? In your dreams,' he said.

'I will put my boot through your balls and we'll see who's dreaming then,' said Rory.

'Calum,' hissed Indy, feeling anger like she'd never felt in her life, 'you are such a bastard. You deserve whatever the judicial system can do to make you pay.'

'I'll destroy you first, all of you,' he snarled. 'You think you're all so high and mighty—'

At that moment, a hand reached around his neck and pulled tight.

'Have you been threatening my daughter?' growled Stu Robicheaux. He was older but taller and stronger, and he had rage on his side.

Savannah was sobbing now.

'Savannah, come with me,' said Chantal gently. 'We need to fix your make-up. Eden, the police?'

'Yes.' Eden beamed. 'I know just the people. This needs to be done quietly and subtly and—' she leaned closer so she could whisper – 'I will destroy your career, not that you have much of a career, but believe me, it will be destroyed. You'll never do this to another woman, because I'll make sure of it.'

Her father tightened his grip around Calum's neck.

Calum tried to straighten himself up but Indy got in there first. She slapped him hard across the face with a hand that had tended many women's bodies before and, for the first time, was punishing a man for hurting one.

Everyone turned to look.

'You absolute piece of shit,' she said loudly. 'When this family is finished with you, you will know about it.'

With Rory on one side, and Steve, who'd materialised from nowhere on the other, they frog-marched Calum from the hall.

'The police will be at the house with one phone call,' said Eden, following them. 'My father-in-law will keep an eye on you till then. Diarmuid's very good with difficult people,' she added. 'He can make some calls. Get his guys to accompany you. Diarmuid,' she leaned in, 'knows some very scary people.'

In one of the bedrooms, the sisters gathered and took care of Savannah. Chantal made up her face again, Indy stroked her hands, Rory stirred sugar into some strong tea and Eden comforted her.

'The police take domestic abuse very seriously.'

'It wasn't—' began Savannah.

Eden held her. 'It was, darling. It's going to take time for you to process, but it was. It's OK, though: it can only get better now.'

'We're here. You and Clary will never have to go through that again.'

'We promise.'

'Let's not tell Mum, not till later.'

Savannah began to cry again. 'I wanted to tell you all but—'

'It's not your fault,' said Indy and Eden in tandem.

'You're not responsible for what he did,' Rory said, her hand shaking as she stroked her sister's hair. 'We should have seen.'

Savannah looked at them all now. 'I couldn't bear to let you see and at the same time, I thought he was right: that I was this dreadful person . . .' She shuddered. She still felt so scared.

Her family were telling her she was safe but she didn't feel it: she still felt the fear.

Eden knelt on the floor in front of her.

'You're still scared, aren't you? It will get better,' she said. 'Slowly but it will. I know just the people to help.'

Agnes Tallisker's present had been a string quartet. And as Meg Robicheaux and her bridesmaids and flower girls processed down through the assembled people into the garden, where a beautiful archway had been decorated with silk flowers, the string quartet played. Meg smiled at the people around her, breathed in the scent of the roses from the hotel garden she had once tended and looked to where the love of her life stood beside the registrar. Stu had always had an amazing ability to recover from all-night benders. And he'd outdone himself today. He looked tanned and healthy. As she got closer, she could smell the Vetiver cologne he wore. His eyes were a bit bloodshot, she thought, but that was OK. She turned and smiled at Rory, who wore the most beautiful dark suit as she escorted Meg down the aisle.

'Thank you, darling,' she said.

Rory grinned. She looked lighter. Meg turned and smiled at

all her attendants and beamed down at her three flower girls. They went and sat down. Should she marry him? Meg thought, looking at Stu. She leaned closer to him so that nobody else could hear.

'I heard,' she said. 'We can't get married unless I know that's never going to happen again.'

'It won't,' he breathed.

She could see anxiety in his eyes.

'Will you go to rehab?'

'Yes.'

'Really go to rehab? Because if you don't, I will leave you here or leave you when you refuse, and that will be it. I will never see you again, Stu Robicheaux.'

'I'd do anything for you, I'm sorry, I'm sorry,' he said, holding her hands and looking down.

'I need you to do it for yourself. It's no good if you're doing it for me. Yes, it will be for us and our future, but you have to do it for you.'

The celebrant gave a little cough as though to say she was aware something deep was being discussed, but that she had another gig on somewhere.

Meg nodded to her. 'Just sorting something out,' she said in a low voice. 'Well?'

'I'll go, if you drive me.'

'That's a deal,' said Meg.

Stu wasn't the only gambler in the family.

She turned and smiled tremulously at her four daughters and she saw Chloe out of the corner of her eye. Poor Chloe, unsure of her welcome.

As if Meg Robicheaux would turn her husband's secret daughter away. What sort of uncaring woman did they think she was? She was Meg, Queen of the Sorrento, ready to take on anything, modern goddess.

Savannah's eyes were red but she looked less stressed. Something had gone on there. Eden was holding onto her twin as if holding her upright. Eden really held them all together, Meg thought. Who'd have believed it. She beamed at her daughters, her grandchildren and her dear friends.

'I think we're ready to get married,' she said to the celebrant.

And amid the sun and the hazy scent of roses with insects buzzing lazily in the background, the string quartet playing, and family and friends watching them happily, Stu and Meg Robicheaux got married for a second time.

Civil ceremonies could go in many directions, and Meg and Stu had decided to make theirs like an ancient Celtic one. Outside, in the garden, under a beautiful woven trellis full of real and fake flowers and Vonnie's pretty silken roses, the celebrant got them to hold hands.

'This handfasting,' she said as she tied the crios around their hands, 'is a sign of a bond that cannot be broken. It is a sign of love that goes back thousands of years on this island. A love of the land and the creatures of the land, a belief in the goodness of people, a belief in the love of two people who have chosen to live their lives together. Your hands tied together, held together, symbolise this.'

Indy stood beside Savannah, her arm around her. Clary was in front of them. Chantal was holding her hand.

'You know, Clary,' whispered Chantal, 'Rory and I are going to have a baby. Not yet but soon.'

'Really?' said Clary, whispering back.

'Yes, really, and I think you should be godmother. You are very good with little children. Minnie and Daisy adore you.'

'Me?' Clary was astonished at the honour.

'Yes, you,' said Chantal. 'You'll be nearly eleven or twelve,' she closed her eyes and prayed, 'so, though you'll be a cousin to the baby, you'll be almost like an auntie, because you're older. It'll be super fun. You're so wise and clever. Would you do that for us and the baby?'

'I'd love that. Will you be getting a puppy too? My friend Alice in school got a baby and a puppy.'

'You want a puppy?' said Chantal.

'Yes, but Daddy won't let us . . .' began Clary.

'Oh, I think Mummy will let you get a puppy,' said Chantal.

Behind her, Savannah felt the tears course down her face. She couldn't quite believe what was happening.

The celebrant was continuing: 'As you hold each other's hands, you know that these hands will love you through your lifetime. These hands will comfort you, cook when you are ill, feed you when you cannot move, wipe away your tears of sorrow, stroke your face at tears of joy.'

The family watched Stu and Meg looking lovingly into each other's eyes.

'As your love endures, remember that love exists in the sky, in the clouds, in the rain. When it rains, we know that the water will give rise to crops that will feed us. We know that the sun will come out. We know that the great cycle of life will continue. That you will be there for each other during the struggle of life and during the great joys of life too.'

Eden thought she might cry.

It had all seemed such a wild proposition at the start and yet now, here, on a day when so many things were happening, this handfasting was the perfect wedding.

She wiped away her own tears of joy.

'Will you, Stuart Robicheaux, pledge yourself, handfast yourself, to this woman for the rest of your life?'

'I will,' said Stu gravely.

'Protect her with your body and your mind and your soul, never raise a hand to harm her but protect her from all comers?'

'I will,' said Stu and he leaned forward and kissed Meg gently on the cheek.

'Will you, Margaret Eleanor Robicheaux, pledge yourself, handfast yourself, to this man for the rest of your life?'

'I shall,' said Meg.

'Will you promise to protect him with your body, mind and soul, never raise a hand to harm him and protect him from all comers?'

'I shall,' said Meg and she leaned forward and kissed him.

'You are handfasted before your family and friends, those gathered here who love you, joined together until the Great Mother takes you away from each other and you get to live in the eternity of her joy.'

Vonnie was ready with the rose petals, and she threw them into the air.

The string quartet started to play something very lively, and Meg and Stu embraced.

'Yeuch,' said some small boy who had broken off playing with his mother's phone for a moment. 'Nobody said there would be kissing.'

'I don't know why we didn't get married that way,' said Ralphie, leaning over so that he was speaking gently into his wife's ear. 'It's much nicer.'

'It is, isn't it?' said Eden. 'Completely lovely.' She leaned against him. He really was a darling, darling man.

16

One Month Later

The first week of August was around the corner and the countryside was golden. As Meg drove, fields of hay shimmered around, golden in the sun, waiting for the moment when the harvesters could shear the field. She was aware that, sitting beside her in the passenger seat, Stu wasn't shimmering with any sort of joy. He'd been silent for the first half-hour of the journey and Meg had let him sit there quietly. But now she was beginning to feel irritated. This was not the way this was supposed to go.

Stu was behaving as if he were going to the guillotine. Meg did not have the bandwidth for his backing out of this. It had been enough to find out about Savannah – oh God, her poor darling girl and what she and Clary had gone through – and try to cope with the anxiety and guilt over not seeing what was wrong in her daughter's life.

'None of us knew, Mum,' Eden had told her. 'That's how people like Calum get away with it. They divide their prey from the herd. Cut them off from everyone.'

Meg had spent a lot of time with Savannah and Clary, walking on the beach, talking in low voices when Clary couldn't hear, about what had happened.

Meg didn't know if she'd ever recover from hearing her daughter's stories.

'I should have stopped it, I should have known: I'm your mother!'

Savannah had smiled gently: she was smiling more these days. Just a little but it was noticeable.

'It's complex, Mum. He cut me off from all of you and he was so persuasive.' She couldn't say Calum's name. Didn't think she ever could again. 'It's not your fault, Mum. Please understand that.'

Now, a month after the wedding, Meg was driving Stu to the addiction centre, a residential facility where he would spend twenty-eight days working on his alcohol and gambling addictions. He had never done residential rehab before. And Stu agreeing to it was the only reason Meg had married him, a fact that still made Eden wince.

'Mum,' she'd said several times in her father's presence, 'I'll never be sure if this remarriage was a good idea.'

'Eden, you can be an awful cow, you know that,' Stu would say. 'I'm not drinking.'

Eden would look over at him. 'Well done, you. Let's have an award over here – Stu Robicheaux, for not drinking.'

'Darling, I just wish you'd support us,' Meg said.

'I do support you, Mum,' Eden said, 'I'm just not sure about Pops. I don't know if he has it in him.'

'That's a terrible thing to say,' Stu had said.

'I'm just telling the truth,' said Eden, 'that's what I do, tell the truth, no matter how tricky.'

'Your form of truth-telling is very vicious,' said her father grimly.

Today, Meg was driving down to Wexford to deliver Stu to the SAOR rehab centre. It had taken this long to get him in. Clearly the country was full of people who needed alcohol and gambling rehab.

'See,' said Stu in one of his lighter moments, 'there're loads of us out there.'

'I didn't marry the rest of them,' said Meg, 'I married you, I want you to get better.'

'Course I'll get better,' he said.

There was another forty-five minutes on the road at least.

Meg decided she needed a coffee. If she had to sit in silence, she needed caffeine. There was a service area a few kilometres away and when it appeared, she drove in, parked the car, put petrol in it, then poked her head back in the door.

'Are you coming?'

'What?' said Stu, still lost in space.

'Are you coming in, because I have to pay and I'm going to get a cup of coffee.'

'Ah, I don't know.'

'Come on in,' she commanded.

He got out of the car and followed her in.

'I'll pay and you can get me coffee,' she said. 'I'll have an almond flat white.'

'I remember when everyone just had an ordinary coffee,' muttered Stu.

She went to pay for the petrol, wondering if she'd have to go to jail if she kicked him out of the car when exiting the service area. What would she say to the judge?

I was bringing him to rehab and he annoyed me so much that I thought I'd just push him out the door, Your Honour. All it took was a little kick. He was annoying. There rests the case for the defence.'

A slightly hysterical giggle escaped her. Was she mad to have married Stu, knowing everything that she did? There were a couple of people in front of her in the queue and she turned around to see her husband at the coffee counter. He was carefully stirring sugars into one of the coffees. Not his, she knew, because he didn't take sugar, but into hers. He did it so gently that she felt a wave of tenderness rise up in her to meet his. She loved him. And if there was any chance she could help him get better, she would. For all that Indy said, rightly, that Meg could not make him get better.

'It's up to him, Mum.'

Back in the car, she took the chocolate bar she'd bought, broke it in two and gave half to him.

'You're going to need this,' she said, 'sugar. Apparently, people need lots of sugar when they give up alcohol.'

Stu looked at her. 'How do you know all of this?'

'I've been researching, darling. Can we talk?'

'Talk about what?' he said dully.

Meg got them back on the motorway. She knew there was no point in kicking him out of the car.

'Talk about us and the future,' she said.

'OK.'

'No, Stu,' she said again. 'Not me give out to you and you listen and be angry.'

He was silent. But she knew he was looking at her, watching her.

'Before, I didn't understand what was going on. I knew you were gambling and I thought you could stop.'

The silence from his side of the car was deafening.

'But I've been researching, Indy's been helping me. She said it's a disease and if we treat it like a disease and you get meetings with a twelve-step group, then you have some hope of getting better. But if you don't, you can't.'

Still silence from the other side of the car.

'You're an addict and I love you, so there's no point wishing you're going to get better, I have to try and be there with you, as you try and get better. But it's up to you.'

'Yeah, well, that's why I'm going to this place,' he muttered.

'You know, Stu, if you're just going there for me, it's not going to work.'

Meg felt her eyes fill up, which she knew was very dangerous when driving. She rubbed a hand over each eye.

'I love you and I'd love us to be together, which is why I married you. Eden thinks I was nuts.'

Stu laughed at this. 'You've got to hand it to Eden,' he said, 'she speaks her mind.'

'She gets that from you,' commented Meg, 'you speak your mind too.'

'Not all the time,' Stu admitted. 'Not when I'm trying to cover stuff up.'

'Yeah, but that's it,' Meg said urgently. 'That's what I've been finding out from reading articles online. This stops you being fundamentally honest. And we can't go forward as a couple unless you are, because I'll always be wondering. I'll always be wondering every time you go out if you're going out to drink and then to gamble, because you've always drunk too much, and when you drink too much, you gamble.'

'I don't always drink and gamble,' Stu said calmly. 'Sometimes I just gamble.'

'Which is worse, do you think? Which is strongest in you?' Meg said.

'Don't know,' Stu admitted. 'I can't stop when I start. I say I'm going to put just one bet on and then, suddenly, I think I'm going to get the money back, win it back. I'm in the hole and I'm stuck and I think I'll win the money back and it will be all right.'

He was animated now as he tried to explain. 'It's like this virus racing through me, this fiery energy, and I think, I'll bet on another horse, I'll make it work. And I'll have a drink and I'll bet again and – and I lose it. Then I have another drink to make up for losing.'

Meg reached out and grabbed his hand. He held hers tightly between both of his.

'I'm sorry I never explained it to you before, but I was ashamed, still am ashamed. I lost us our home.'

It was the first time he'd ever enunciated this fact to her. Meg felt her eyes fill up again and, this time, she didn't rub the tears away.

'I know,' she croaked. 'I was very angry for a long time about that. I was angry about Lori. And about poor Chloe. I was angry about so many things. But this is new, this is a new start, and this place we're going to is part of it. But only if you take it, only if you actually enter into it, for you first, not for us, you've to do it for you. Because if you don't want to do it, it's a waste of time and I won't be there when you come out. From now on, it's transparency, Stu. Transparency all the way.'

He squeezed her hand even more tightly. 'I want it to work,' he said. 'I'll make it work.'

'OK, then,' said Meg. 'Let's make it work.'

How do you feel? The very word *feel* made Savannah want to throw up. At the thought of feelings, the anxiety in her chest rose like she'd been thrown into a pool and the water was filling her up from the inside, about to drown her. That was it, it was a drowning sensation.

'Breathe through it,' said the therapist.

'I can't,' said Savannah.

'You can, breathe in and breathe out.'

Somehow she managed. 'It's the word feelings, I . . . when people say how do I feel, it's like I've a door locked and I open that door and everything comes tumbling out. I feel *everything*.'

'Perhaps because up to now everything was locked carefully away.'

'Yes, everything was locked away,' Savannah agreed, leaning back in the chair and trying to breathe. She'd been doing the sessions for three weeks now, two a week. It was very intense. But it was helping. It had taken three sessions before she'd been able to relax even a little bit. And then, things had come tumbling out of her.

'I have the idea of water,' she said to the therapist, who did not get up and offer her a glass. There were glasses with water on a low shelf near her. But that wasn't what Savannah meant and the therapist, Claire, knew it.

'Talk of feelings makes me feel this drowning sensation and then when I talk, it's like all the liquid is pouring out of me, like I'm draining it out, and yet there's still more, more and more and more. It's like I'm undammed. The dam has broken. Do you think I'll ever be better?' she asked suddenly.

Claire looked at her and did that thing that Savannah found deeply annoying. She turned the question back.

'Do you think you'll ever be better?'

Savannah laughed. 'I knew you'd say that,' she said.

'Excellent. So do you think you'll ever be better?'

'I don't know, better than what? Better to be like what I was before. I'm trying to remember before, but it's difficult. Because all I can think of is life with him.' She didn't say Calum's name anymore.

When she spoke to Clary about her father, she said Daddy. The fact that Daddy had gone from their lives was something tricky for Savannah to explain. And yet Clary had so far not made the slightest noise about seeing him.

Eden said he'd left the country, but he'd be back. Eden had said: 'Men like him always come back.'

His lawyers had sent Savannah a terse message that her husband would be back and they could resume their separation discussions then. An email which had made her hyperventilate. But she'd rung Eden. Eden had instructed her to ring any time she got upset.

'I got an email and—'

'Read it out to me,' said Eden calmly.

She hadn't said she was busy or that she was in a meeting. All Savannah could hear was some movement of chairs and a door shutting. And then Savannah was speaking to her again. 'Read it out to me and breathe.'

Everyone wanted her to breathe. How did they think she'd survived this long without breathing?

Savannah had read out the email.

'That's OK, it's good, he's going through the lawyers,' said Eden. 'He'll continue to go through the lawyers. You're safe, you don't have to see him again, ever, if you don't want to.'

'I don't want to see him,' Savannah had said.

'Diarmuid has the best lawyers. Let them handle it. You won't have any trouble from Calum ever again.'

'I'm terrified of seeing him again,' she said out loud now and Claire nodded.

'Can you tell me where that sensation of terror comes from?' Claire asked.

Savannah's hands reached down to her torso, automatically touching her chest and then her belly.

'Everywhere,' she said, 'everywhere. I can't bear the thought of having to see him or hear him or have him near me. I close down, lock myself into myself to be safe. Because I'm scared.'

'And you've been scared for a long time,' said Claire.

'Yes.'

'Savannah, I'm aware that what you have described, the relationship, the marriage, has been a very dark relationship. It was a relationship of emotional and physical abuse. It will take time to work through it, time for you not to be scared at the very thought of your ex-husband's name,' Claire said gravely. She used the word 'ex-husband', even though it would be a long time before Calum was an actual ex, but Savannah appreciated that so much.

'Yes,' said Savannah, sighing.

The session was nearly at an end when a thought came into her head. She'd been surfing the net, looking up information on women like herself, women who'd been – she hated the term, hated it, and yet it made sense – emotionally abused. Because Calum had hurt her physically on three occasions. Her finger still still ached, she thought, flexing it.

But abuse was abuse, the therapist explained. Calum's abuse of her was an emotional onslaught designed to destroy her. It was verbal, was the removal of affection, was the taking away of relationship, the silent treatment, the coldness, the sarcasm, the utter contempt.

That was emotional abuse, but was that her life? Had it been?

She and the therapist spoke about this endlessly. And sometimes Savannah slipped into thinking, *Was it that bad? Why didn't I do something about it, if it was that bad?*

She was drawn to reading about abuse online and she

compared herself to other abused people. Women who'd had jaws broken, been admitted to hospital. Was her abuse not so bad because her jaw had not been broken? Once, she'd read a negative comment from someone who'd angrily asked why none of the women had stood up to their attackers. 'Had they no backbone?' Savannah had winced at that.

Backbone to stand up to the person who controlled their every move?

Claire always brought her back to the central tenet of their therapy which was that nobody was allowed to treat her that way. Just because she had become used to it, did not make it right.

'I swing between two trains of thought,' said Savannah guiltily, 'between horror and thinking about him and the joy of being free of him, and then, then I think, was it *that bad*? Was it so awful, am I imagining it?'

And then she paused because this was strict therapy and what she wanted to explain was something she'd seen on social media. But she went ahead with it anyway.

'I read an amazing thing,' she said, 'about the type of tactics people use when they're emotionally abusing someone. They gaslight them. They say, "you're crazy, you're emotional, you're insane". They belittle you, they do all those things. And you—' she paused, – 'you do everything you can to make that not matter, to fix the relationship.' She felt shamed admitting this.

'If he said I was stupid, I was stupid. If he said I was over emotional, I was over emotional. And then I read this thing and it said you don't have to set yourself on fire to keep somebody else warm. I read it yesterday and it meant something to me, because I've been putting myself on fire for years to keep him warm. And I put myself on fire but I didn't know if he wanted to be warm. He might have wanted to be cold. But I would have done anything to make him happy, because then the torture would stop.'

'This has been a wonderful session,' said Claire. 'And that's a marvellous quote. Hold on to that if ever you doubt yourself. *You don't have to put yourself on fire to keep somebody else warm.* It's a wonderful way of putting it. You were never responsible for Calum's moods. But he made you responsible. And you took that burden. So our job here is to let you see that you do not take that burden for anyone. That was his burden. You have put out the fire.'

'Yes, thank you,' said Savannah.

Savannah picked up Clary from her friend Daniel's house. Daniel's mother had been such a tower of strength during the past month.

Savannah had not known what to say to people so she'd said nothing. Nothing about Calum leaving. And nobody had asked about him because they weren't used to seeing Calum, as it turned out.

Savannah was the one who took Clary to school, brought her to play dates.

Calum was always too busy.

The first week, when she'd gone round to pick up Clary from the play date she'd had in Daniel's house, Joyce had taken one look at Savannah and said, 'I'm not trying to be rude, but you look dreadful, Savannah. Come in for a minute, for a cup of tea and some sugar.'

'I can't eat sugar,' said Savannah, anxiously. She was quivering. She shook all the time as every bit of adrenaline in her body was speeding through her.

'Come in. You can tell me all about the wedding at the weekend,' said Joyce.

'Yes,' said Savannah mechanically.

'It looked lovely in the paper, I saw the picture today,' said Joyce. 'You've a beautiful family. They didn't have a picture of you. Come into the kitchen and sit, Savannah. You're deathly white.'

Savannah knew many people who would be interested in

knowing what was wrong with her for all the wrong reasons. But Joyce was not one of them.

She led the way into her kitchen, which was messy and homely.

'They're out the back on the trampoline with the dog.' The dog was a Labrador retriever called Sweetie.

Savannah loved dogs, adored that little pup her father had brought home all those years ago, and she peered out the window.

'Don't worry,' said Joyce, mistaking her look for concern. 'Sweetie is the most good-natured dog. I know people who don't have dogs get nervous but she really is great with kids, and she loves bouncing. She goes to the side when they're bouncing manically and then when they're tired and they sit down, she goes into the middle and jumps up and down. Very clever dog.'

Savannah laughed and then hiccupped and it turned into a cry.

Joyce went over and hugged her. At first Savannah couldn't bear the touch and then she let herself be enfolded and leaned against Joyce's shoulder.

'I'm sorry, I don't know what's wrong with me.'

'You're shaking and you're going to sit down, have a cup of tea and something to eat, because, Savannah, you do not eat. I don't think I've ever seen a morsel pass your lips. That's no criticism, no judgement, you'll find no judgement here,' said Joyce. 'But you need to sit down. Clary said something about her dad leaving.'

Savannah looked up, eyes huge. 'Yes.'

'It's OK, she's really happy about it,' said Joyce 'and that's good. Because he obviously needed to go.'

Her eyes were gentle as she looked at Savannah. And then Savannah couldn't keep it all in anymore.

'He was awful, awful. We were frightened of him, Joyce,' she said. 'He frightened me for years and he bullied me. Bullying and shouting and he had all these rules.'

'I know people like that,' said Joyce, softly. 'It's never easy to get out of that.'

'No,' said Savannah sadly, 'it's not. And my sister helped me because she overheard him at the wedding and—' she shivered – 'she made him go.'

'He went?'

'Yes, he went. Eden had the locks changed, the gate code changed, and he can't get back in. But I'm still scared.'

Joyce sat her down at the table, made some tea and put lots of sugar in it.

'Drink that, I've made some scones.'

Savannah could feel her stomach contract. 'No, I – I—'

'I know you don't eat and I know eating is very hard when you're stressed, but I think you should, just a little bit, maybe even a quarter of a scone.'

'OK,' said Savannah.

'Because you've got to show Clary that human beings eat, that women eat, that it's OK.'

Their eyes met.

'I was bulimic for years,' said Joyce. 'Then when I had the kids, I realised that I had to stop, because they'd know, they'd find out and they'd think that was normal. I didn't want them to think that was normal. It was normal for me, but it wasn't healthy. That's the right word,' she corrected herself. 'Healthy rather than *normal*. I mean, what's normal?'

'I don't think I've ever been normal,' said Savannah.

'It's overrated,' said Joyce.

Savannah drank the sweet tea and found something very comforting about it. She ate half a scone and instead of sitting in her stomach like a lump that she would want to expel or exercise out of her system, she allowed it to sit there, nourishing her.

'The thing is, Joyce,' she said, 'I don't feel safe in the house.'

'You think he'll come back even with the locks changed? You can always get some sort of court order to keep him away.'

'No, it's not that, it's the house, I don't like it. It's beautiful but it's all him.' She couldn't say his name. 'You do believe me, don't you?' she added suddenly. She never thought anyone would believe her because Calum was so good, so practised. Everyone loved him. Joyce looked at her with cool eyes.

'I believe you. I saw the two of you out together and it was obvious to me that you were a trophy. He didn't need to be kind to you because he had already won you. He needed to be kind to all the other trophies he hadn't won, all the other people he needed to engage with. Did you know Daniel hated him and children are amazing litmus tests of human beings? Same as dogs,' she said.

'I'd love a dog,' said Savannah. 'I've always wanted a dog but—'

'But he wouldn't let you have one.'

Savannah nodded. 'Am I pitiful?' she asked. 'Thirty-seven, my own business and I couldn't get my own dog.'

'No, you're not pitiful at all. My sister, whom I can introduce you to, was in a very similar relationship for many years. She can give you all the details, I'll put you in touch with her. She's a clever, wise woman and she got caught that way too. These men are good at pulling you into their world and then you're stuck. Why do you have to stay in that house?' Joyce asked suddenly.

'I mean, it's the family home and—'

'Do you own the business?'

'Yes.'

'And does he have his own business?'

'Yes.'

'Well, then, that house can be split between the two of you. Find somewhere else to live, rent somewhere where he's never been, where he can never come, where you can be safe. And get a dog or two.'

Savannah laughed. Clary would love that. It seemed so easy when Joyce said it: get a house, move out. 'All you need is to find a house, rent it, get movers to move your stuff, and you're gone.'

'That's just what I'll do,' said Savannah.

'Honesty,' said Eden, looking out over the assembled party in front of her, 'is what we're supposed to be about.'

One hundred and fifty faces looked up at her. Faces of all ages, but certainly there were more older male faces than female ones. She repeated the sentence.

'Honesty is what we're supposed to be about. But we can't really be honest,' she said. 'We can have honesty in what we hope for, say we hope for climate change or we hope for the health care system to work properly or for homeless people to be housed. But there are so many parts of our lives where we, women, can't be absolutely honest. Where we have to weigh our words carefully.'

The audience were with her at this point. Behind her, stood Agnes and she knew Agnes was with her. Ralphie was there too and Diarmuid. She could feel his tall stately presence behind her. And she knew that he was supporting her. But she also knew that if the party turned against her, really turned against her, Diarmuid's support would fizzle away like a spent match. Except that Agnes's support would not wither away. Agnes was with her. And for many of the party faithful, Agnes was the strong member of the Tallisker family. Agnes was the one who'd run surgeries and stepped in and found homes for people, defused difficult scenes, handled both the minutiae and the generalities of political life. Been there through years of party politics, international politics, moments of distress and trauma. Agnes had always been there by Diarmuid's side, sometimes showing him the right way to do things when it came to comforting people who'd been involved in tragedy. There'd been enough tragedy over the years. Agnes was the one people looked to, to see which way to sway. Tonight Agnes was on Eden's side.

'I know many of you think that I'm a shoe-in for the nomination for Fergal Maguire's seat, that my family-in-law will have tied up the seat for me.'

Eden did not know how she hadn't said Feral Maguire.

It was very hard to get his name right. She had to stop referring to him as Feral in private. Feral was there in person, teeth glittering. He really had huge canines, she thought, trying not to look at him. Word was that he'd head butted a constituent once and it had been nicely covered up.

There was definitely something of the night about Fergal.

'It would be an honour to serve—' Eden paused. She'd had trouble writing this bit. She couldn't possibly say, in Fergal's place, because really! An honour to serve in place of Fergal, the head butter. So she'd amended the speech. 'An honour to serve all of you in the Dáil. And because of my relationship with Diarmuid and the whole Tallisker family, I'm sure many of you feel that I've come up through the ranks very quickly. But my work in politics in Trinity showed my commitment to public representation from the very start. And when I began in politics, honesty was what I was looking for. But even then, I had secrets and I kept them close to me, because I was terrified that they would derail my political career. Even though those same secrets were the thing that had pushed me into politics.'

She definitely had everyone's attention now. She could see the cogs of their minds moving. What was she going to say next? Secrets? Something juicy, she could see them hoping.

'So tonight I'm here to give you the reasonably unadulterated story of me. Because I'm not going to stand on the ticket for the party without honesty. I can be diplomatic, hardworking, and I can work with anyone, but I'm here tonight putting out my core values, explaining who I am to you, so that when you choose who goes forward, you will choose knowing all the facts. Knowing who I am, knowing what I stand for. And you can decide if that's what you want for this party.'

'You're doing brilliantly,' whispered a voice behind her: Ralphie.

She took a deep breath.

'I've campaigned for women's rights for years but I never told you my own story because I was afraid – afraid that my story would mean I got drummed out of politics. I'd be no use and, worse, I'd be humiliated for being human, for being a scared seventeen -year-old. I was afraid of the Twitter trolls, the Facebook venom, the letters . . . I kept silent and that did nobody any good—' She paused, looked over the audience. 'When I was seventeen I got pregnant. It was the year of my final school exams and my boyfriend wasn't able for it and neither was I. I was too young to become a mother. So I did what thousands of Irish women had done before me. I got the boat to London where I had an abortion.'

There was a harsh intake of breath. No matter that abortion was now legal in this country actually saying that you'd had one and being a political representative was a bit like being Bill Clinton on the impeachment stand. Low murmurings began. But Eden stood up straighter.

'I know that's shocking to many of you. For some of you, it goes against your religious beliefs. But it was not against my religious beliefs.' She stared at them all. 'I think it's very hard to judge other people unless you're in their shoes. For so many years women have been judged by white middle-aged males.' She caught the eyes of many of the white middle-aged males now. 'And they've judged harshly. They've made the decisions, decided what was acceptable for us. Some political campaigns around the world are run on where the candidate stands on abortion – people, who do not care about the rights of children once they're out of the womb and living in poverty, claim to care deeply about them when they're in utero. Caring for one and not the other is not being pro-life. Pro-life is caring for *all* children.'

She could see the women in the room sit up straighter. She

knew she was risking her political career on this. Perhaps it would all fall apart, but then she could run as an independent. She didn't know. All she did know was that honesty was what she wanted from now on: no more lying, no more waiting for another letter to come into her house, threatening her, blackmailing her.

'I don't regret my choice now and I've thought of it often. I still don't have children but that's not the reason. That decision is between me and my husband. Some things are private. But because abortion is such a political football, I'm telling you all this now. There will be no skeletons falling out of my cupboards when I'm in parliament. Nobody will find any drink driving or crazy behaviour in my life. This is me standing in front of you, honestly. You know my policies, you know I fight for climate change, I fight for women's rights, I fight for the rights of women not to live in fear in their own homes because they're being abused, I fight for children's rights. I had an abortion. I'm a woman. There you have it. You can make the decision based on that.'

The clapping came from behind her first. She knew it was Agnes, Ralphie – and Diarmuid, because he had a very particular way of clapping. It was those huge hands. He could make a clapping noise that would be heard miles away. And then the women in the audience began to clap and stand up. There were more men for sure in the room, but the women were standing and some of the men, the younger men. And wow, Feral – Feral was standing. Eden wondered if he'd had a daughter who'd taken the boat. Many of the old white men here would have had daughters and granddaughters who'd had abortions and maybe they'd known and maybe they hadn't. But suddenly here was somebody putting it up to them, saying *this is life, this is reality: choose.* The clapping was deafening now. Perhaps, thought Eden, perhaps they would choose her.

*

The sisters thought that the Sorrento Hotel would be the perfect place for the new photo as a fivesome instead of a foursome. It would probably be the last time they would ever be there, Indy said, looking at it mournfully. More than a year had passed since the wedding. The acers were beginning to glow gold in the garden in the October sun and the place looked so beautiful.

Indy, who'd found she had green fingers with her own garden, looked at the now forlorn raised flower beds near the verandah and sighed.

'It's a waste, seeing all this life here, and it's going to be dug up.'

Eden had stared at it all and said, 'It's lovely, but you know you wouldn't catch me gardening.'

Indy had laughed. 'No, I don't expect I would, but I like it. There's something very calming about the fingers in the earth.'

'Makes a change from having them inside women,' said Eden.

'You really need that media training,' Indy had said.

'I wouldn't say that in public,' Eden had pointed out.

'Yeah, that's good,' said Indy, 'because I can't see that going down well on a political programme. I mean, there'd be a lot of guys in the audience who will have to turn around and puke.'

'Yeah,' said Eden. 'Isn't it funny, stuff that women have to put up with that make men want to get sick.'

'Breastfeeding,' Indy said. 'You have no idea, mention breastfeeding and grown men with many children turn pale.'

'Or periods,' said Eden, an evil grin on her face. 'Periods – you have no idea. I brought up the subject of period poverty recently, and I swear all the guys went white.'

'Not the younger guys?' Indy said.

'No, not the younger guys, but the older ones, the ones who talk about "women's problems" in inverted commas: they can't cope with female body issues. They're the ones who still think that period fluids are blue because that's what we see on the adverts.'

Now Indy really did laugh.

'Oh,' she said, 'makes me laugh so much, that blue liquid. When fifty per cent of the population know it's not blue.'

The two sisters grinned.

Indy turned her face up to the autumn sun. One day she and Steve might have a house in the country, but for now their semi-d suited her perfectly, because it was close to public transport and Minnie and Daisy would need that when they were older. Older. The thought still filled her with horror. Eight and seven now, but soon, all too soon, they'd be growing up and . . .

She knew what happened next from people she worked with. Women who started off with adorable little girls and boys and over the years had started talking about parties, nightclubs, teenage drinking and people getting sick in cars. Parenting was not for the faint hearted. That was why Indy thought she understood her parents better than Eden and Rory. Rory had a vision that parents had to be perfect. It wasn't like that: parents were just people and people messed up. Mind you, Dad had messed up rather spectacularly. Still, he'd got a place in rehab and since he'd left, he was making a go of it.

Back last summer, they'd had a family day where everyone came and told him how he'd hurt them. Dad had cried nonstop.

Savannah hadn't been able to cope with it and had left the group-therapy room.

Eden had gone with her.

She'd found her sister in the garden sitting on a bench, sobbing, and had held her until the sobs subsided.

Eden didn't try to predict why it had all upset her sister. She now knew what she didn't know, as Agnes would put it.

'Do you want to talk about it?' she asked finally.

Savannah wiped down her face with one sleeve. Her clothes were different now: no longer beautiful garments but long-sleeved T-shirts and jeans, or fleeces, if it was cooler. It was as if she'd shed the garments of the old Savannah and was considering what to wear as the new one.

'I can't stand the pain,' Savannah said. 'Any pain. Dad's pain, the pain of anyone listening pain—' She broke off. 'He isn't a bad person.'

'No,' agreed Eden. 'Nothing bad about him. Just an addict. Gambling, mainly, but when he loses, he turns to hash and booze to flatten the pain.'

They'd all got handouts from the rehab. The simple language had demystified the whole thing. Not that it was easier to handle – but easier to understand.

'Calum was bad. I let him be bad. I let him hurt Clary.'

Eden put her arms around her sister again. 'He's her father. You weren't responsible for his behaviour towards you or Clary. He was. You got out when you could.'

'But not soon enough.'

'You got out when you could. That's enough,' said Eden. 'You're a fabulous mother, Savannah. You are not to blame for what Calum did. You handled it the way you could. Given how strong you were at the time. Don't look back and blame yourself for what Calum did to you both. You were brave when you had to be. That's enough.'

She knew a lot more about physical and emotional abuse now because of her work with the women's abuse charities. The Freedom Party now had a very muscular legal approach to how legislation on abuse should be handled.

The rehab counsellor had explained that nobody could make Stu stop gambling or stop drinking.

'It really is up to him,' she said, 'absolutely nothing you can do. If he doesn't want to go along with it, he can spend twenty-eight days in here and that's money down the drain.'

'I'm hopeful after today,' Mum had said as they'd driven away. 'I suppose you all think I'm stupid for having just married him?'

'No,' said Indy, 'it was an act of faith, faith in him. I think it will work, Mum, because he loves you.'

Her mother had smiled.

Now Indy had put out lemonade, some strawberries she'd dipped in chocolate, watermelon, a bottle of wine, just one, and some glasses for cool drinks. Eden was bringing Chloe. They were last to arrive. Savannah had come in and asked for coffee, which she'd had with two sugars to Indy's amazement. Savannah still looked taut and anxious, but she was less shaky. And as Indy hugged her tightly, she could sense slightly less tension in her sister's body.

Rory was quieter, the belligerent teenager vanished from her persona. She hugged Indy warmly. 'Thank you for doing this,' she said. 'I couldn't really spring it on poor Chantal.'

Chantal's bump was very obvious now. She only had another three months to go, and Rory was, the other sisters agreed, wildly amusing as she ran around after Chantal, barely letting her hold as much as a handbag unless she hurt herself.

'You can't be too careful,' said Rory. 'She's very delicate. I should have carried this baby. I mean, I'm stronger and bigger than she is.'

'You can carry the next one,' said Indy mischievously.

'I will,' said Rory gravely. 'We're going to use the same sperm donor so they'll be related either way.'

Steve was organising his camera.

'I'll miss this old place,' said Indy, walking round, dead-heading the odd rose.

'Is Frank ever going to get around to turning this into apartments?'

'Who knows?' said Savannah. She and Clary were bringing round the dogs, two golden cocker spaniels mixed with a bit of something else. They'd been abandoned as part of a puppy-farm haul, left to drown because an accident with a kennel door left open meant they weren't pure bred.

Savannah had taken two.

Eden had said that Savannah had nearly taken the entire litter but she'd explained that six puppies was probably too much.

She and Ralphie had taken two as well, but Raspberry the cat still came into their house and made sure the puppies knew who was boss.

'Raspberry still rules the roost.'

The odd nasty letter also arrived but they'd managed to track down the sender. It transpired that somebody had been very upset about the water-treatment plant in Wicklow. A police warning had been issued and Eden was working out whether to progress with a case against the person who kept sending the letters.

'They're not aggressive,' she said. 'He's quite an elderly man and I do feel a bit sorry for him. He tells me things when I talk to him.'

'He still writes you mean letters,' said Ralphie, who got annoyed on her behalf and was all in favour of prosecution.

'I know, but he's miserable. His wife died. He wants to give out to someone. And he doesn't say I know what you did any more. He just blathers on about why we shouldn't have done what we did and gives out about the wind power and the turbines in the area.'

All the dogs wanted to be in the pictures.

While Savannah and Clary were determinedly trying to train theirs, Eden's and Ralphie's just raced around the huge garden in the Sorrento, nearly knocking Stu off his feet.

'Eden, your hounds are growing wild,' he yelled happily, carrying a basket with a picnic lunch in it.

'Eden, you're supposed to teach them how to sit, and stand and fetch and stuff,' said Clary. She'd grown into a very different little girl in the past year. She was no longer quiet, watchful. Instead, she was energetic, full of joy. Her friend Daniel and his mum were there too.

'Daniel, why don't you take my dogs,' said Eden, who didn't

really mind who took the dogs, as long as she didn't have to clean up their poops. 'Here are their leads and the two of you can train them. Right, OK, that's your job for today. I want them totally trained; I mean, I'm sure you can do it in a day.'

'Eden,' giggled Clary, 'you can't train them in a day.'

'Auntie Eden probably could,' said Savannah, smiling. 'Auntie Eden can do anything.'

Eden winked at her twin sister. Eden had managed to put the frighteners on Calum Desmond. He wasn't contesting the divorce and wanted nothing out of it, and had instead settled quite a bit of money upon Savannah. Eden had got Diarmuid Tallisker's pals to have a quiet word with him and tell him he'd better not frighten any other women ever again or they'd find him.

'He really thinks they're very dangerous men,' said Eden gleefully.

Ralphie had looked at her. 'They can be dangerous enough, you know, honey. If they thought he was beating up a woman ever again, I wouldn't say he'd get off lightly.'

'I'd beat him up myself if he did that,' Eden said, cold now. 'Actually, I'd get my sharpest kitchen knife and cut him to shreds.'

'You're funny when you're trying to be scary,' Ralphie said.

Eden smiled as if she really was trying to be scary. She wasn't. She was being honest. Nothing would ever make Calum pay for what he'd done to her sister and Clary but if he ever returned to hurt them, Eden would be there.

Stu and Chloe were in charge of the bouncy castle. It was going a bomb with Vonnie's grandchildren and two friends of Minnie's and Daisy's. Daniel and Clary had gone off with the dogs and Chloe kept peering round to make sure they were all right.

All the small girls wanted Chloe to bounce with them while the boys wanted Stu to keep climbing up the squishy ladder and slide down frontwards so they could giggle at him.

Steve was assisting in between working on the barbecue. Ralphie was in charge of drinks, which were mainly soft drinks, but some people were drinking wine. Not Stu, though. He'd got the message this time.

Rory wasn't drinking, either.

She knew she was more like her father than any of her sisters. Genetics, environment? Who knew. But she did not drink well and she did not want Chantal and their beloved baby to live with a heavy drinker. For the moment, she was managing not to drink but she could see her father very clearly within her. The urge to deal with feelings with a nice glass of wine was still there. She'd spoken to her father about it.

He'd said that he'd bring her to some of his twelve-step meetings if she wanted to go.

'I'm not that bad,' she'd said, outraged.

Stu had laughed. 'Funny: that's just what I used to say.'

Rory had gone back to hug Chantal. Chantal, now her fiancée, was her lodestone. With Chantal beside her, she would be safe.

Stu looked wistfully around the Sorrento. 'We'll miss the old place,' he said now to Meg, who was standing beside him. 'It's so beautiful. We had some fun here.'

'Yes,' agreed Meg. 'But life changes and we embrace the change.'

'For sure,' Stu said.

'You don't have to miss it,' said Sonya, coming up between them and putting an arm around each of them.

'What do you mean?' asked Meg.

'You are standing on Robicheaux land again,' Sonya announced. 'I bought it off your old pal, Frank – who drives a useless bargain, it has to be said. He never did get planning permission for all his apartments.'

'You're going to build apartments here?' asked Stu, aghast.

'No, you idiot,' said Sonya, the way only an older sister could. 'I thought we could renovate it and run it again like it

324

used to be, the Sorrento Hotel, only without the craziness and the owner going off gambling.'

There was a stunned silence.

'Really?' said Meg.

'Only if you're up for it. We'll figure a way to share it out. I still have the money my mother left me. Just because you ran through yours, Stu,' Sonya added, 'didn't mean I did the same. I invested mine and, let's face it, I've no family to leave it to. So we could get the Sorrento up and running again.'

'Wow,' said Indy.

'There's a certain notoriety to it, given that it's the setting for such a bestselling book,' added Eden. 'Albeit just the setting in a vague way. *Any resemblance to real people, etc., is purely coincidental—*'

Everyone laughed.

Rory's book had been a success but she had – with Savannah's help - learned how to control the narrative.

'I did it for so long,' Savannah said. 'Told one story and lived another. You decide what you want to say and say it. Don't let this book destroy our family.'

Meg looked at Eden. 'You knew about Sonya buying the hotel, didn't you?'

'I just knew because Aunt Sonya was talking to me about the whole planning situation and what we'd have to do and – you know it's doable. It'll take money but we could come up with some investors. Diarmuid's great at that sort of thing. Sleeping partners, not ones you sleep with,' she said to her father and then winked.

'None of your cheek, madam,' he said.

'Only teasing, Pops, darling,' she said.

'So the Sorrento could live again,' Rory said.

Steve's voice was heard over all others. 'Photograph, everyone. Can we get the whole family together for the first one and then the five girls.'

For a moment, Chloe looked unsure.

'Is it all right, me being in the photo?' she asked Meg, who was helping her down from the bouncy castle.

'You're stuck with us, darling,' said Meg, linking her arm through Chloe's. 'Too late to back out now. And wait till I tell you Sonya's news about the hotel . . .'

17

A Year Later

The locals loved the fact that the Sorrento was open again. It wasn't quite the grand hotel it had been, but a more relaxed version where people could have light meals at lunchtime and, in the evenings, a set meal in the dining room was available with organic foods, choices of vegetarian, vegan or fish.

Sonya Robicheaux ran the place with her sister-in-law, Meg.

Lorelei from La Maison Beauty Salon popped in all the time for the morning yoga classes that Meg ran in the barn. The women who'd wondered how Meg stayed so lean and fit understood it more as they watched their Amazonian yoga instructor bend gracefully and lean into an asana as if she'd been born a yogi.

Stu was heavily involved in the garden. Apparently, he'd got really into gardening when he'd been in the rehab place and he said there was such joy to be had in feeling life in the earth.

Of course, some of his old drinking pals thought this was stone mad but each to his own. Stu had given up gambling, but then so had Ferdie, and Ferdie had been sitting in bookies studying the form since he'd been about ten. They went to their twelve-step meetings, took one day at a time and avoided the same side of the street as the bookies'.

Ferdie had a green beanie hat he wore now and he helped Stu with the Sorrento's gardens so that the endless weddings that people wanted there were supplied with more and more corners of verdant beauty for the happy couples to be photographed in.

Rory and her partner, Chantal, had just been married in the hotel and their daughter, Lily, had been a flower baby, helped along by her big cousins, Clary, Minnie and Daisy. Lorelei's son, Artie, had been her best man.

The whole huge Robicheaux family had been there: cousins, aunties, dogs, the sisters, all five of them, and a host of publishing people who'd planned to stay for an appropriate amount of time and then decamp back to the city had ended up having to be poured into a mini-bus at the end of the night screaming about how they wanted just one more Gimlet and a bit more ABBA . . .

Rory's book had won big awards as it was, apparently, a 'searing emotional journey . . .' or was it a 'searching emotional journey . . .' Nobody could remember.

But the newspapers said it had been translated into loads of languages and there was a small but steady fan trail of twenty-somethings who made the pilgrimage to the Sorrento to have coffee where Rory Robicheaux grew up.

She was writing something for Netflix now, apparently. All about sex, someone in the pub had said.

'Sex?' said the pink-haired lady, who had acquired a fluffy beige teacup chihuahua called Muffin, who sat in her handbag on the seat while she ate her lunch on the terrace.

'Ah well, probably not,' said the landlord, who didn't want any elderly ladies having heart attacks on the premises.

'Loads of sex,' whispered his wife, who was in a book club with the pink-haired lady and knew her very well.

'Goodie gum drops!' The elderly lady clapped her hands.

Eden Tallisker had indeed been elected to parliament and was already shadow social welfare spokesperson. She was always in the newspapers, relentless in her campaigns for social justice and legal changes to make the world a safer place for women.

She had recently caused a Twitter storm by saying she didn't want children. That no, this had nothing to do with her abortion when she was younger. And that no, it didn't make her strange/weird.

'Saying it makes me honest,' she'd said cheerfully on every radio and television show. 'Not every woman wants children. And by the way, period blood isn't blue.'

Indy, the midwife, had been approached about appearing in a television series on midwives but had declined because she said she had to be focused one hundred per cent when she was in a delivery room.

The view in the area was that Indy was a great loss to the telly as she was so stunning, but they'd always been unusual, those Robicheaux girls.

Savannah, the one with the scented candle and lotion company, was seeing it go from strength to strength. All the posh stores around the world were stocking her products and she'd moved her factory further down the coast to cope with demand. The black and cream boxes were everywhere, on every 'must have' and 'hottest thing' list online.

Yet when you met Savannah Robicheaux in the flesh – she'd gone back to Robicheaux, as she'd split up from her husband – she was nothing like the titan of business you'd imagine. She wore jeans, trainers, a simple white shirt in summer and a sweater in winter. Her skin was amazing – 'my own products', she always said – and she wore almost no make-up. Chloe, the sister – well, half-sister – who'd come from Cork and seemed to have been with the family forever – was now working with Savannah when she wasn't in college.

They'd become very close, both a little fey and artistic. Chloe and Anthony, the company's trained Nose, often went off on adventures looking for new things.

Anthony and Philip were getting married themselves soon and Vonnie, who adored them, was arranging things. Since the success of Stu and Meg's wedding, local people were asking her to give them a hand with wedding plans, and she loved it.

'Who knew I'd be so good at this?' she said delightedly.

As for Stu and Meg, they walked a lot. Along Killiney beach, holding hands, sometimes picking up shells, and talking. Endlessly.

They chatted with the dog walkers and sometimes brought along their grand-dogs, who had no training whatsoever and got their leads crossed at all available opportunities.

Stu, always the sun lover, adored it when the sun shone on their walks, but Meg felt most alive on those days when the wind rushed in from the Irish Sea, when her hair whipped around even when it was in a plait, when she could feel spray on her face. This was life, she thought: the wind, the spray, the sun, the noise of the waves. Sometimes she closed her eyes and just walked, letting Stu guide her.

'You're amazing,' he said sometimes, smiling as she did this, and he'd whirl around to kiss her. 'I could lead you right into the sea and you'd never know until your feet were wet.'

Meg laughed joyously. 'I trust you to keep me safe,' she said. 'The way you trust me.'

In response, he squeezed her hand and they kept walking, the beach and life stretching out in front of them.

Acknowledgements

I like to say that I just have too many tabs open in my brain. Which is true of both my brain and my phone. You can tell a lot about a person by their phone history and mine roams between pebble mosaics (yeah, really) and patterns for African violet crochet flowers. It also covers what supplements are really good for fatigue and is there actually a glowy sort of cream yoke that you put on under your base/foundation (what you call this depends on your age) that stays all day and makes you glow. (I know there are lots of them but one that stays......) Oh yeah, and how do you stop eyeliner sliding down if you have oily eyelids. First world problems.

Bearing this in mind and my capacity for losing stuff, I need to explain that while I have written many, many names on my beloved notecards for the acknowledgements, I have managed to lose them all. So I KNOW I am going to leave people out and I will wake up in the middle of the night and remember this and be devastated. I am so sorry. Just – you know, am a flawed human being with head like a sieve.

Thanks, in no particular order, to my wonderful Curtis Brown family, including Jonathan Lloyd, Lucy Morris, Caoimhe White, Olivia Edwards and the huge team who never stop working and being fabulous.

To the superb Communications Clinic team of Terry Prone, Aileen Gaskin and Robyn Keleghan.

To my friend and colleague, Gillian Glynn O' Sullivan (and the gorgeous Pippa!!) To the marvellous Orion team of Charlotte Mursell, Sarah Benton, Virginia Woolstencroft, Helena

Fouracre, Sanah Ahmed, Jake Alderson and all the people who do so much and whose names are on notecards. Imagine the monkey with its head in its hands emoji here. To the dear Hachette Ireland team of Breda Purdue, Jim Binchy, Elaine Egan, Ruth Shern, Siobhan Tierney and Joanna Smyth.

This book was written with the help of two spectacular community midwives, Debbie FitzGerald and Clodagh Manning and all mistakes are mine. Thanks to Lisa for talking to me about Rory's take on the LGBTQ+ community. Being really, er, vicious to homophobes was my idea, not hers. I had to remember I was not writing a thriller...

Thanks too to the women who spoke to me for this book. During the Pandemic, abuse of women and children hit a huge level and I am deeply grateful with the people who shared their stories with me. Funding for women and children in this situation is so often purely community based. That needs to change. Violence and abuse against women, children, anyone vulnerable, needs to be funded by governments.

Thanks to dear Pam and Marcus Magnier for stellar property advice for my last book.

Thanks also to retired Detective Inspectors Pauline McDonagh and Joe O'Hara, Gardai Helen Cuddy, Sean Callaghan and Aoife Hayes.

A huge thank you to my darling Eddie and Alison Cowzer and to Honor Savage, the wisest woman ever: you were all there when it mattered. Thanks also to Mary Mullins for so much kindness and advice.

To all my friends in Enniskerry, (Wendy, thank you, always, especially) who are always in my corner. You know who you are. I am lucky to live in a beautiful part of the world among lovely people.

The people who keep me going all the time are my close friends and loved ones. To Murray and Dylan, my beautiful sons: you are the kindest, most beautiful human beings on the planet. My heart bursts with love for you both. I am so lucky to be your mother. To PJ, who has been there for me with love and kindness: merci et bisous. To Licky, Scamp and Princess Dinky who are precious jewels.

To my beloved Mum, who is always there for us, does so much for others and should have written her own books, and to my darling brother and sister, Lucy, and Francis, who have given me unceasing love and support and are such wonderful people. To dearest Dave, Anne, Laura, Naomi, Emer, Robert, Katie and now baby Rory! I am so lucky and proud to have all of you in my life. Love you all. And kisses and biscuits for Lola, Hugo, Alice and Bailey.

To Wendy Hutson (and Reggie!) and Margaret Fagan, true friends. To my wise women: Gai Griffin, Lynn McKee, Marian Keyes, Tricia Scanlan, Clodagh Finn, Lisa and Shona Redmond, Catherine Lee: I couldn't do it without you all. To healer extraordinaire Aidan Storey and Murtagh Corrigan. To Mary Canavan for so many years. To dear Mick and Molly McNiffe, Eva Berg, Thelma O'Reilly, Fiona O'Brien, Rosie O'Keefe, Bernie Kinsella, Barbara Durkan, Jane Owens, Grainne Whitelaw, Susan Zaidan. To the always amazing Stella O'Connell for being there, and to Bernadette Kelleher-Nolan and Finola Murphy.

To Emma, Richard and Kit Davies, Lottie, Little James, Tiggy, Nell, Alan, Richard, Dorothy, Cindy, Matt, Bea, Katie, Louise, Lizzie, Vickey, and to the beautiful Extendables who are glorious. (hugs to all animals, esp Juno, the Treasure, Charlie, Pickle, Kiki, Pebbles, Lucy, including Satara and Rory's lovely dog, whose name escapes me. Kisses to all!)

Huge thanks to Cindy Ireland, James, Georgina and Caroline. To the Party At Don and William's crew – I love you all!!!!!! Many more parties!

To my family in the West, much love to Mary and Leah, Catherine, Mary, Celia, Maggie and Chris. I know how much you all miss darling Matt. To my walking pals, the ever-wise Steph, darlings Martina, Judy, Brenda, Caroline,

Niall, Debbie, Anne, Alice, Declan, Aidan, Loulou, Ruth, Julie, Anne, James, Denis, Ray, Marguerite, Lisa, Charlotte, Tara, Diarmuid, Samantha, Janet, Mara, Rita, Fanchea, Julie, Aoife, Bridin, Ellen, Rob and for all of you.

Writing is never lonely, not with gorgeous writer friends like the amazing Erica James, Louise O'Neill, Sheila O'Flanagan, Rachel Hore, Michelle Dunne and Emma Murray (not to miss out on the bunnies, Anya and Ava, and Sam and his father, Sabah, who is an angel). Talks with Sinead Moriarty, Claudia Carroll, Audrey Magee never have enough time! We are all always writing!!!!

Thanks to the fabulous friends I made on Ireland's Dancing With The Stars – I never did learn to tango, but Maurizio Benenato says he will teach me! You guys are all fabulous – it was a wonderful experience. The sparkles!!!!!

Thanks to Cliona and John Sherwin, Frank Delaney and the whole marvellous team on the Tracks and Trails show. It was a wonderful shoot in exquisite Kerry and I think I'll become a broadcaster now!

Thank you to the booksellers who tirelessly sell my books all around the world and to my readers, without whom I would be both out of a job and devastated. Your support means the world to me. Thank you so much.

Finally, thanks to my UNICEF family who are working tirelessly in the field right now in Ukraine, Afghanistan, Yemen and in any one of the war zones or disaster areas on our planet. We always need your help.

Credits

Cathy Kelly and Orion Fiction would like to thank everyone at Orion who worked on the publication of *The Wedding Party* in the UK.

Editorial
Charlotte Mursell
Sanah Ahmed

Copyeditor
Marian Reid

Proofreader
Linda Joyce

Audio
Paul Stark
Jake Alderson

Contracts
Anne Goddard
Humayra Ahmed
Ellie Bowker

Production
Ruth Sharvell

Design
Charlotte Abrams-Simpson
Joanna Ridley
Nick May

Editorial Management
Charlie Panayiotou
Jane Hughes
Bartley Shaw
Tamara Morriss

Finance
Jasdip Nandra
Afeera Ahmed
Elizabeth Beaumont
Sue Baker

Marketing
Helena Fouracre

Publicity
Virginia Woolstencroft

Sales
Jen Wilson
Esther Waters
Victoria Laws
Rachael Hum
Anna Egelstaff
Frances Doyle
Georgina Cutler

Operations
Jo Jacobs
Sharon Willis

If you loved *The Wedding Party*, discover Cathy Kelly's other bestselling stories, told with her trademark sparkling warmth, humour and honesty.

Other Women

'A burst of warmth and wit, twists and turns'
Marian Keyes

Three women. Three secrets. Three tangled lives . . .

Sid wears her independence like armour. So when she strikes up a rare connection with unlucky-in-love Finn, they are both determined to prove that men and women can just be friends. Can't they?

Marin has the perfect home, attentive husband, two beloved children – and a secret addiction to designer clothes. She knows she has it all, so why can't she stop comparing herself to other women?

Bea believes that we all have one love story – and she's had hers. Now her life centres around her son, Luke, and her support group of fierce single women. But there's something that she can't tell anyone . . .

'Honest, funny, clever, it sparkled with witty wry
observations on modern life'
Marian Keyes

The Family
Gift

Freya Abalone has a big, messy, wonderful family. She has
an exciting career as a celebrity chef. She has a
new home that makes her feel safe.

**But behind the happy front, Freya feels pulled in a
hundred directions.** Life has thrown Freya some
lemons – and she's learned how to juggle! But she's
keeping a secret from her family, and soon
something is going to crashing down . . .

All families have their struggles and strengths.
So can Freya pull everyone – and herself – together
when they need it most?

The Year that Changed Everything

Three women. Three birthdays.
One year that will change everything . . .

Ginger isn't spending her thirtieth the way she would have planned. Tonight might be the first night of the rest of her life – or a total disaster.

Sam is finally pregnant after years of trying. When her waters break on the morning of her fortieth birthday, she panics: forget labour, how is she going to be a mother?

Callie is celebrating her fiftieth at a big party in her Dublin home. Then a knock at the door mid-party changes everything . . .

Help us make the next generation of readers

We – both author and publisher – hope you enjoyed this book. We believe that you can become a reader at any time in your life, but we'd love your help to give the next generation a head start.

Did you know that 9 per cent of children don't have a book of their own in their home, rising to 13 per cent in disadvantaged families*? We'd like to try to change that by asking you to consider the role you could play in helping to build readers of the future.

We'd love you to think of sharing, borrowing, reading, buying or talking about a book with a child in your life and spreading the love of reading. We want to make sure the next generation continue to have access to books, wherever they come from.

And if you would like to consider donating to charities that help fund literacy projects, find out more at www.literacytrust.org.uk and www.booktrust.org.uk.

THANK YOU

*As reported by the National Literacy Trust